4

BRIAN K. VAUGHAN writer
CLIFF CHIANG artist
MATT WILSON colors
JARED K. FLETCHER letters

image®

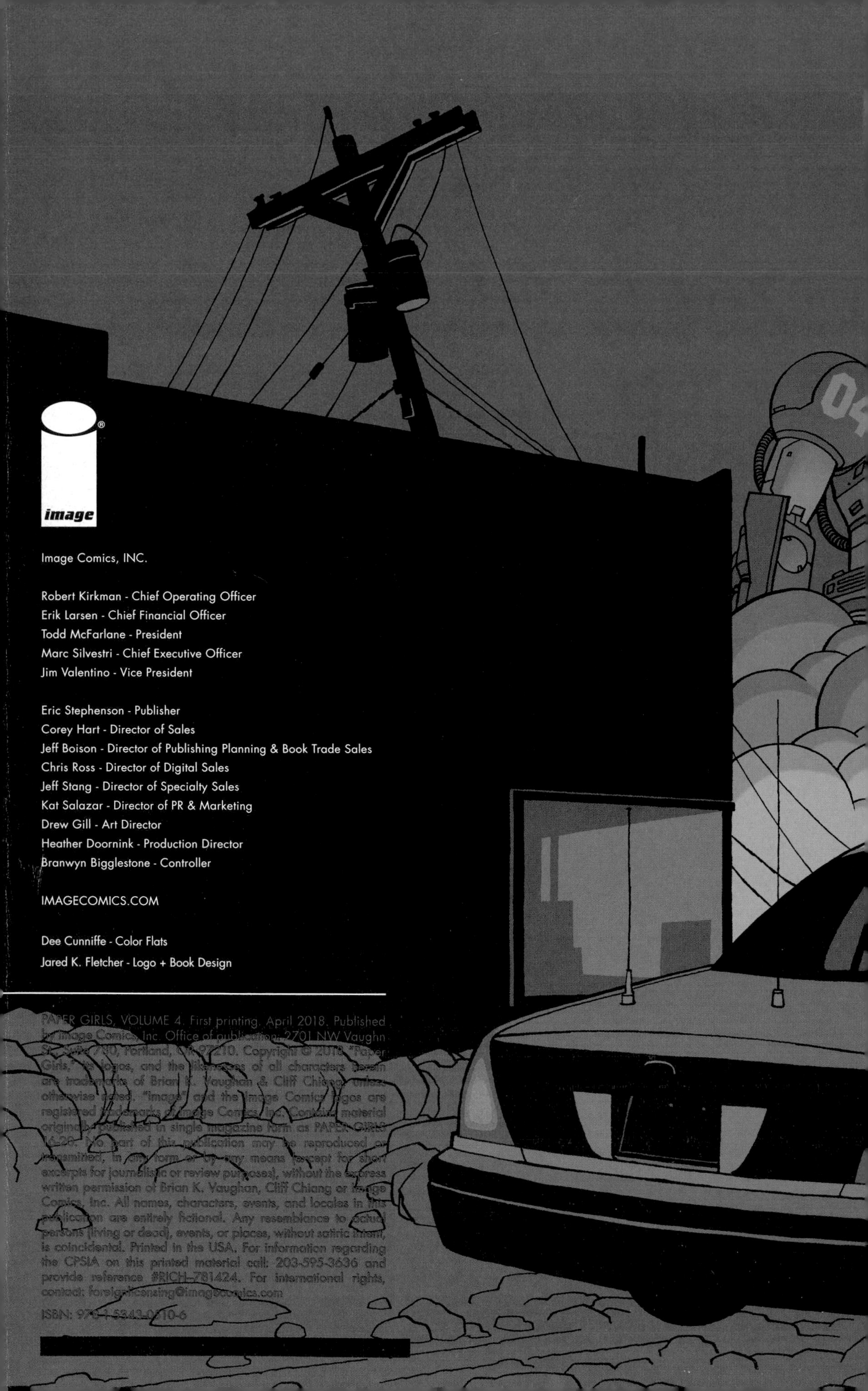

Image Comics, INC.

Robert Kirkman - Chief Operating Officer
Erik Larsen - Chief Financial Officer
Todd McFarlane - President
Marc Silvestri - Chief Executive Officer
Jim Valentino - Vice President

Eric Stephenson - Publisher
Corey Hart - Director of Sales
Jeff Boison - Director of Publishing Planning & Book Trade Sales
Chris Ross - Director of Digital Sales
Jeff Stang - Director of Specialty Sales
Kat Salazar - Director of PR & Marketing
Drew Gill - Art Director
Heather Doornink - Production Director
Branwyn Bigglestone - Controller

IMAGECOMICS.COM

Dee Cunniffe - Color Flats
Jared K. Fletcher - Logo + Book Design

PAPER GIRLS, VOLUME 4. First printing. April 2018. Published by Image Comics, Inc. Office of publication: 2701 NW Vaughn St., Suite 780, Portland, OR 97210.

ISBN: 978-1-5343-0510-6

[redacted]

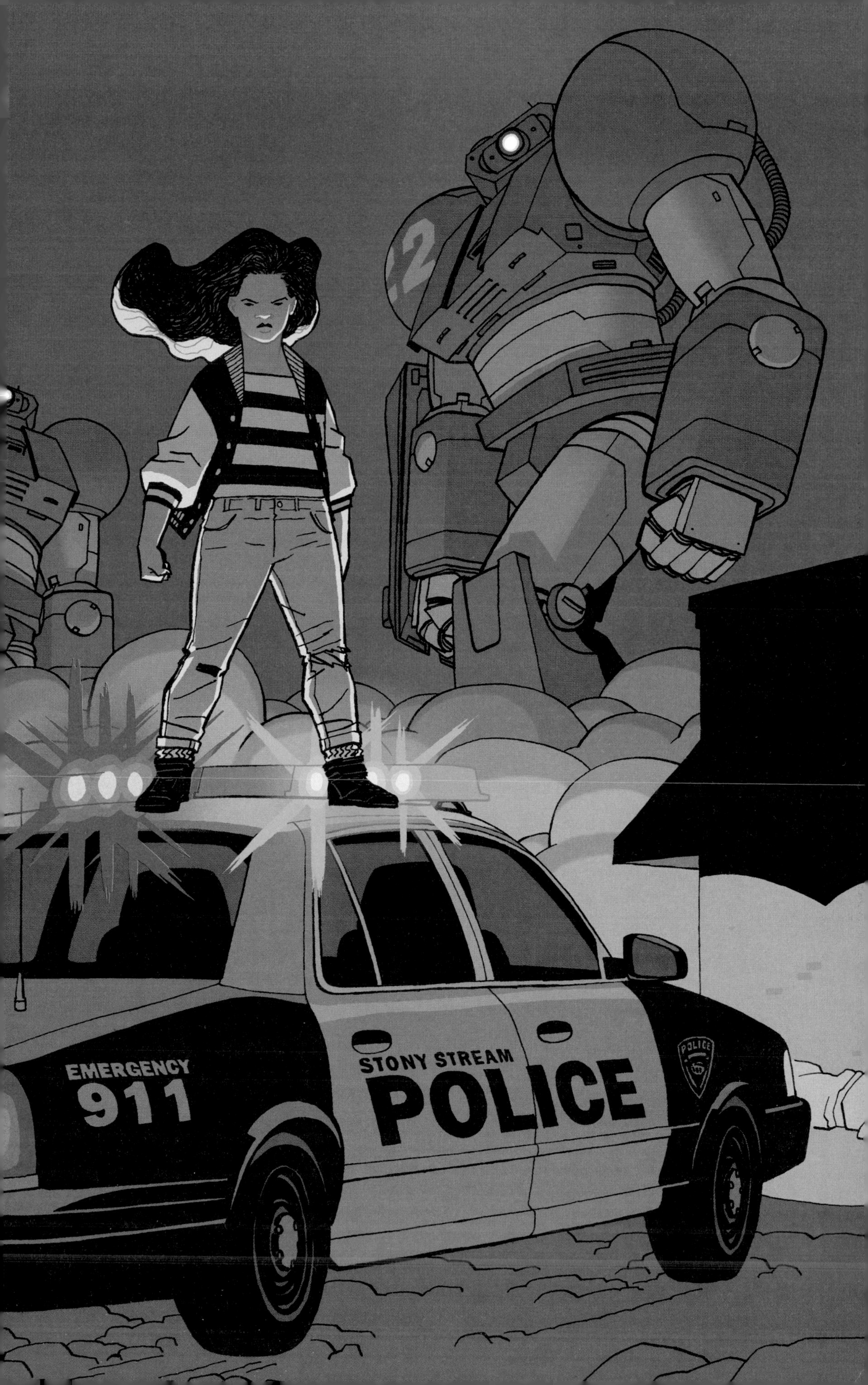
EMERGENCY
911
STONY STREAM
POLICE

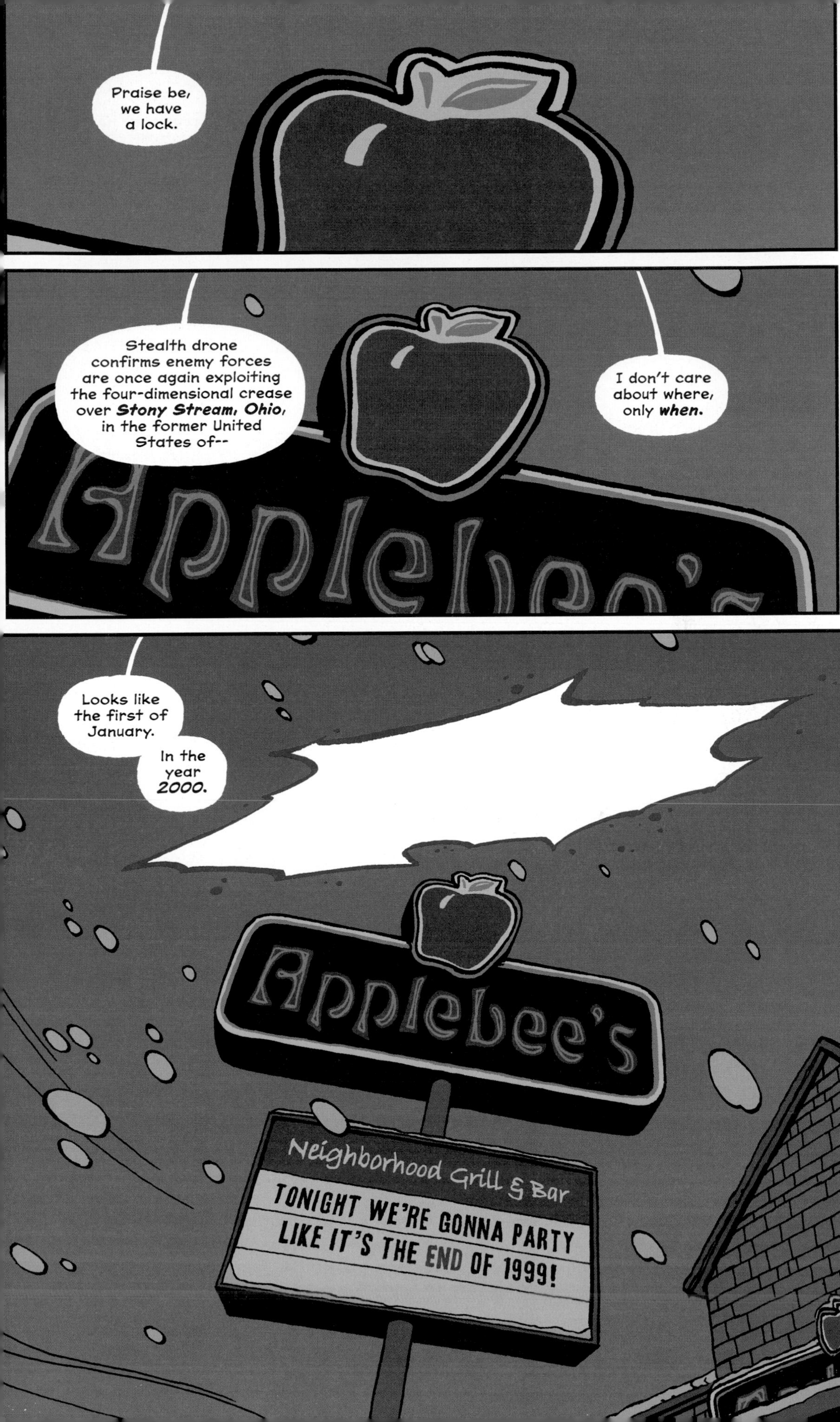
Praise be, we have a lock.
Stealth drone confirms enemy forces are once again exploiting the four-dimensional crease over ***Stony Stream, Ohio,*** in the former United States of--
I don't care about where, only ***when.***
Applebee's
Looks like the first of January.
In the year ***2000.***
Applebee's
Neighborhood Grill & Bar
TONIGHT WE'RE GONNA PARTY LIKE IT'S THE END OF 1999!

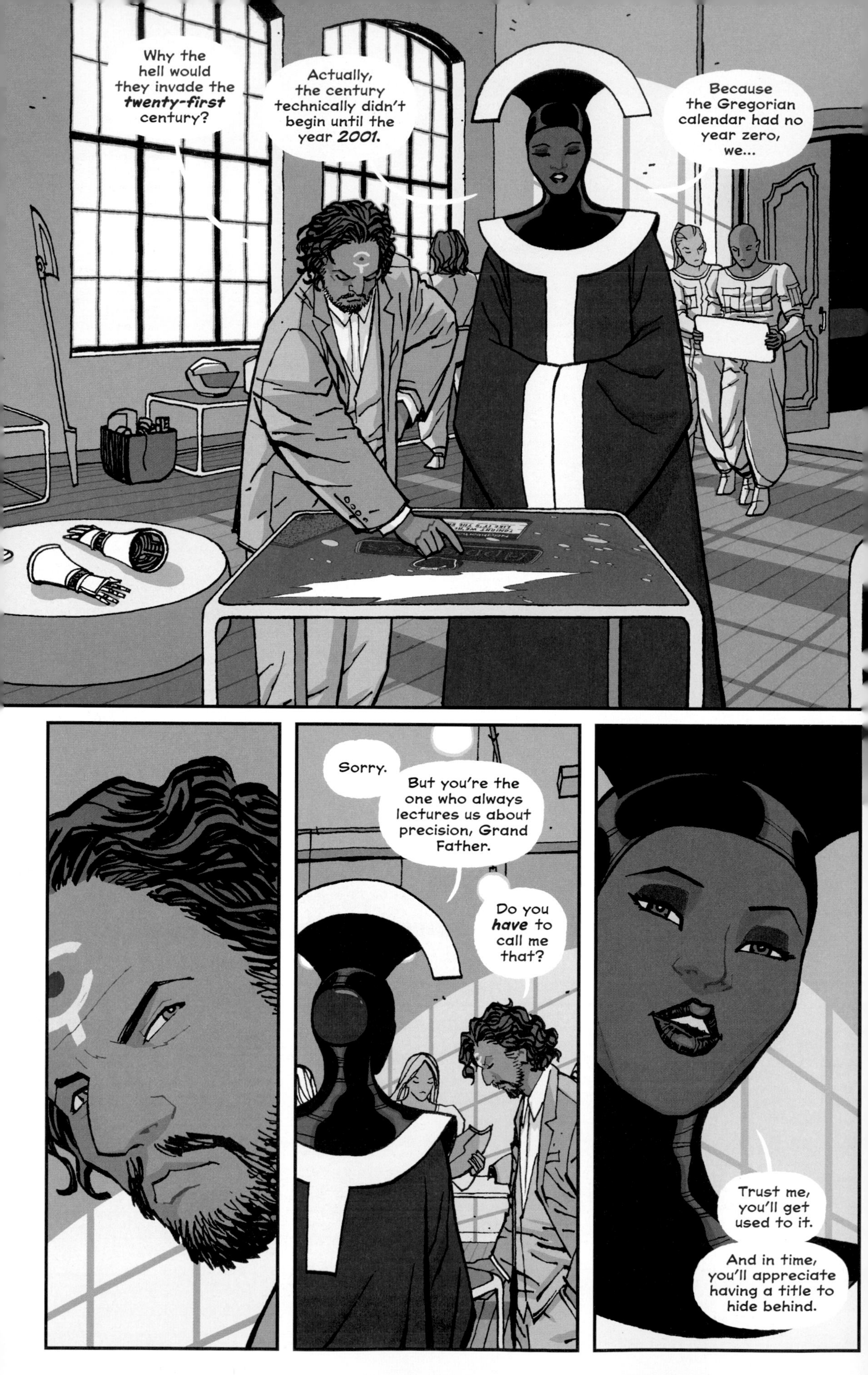
Why the hell would they invade the *twenty-first* century?
Actually, the century technically didn't begin until the year *2001.*
Because the Gregorian calendar had no year zero, we...
Sorry.
But you're the one who always lectures us about precision, Grand Father.
Do you *have* to call me that?
Trust me, you'll get used to it.
And in time, you'll appreciate having a title to hide behind.

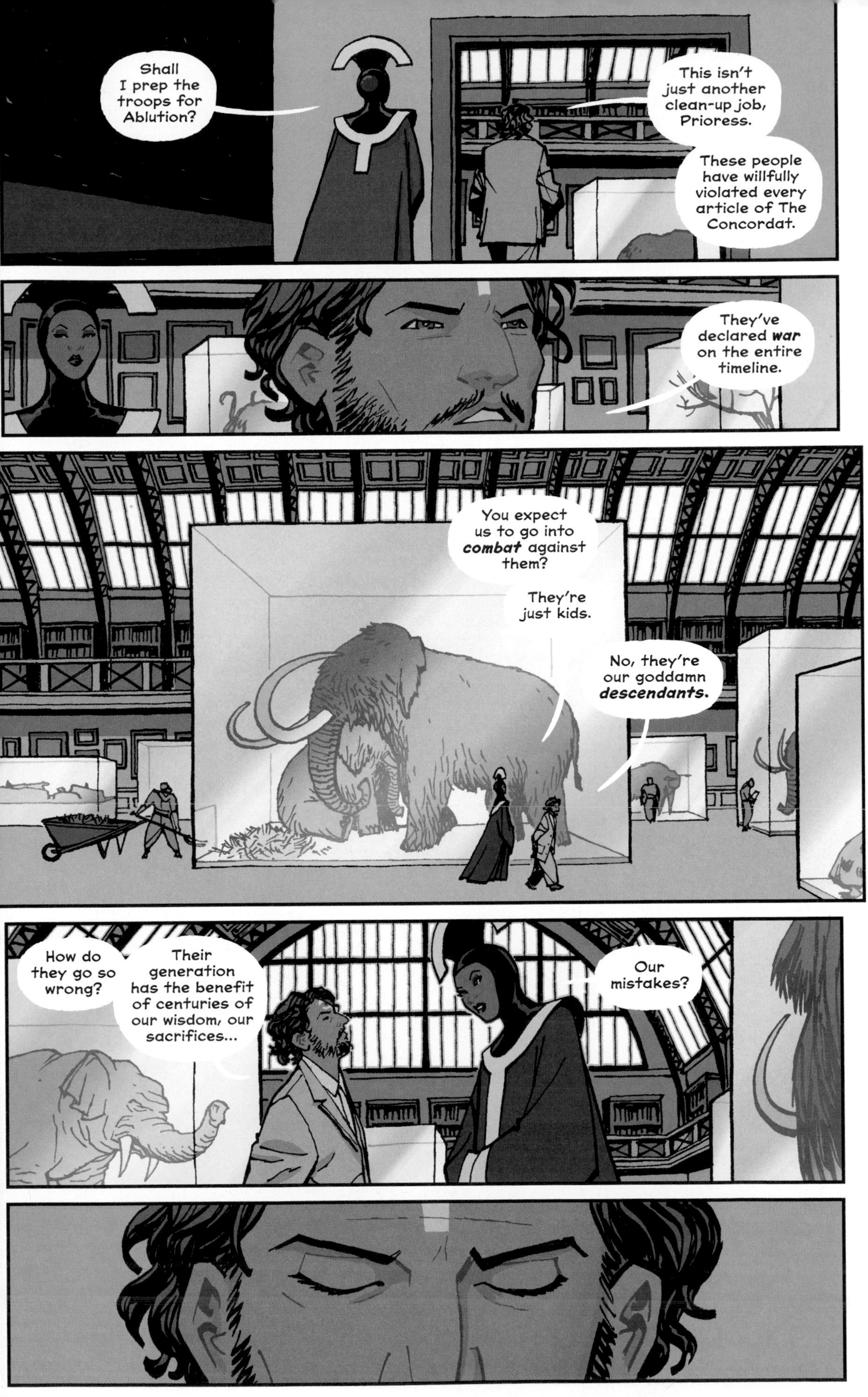
Shall I prep the troops for Ablution?
This isn't just another clean-up job, Prioress.
These people have willfully violated every article of The Concordat.
They've declared **war** on the entire timeline.
You expect us to go into **combat** against them?
They're just kids.
No, they're our goddamn **descendants.**
How do they go so wrong?
Their generation has the benefit of centuries of our wisdom, our sacrifices...
Our mistakes?

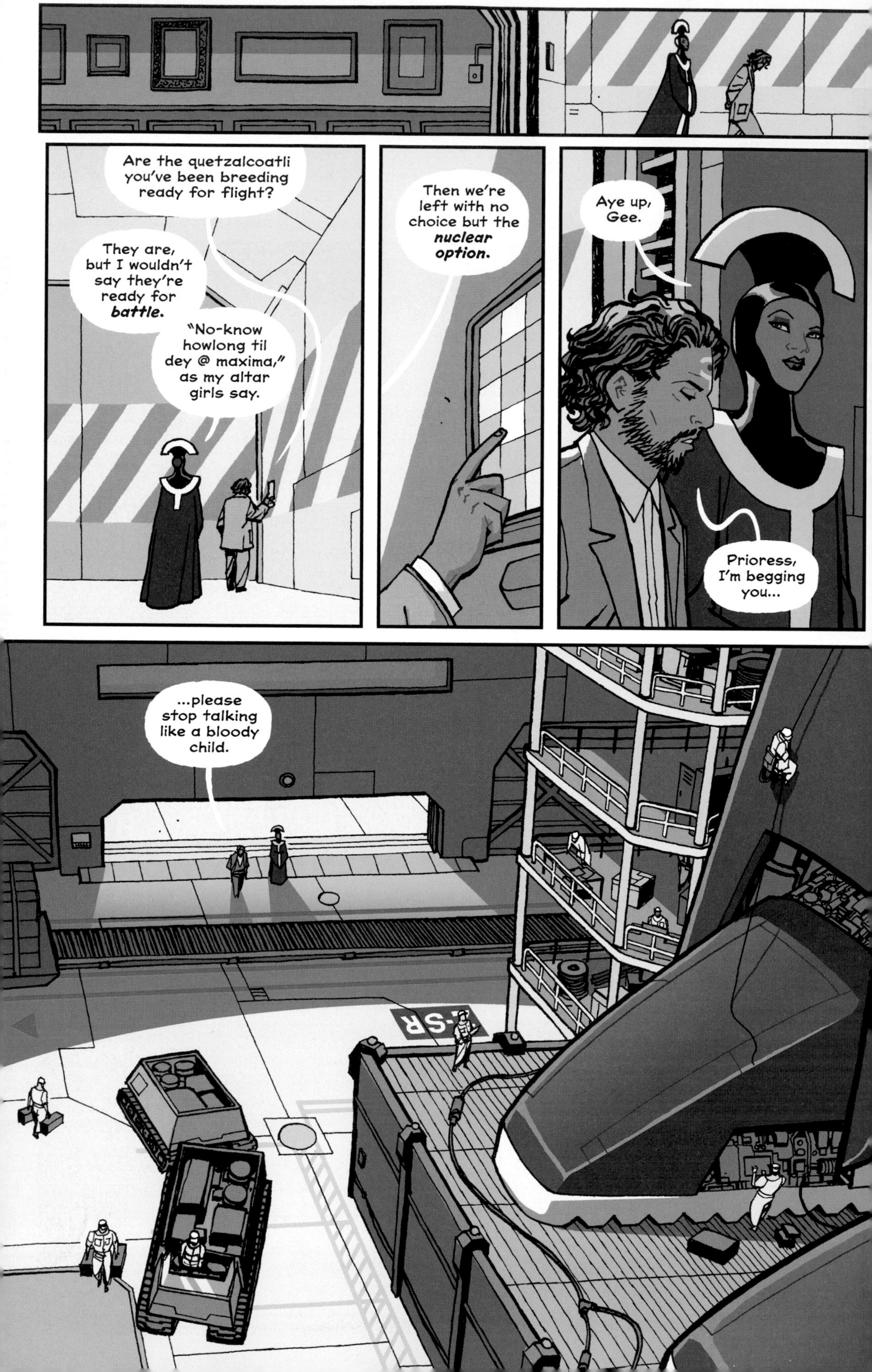
Are the quetzalcoatli you've been breeding ready for flight?
They are, but I wouldn't say they're ready for ***battle.***
"No-know howlong til dey @ maxima," as my altar girls say.
Then we're left with no choice but the ***nuclear option.***
Aye up, Gee.
Prioress, I'm begging you...
...please stop talking like a bloody child.

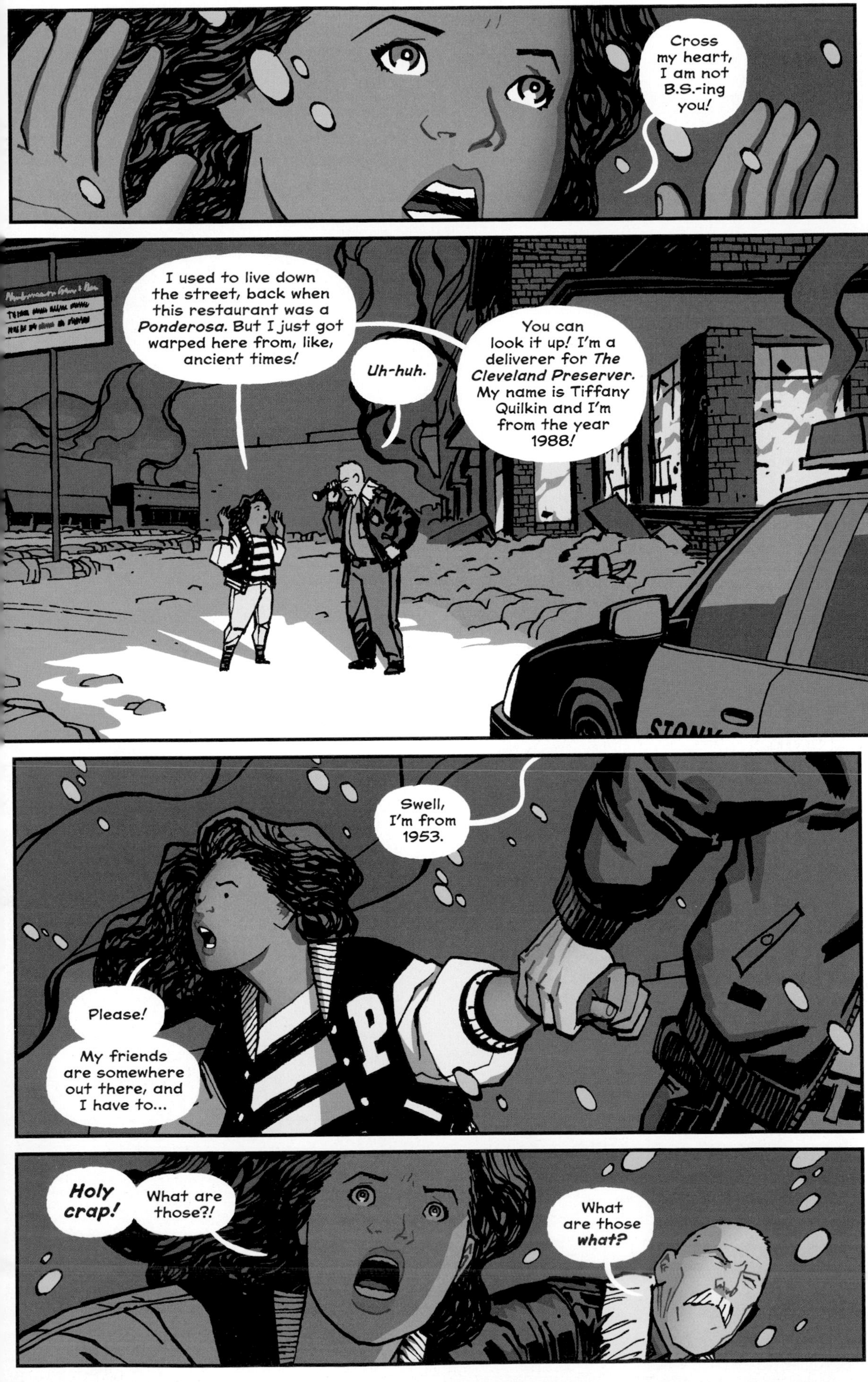
Cross my heart, I am not B.S.-ing you!
I used to live down the street, back when this restaurant was a *Ponderosa*. But I just got warped here from, like, ancient times!
Uh-huh.
You can look it up! I'm a deliverer for *The Cleveland Preserver*. My name is Tiffany Quilkin and I'm from the year 1988!
Swell, I'm from 1953.
Please!
My friends are somewhere out there, and I have to...
Holy crap!
What are those?!
What are those *what?*

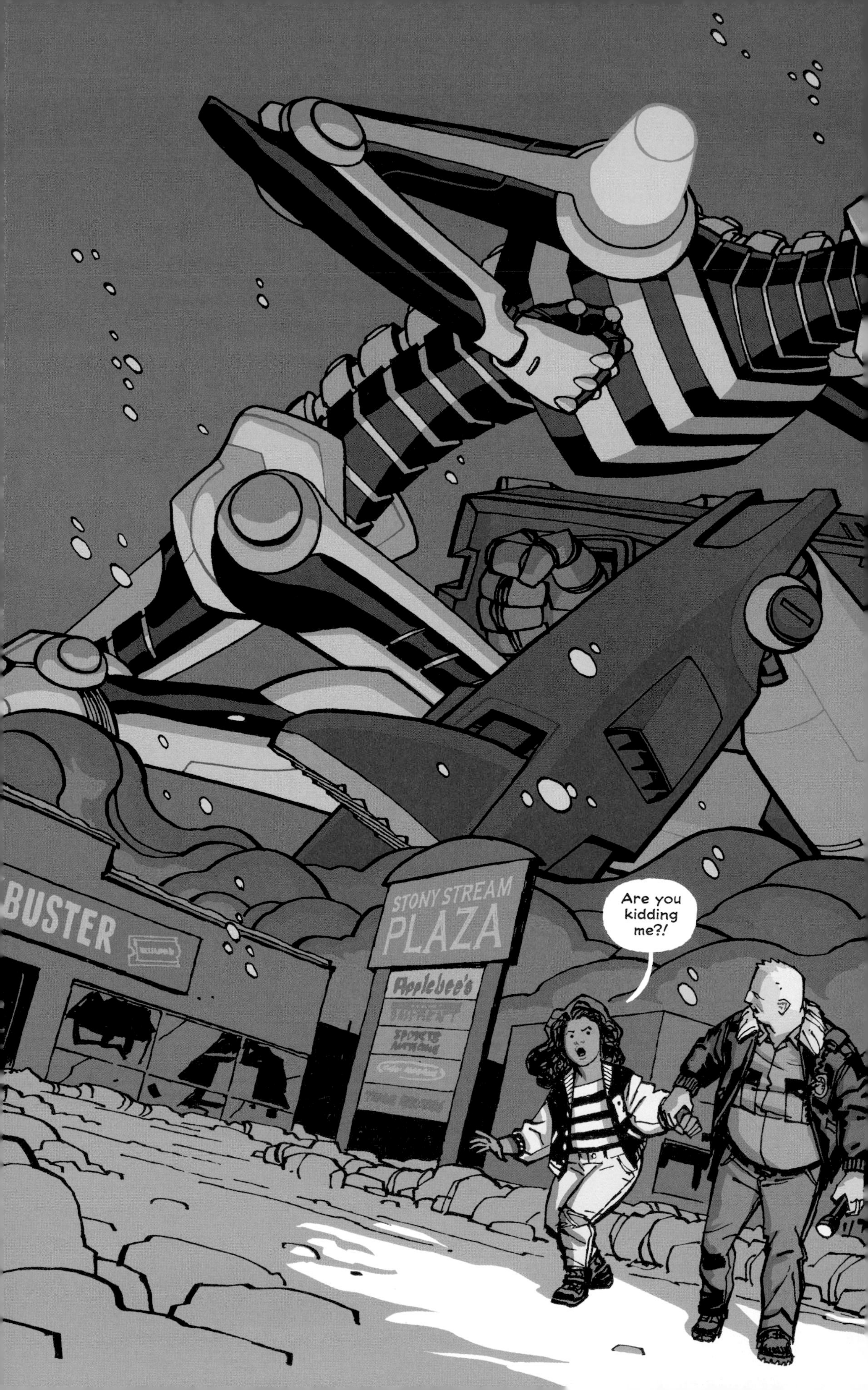

BUSTER
STONY STREAM PLAZA
Applebee's
Are you kidding me?!

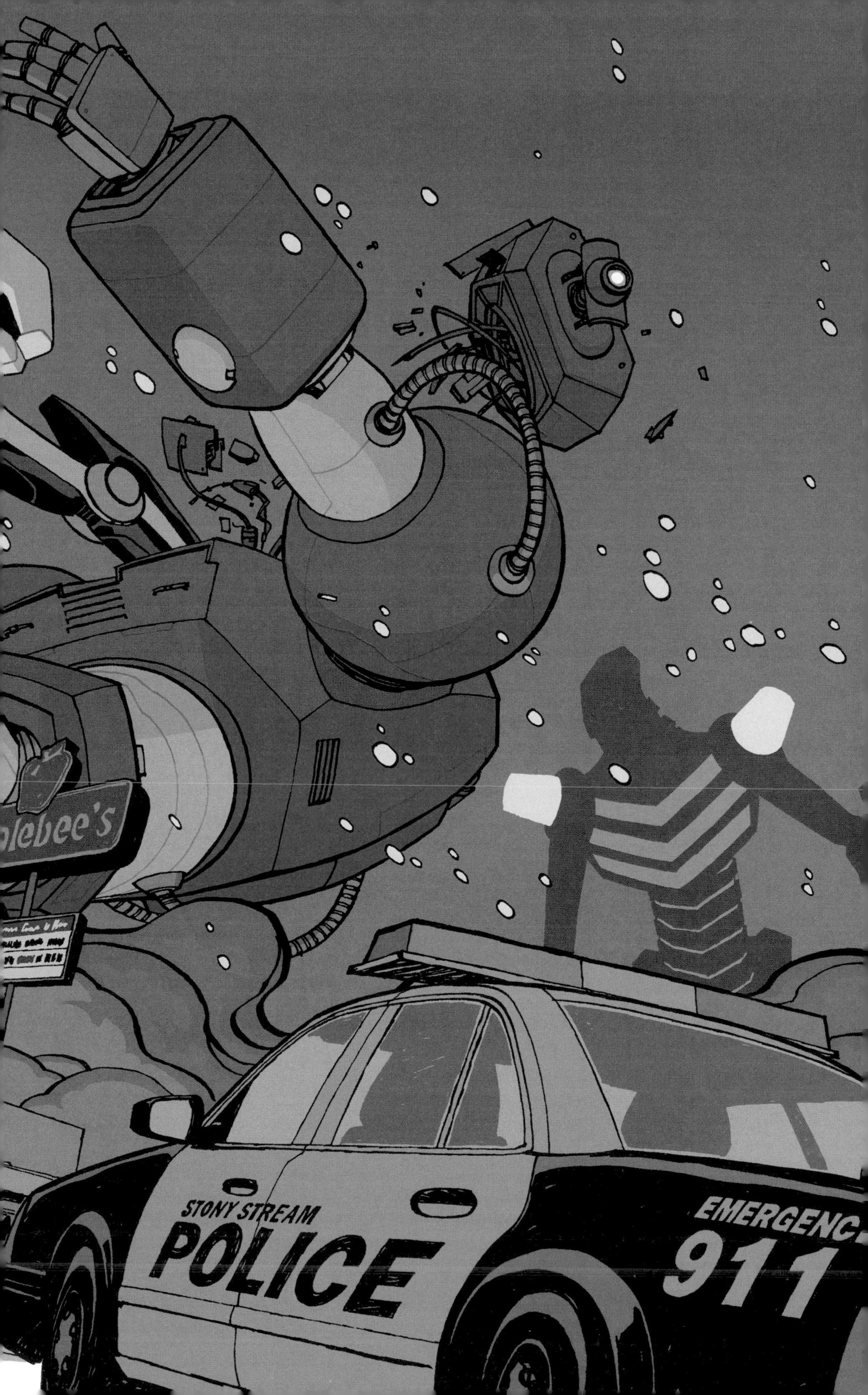
olebee's
STONY STREAM
POLICE
EMERGENC
911

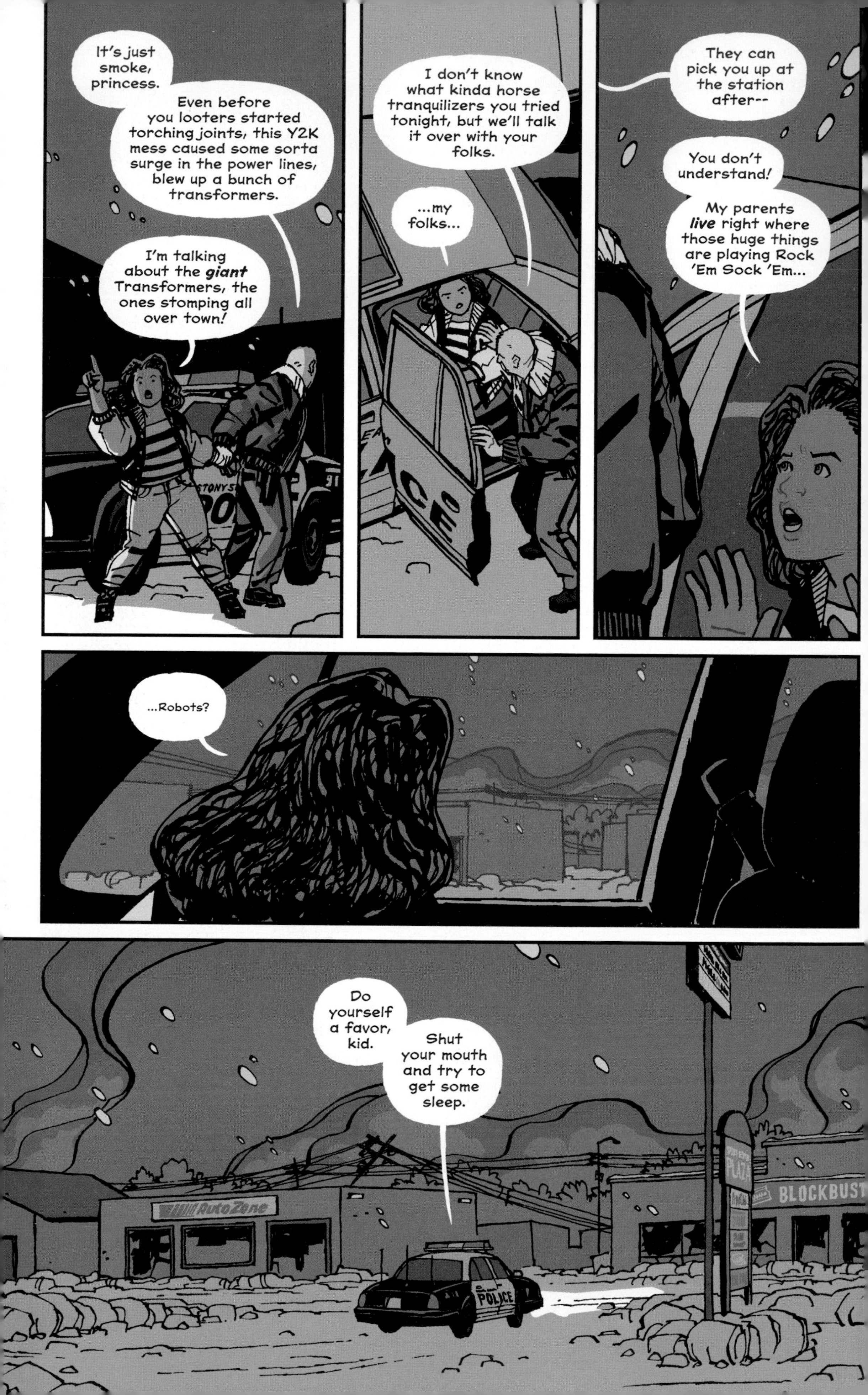
It's just smoke, princess.
Even before you looters started torching joints, this Y2K mess caused some sorta surge in the power lines, blew up a bunch of transformers.
I'm talking about the *giant* Transformers, the ones stomping all over town!
I don't know what kinda horse tranquilizers you tried tonight, but we'll talk it over with your folks.
...my folks...
They can pick you up at the station after--
You don't understand!
My parents *live* right where those huge things are playing Rock 'Em Sock 'Em...
...Robots?
Do yourself a favor, kid.
Shut your mouth and try to get some sleep.
AutoZone
PLAZA
BLOCKBUST
POLICE

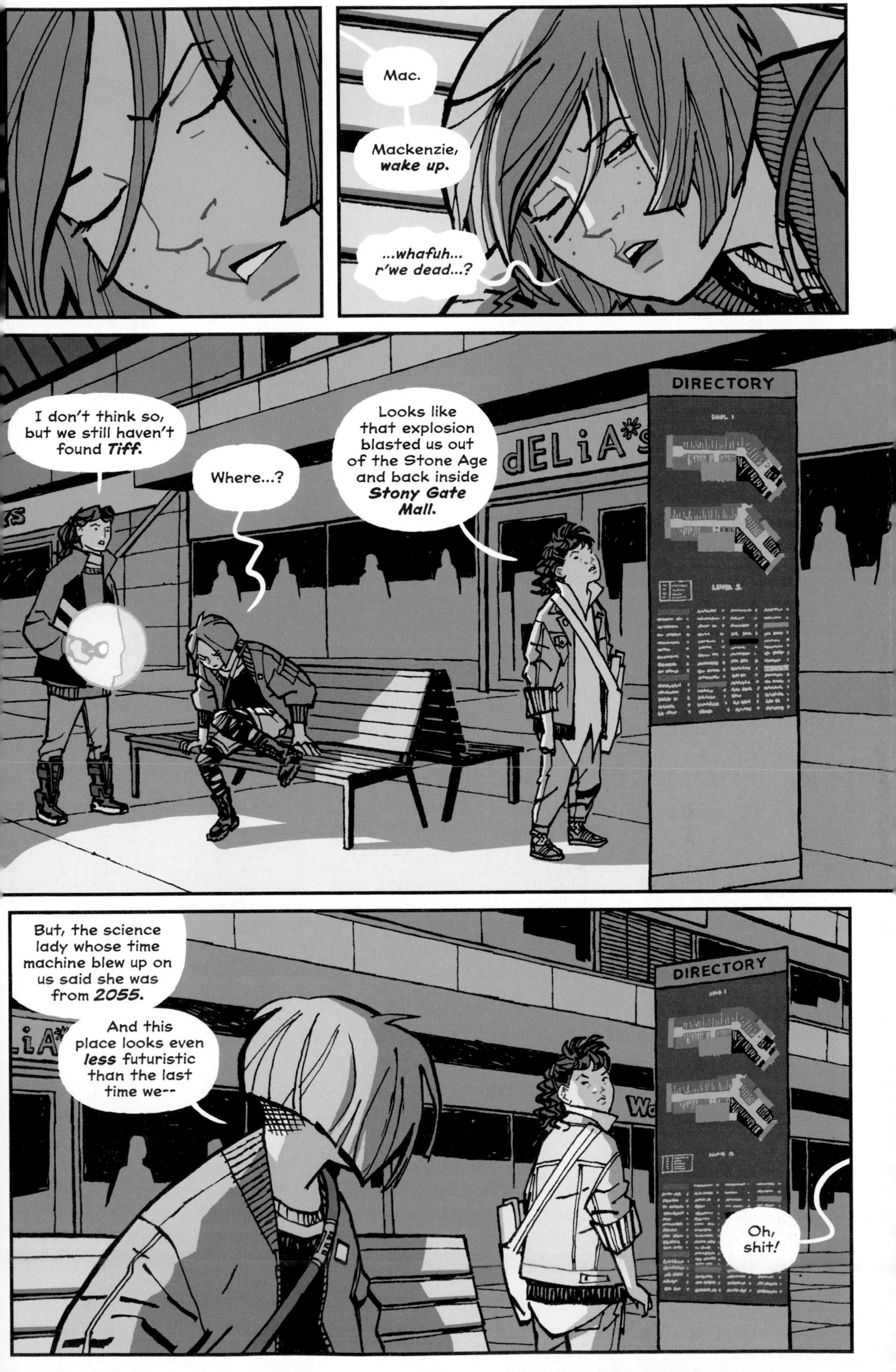

Mac.
Mackenzie, **wake up.**
...*whafuh... r'we dead...?*
I don't think so, but we still haven't found ***Tiff.***
Where...?
Looks like that explosion blasted us out of the Stone Age and back inside ***Stony Gate Mall.***
dELiA*s
DIRECTORY
But, the science lady whose time machine blew up on us said she was from ***2055.***
And this place looks even ***less*** futuristic than the last time we--
DIRECTORY
Oh, shit!

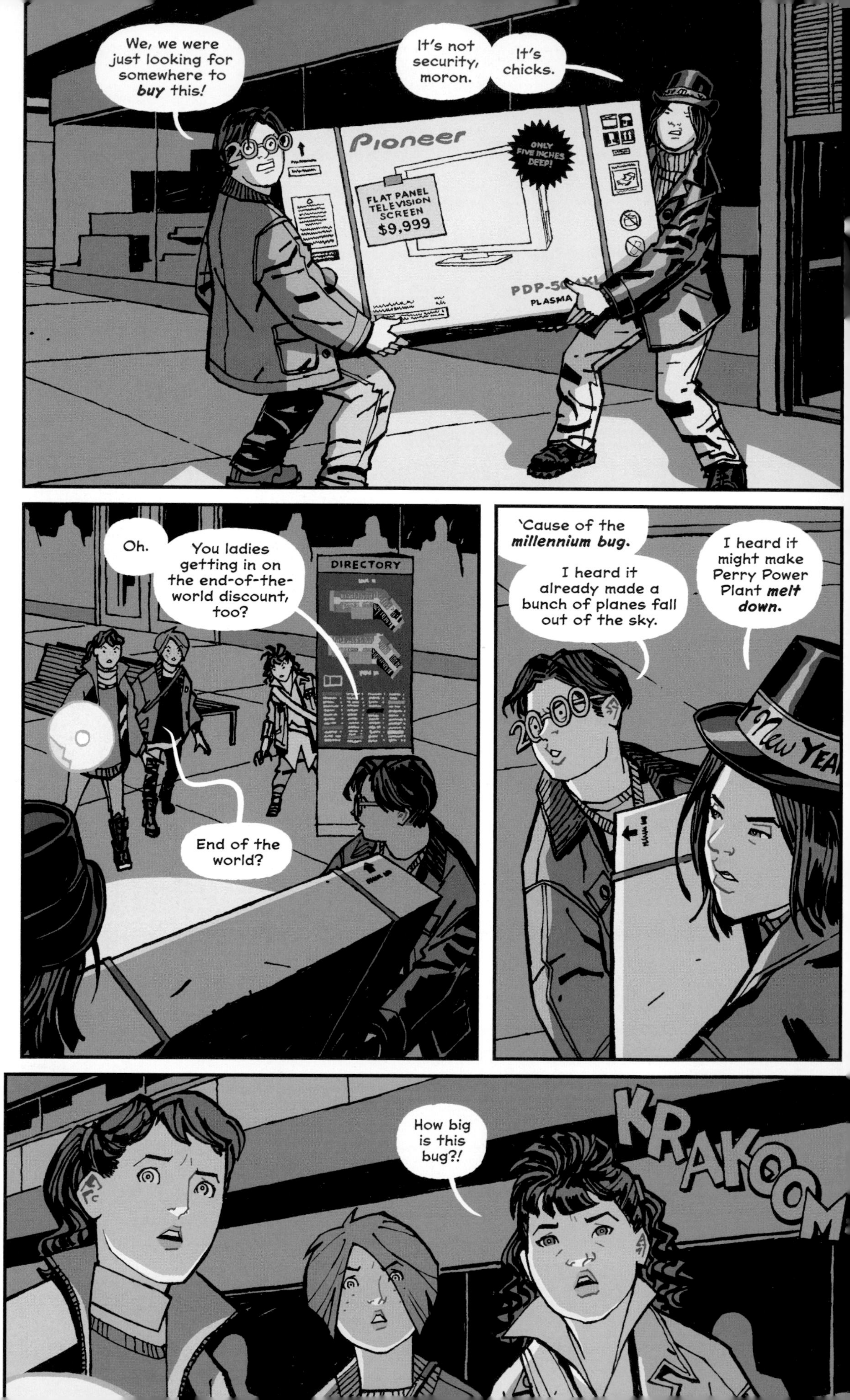
We, we were just looking for somewhere to **buy** this!
It's not security, moron.
It's chicks.
Pioneer
FLAT PANEL TELEVISION SCREEN $9,999
ONLY FIVE INCHES DEEP!
PLASMA
Oh.
You ladies getting in on the end-of-the-world discount, too?
DIRECTORY
End of the world?
'Cause of the **millennium bug.**
I heard it already made a bunch of planes fall out of the sky.
I heard it might make Perry Power Plant **melt down.**
How big is this bug?!
KRAKOOM

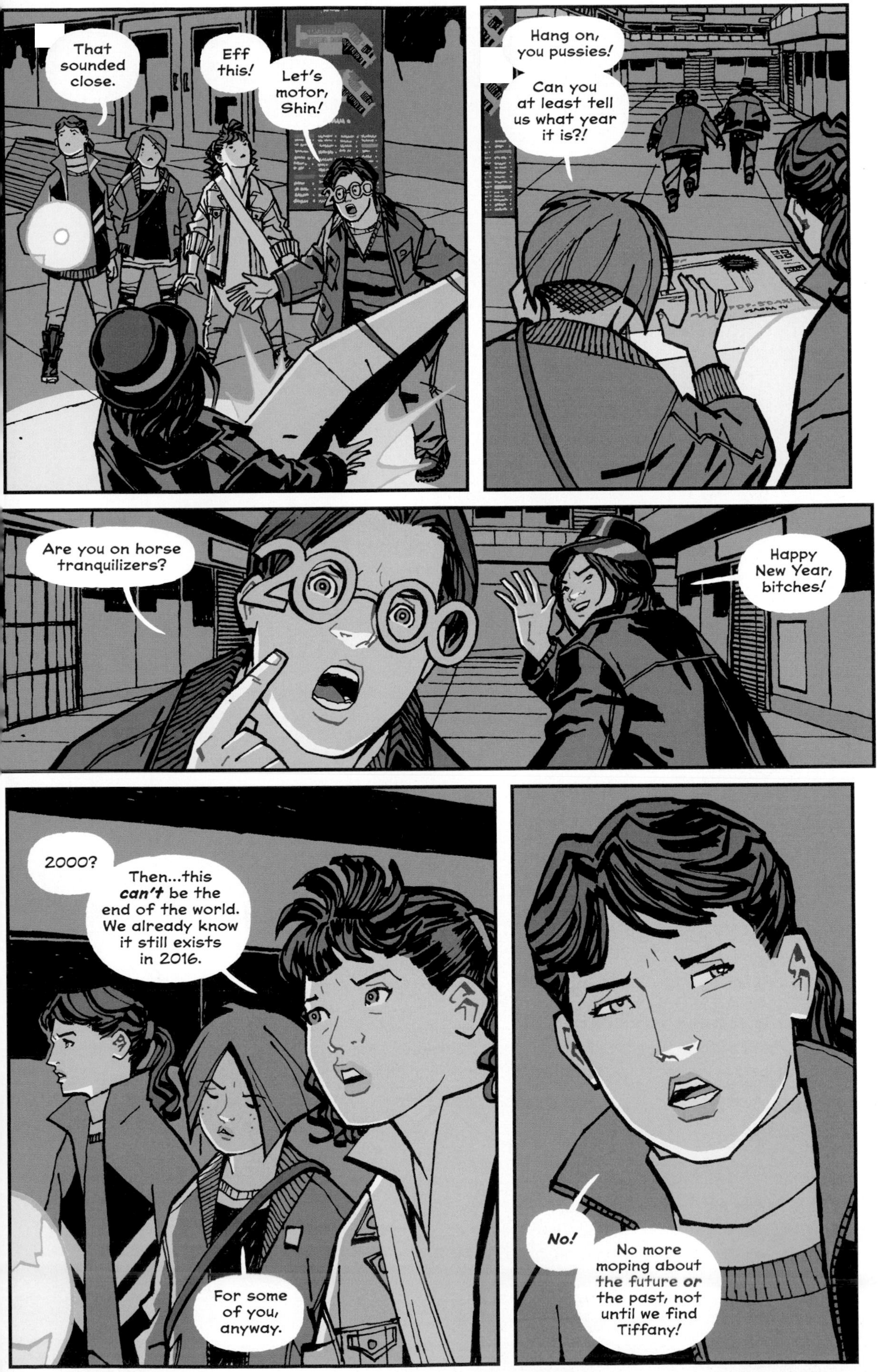
That sounded close.
Eff this!
Let's motor, Shin!
Hang on, you pussies!
Can you at least tell us what year it is?!
Are you on horse tranquilizers?
Happy New Year, bitches!
2000?
Then...this *can't* be the end of the world. We already know it still exists in 2016.
For some of you, anyway.
No!
No more moping about the future *or* the past, not until we find Tiffany!

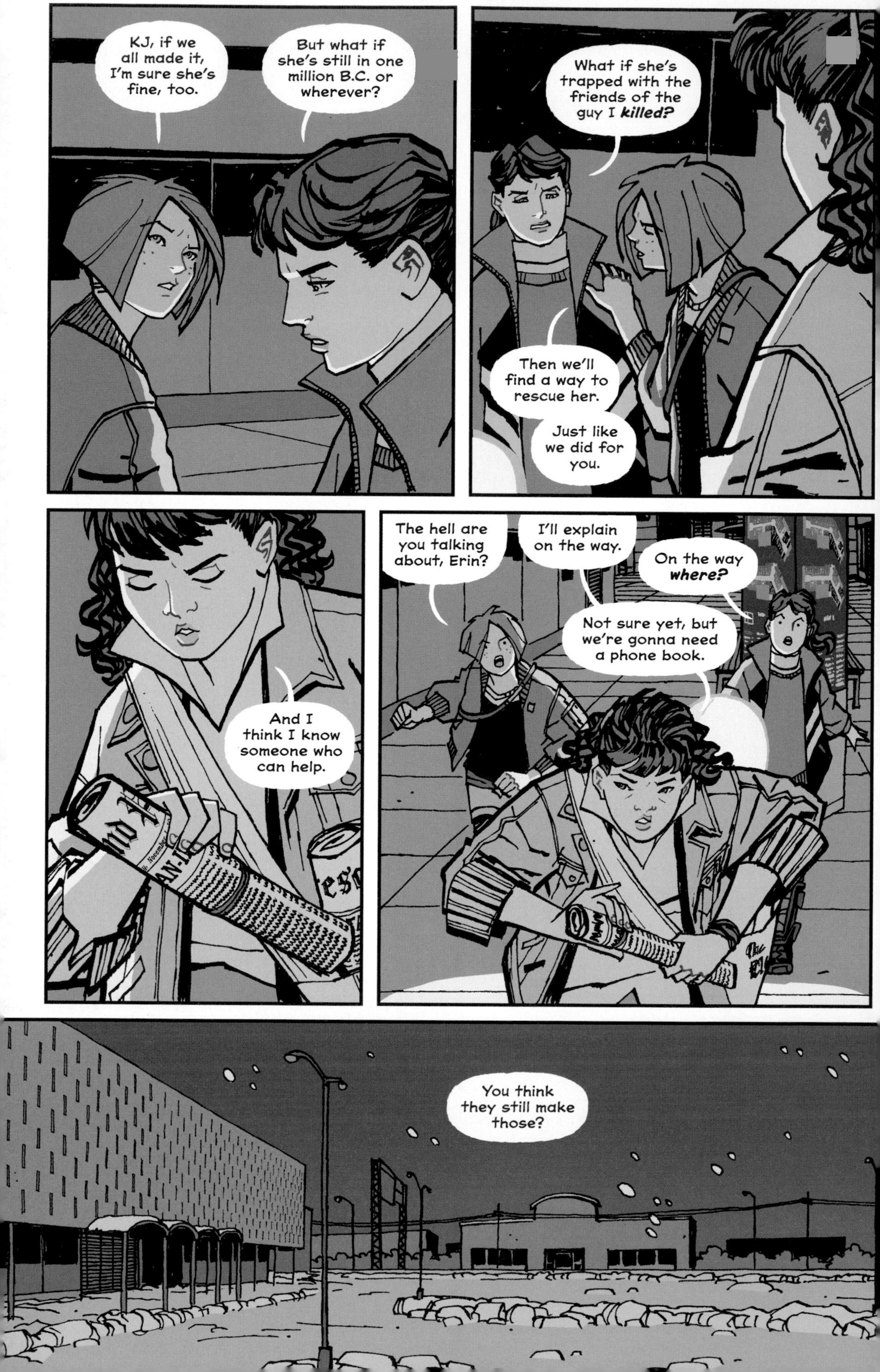
KJ, if we all made it, I'm sure she's fine, too.
But what if she's still in one million B.C. or wherever?
What if she's trapped with the friends of the guy I *killed?*
Then we'll find a way to rescue her.
Just like we did for you.
And I think I know someone who can help.
The hell are you talking about, Erin?
I'll explain on the way.
On the way *where?*
Not sure yet, but we're gonna need a phone book.
You think they still make those?

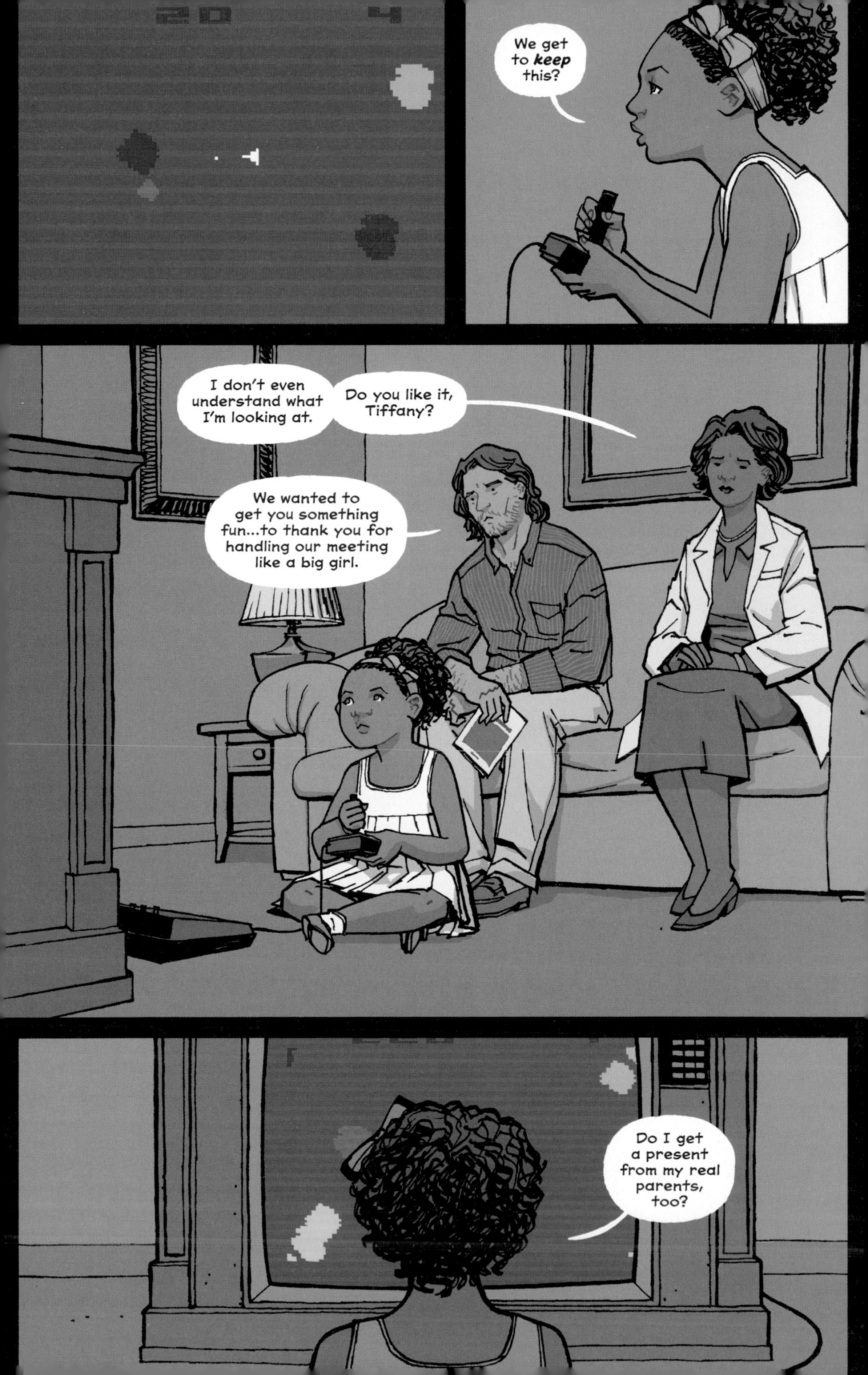

We get to *keep* this?
I don't even understand what I'm looking at.
Do you like it, Tiffany?
We wanted to get you something fun...to thank you for handling our meeting like a big girl.
Do I get a present from my real parents, too?

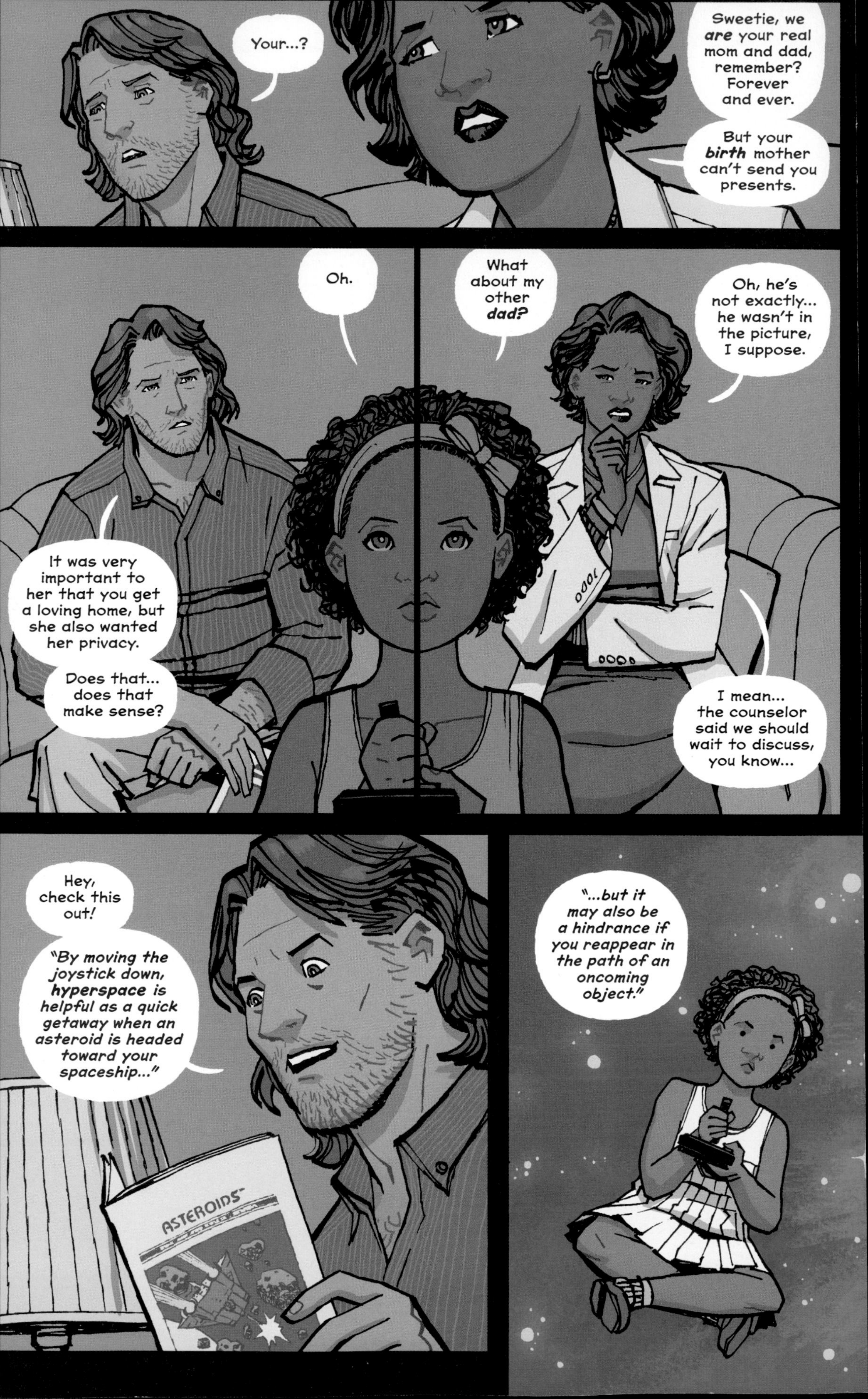
Your...?
Sweetie, we **are** your real mom and dad, remember? Forever and ever.
But your **birth** mother can't send you presents.
Oh.
What about my other **dad?**
Oh, he's not exactly... he wasn't in the picture, I suppose.
It was very important to her that you get a loving home, but she also wanted her privacy.
Does that... does that make sense?
I mean... the counselor said we should wait to discuss, you know...
Hey, check this out!
*"By moving the joystick down, **hyperspace** is helpful as a quick getaway when an asteroid is headed toward your spaceship..."*
ASTEROIDS
"...but it may also be a hindrance if you reappear in the path of an oncoming object."

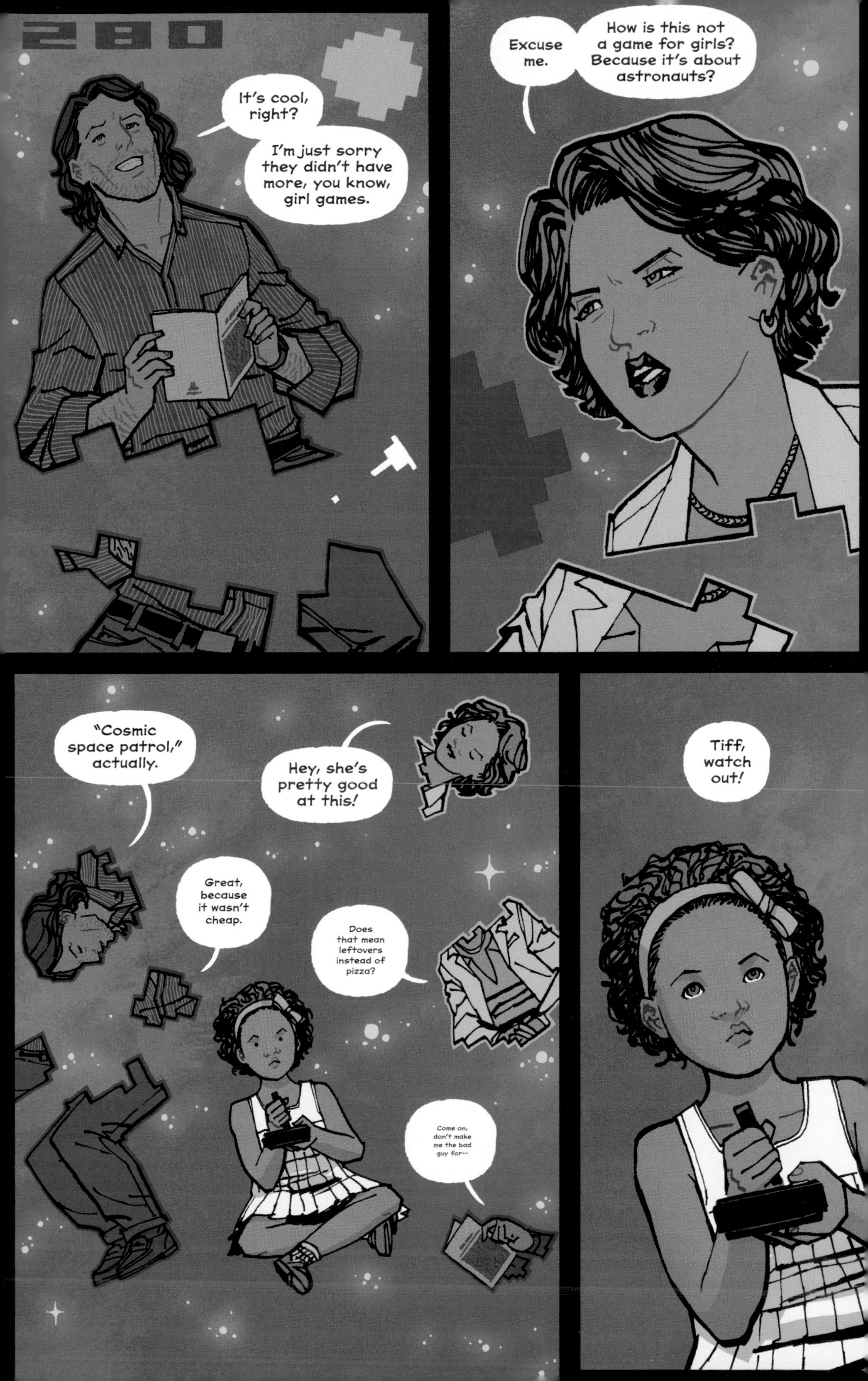
280
It's cool, right?
I'm just sorry they didn't have more, you know, girl games.
Excuse me.
How is this not a game for girls? Because it's about astronauts?
"Cosmic space patrol," actually.
Hey, she's pretty good at this!
Great, because it wasn't cheap.
Does that mean leftovers instead of pizza?
Come on, don't make me the bad guy for--
Tiff, watch out!

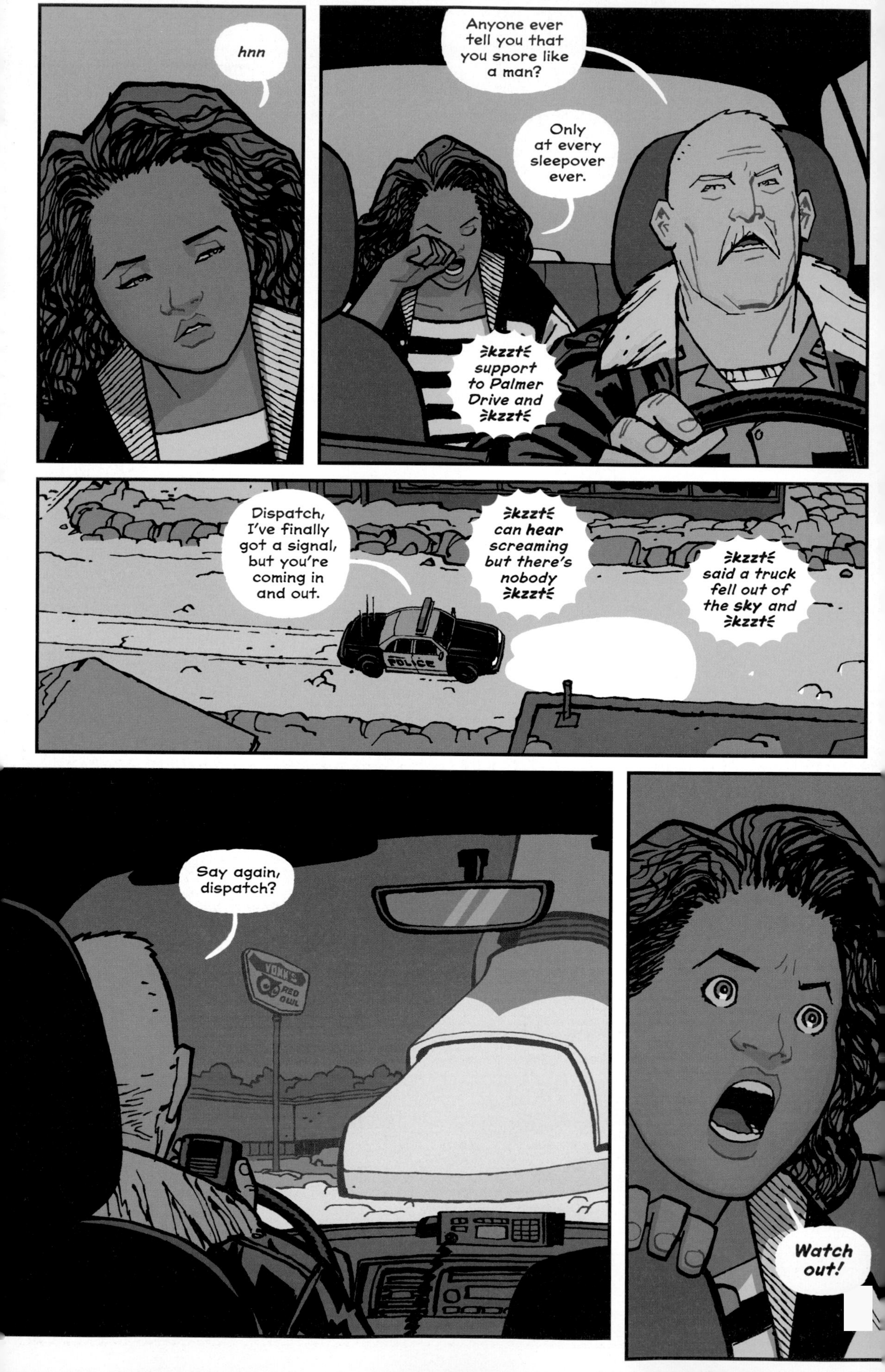
hnn
Anyone ever tell you that you snore like a man?
Only at every sleepover ever.
kzzt support to Palmer Drive and kzzt
Dispatch, I've finally got a signal, but you're coming in and out.
kzzt can hear screaming but there's nobody kzzt
kzzt said a truck fell out of the sky and kzzt
Say again, dispatch?
YORK'S RED OWL
Watch out!

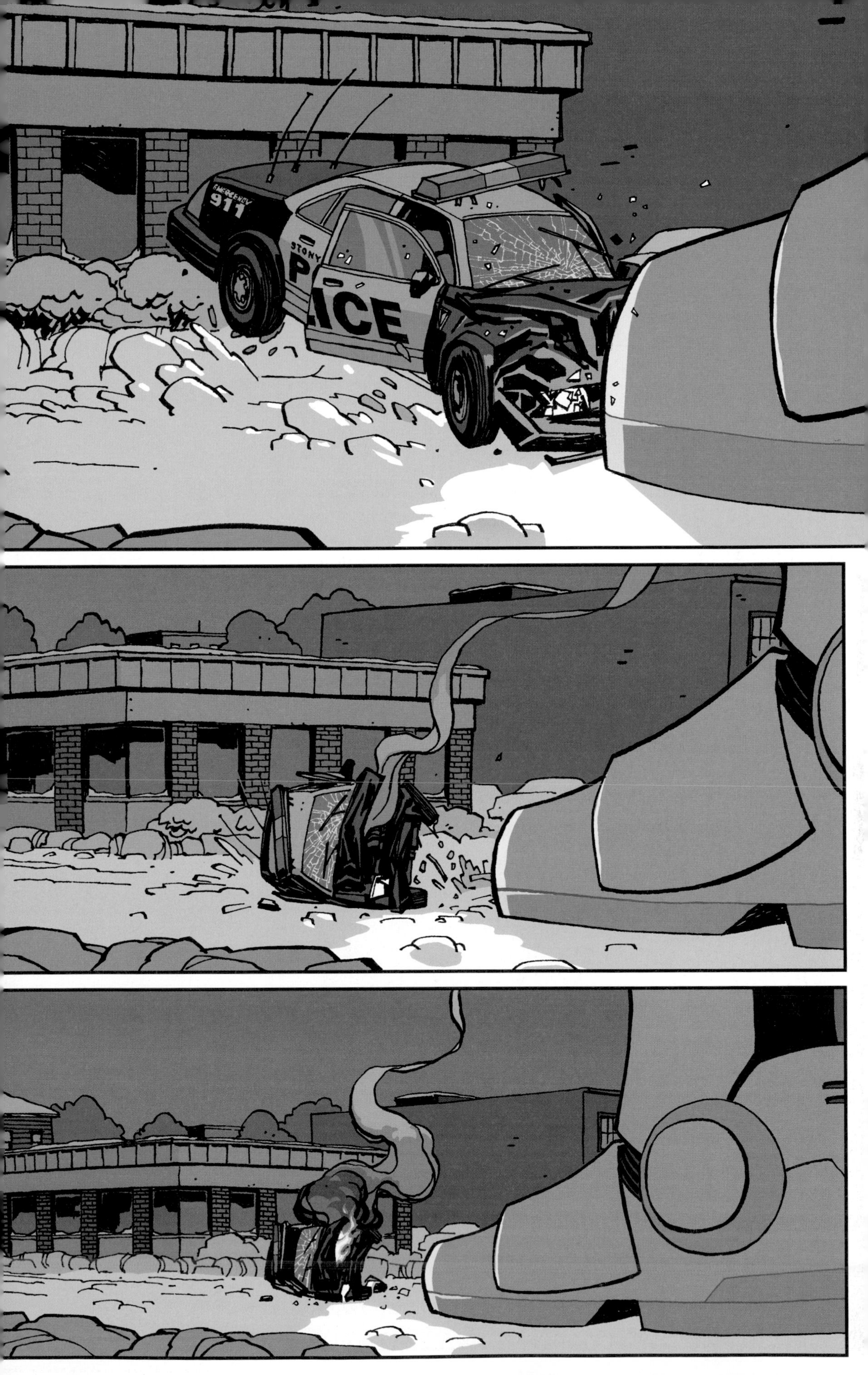
EMERGENCY
911
STONY
P
ICE

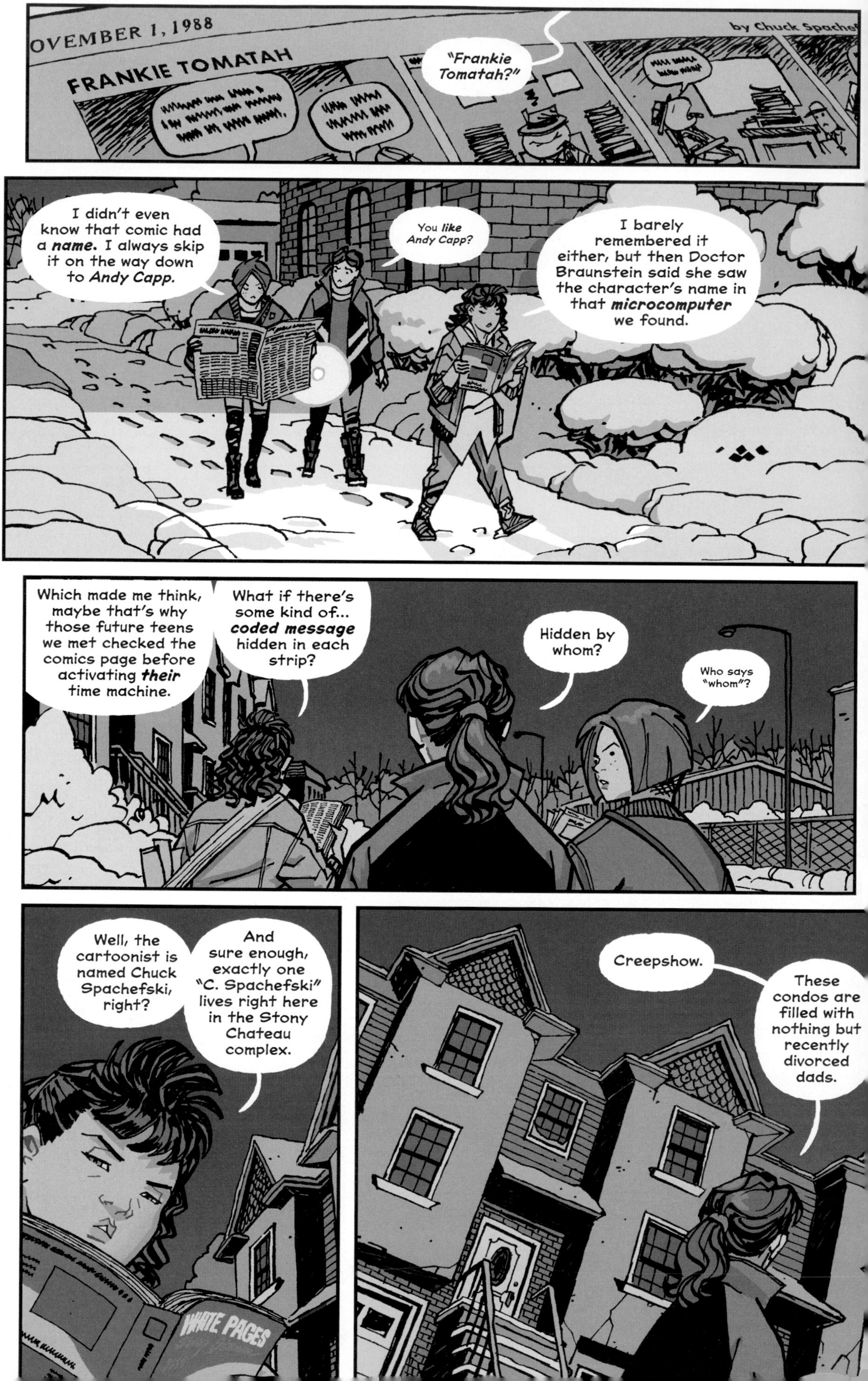

OVEMBER 1, 1988
FRANKIE TOMATAH
by Chuck Spache
"Frankie Tomatah?"
I didn't even know that comic had a name. I always skip it on the way down to Andy Capp.
You like Andy Capp?
I barely remembered it either, but then Doctor Braunstein said she saw the character's name in that microcomputer we found.
Which made me think, maybe that's why those future teens we met checked the comics page before activating their time machine.
What if there's some kind of... coded message hidden in each strip?
Hidden by whom?
Who says "whom"?
Well, the cartoonist is named Chuck Spachefski, right?
And sure enough, exactly one "C. Spachefski" lives right here in the Stony Chateau complex.
WHITE PAGES
Creepshow.
These condos are filled with nothing but recently divorced dads.

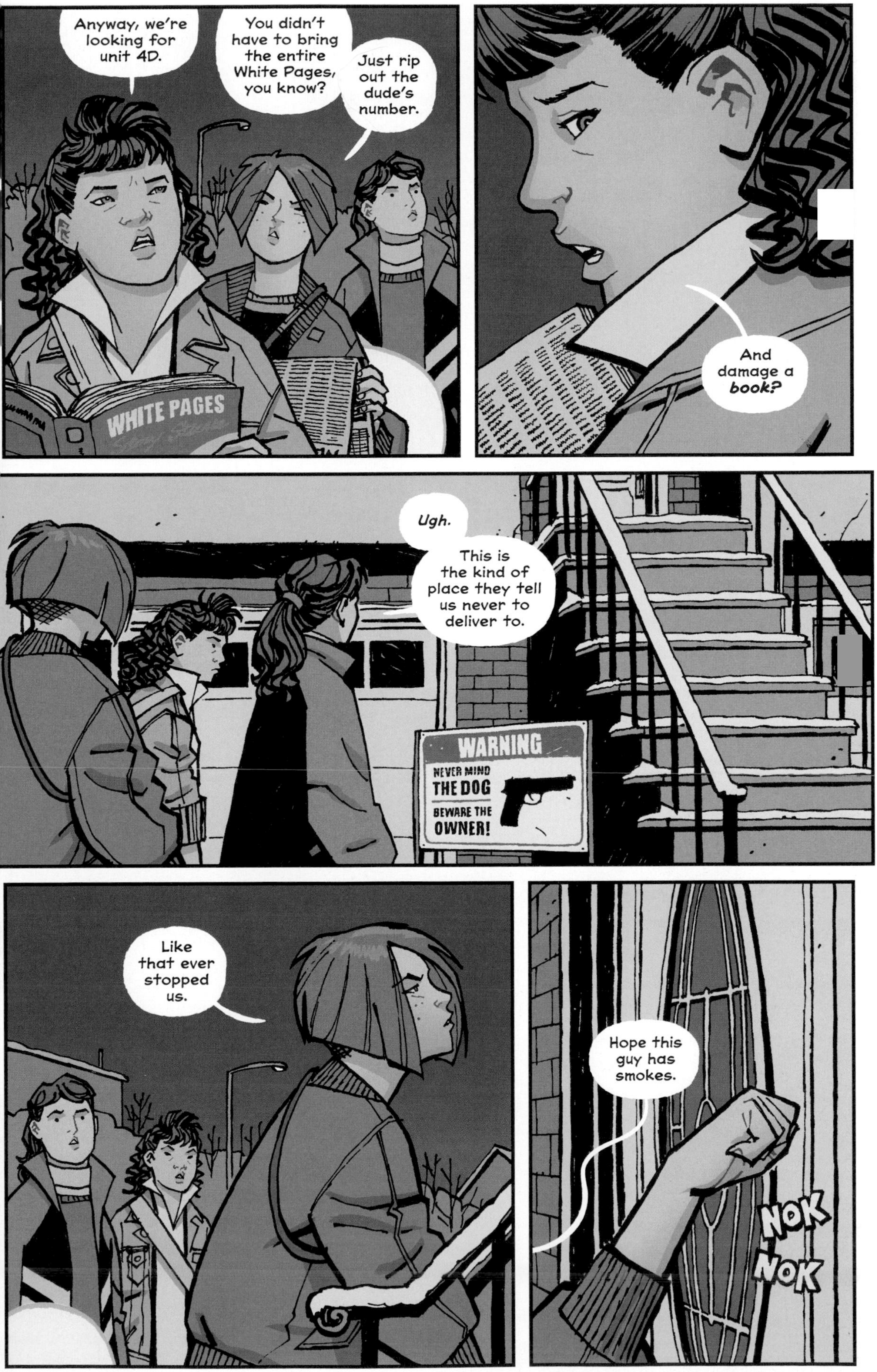
Anyway, we're looking for unit 4D.
You didn't have to bring the entire White Pages, you know?
Just rip out the dude's number.
WHITE PAGES
And damage a *book?*
Ugh.
This is the kind of place they tell us never to deliver to.
WARNING
NEVER MIND THE DOG
BEWARE THE OWNER!
Like that ever stopped us.
Hope this guy has smokes.
NOK
NOK

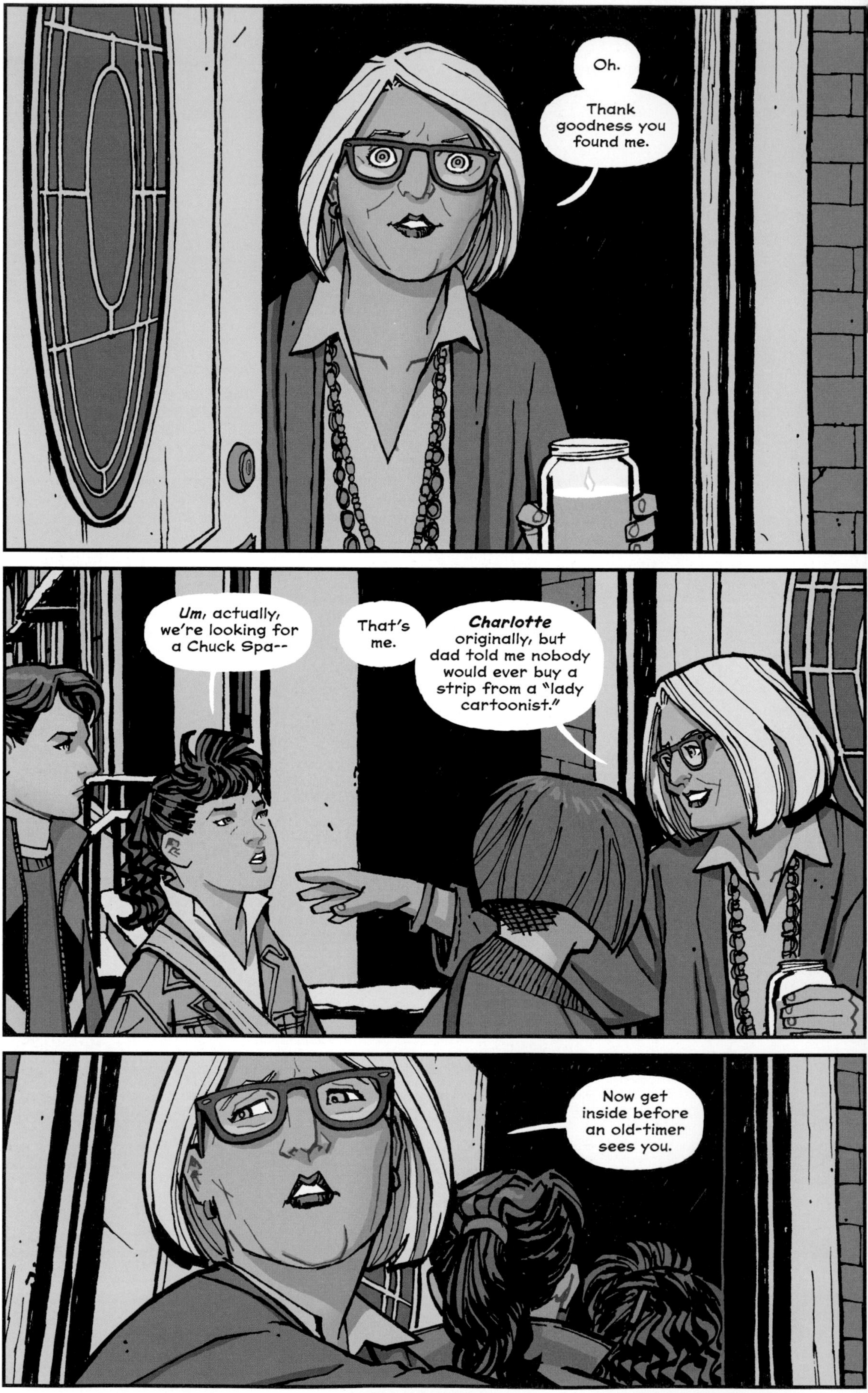
Oh.
Thank goodness you found me.
Um, actually, we're looking for a Chuck Spa--
That's me.
Charlotte originally, but dad told me nobody would ever buy a strip from a "lady cartoonist."
Now get inside before an old-timer sees you.

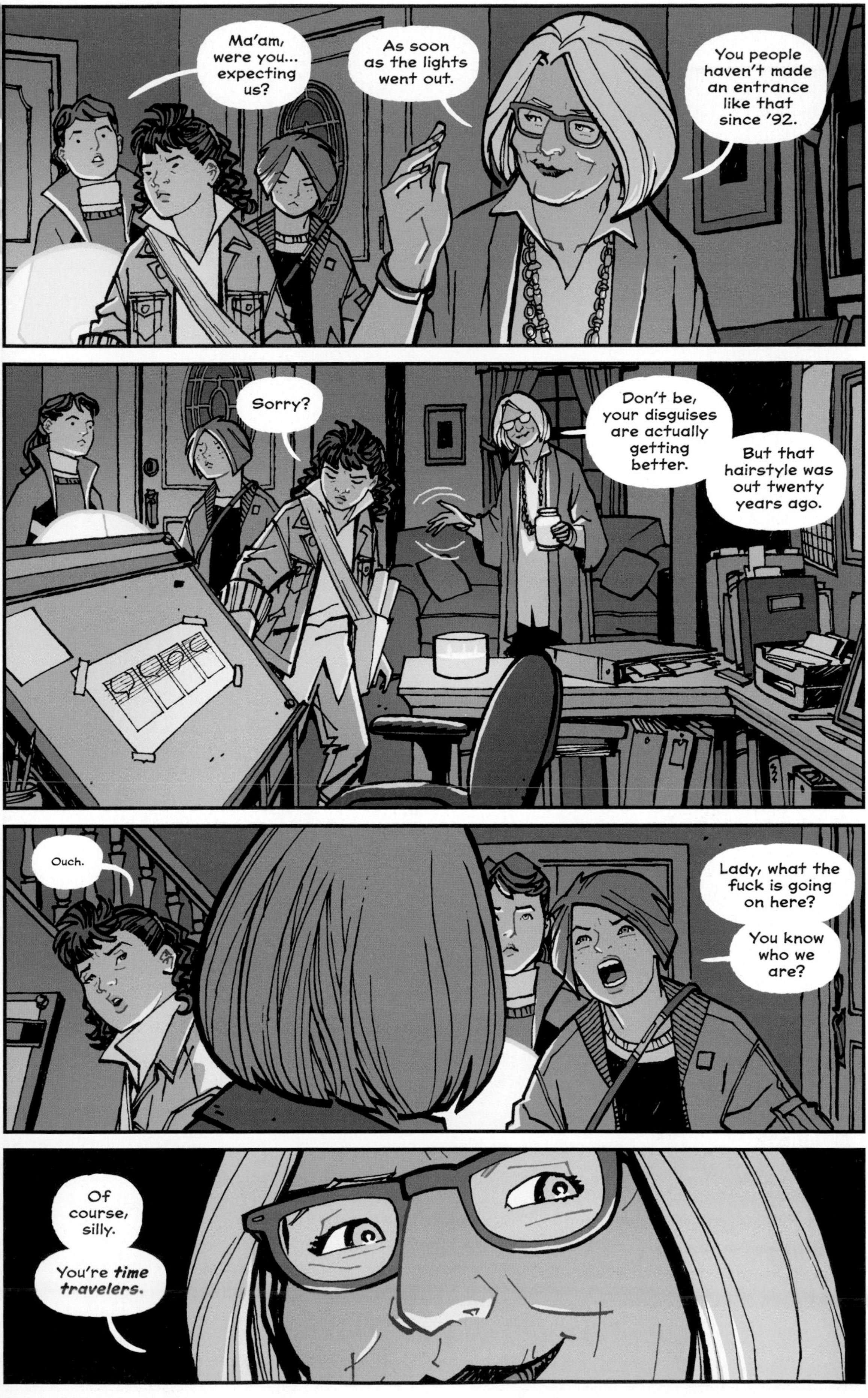

Ma'am, were you... expecting us?
As soon as the lights went out.
You people haven't made an entrance like that since '92.
Sorry?
Don't be, your disguises are actually getting better.
But that hairstyle was out twenty years ago.
Ouch.
Lady, what the fuck is going on here?
You know who we are?
Of course, silly.
You're *time travelers.*

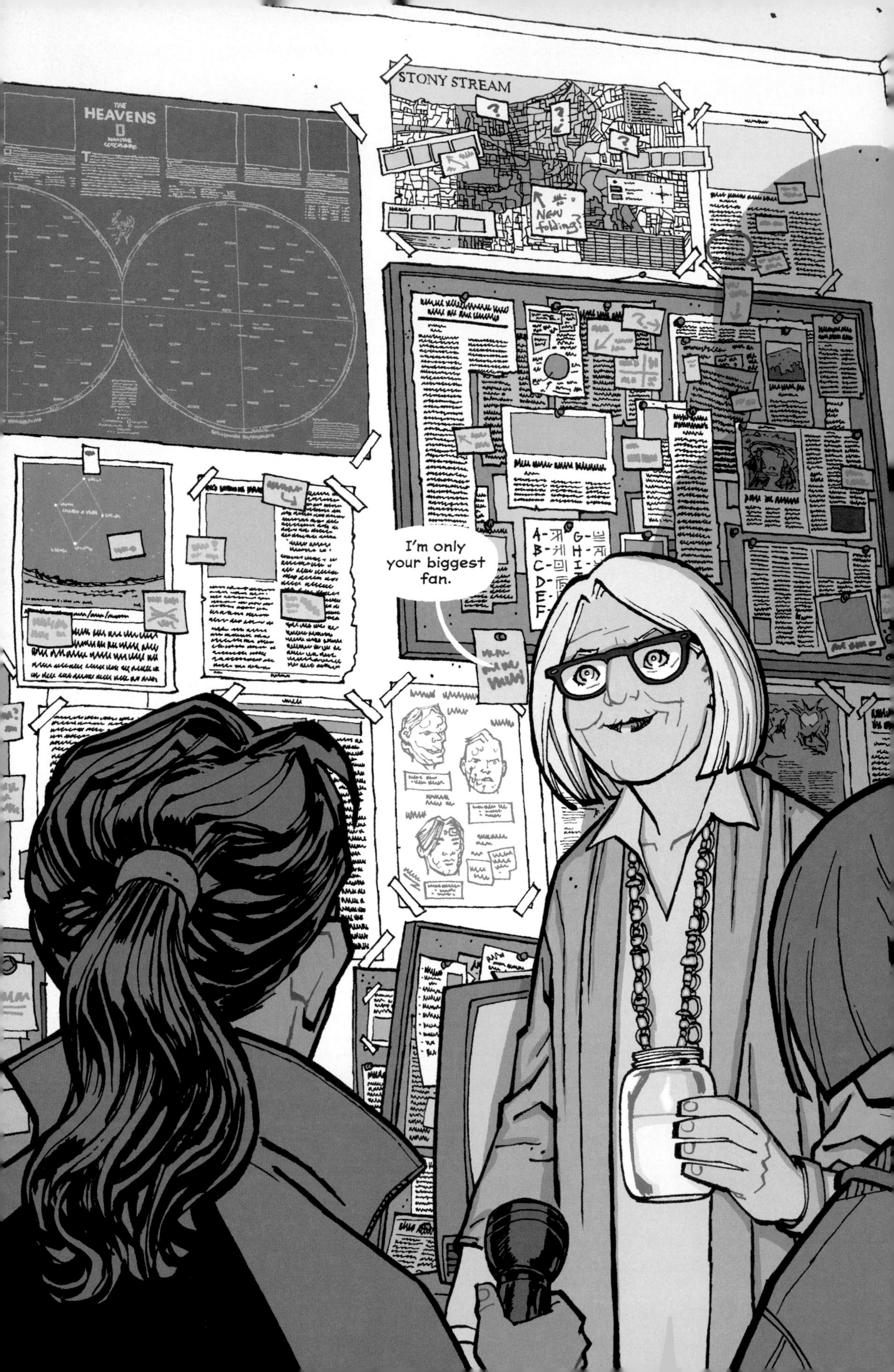
THE HEAVENS
STONY STREAM
New folding?
I'm only your biggest fan.

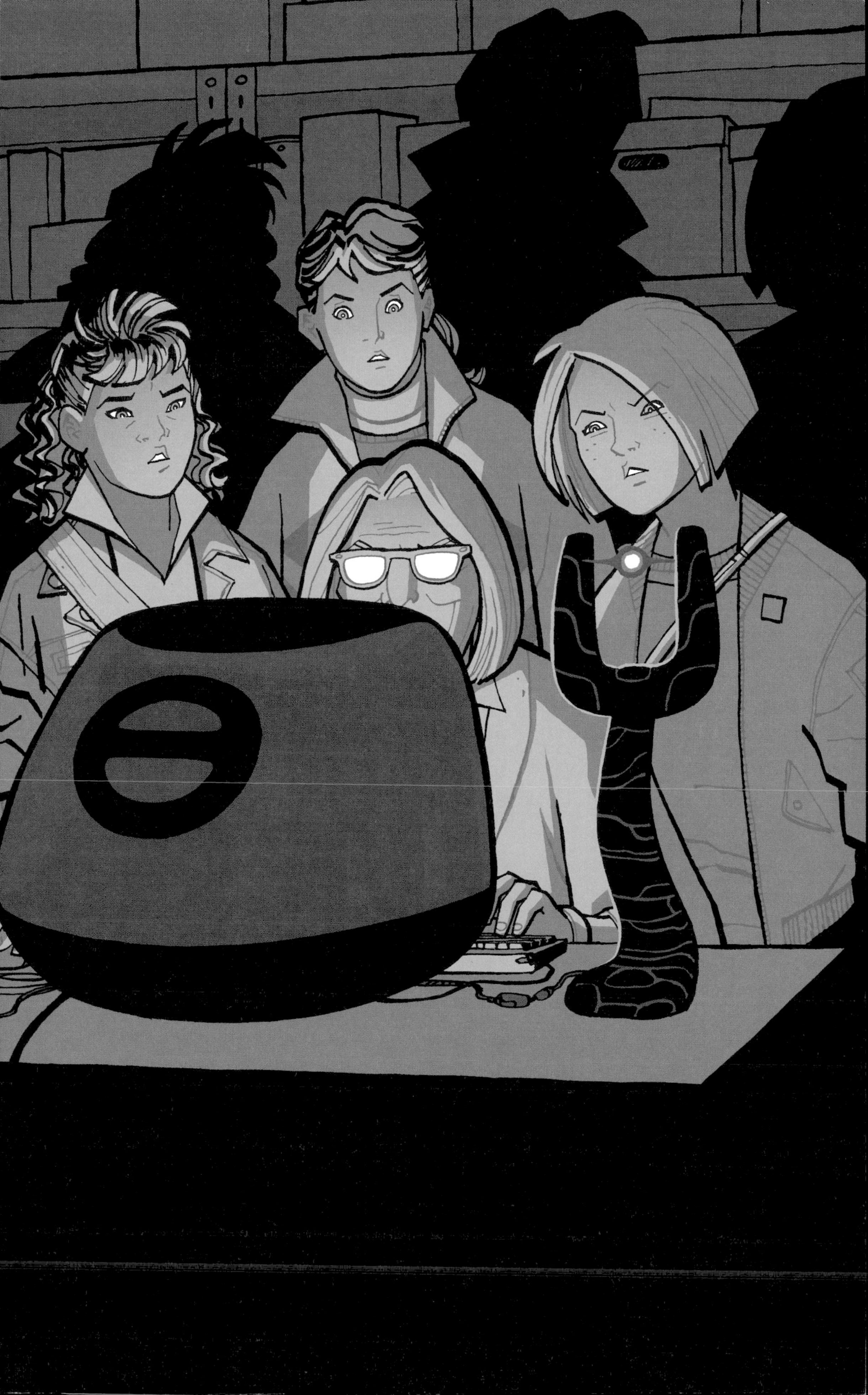

"THE END OF THE WORLD?!?
Y2K Insanity!
Will computers melt down?
Will society?"

-**Time Magazine** cover,
January 18, 1999

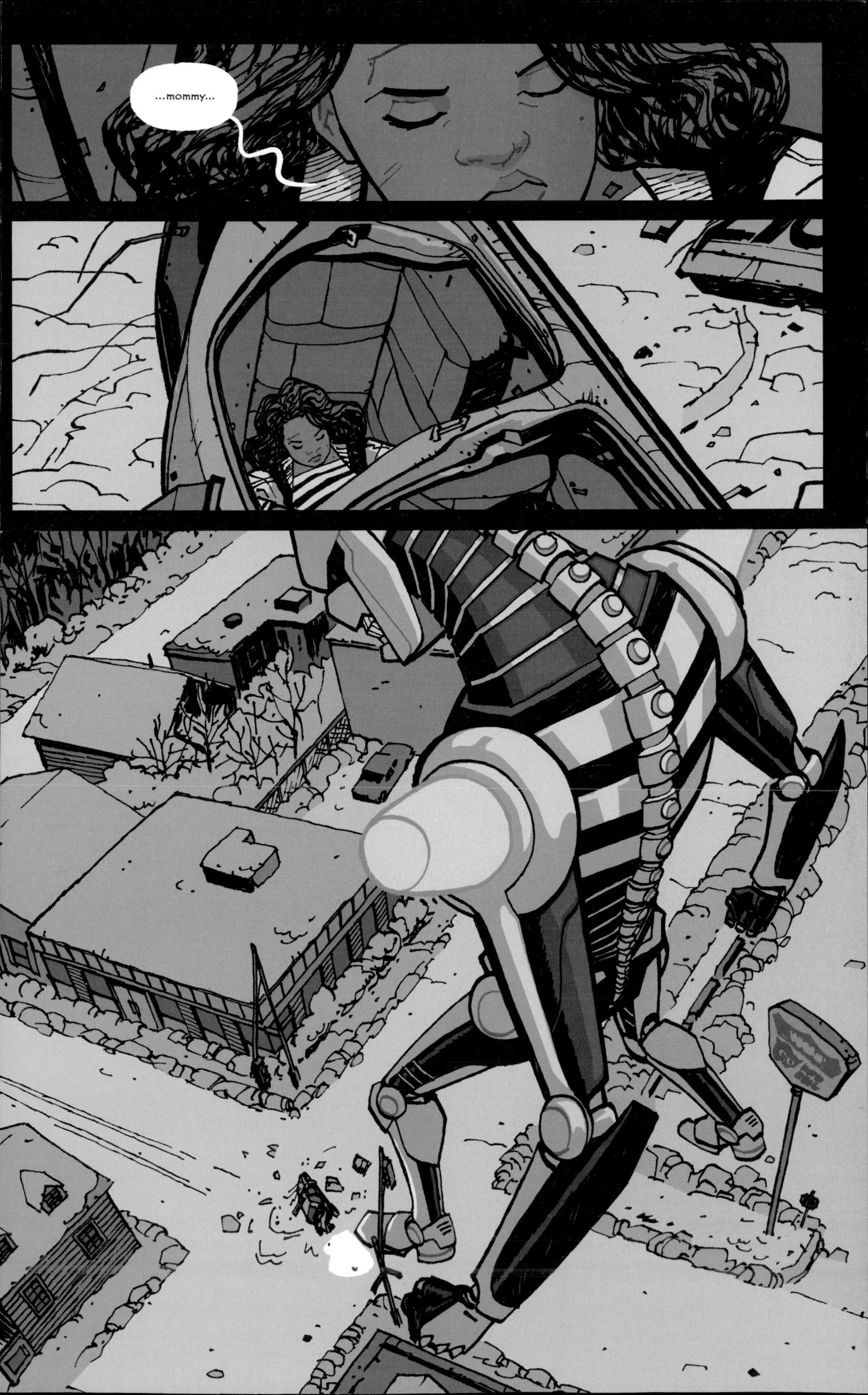
...mommy...

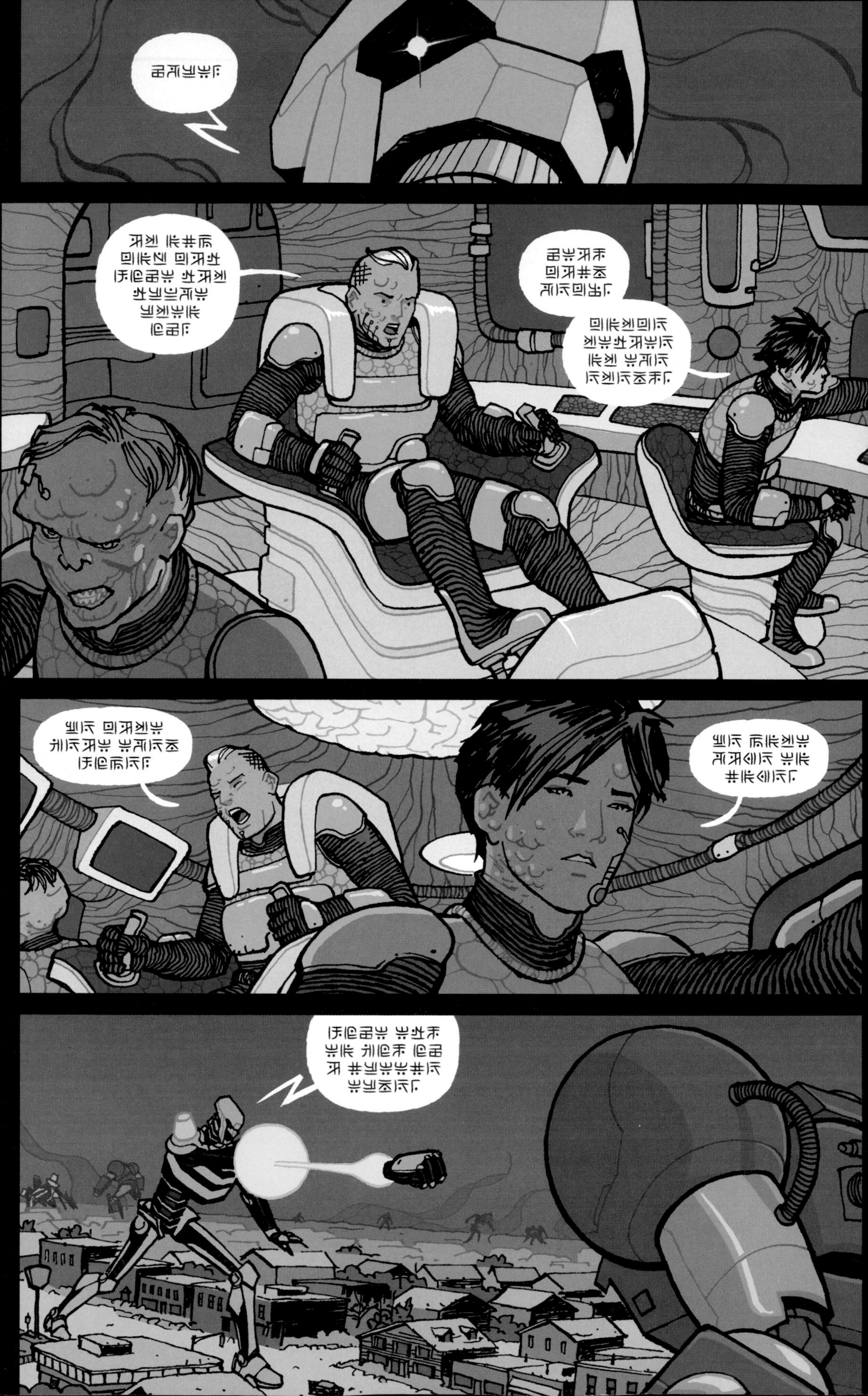

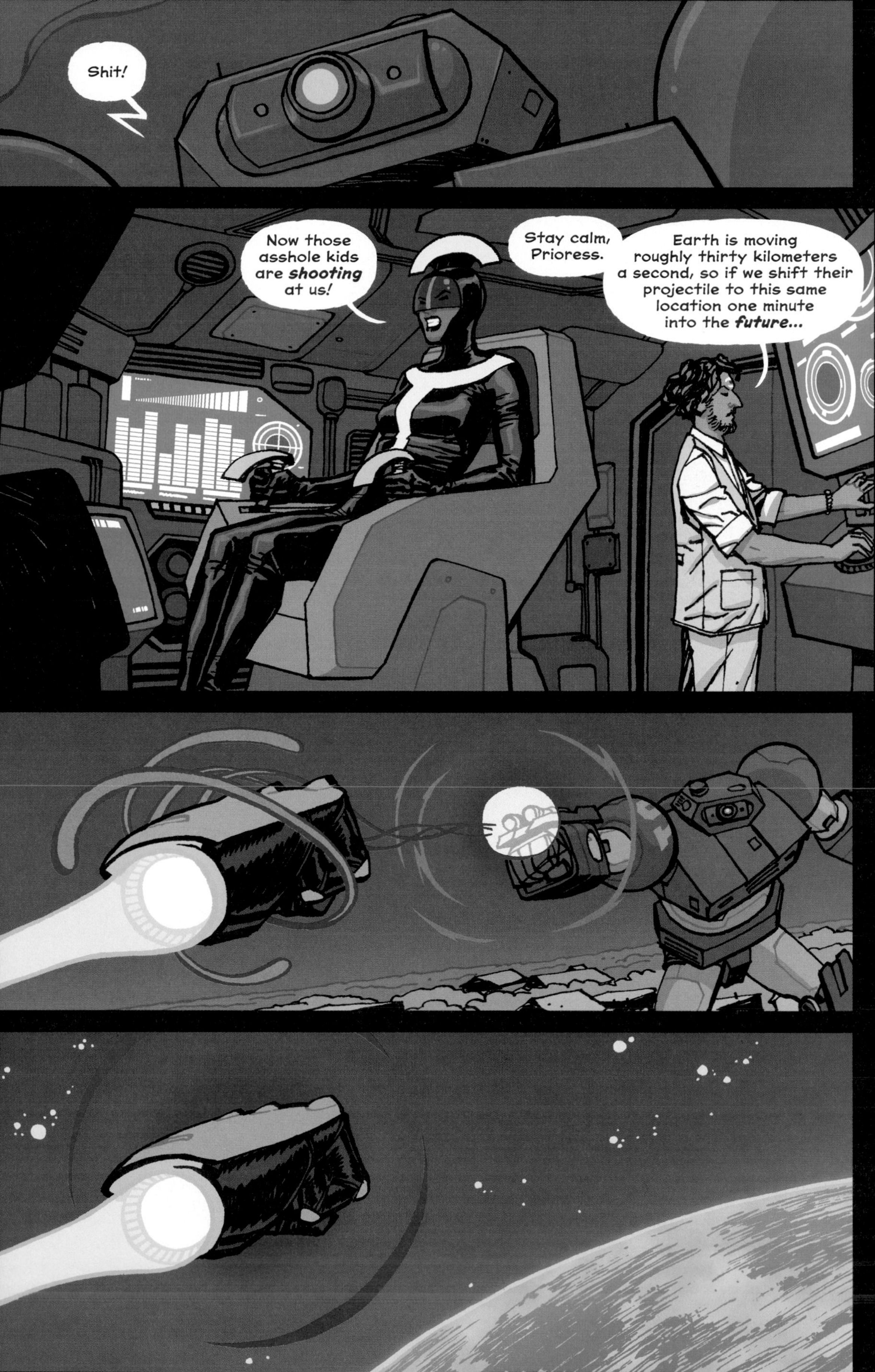
Shit!
Now those asshole kids are shooting at us!
Stay calm, Prioress.
Earth is moving roughly thirty kilometers a second, so if we shift their projectile to this same location one minute into the future...

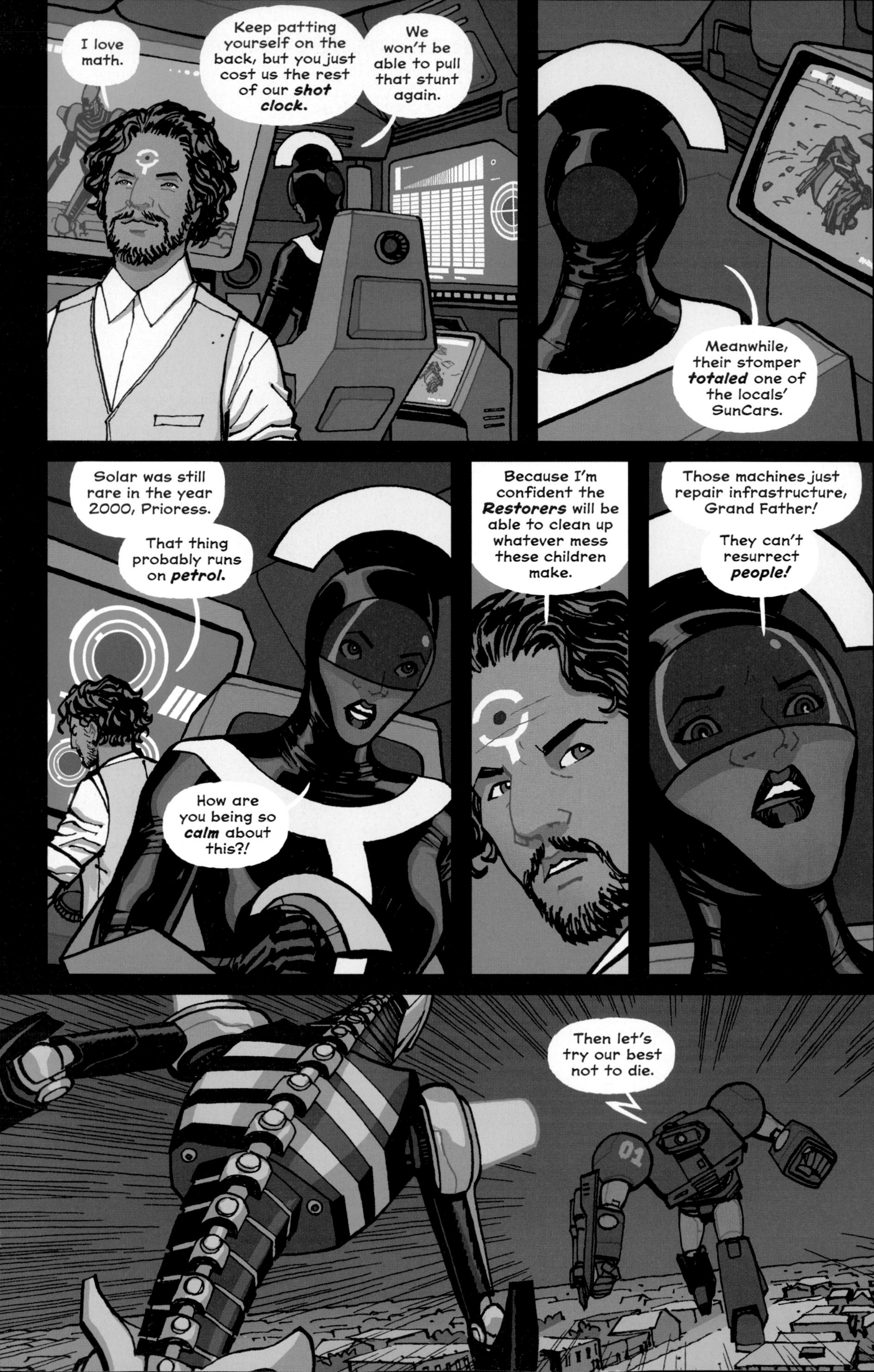
I love math.
Keep patting yourself on the back, but you just cost us the rest of our *shot clock.*
We won't be able to pull that stunt again.
Meanwhile, their stomper *totaled* one of the locals' SunCars.
Solar was still rare in the year 2000, Prioress.
That thing probably runs on *petrol.*
How are you being so *calm* about this?!
Because I'm confident the *Restorers* will be able to clean up whatever mess these children make.
Those machines just repair infrastructure, Grand Father!
They can't resurrect *people!*
Then let's try our best not to die.
01

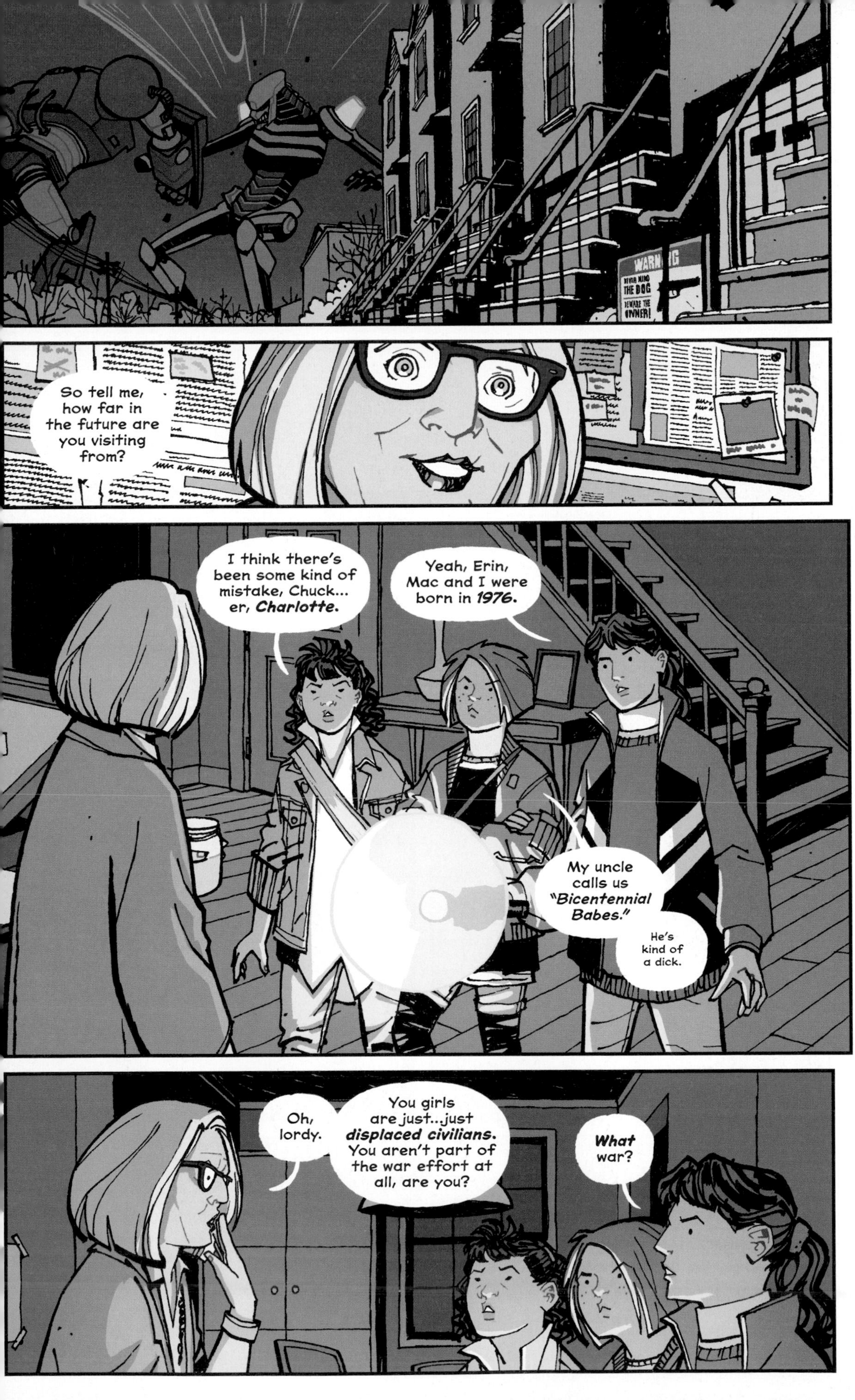
So tell me, how far in the future are you visiting from?
I think there's been some kind of mistake, Chuck... er, **Charlotte.**
Yeah, Erin, Mac and I were born in ***1976.***
My uncle calls us ***"Bicentennial Babes."***
He's kind of a dick.
Oh, lordy.
You girls are just...just ***displaced civilians.*** You aren't part of the war effort at all, are you?
What war?

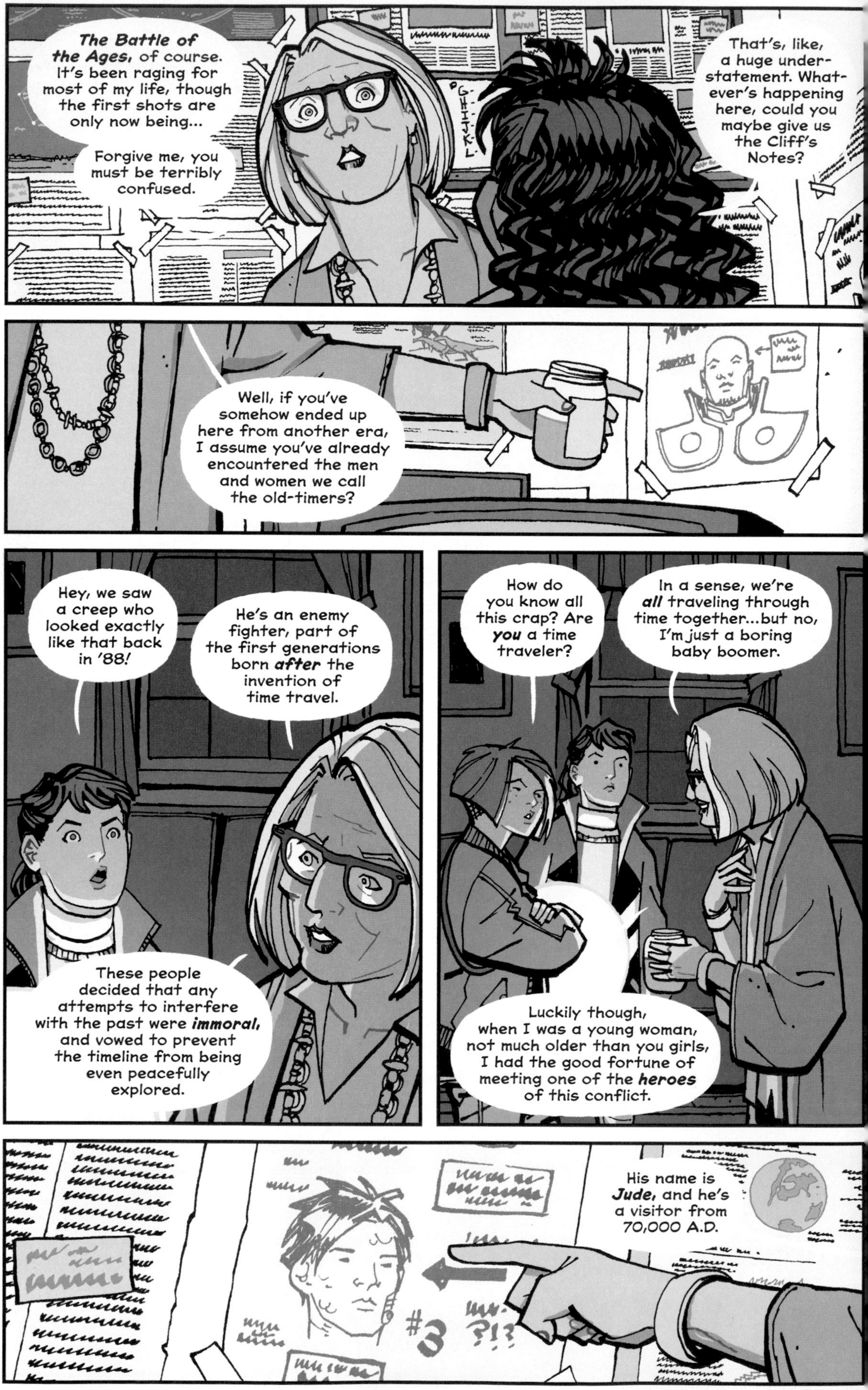
The Battle of the Ages, of course. It's been raging for most of my life, though the first shots are only now being...
Forgive me, you must be terribly confused.
G- H- I- J- K- L-
That's, like, a huge understatement. Whatever's happening here, could you maybe give us the Cliff's Notes?
Well, if you've somehow ended up here from another era, I assume you've already encountered the men and women we call the old-timers?
Hey, we saw a creep who looked exactly like that back in '88!
He's an enemy fighter, part of the first generations born after the invention of time travel.
These people decided that any attempts to interfere with the past were immoral, and vowed to prevent the timeline from being even peacefully explored.
How do you know all this crap? Are you a time traveler?
In a sense, we're all traveling through time together...but no, I'm just a boring baby boomer.
Luckily though, when I was a young woman, not much older than you girls, I had the good fortune of meeting one of the heroes of this conflict.
His name is Jude, and he's a visitor from 70,000 A.D.
#3
?!?

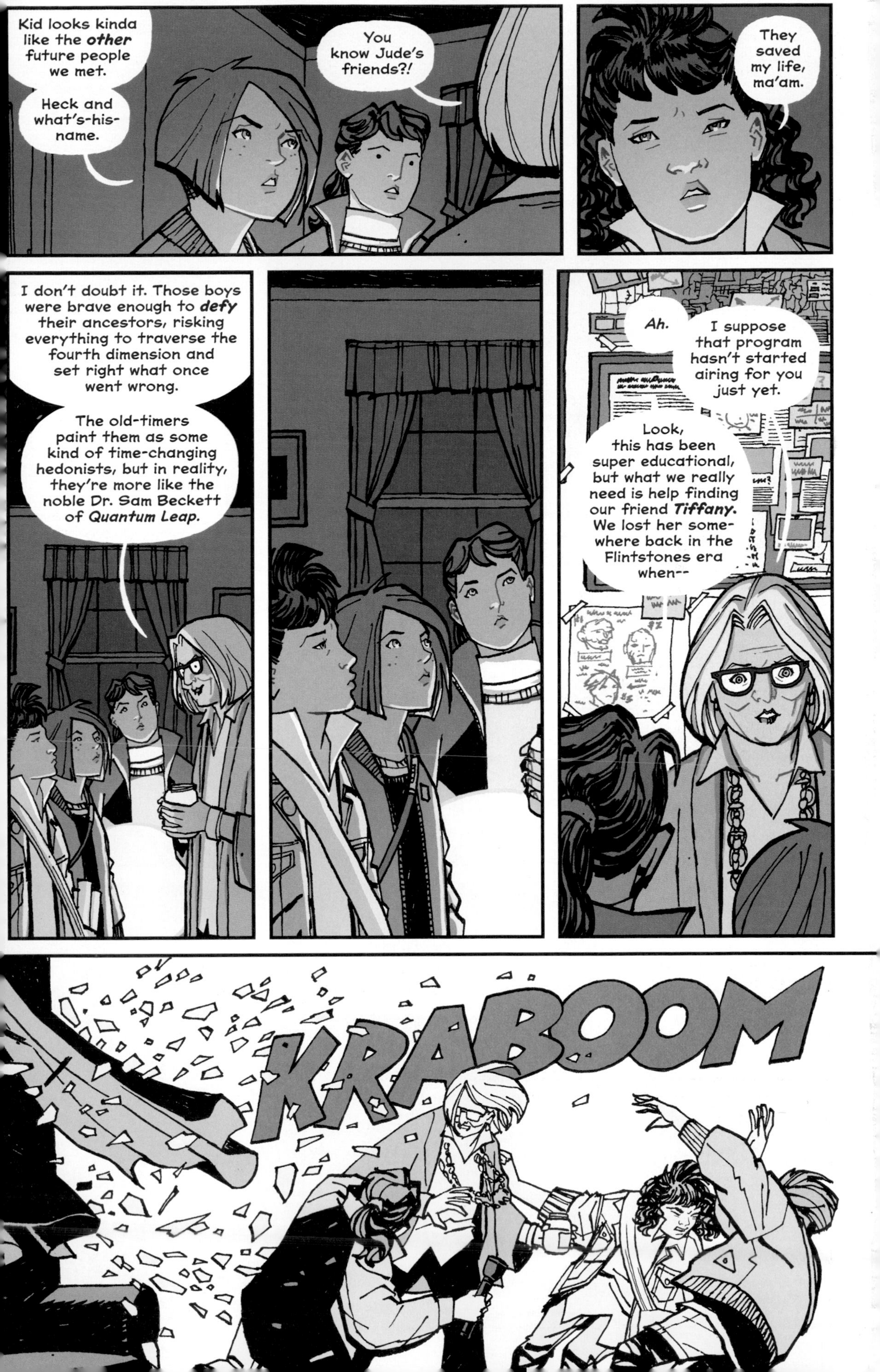

Kid looks kinda like the *other* future people we met.
Heck and what's-his-name.
You know Jude's friends?!
They saved my life, ma'am.
I don't doubt it. Those boys were brave enough to *defy* their ancestors, risking everything to traverse the fourth dimension and set right what once went wrong.
The old-timers paint them as some kind of time-changing hedonists, but in reality, they're more like the noble Dr. Sam Beckett of *Quantum Leap.*
Ah.
I suppose that program hasn't started airing for you just yet.
Look, this has been super educational, but what we really need is help finding our friend *Tiffany.* We lost her somewhere back in the Flintstones era when--
KRABOOM

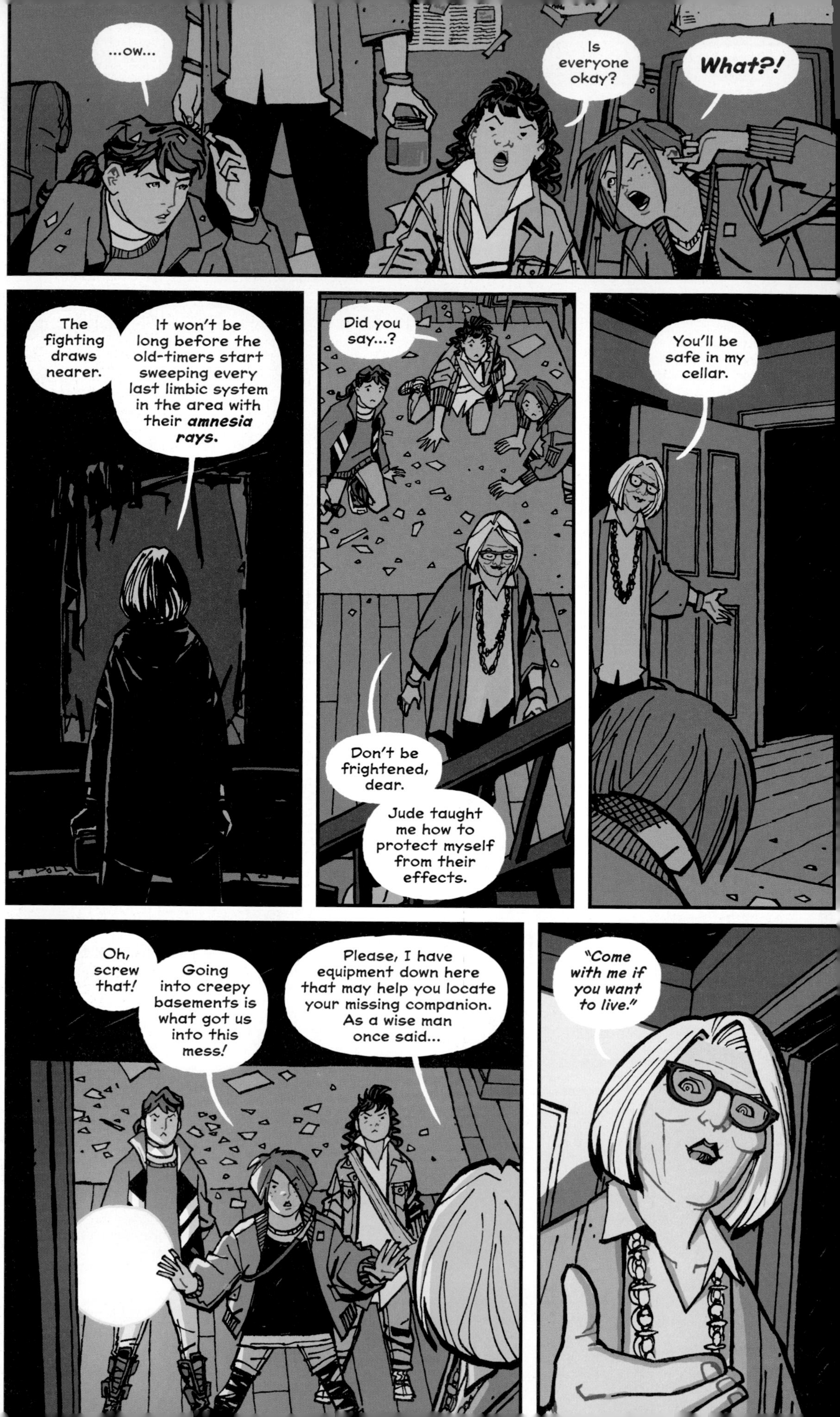

...ow...
Is everyone okay?
What?!
The fighting draws nearer.
It won't be long before the old-timers start sweeping every last limbic system in the area with their *amnesia rays.*
Did you say...?
Don't be frightened, dear.
Jude taught me how to protect myself from their effects.
You'll be safe in my cellar.
Oh, screw that!
Going into creepy basements is what got us into this mess!
Please, I have equipment down here that may help you locate your missing companion. As a wise man once said...
"Come with me if you want to live."

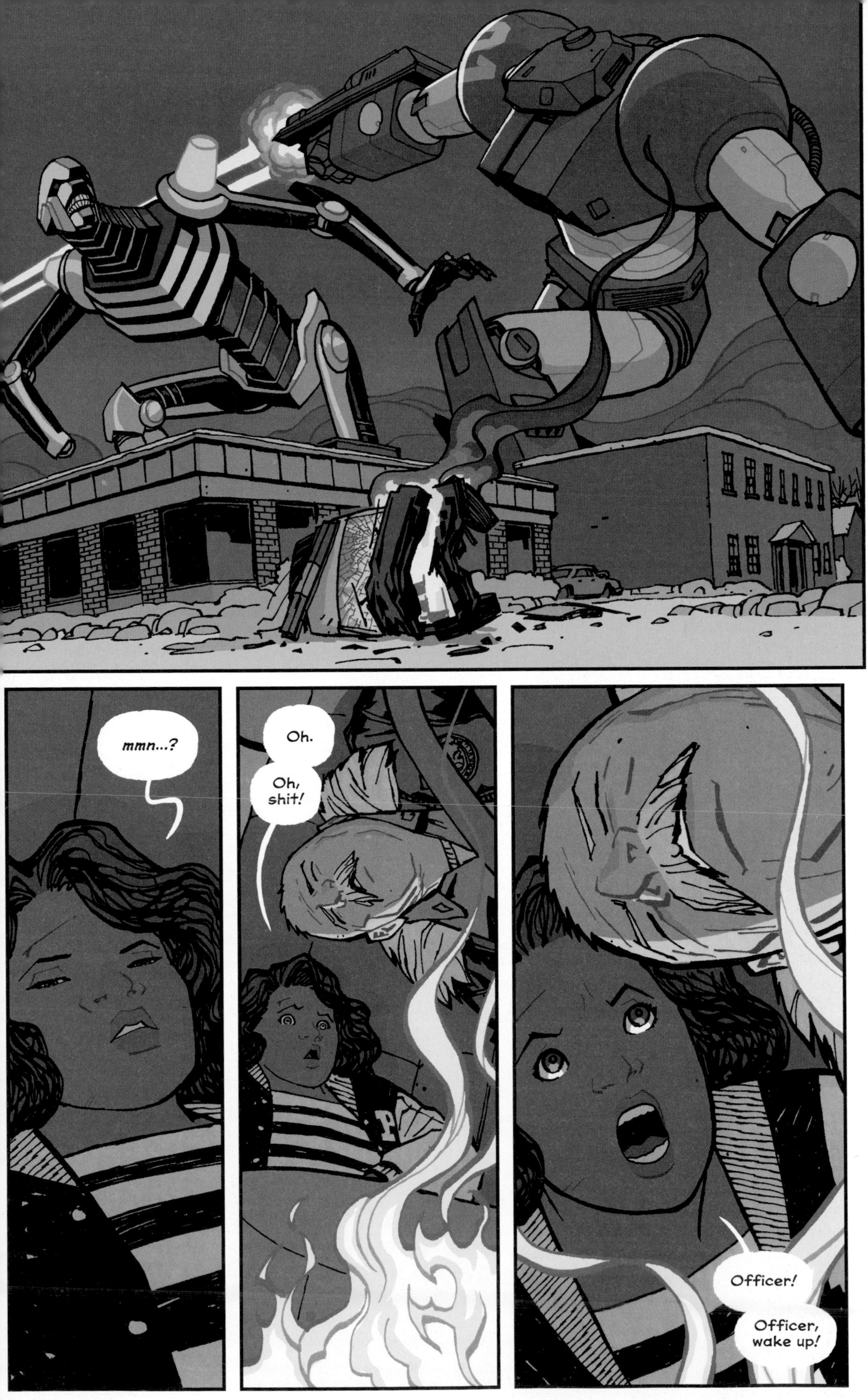
mmn...?
Oh.
Oh, shit!
Officer!
Officer, wake up!

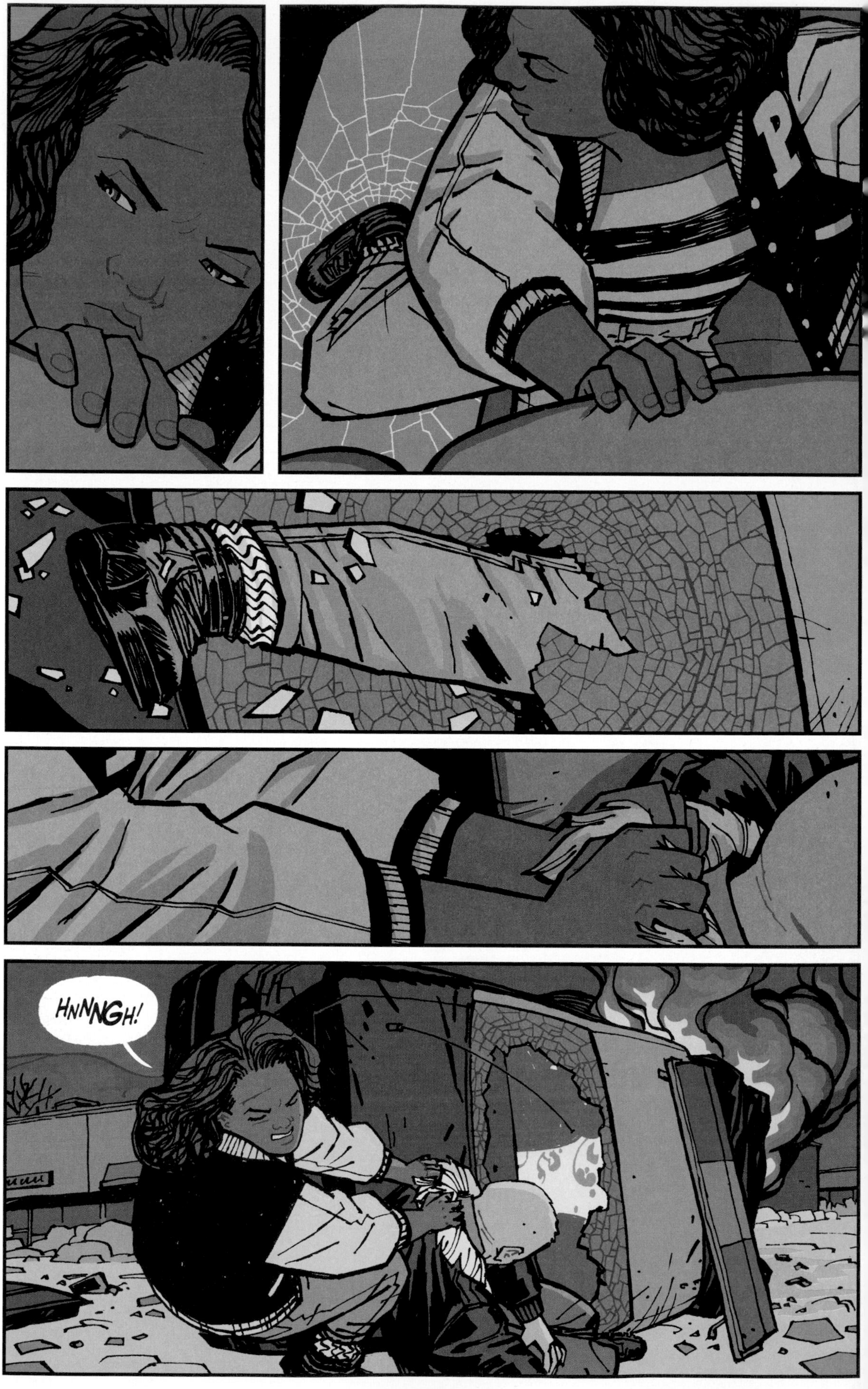
HNNNGH!

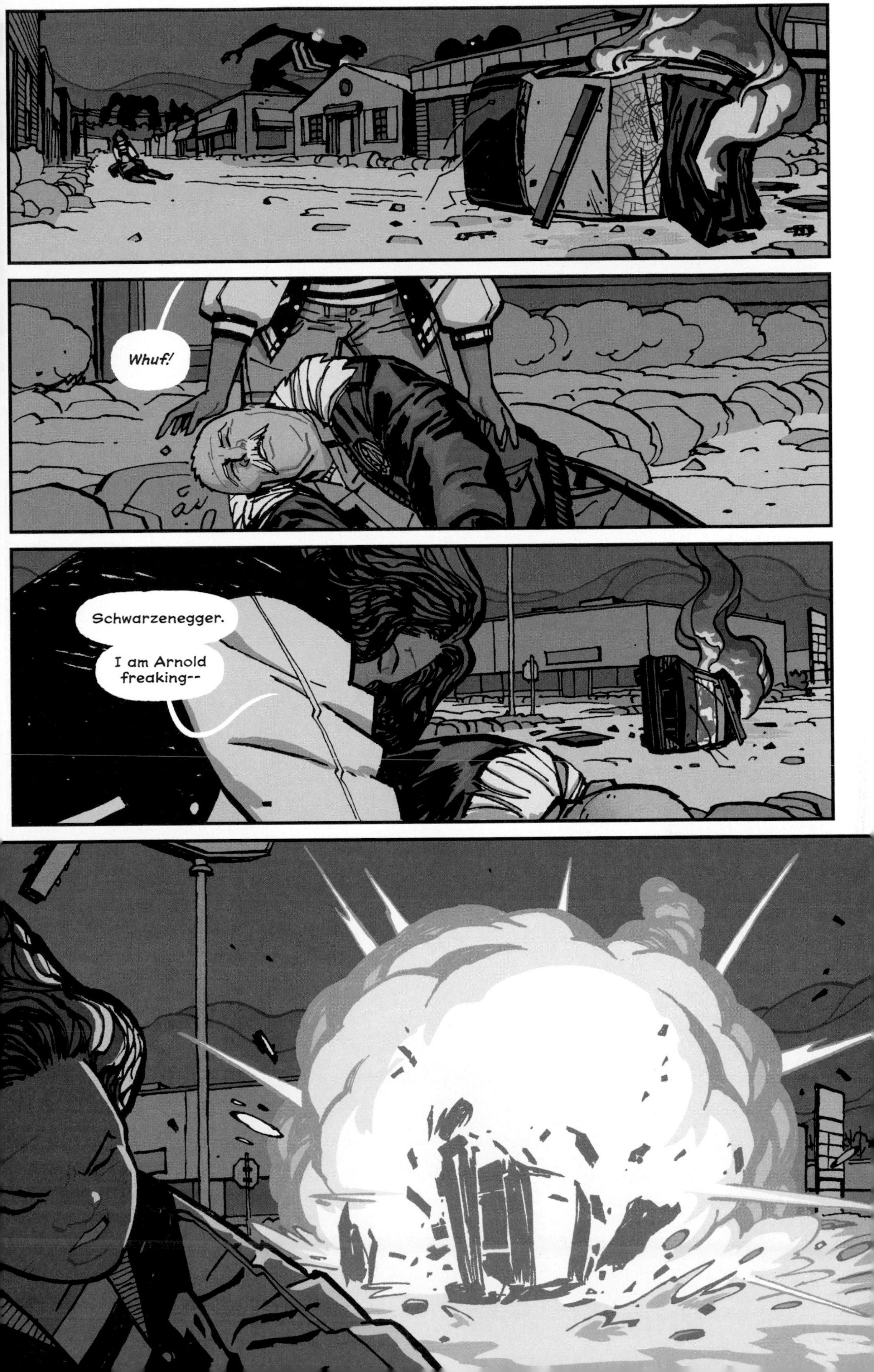
Whuf!
Schwarzenegger.
I am Arnold freaking--

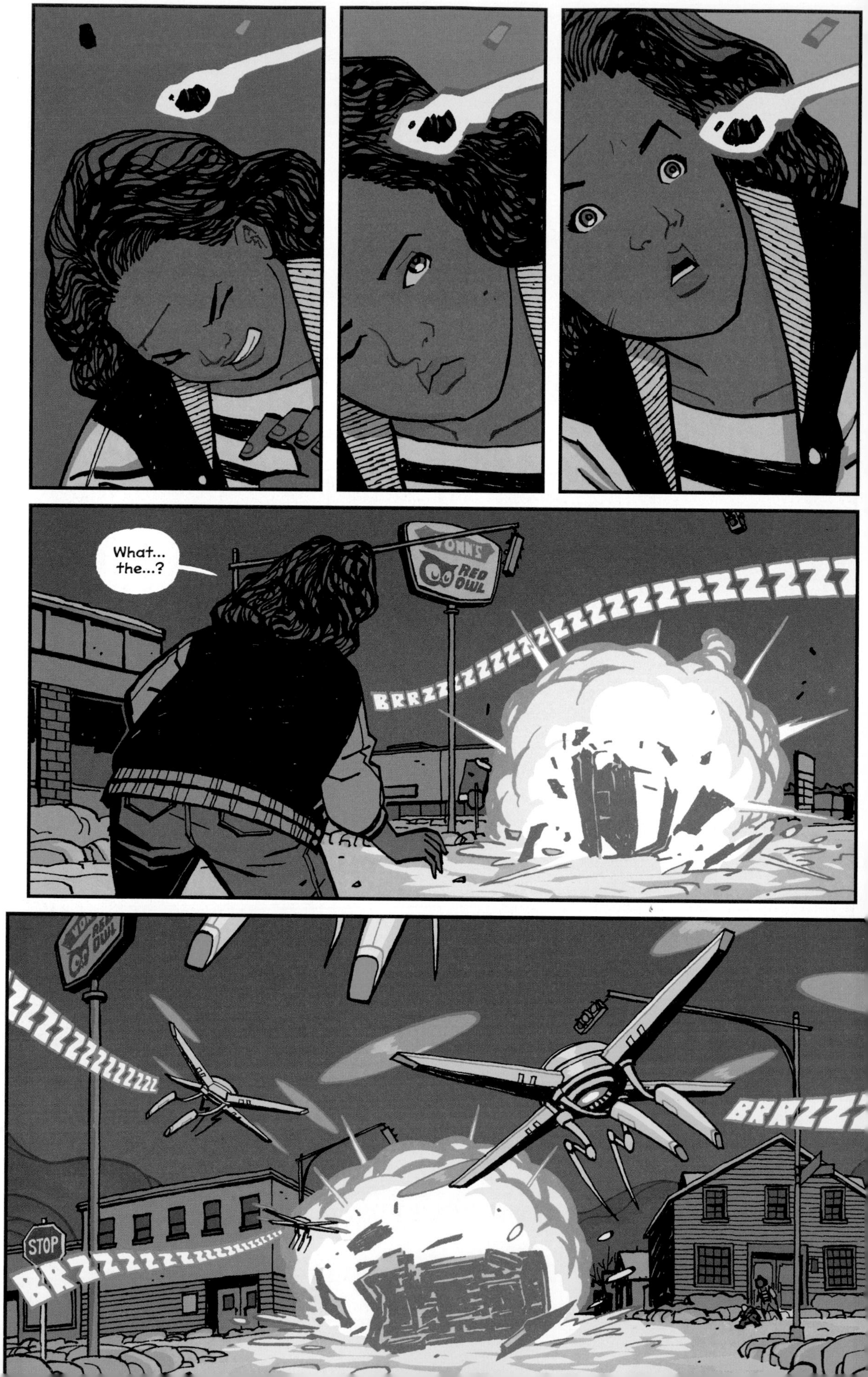
What... the...?
RED OWL
BRRZZZZZZZZZZZZZZZZZZZZZZ
ZZZZZZZZZZZZZZ
BRRZZZ
STOP
BRZZZZZZZZZZZZZZZ

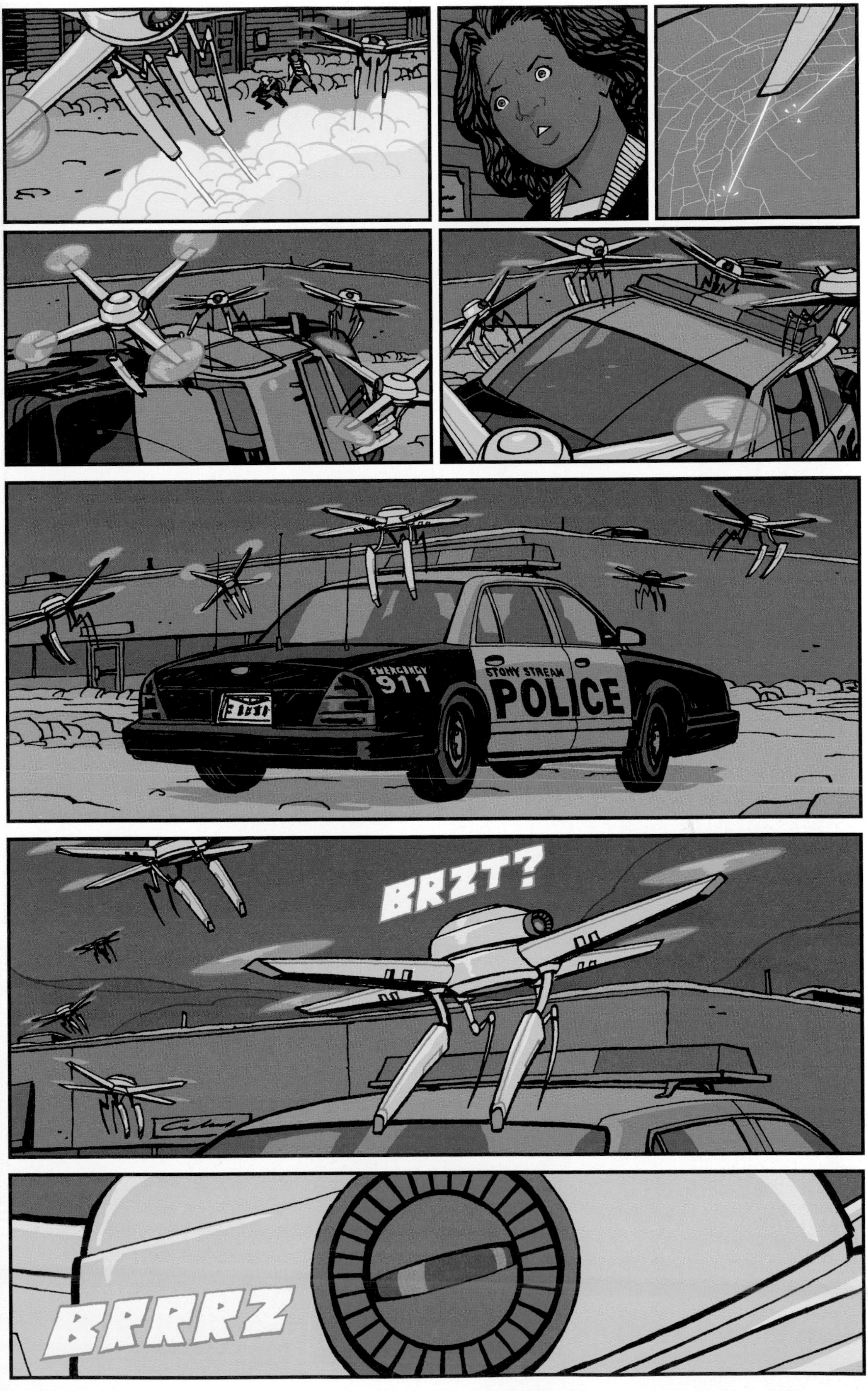
EMERGENCY
911
STONY STREAM
POLICE
BRZT?
BRRRZ

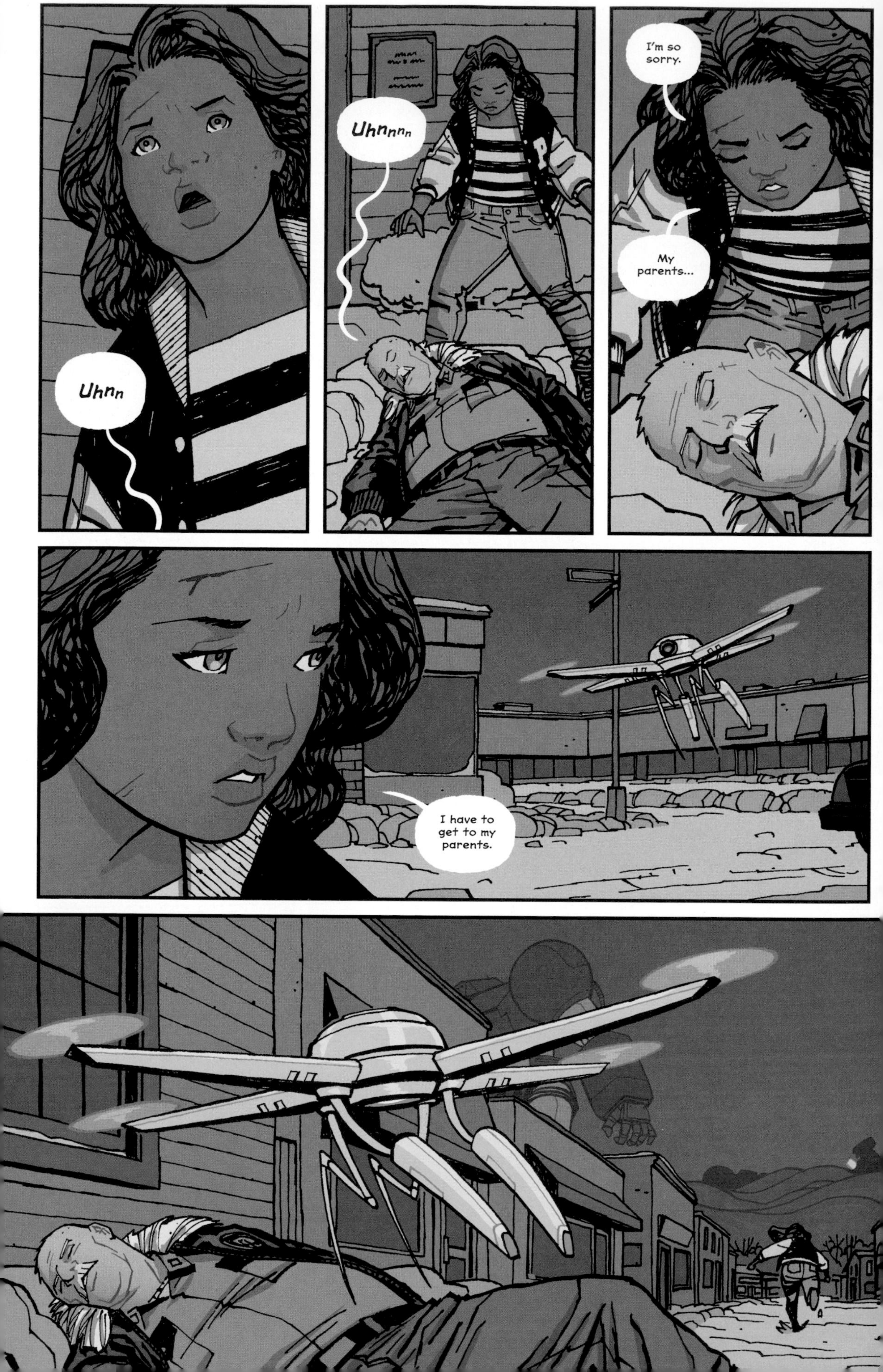
Uhnn
Uhnnnn
I'm so sorry.
My parents...
I have to get to my parents.

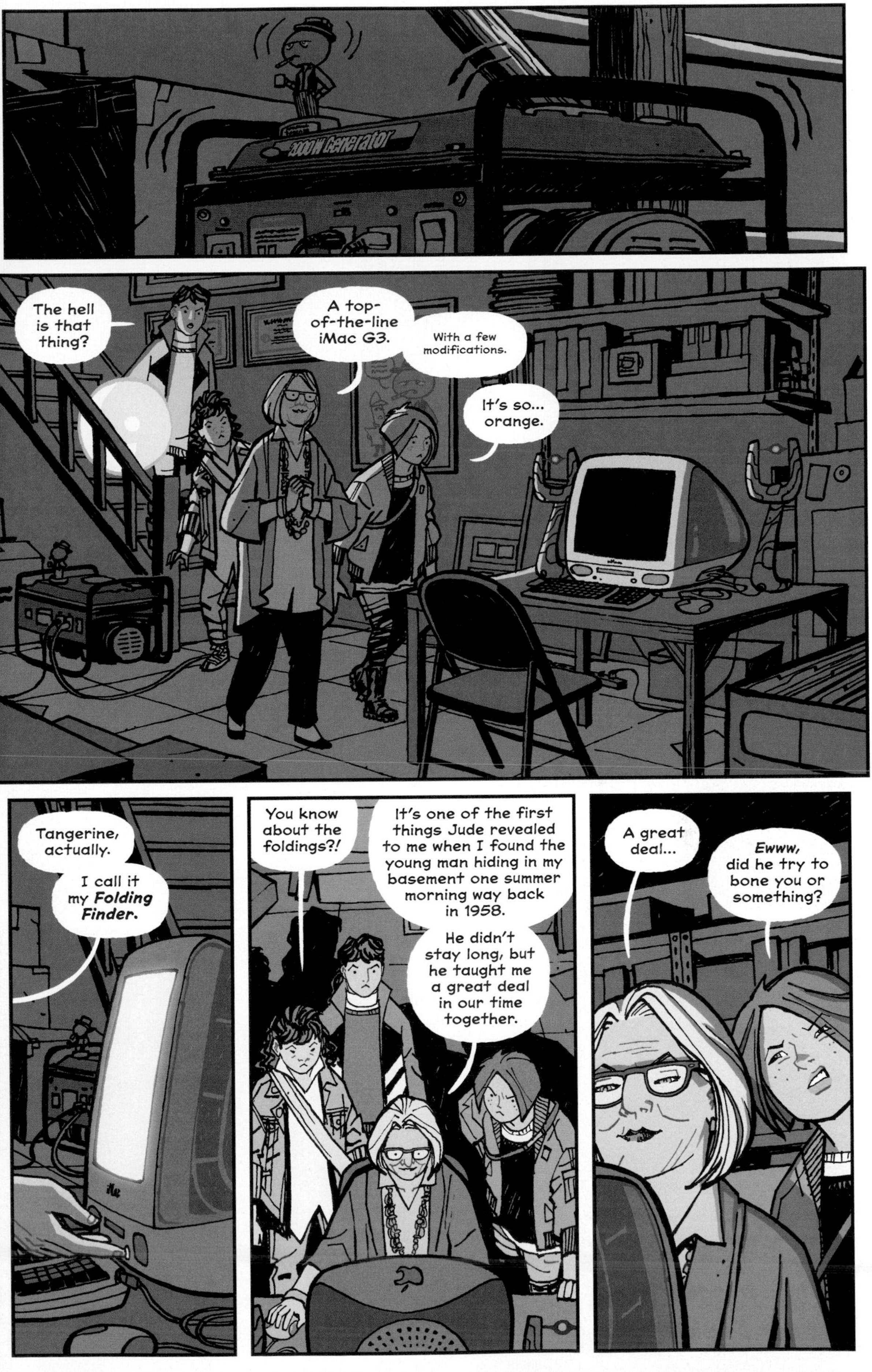
2000W Generator
The hell is that thing?
A top-of-the-line iMac G3.
With a few modifications.
It's so... orange.
Tangerine, actually.
I call it my *Folding Finder*.
You know about the foldings?!
It's one of the first things Jude revealed to me when I found the young man hiding in my basement one summer morning way back in 1958.
He didn't stay long, but he taught me a great deal in our time together.
A great deal...
Ewww, did he try to bone you or something?

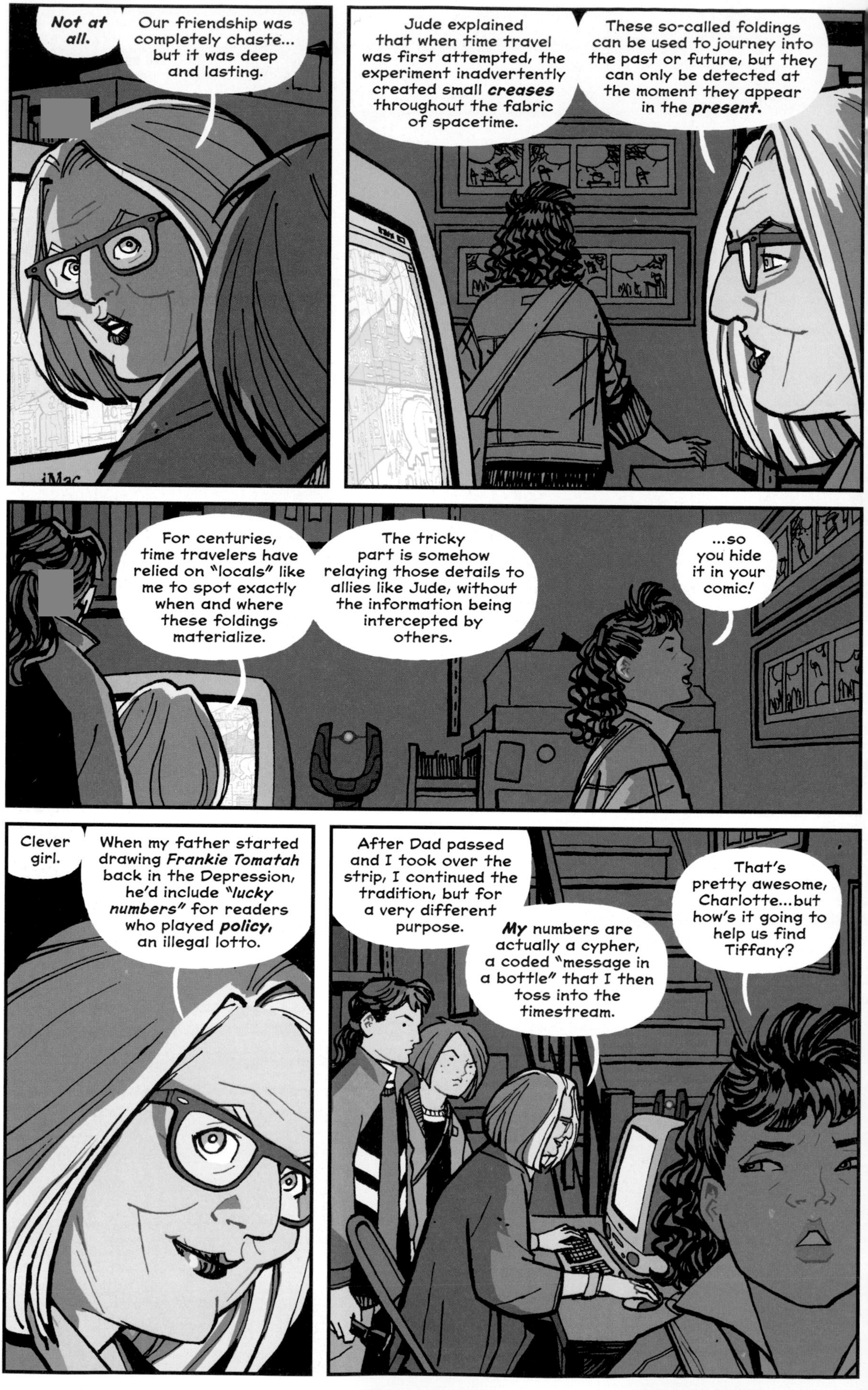
Not at all.
Our friendship was completely chaste... but it was deep and lasting.
Jude explained that when time travel was first attempted, the experiment inadvertently created small creases throughout the fabric of spacetime.
These so-called foldings can be used to journey into the past or future, but they can only be detected at the moment they appear in the present.
For centuries, time travelers have relied on "locals" like me to spot exactly when and where these foldings materialize.
The tricky part is somehow relaying those details to allies like Jude, without the information being intercepted by others.
...so you hide it in your comic!
Clever girl.
When my father started drawing Frankie Tomatah back in the Depression, he'd include "lucky numbers" for readers who played policy, an illegal lotto.
After Dad passed and I took over the strip, I continued the tradition, but for a very different purpose.
My numbers are actually a cypher, a coded "message in a bottle" that I then toss into the timestream.
That's pretty awesome, Charlotte...but how's it going to help us find Tiffany?

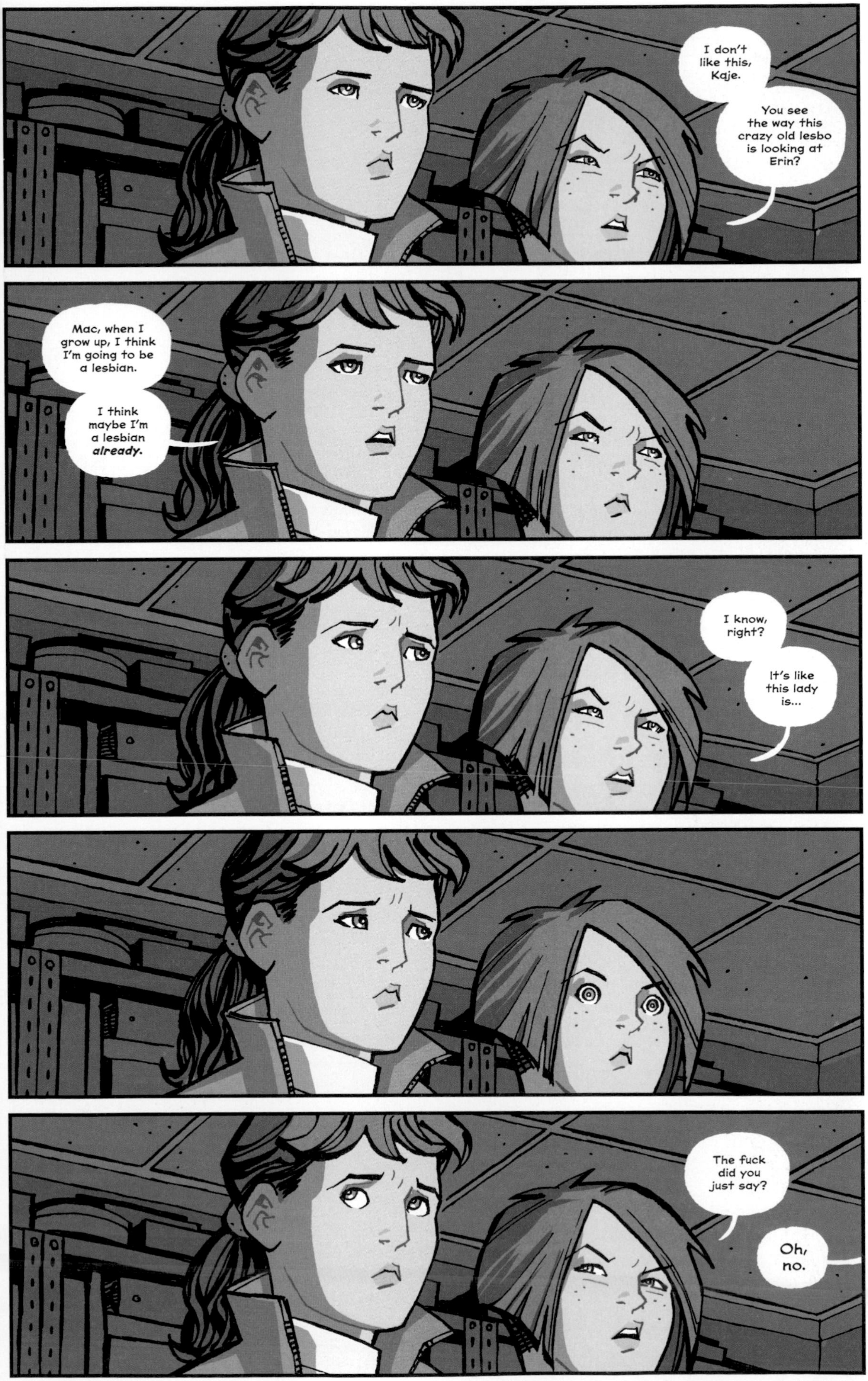
I don't like this, Kaje.
You see the way this crazy old lesbo is looking at Erin?
Mac, when I grow up, I think I'm going to be a lesbian.
I think maybe I'm a lesbian *already.*
I know, right?
It's like this lady is...
The fuck did you just say?
Oh, no.

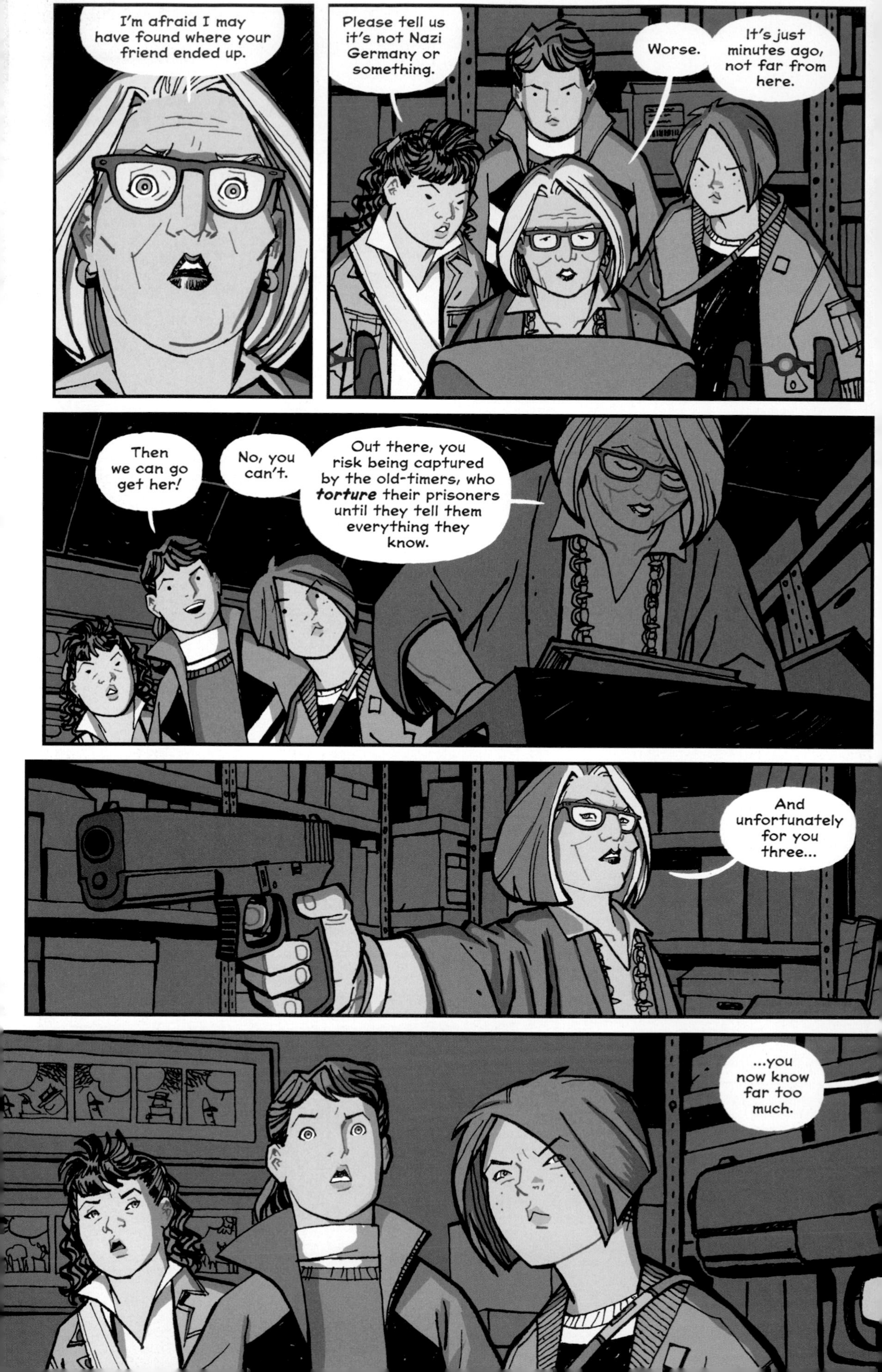
I'm afraid I may have found where your friend ended up.
Please tell us it's not Nazi Germany or something.
Worse.
It's just minutes ago, not far from here.
Then we can go get her!
No, you can't.
Out there, you risk being captured by the old-timers, who *torture* their prisoners until they tell them everything they know.
And unfortunately for you three...
...you now know far too much.

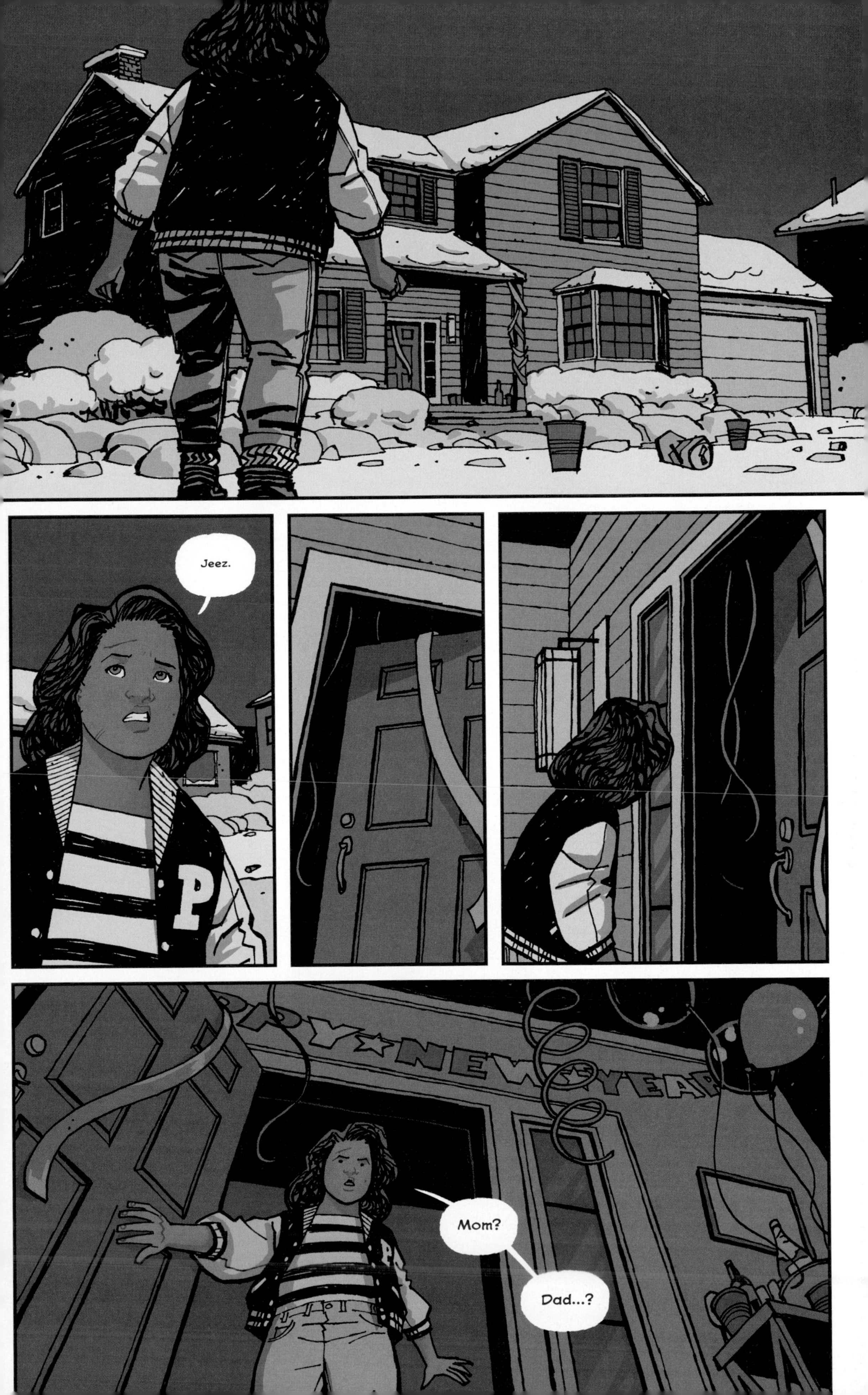
Jeez.
Mom?
Dad...?

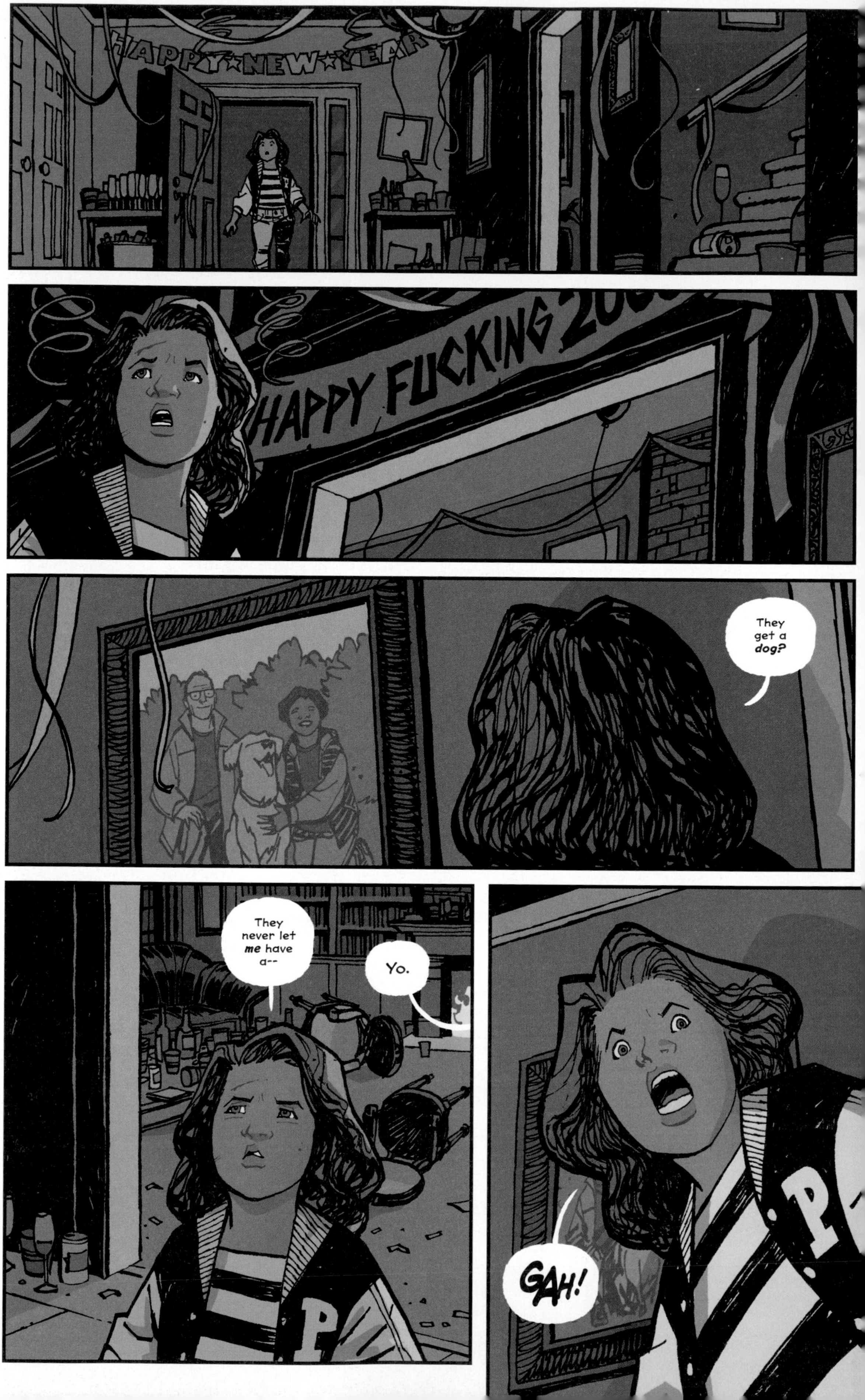
HAPPY★NEW★YEAR
HAPPY FUCKING 2000
They get a dog?
They never let me have a--
Yo.
GAH!

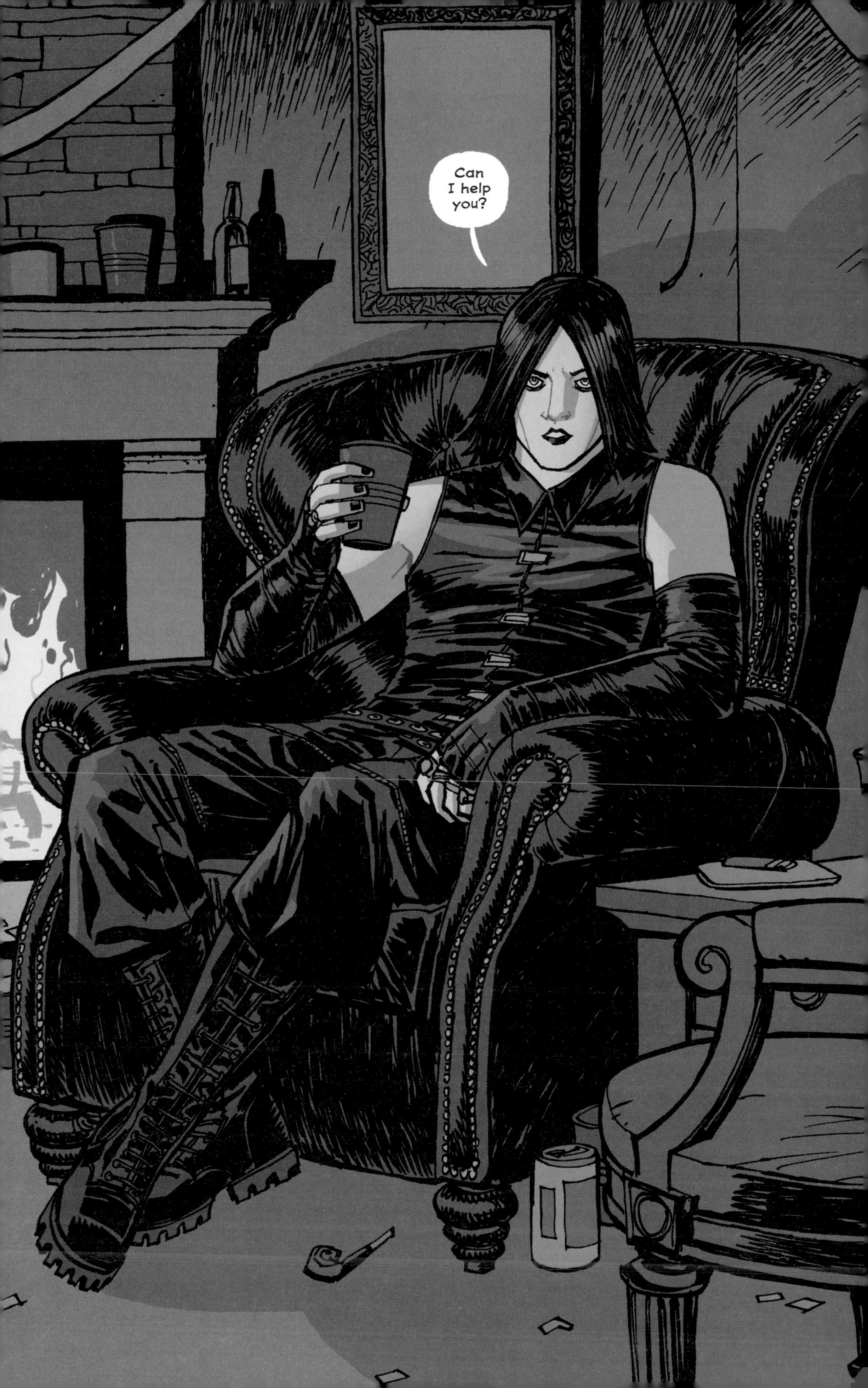
Can I help you?

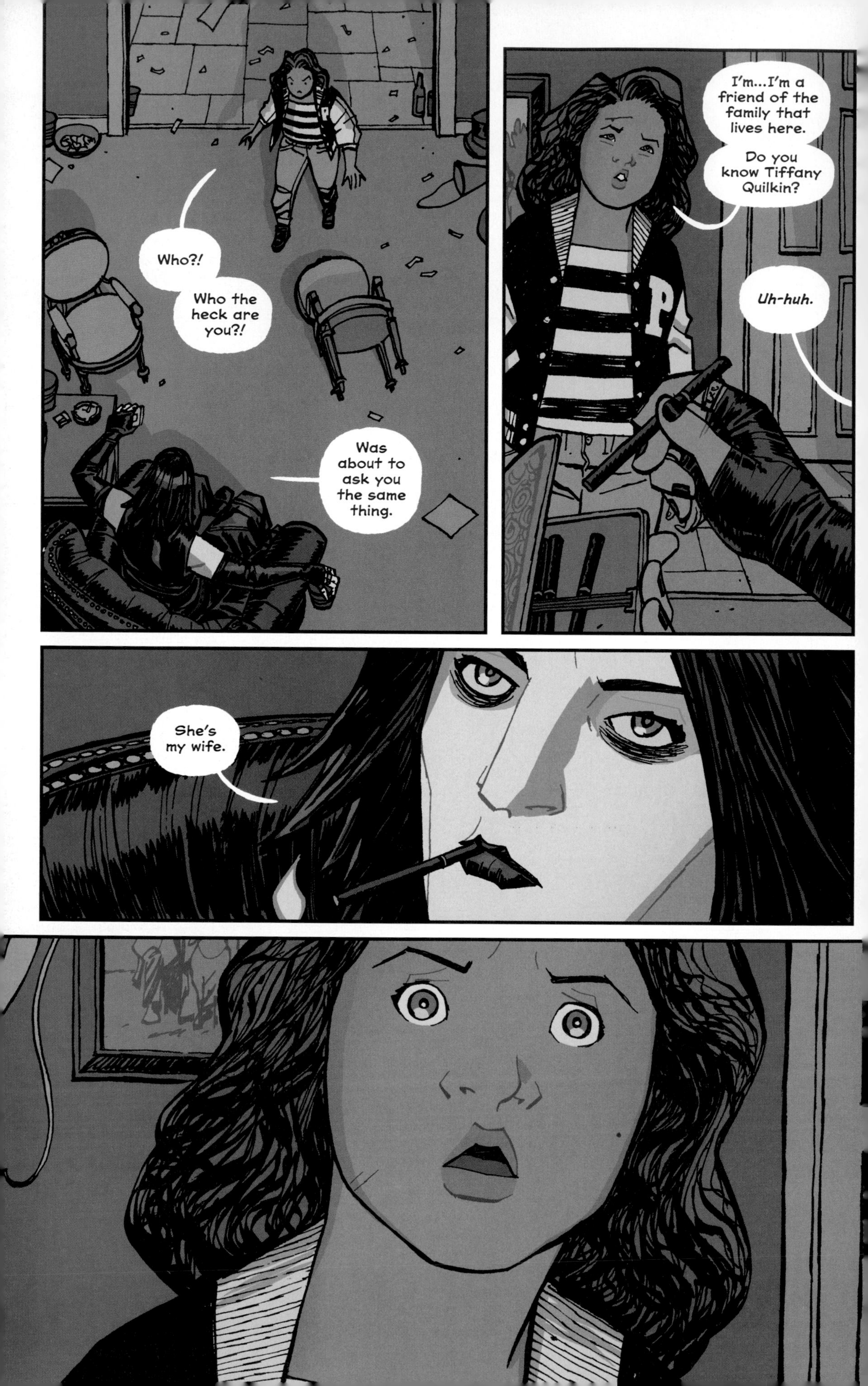
Who?!
Who the heck are you?!
Was about to ask you the same thing.
I'm...I'm a friend of the family that lives here.
Do you know Tiffany Quilkin?
Uh-huh.
She's my wife.

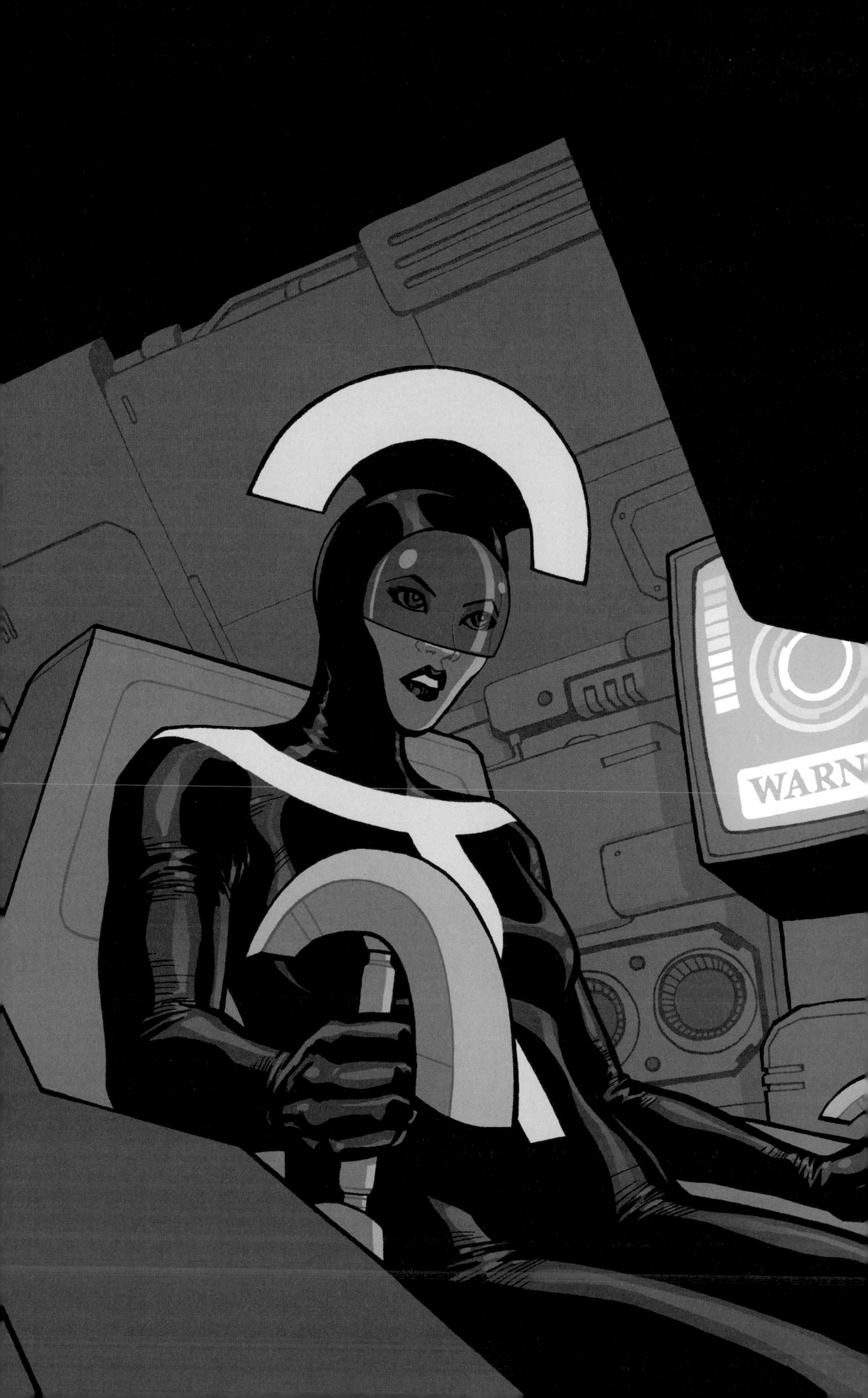
WARN

REMEMBER
Turn your computer off
before midnight on
12/31/99

-Warning Sticker from **Best Buy** circa 1999

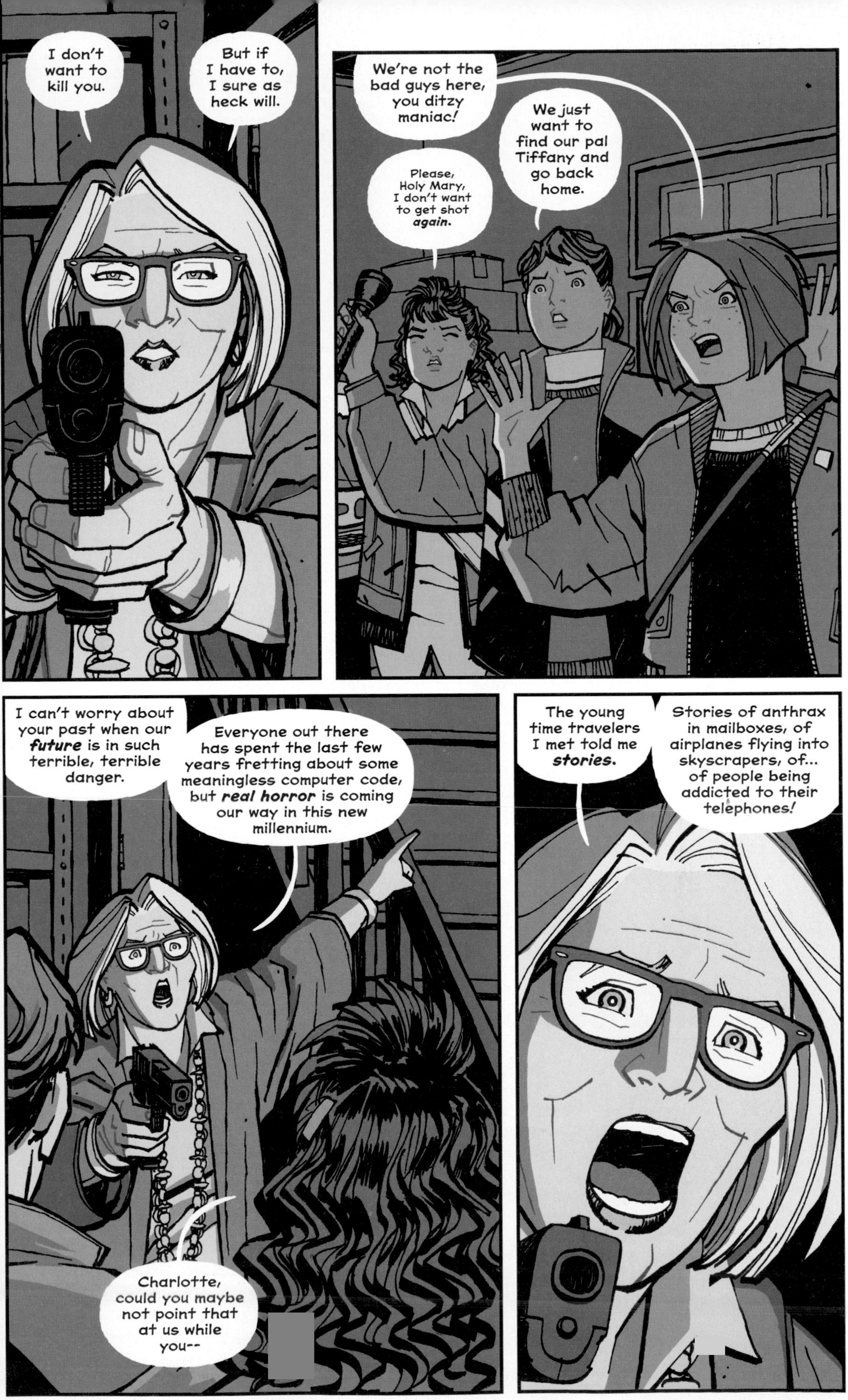
I don't want to kill you.
But if I have to, I sure as heck will.
We're not the bad guys here, you ditzy maniac!
We just want to find our pal Tiffany and go back home.
Please, Holy Mary, I don't want to get shot again.
I can't worry about your past when our future is in such terrible, terrible danger.
Everyone out there has spent the last few years fretting about some meaningless computer code, but real horror is coming our way in this new millennium.
Charlotte, could you maybe not point that at us while you--
The young time travelers I met told me stories.
Stories of anthrax in mailboxes, of airplanes flying into skyscrapers, of... of people being addicted to their telephones!

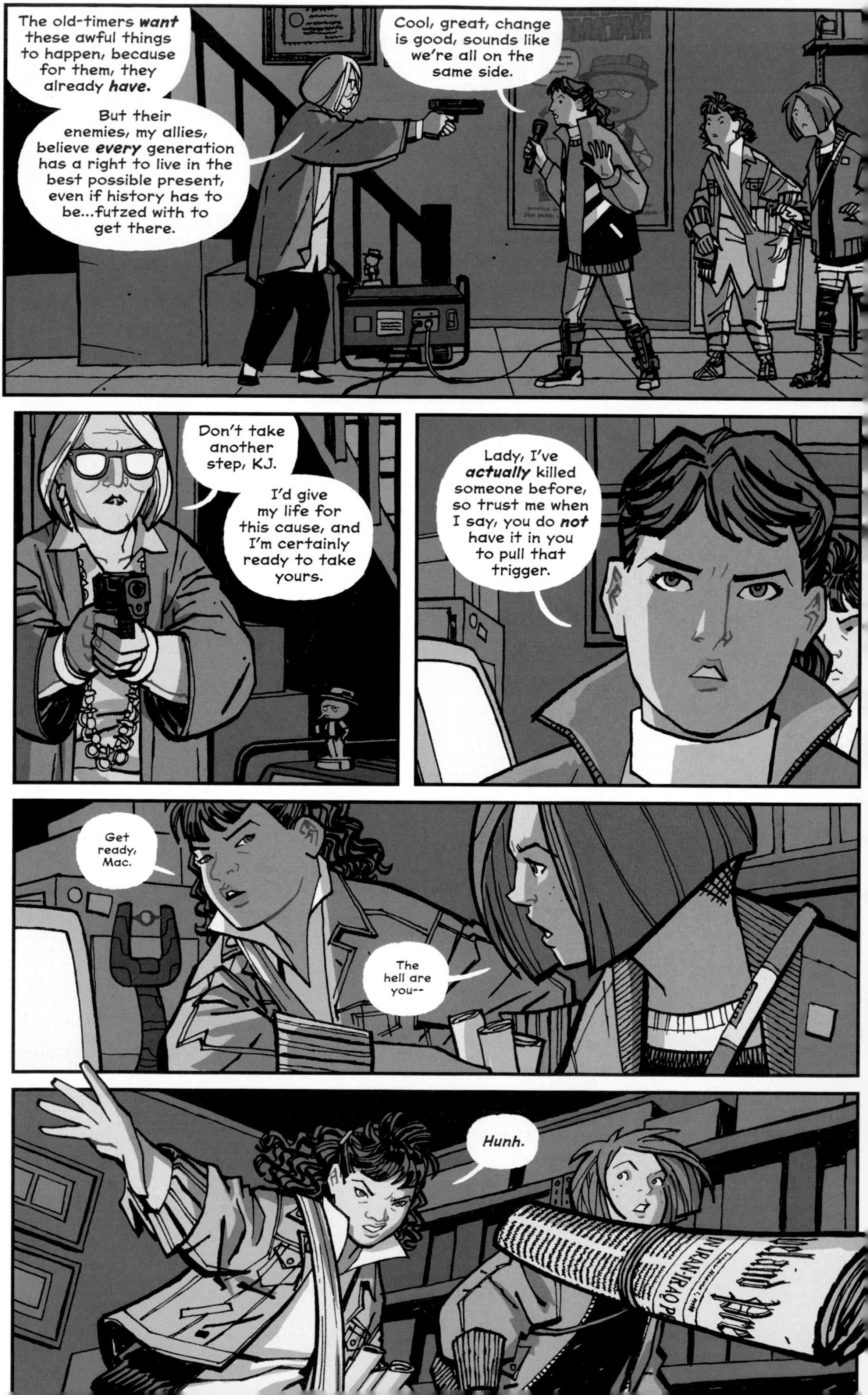

The old-timers *want* these awful things to happen, because for them, they already *have*.
But their enemies, my allies, believe *every* generation has a right to live in the best possible present, even if history has to be...futzed with to get there.
Cool, great, change is good, sounds like we're all on the same side.
Don't take another step, KJ.
I'd give my life for this cause, and I'm certainly ready to take yours.
Lady, I've *actually* killed someone before, so trust me when I say, you do *not* have it in you to pull that trigger.
Get ready, Mac.
The hell are you--
Hunh.

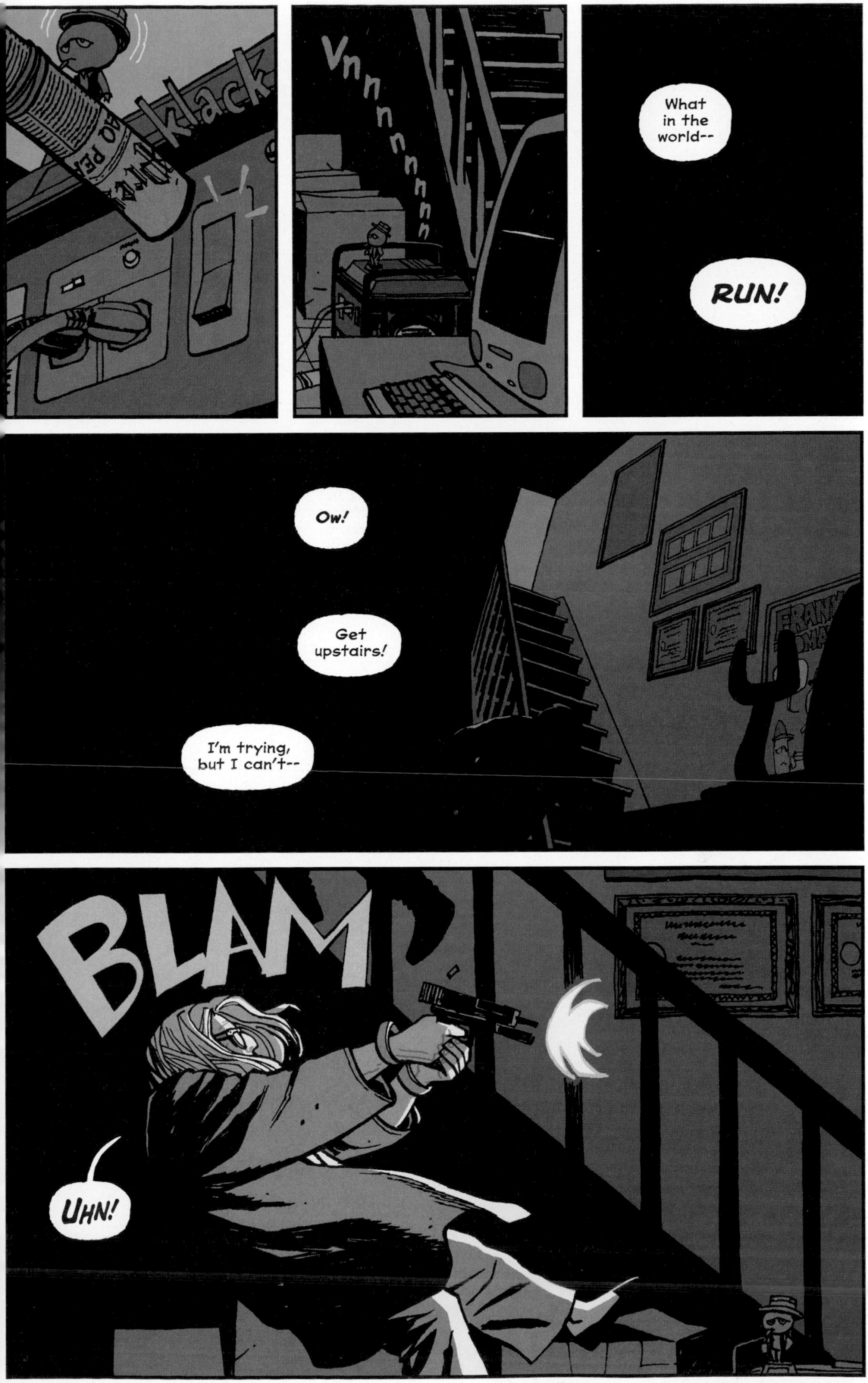
klack
Vnnnnnnnn
What in the world--
RUN!
Ow!
Get upstairs!
I'm trying, but I can't--
BLAM
UHN!

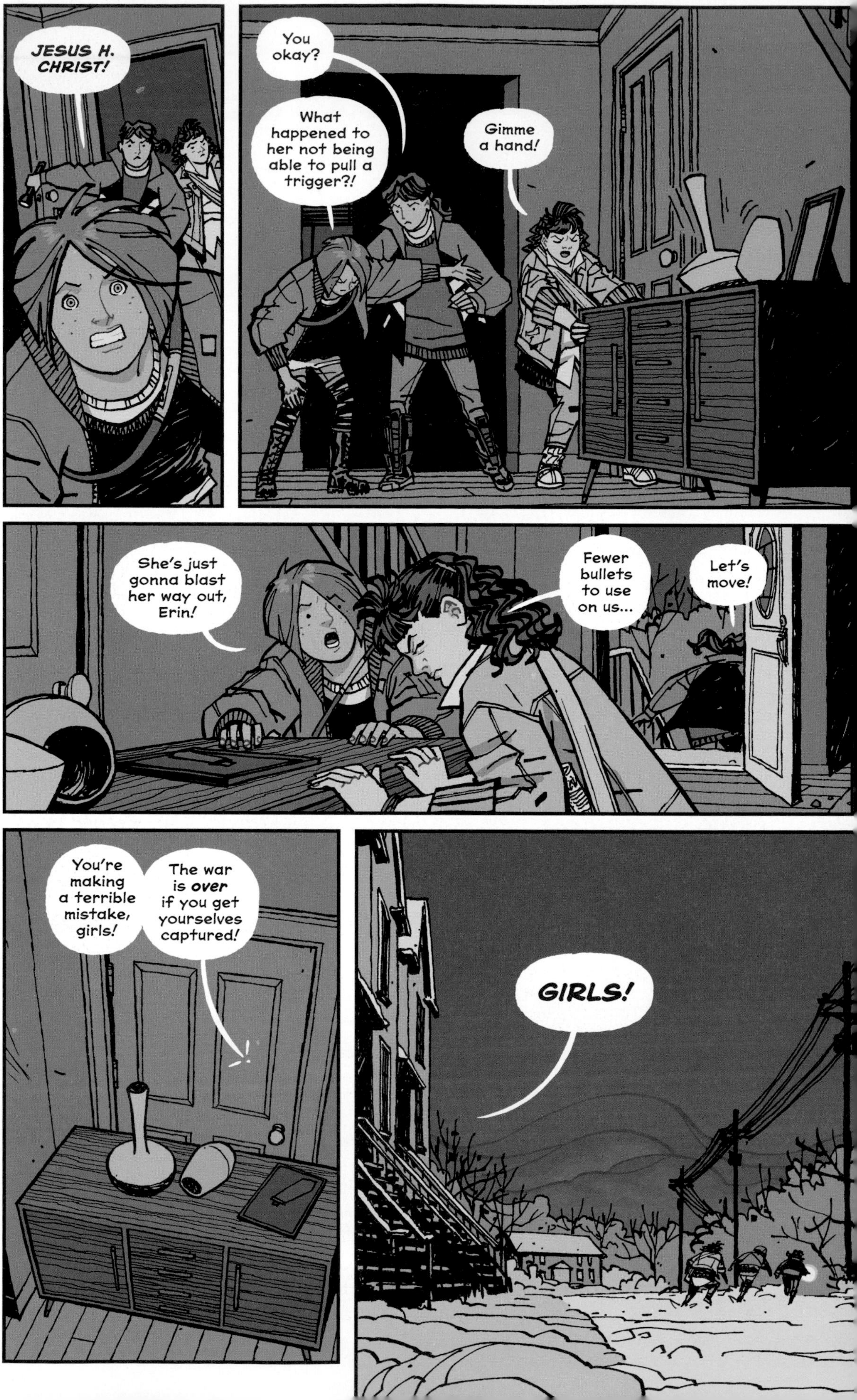
JESUS H. CHRIST!
You okay?
What happened to her not being able to pull a trigger?!
Gimme a hand!
She's just gonna blast her way out, Erin!
Fewer bullets to use on us...
Let's move!
You're making a terrible mistake, girls!
The war is *over* if you get yourselves captured!
GIRLS!

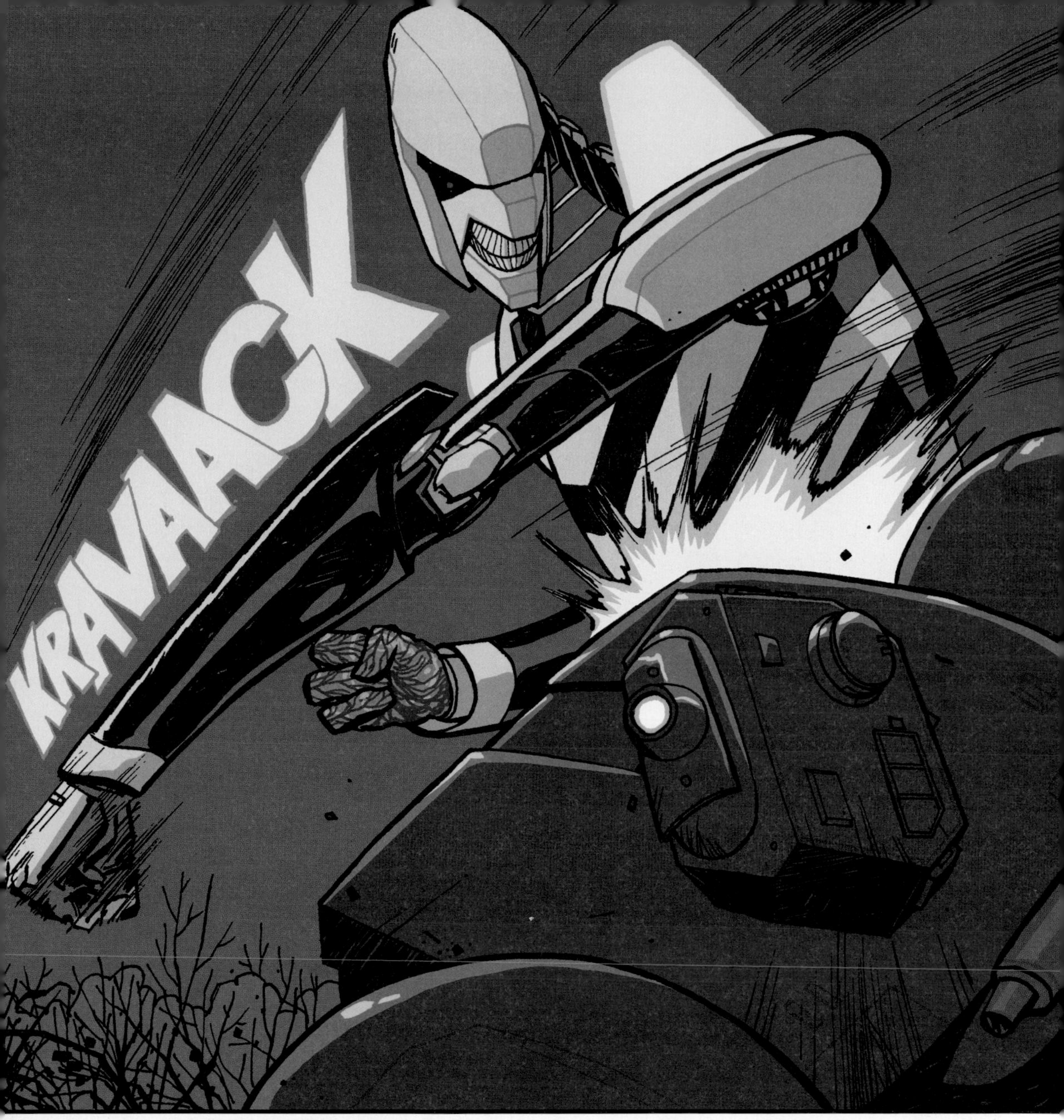
KRAVAACK

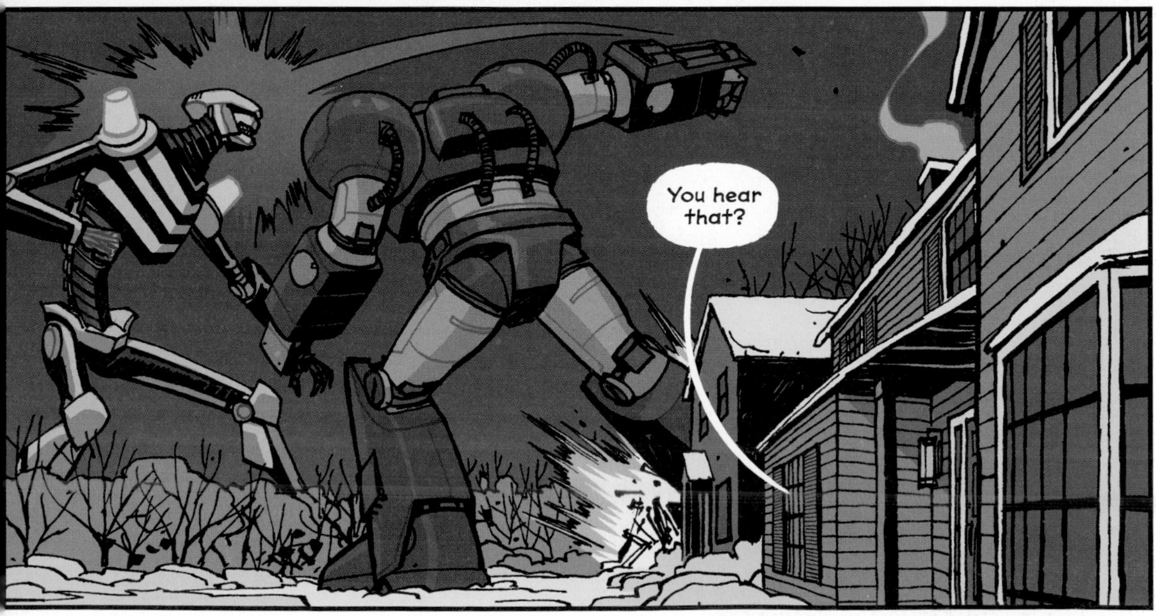
You hear that?

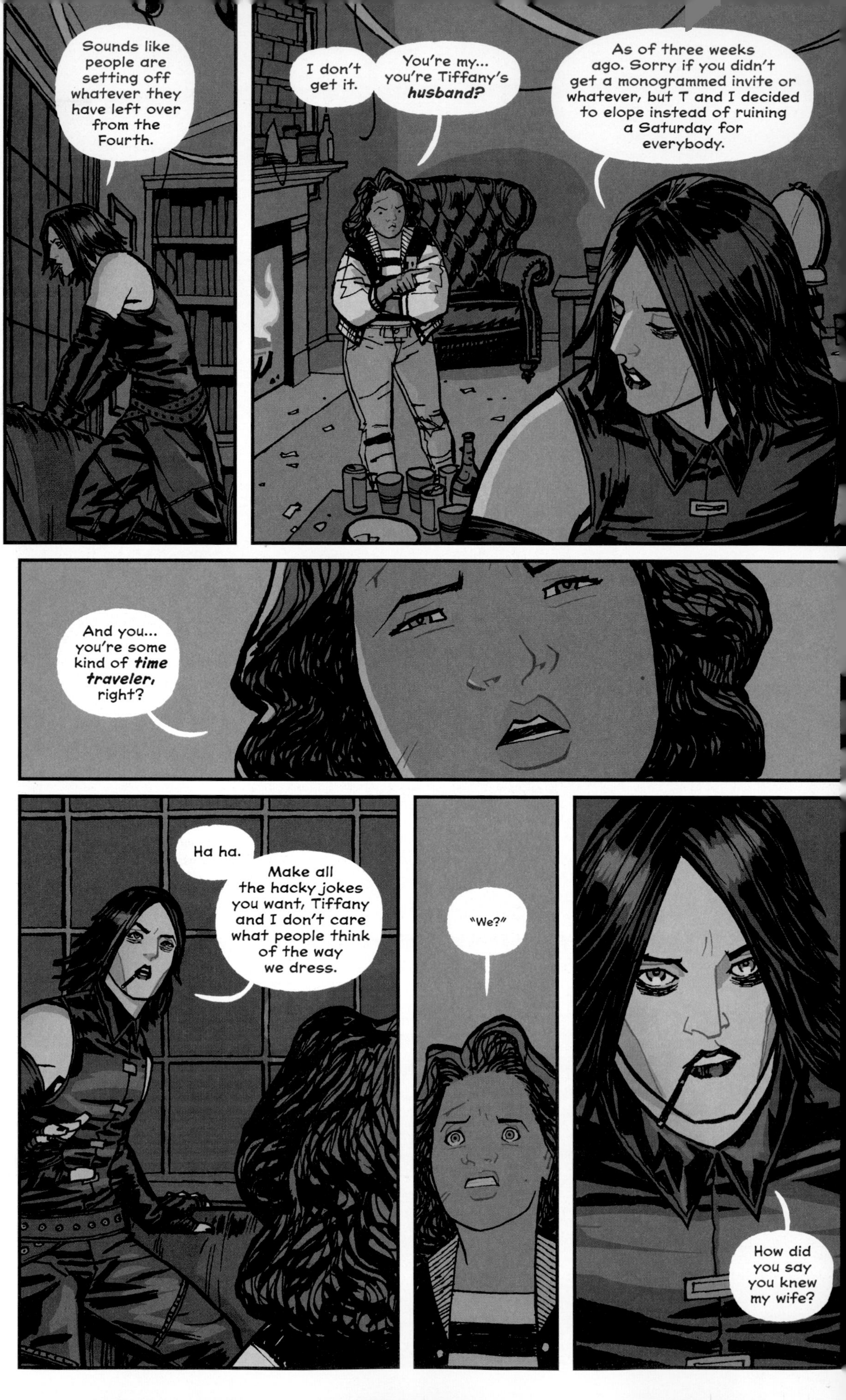
Sounds like people are setting off whatever they have left over from the Fourth.
I don't get it.
You're my... you're Tiffany's **husband?**
As of three weeks ago. Sorry if you didn't get a monogrammed invite or whatever, but T and I decided to elope instead of ruining a Saturday for everybody.
And you... you're some kind of ***time traveler,*** right?
Ha ha.
Make all the hacky jokes you want, Tiffany and I don't care what people think of the way we dress.
"We?"
How did you say you knew my wife?

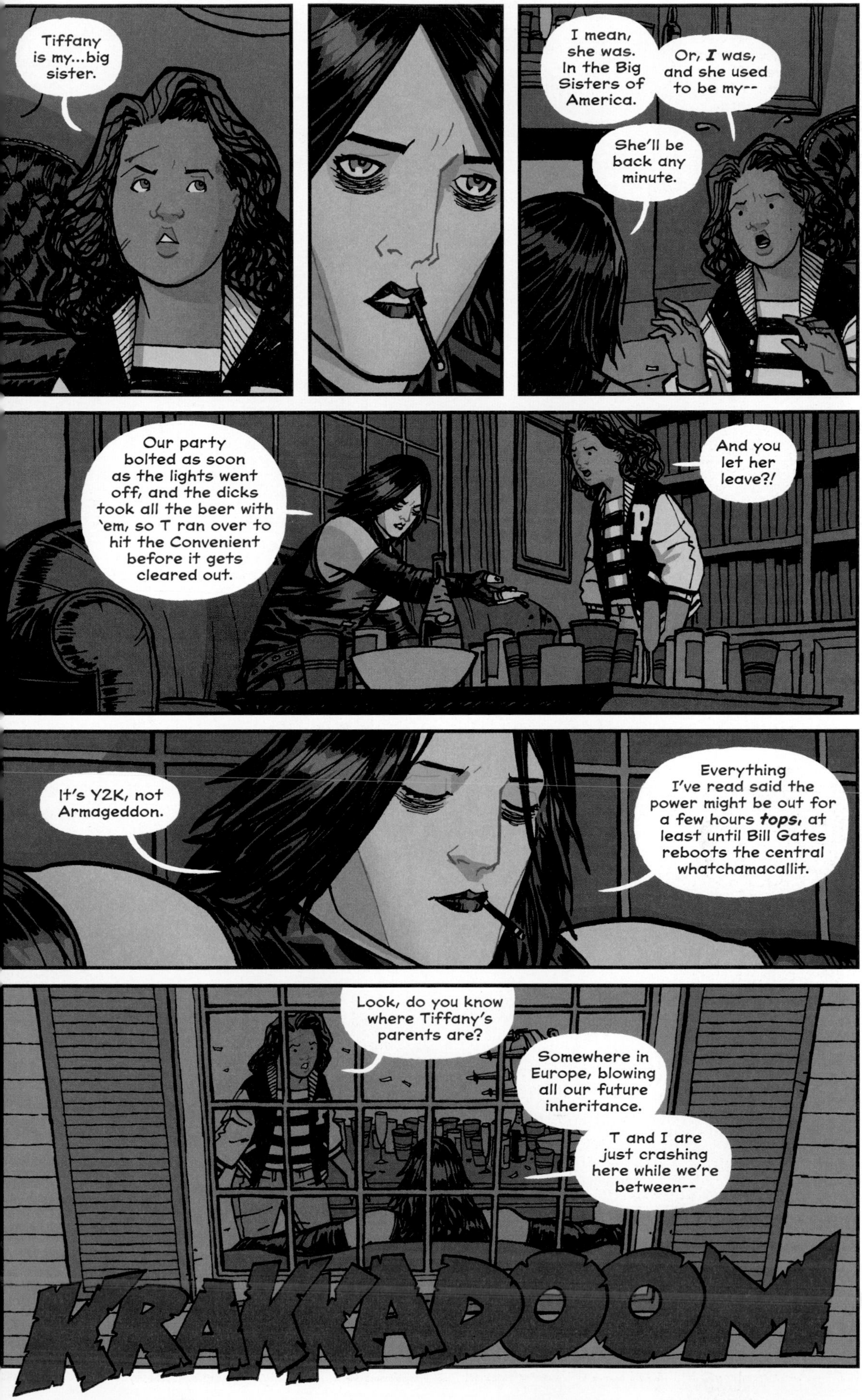
Tiffany is my...big sister.
I mean, she was. In the Big Sisters of America.
Or, I was, and she used to be my--
She'll be back any minute.
Our party bolted as soon as the lights went off, and the dicks took all the beer with 'em, so T ran over to hit the Convenient before it gets cleared out.
And you let her leave?!
It's Y2K, not Armageddon.
Everything I've read said the power might be out for a few hours tops, at least until Bill Gates reboots the central whatchamacallit.
Look, do you know where Tiffany's parents are?
Somewhere in Europe, blowing all our future inheritance.
T and I are just crashing here while we're between--
KRAKKADOOM

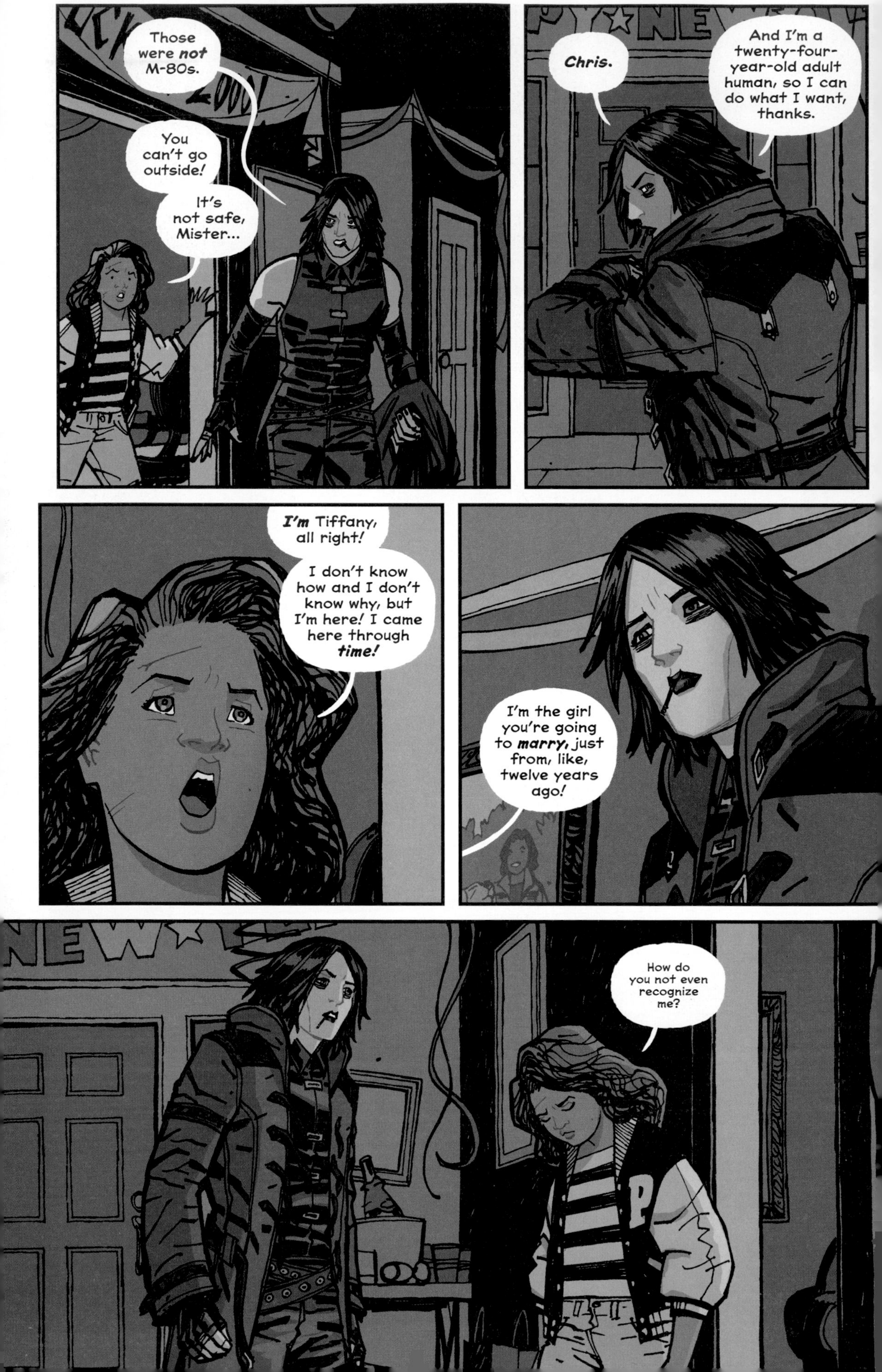
Those were *not* M-80s.
You can't go outside!
It's not safe, Mister...
Chris.
And I'm a twenty-four-year-old adult human, so I can do what I want, thanks.
I'm Tiffany, all right!
I don't know how and I don't know why, but I'm here! I came here through *time!*
I'm the girl you're going to *marry,* just from, like, twelve years ago!
How do you not even recognize me?

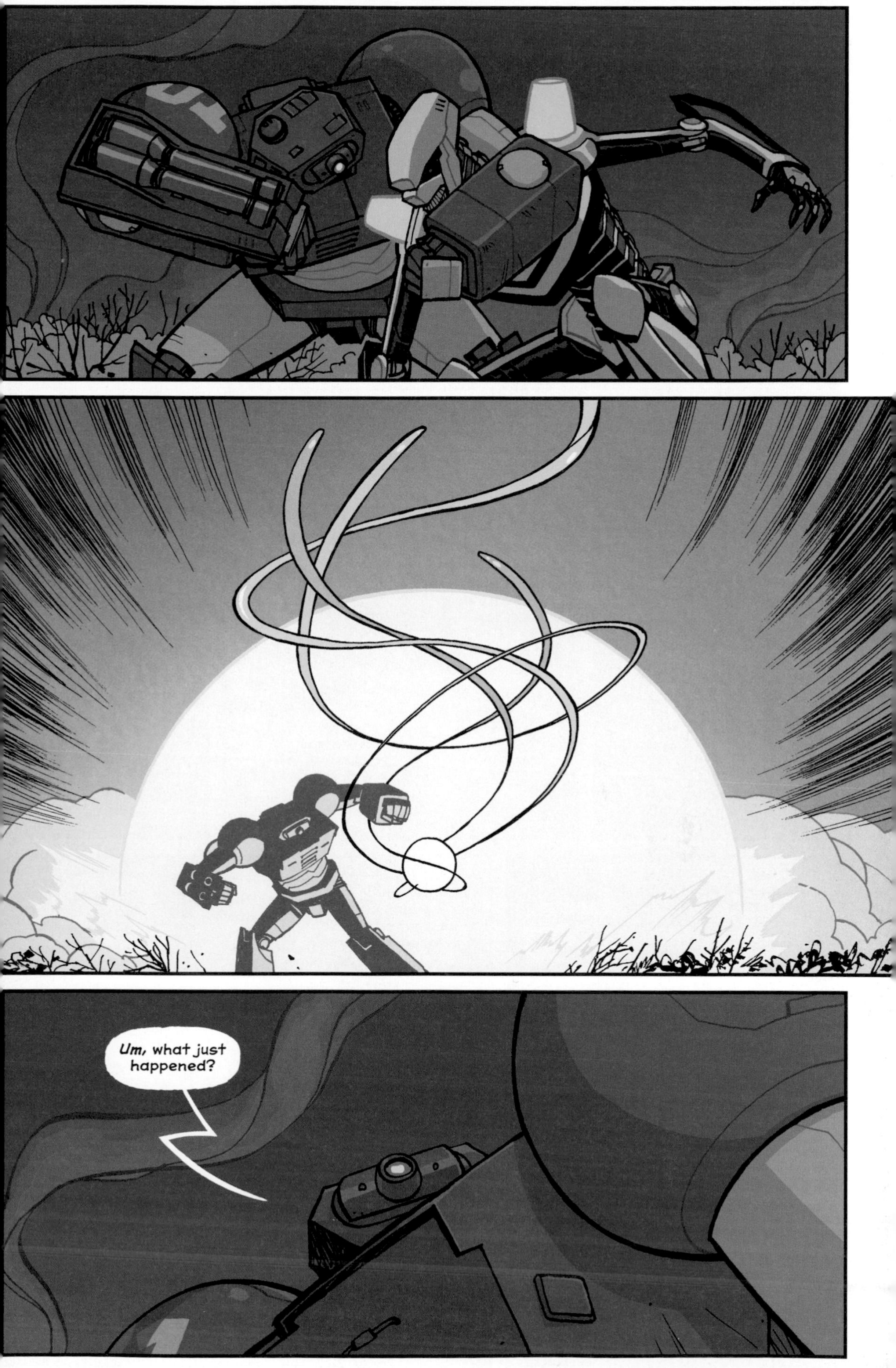
Um, what just happened?

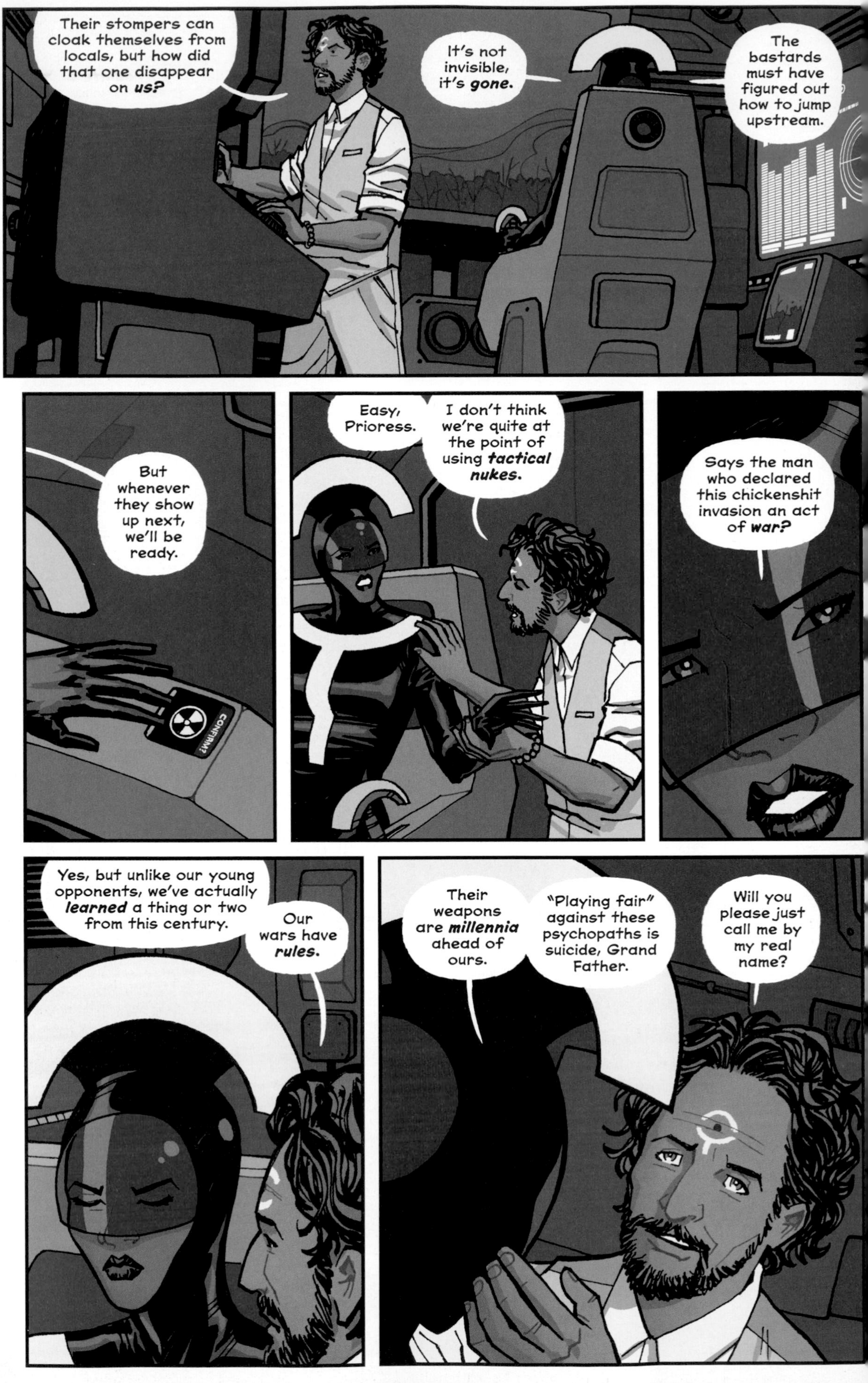
Their stompers can cloak themselves from locals, but how did that one disappear on *us?*
It's not invisible, it's *gone.*
The bastards must have figured out how to jump upstream.
But whenever they show up next, we'll be ready.
CONFIRM?
Easy, Prioress.
I don't think we're quite at the point of using *tactical nukes.*
Says the man who declared this chickenshit invasion an act of *war?*
Yes, but unlike our young opponents, we've actually *learned* a thing or two from this century.
Our wars have *rules.*
Their weapons are *millennia* ahead of ours.
"Playing fair" against these psychopaths is suicide, Grand Father.
Will you please just call me by my real name?

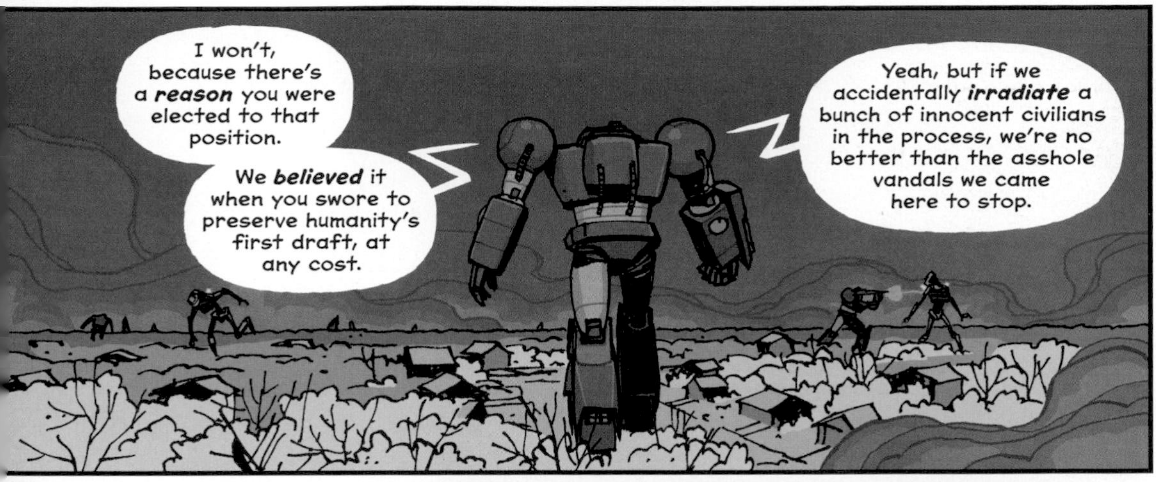
I won't, because there's a reason you were elected to that position.
We believed it when you swore to preserve humanity's first draft, at any cost.
Yeah, but if we accidentally irradiate a bunch of innocent civilians in the process, we're no better than the asshole vandals we came here to stop.

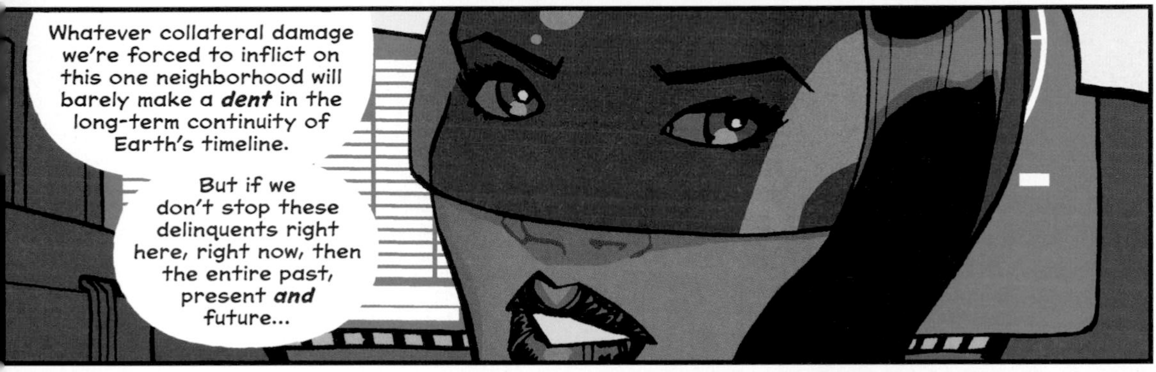
Whatever collateral damage we're forced to inflict on this one neighborhood will barely make a dent in the long-term continuity of Earth's timeline.
But if we don't stop these delinquents right here, right now, then the entire past, present and future...

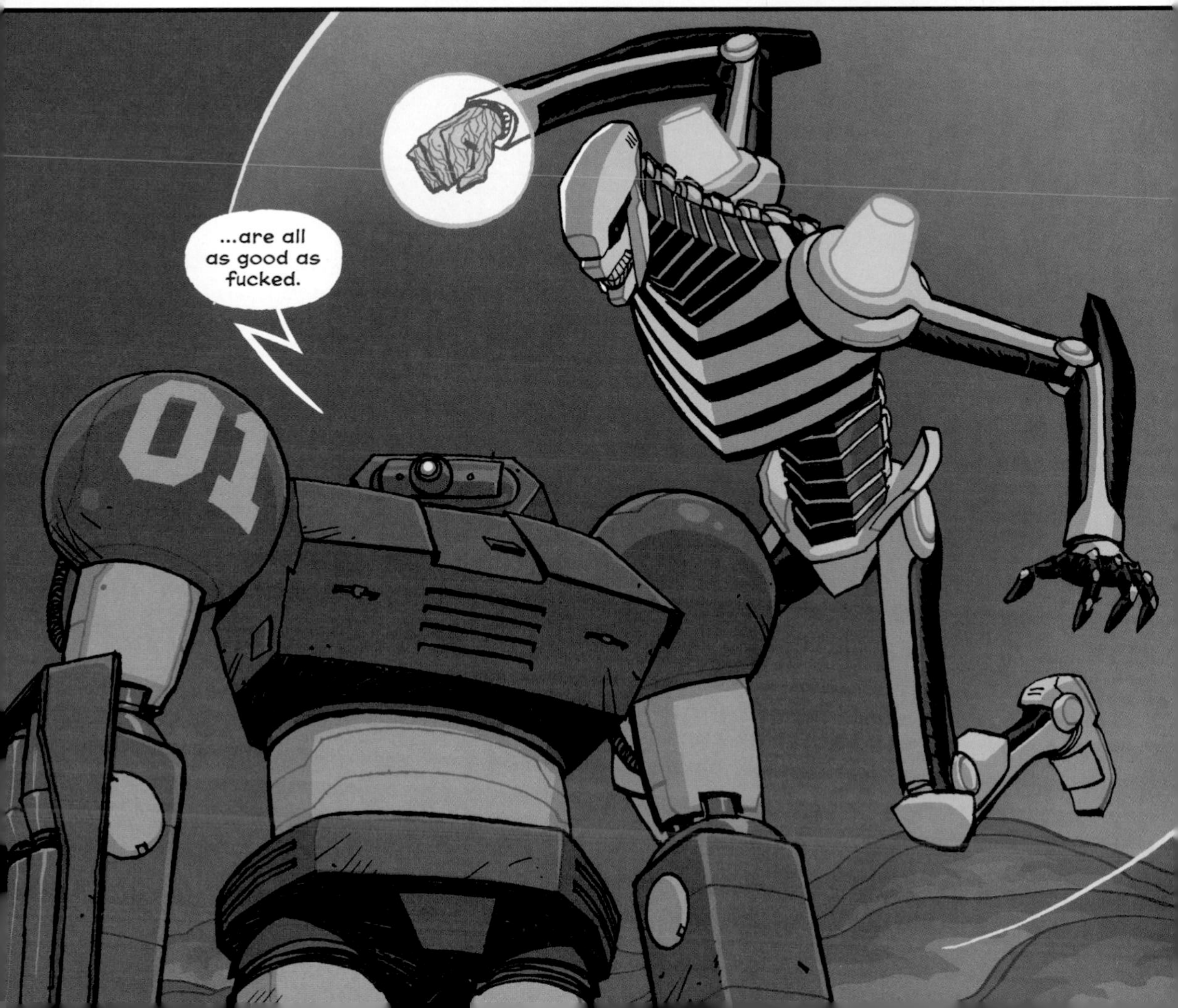
...are all as good as fucked.
01

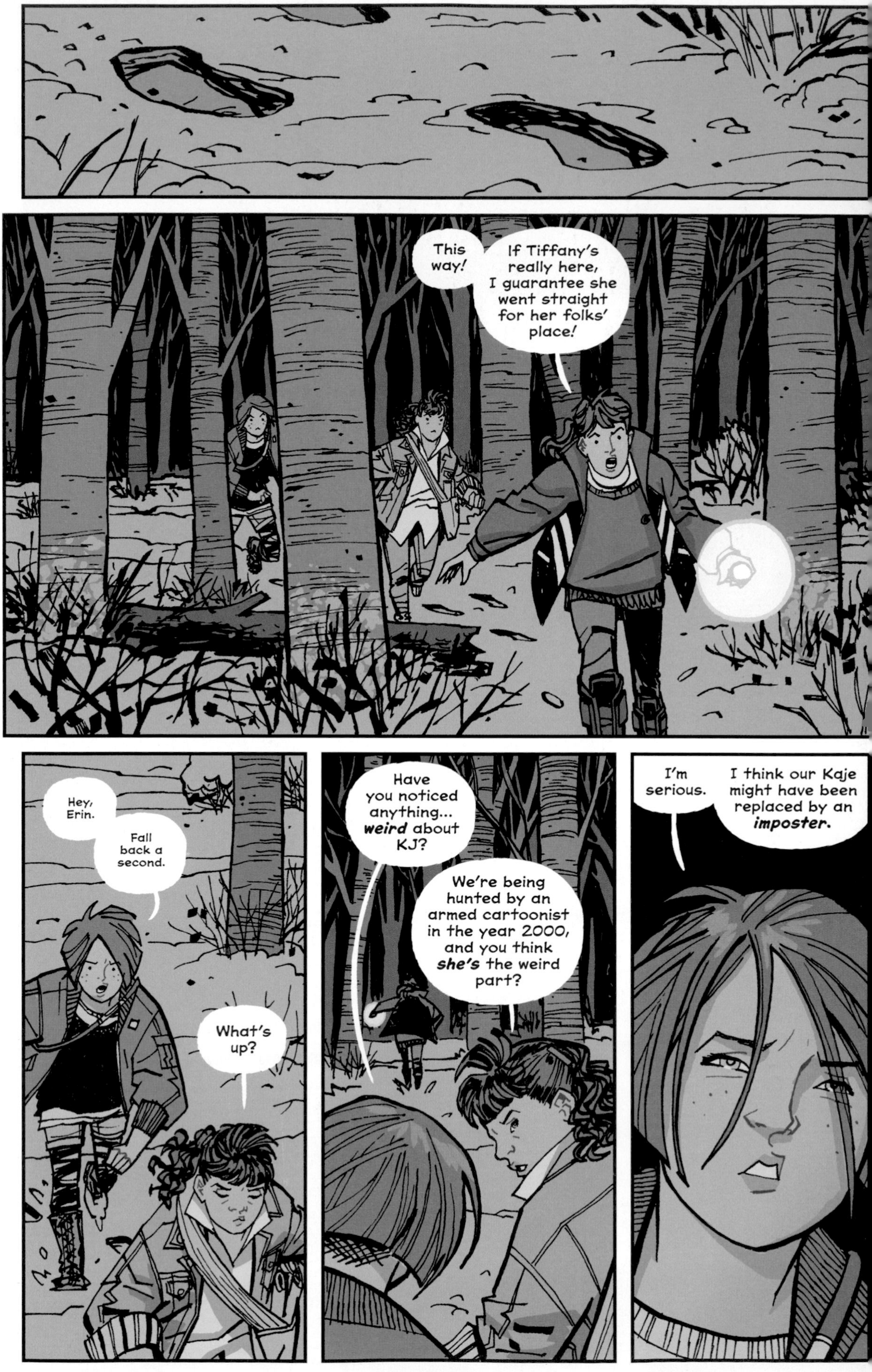
This way!
If Tiffany's really here, I guarantee she went straight for her folks' place!
Hey, Erin.
Fall back a second.
What's up?
Have you noticed anything... *weird* about KJ?
We're being hunted by an armed cartoonist in the year 2000, and you think *she's* the weird part?
I'm serious.
I think our Kaje might have been replaced by an *imposter*.

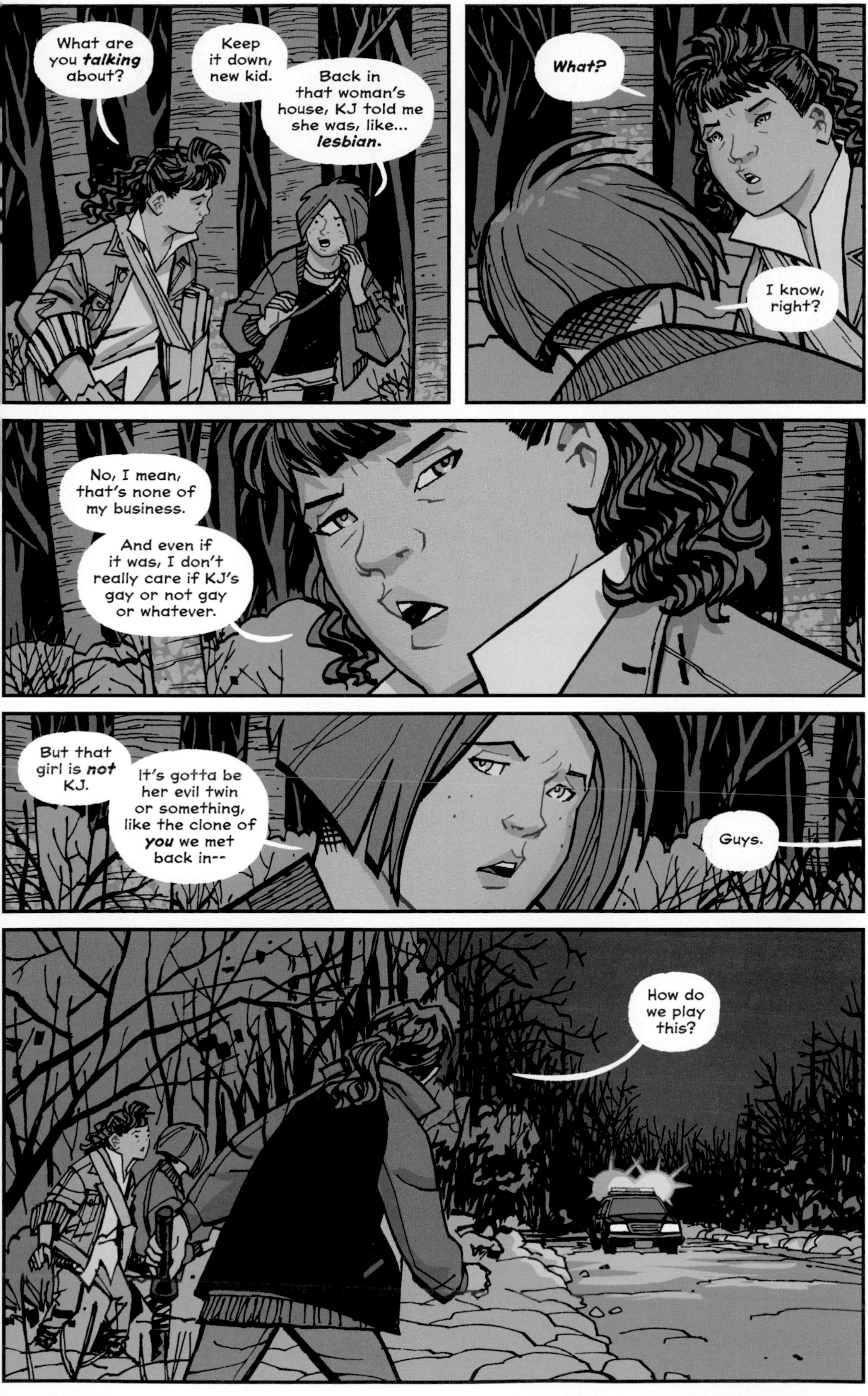

What are you *talking* about?
Keep it down, new kid.
Back in that woman's house, KJ told me she was, like... *lesbian.*
What?
I know, right?
No, I mean, that's none of my business.
And even if it was, I don't really care if KJ's gay or not gay or whatever.
But that girl is *not* KJ.
It's gotta be her evil twin or something, like the clone of *you* we met back in--
Guys.
How do we play this?

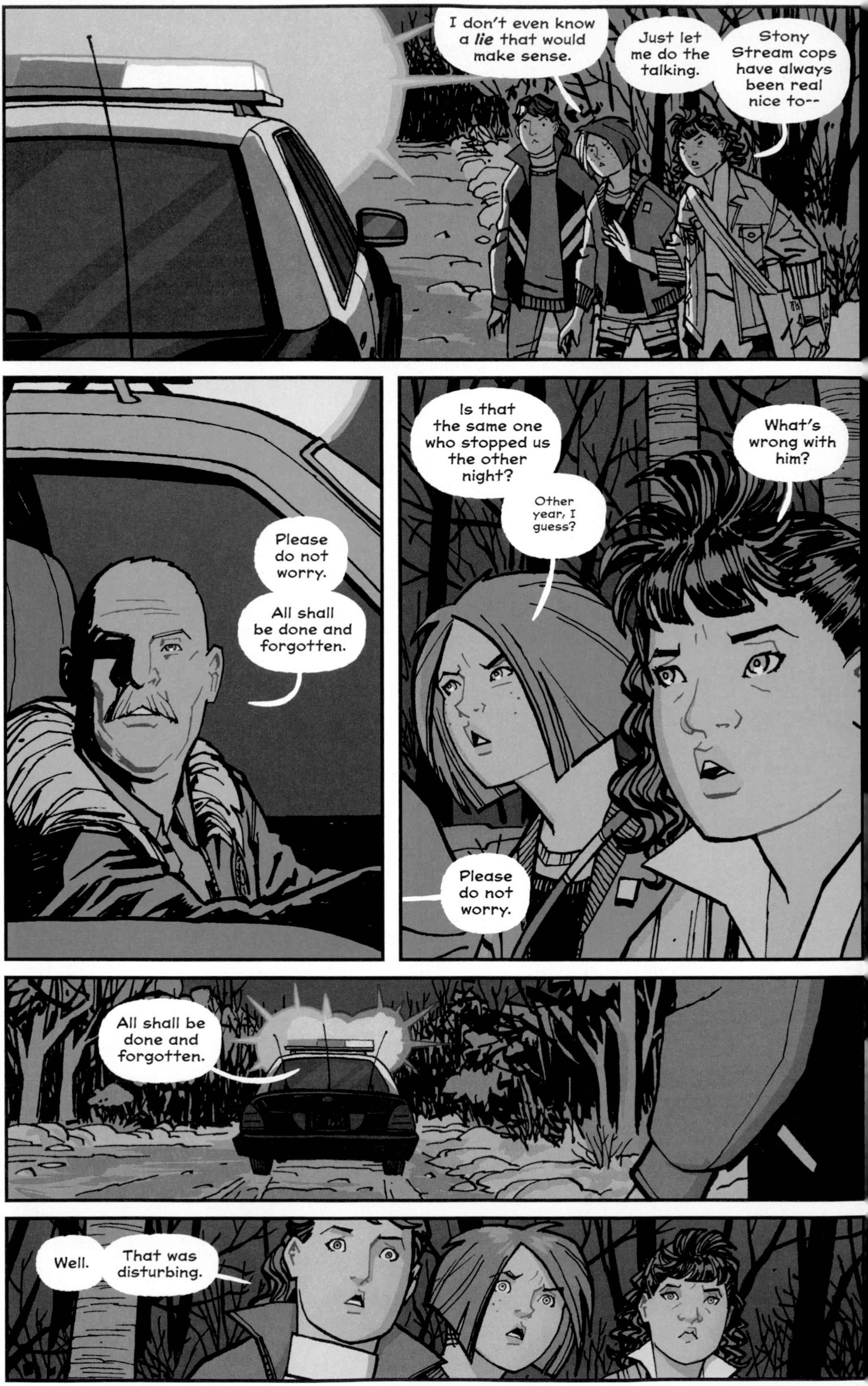
I don't even know a *lie* that would make sense.
Just let me do the talking.
Stony Stream cops have always been real nice to--
Please do not worry.
All shall be done and forgotten.
Is that the same one who stopped us the other night?
Other year, I guess?
What's wrong with him?
Please do not worry.
All shall be done and forgotten.
Well.
That was disturbing.

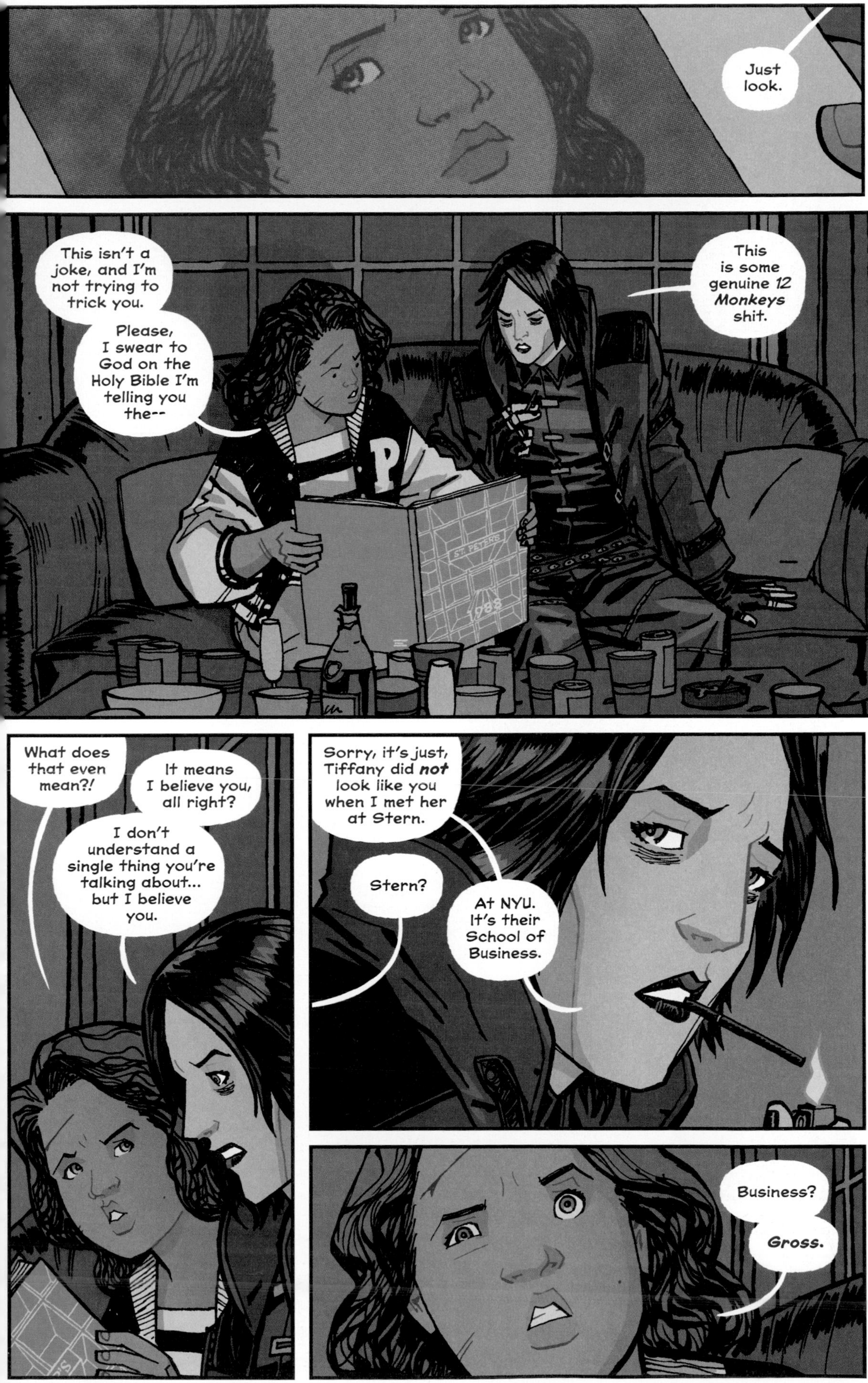
Just look.
This isn't a joke, and I'm not trying to trick you.
Please, I swear to God on the Holy Bible I'm telling you the--
This is some genuine 12 *Monkeys* shit.
ST. PETERS
1988
What does that even mean?!
It means I believe you, all right?
I don't understand a single thing you're talking about... but I believe you.
Sorry, it's just, Tiffany did ***not*** look like you when I met her at Stern.
Stern?
At NYU. It's their School of Business.
Business?
Gross.

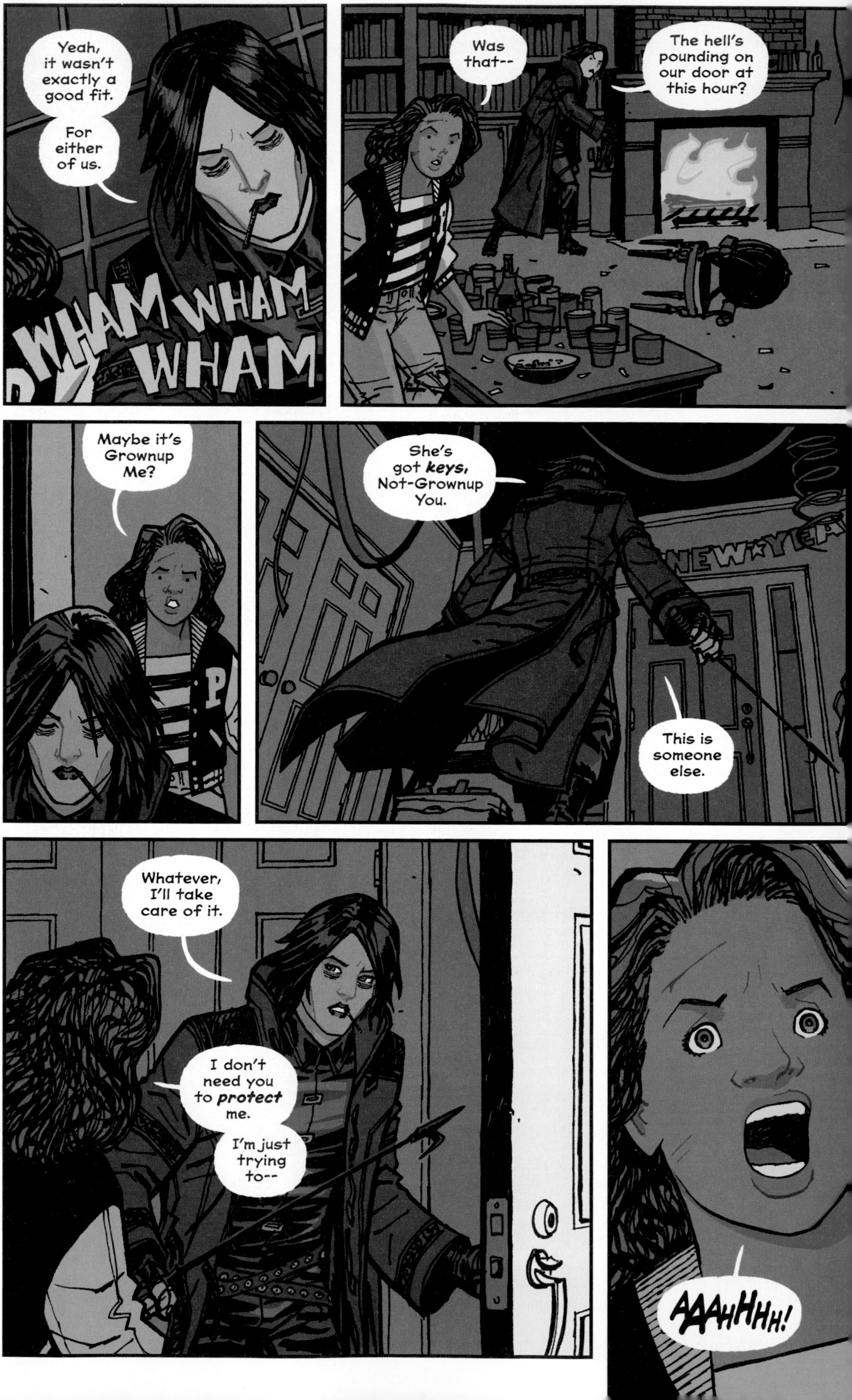
Yeah, it wasn't exactly a good fit.
For either of us.
WHAM WHAM WHAM
Was that--
The hell's pounding on our door at this hour?
Maybe it's Grownup Me?
She's got **keys,** Not-Grownup You.
NEW☆YEA
This is someone else.
Whatever, I'll take care of it.
I don't need you to **protect** me.
I'm just trying to--
AAAHHHH!

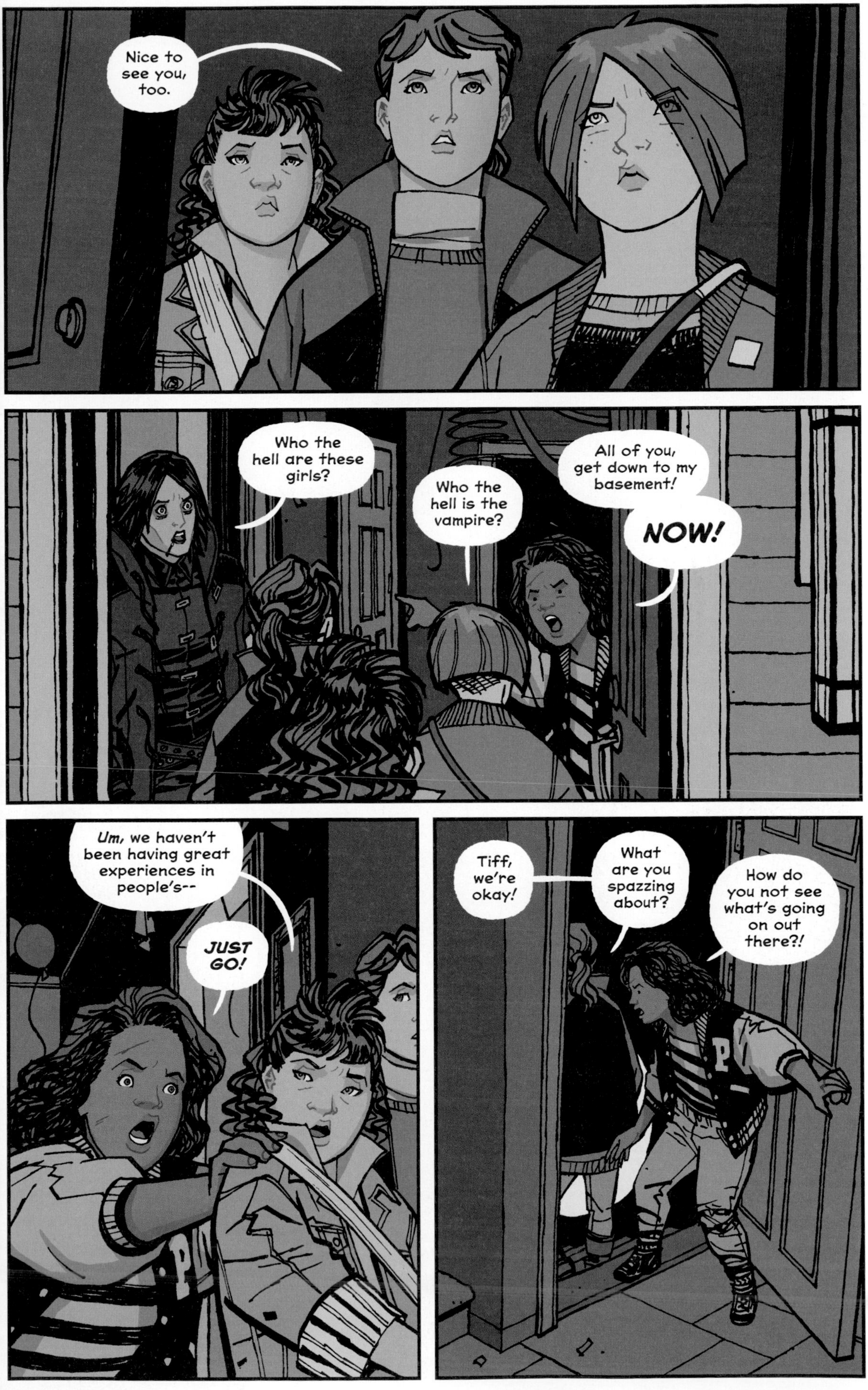
Nice to see you, too.
Who the hell are these girls?
Who the hell is the vampire?
All of you, get down to my basement!
NOW!
Um, we haven't been having great experiences in people's--
JUST GO!
Tiff, we're okay!
What are you spazzing about?
How do you not see what's going on out there?!

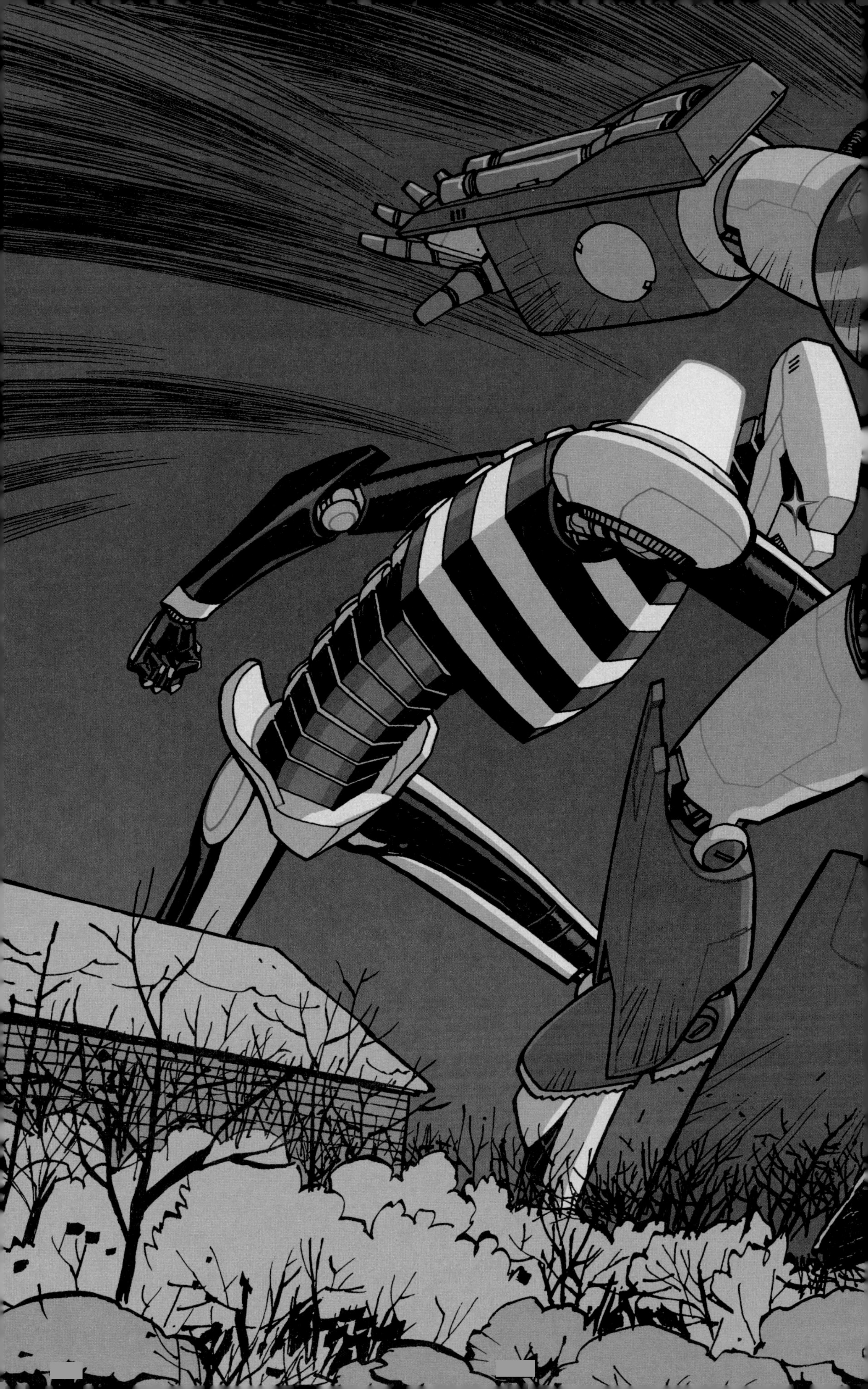

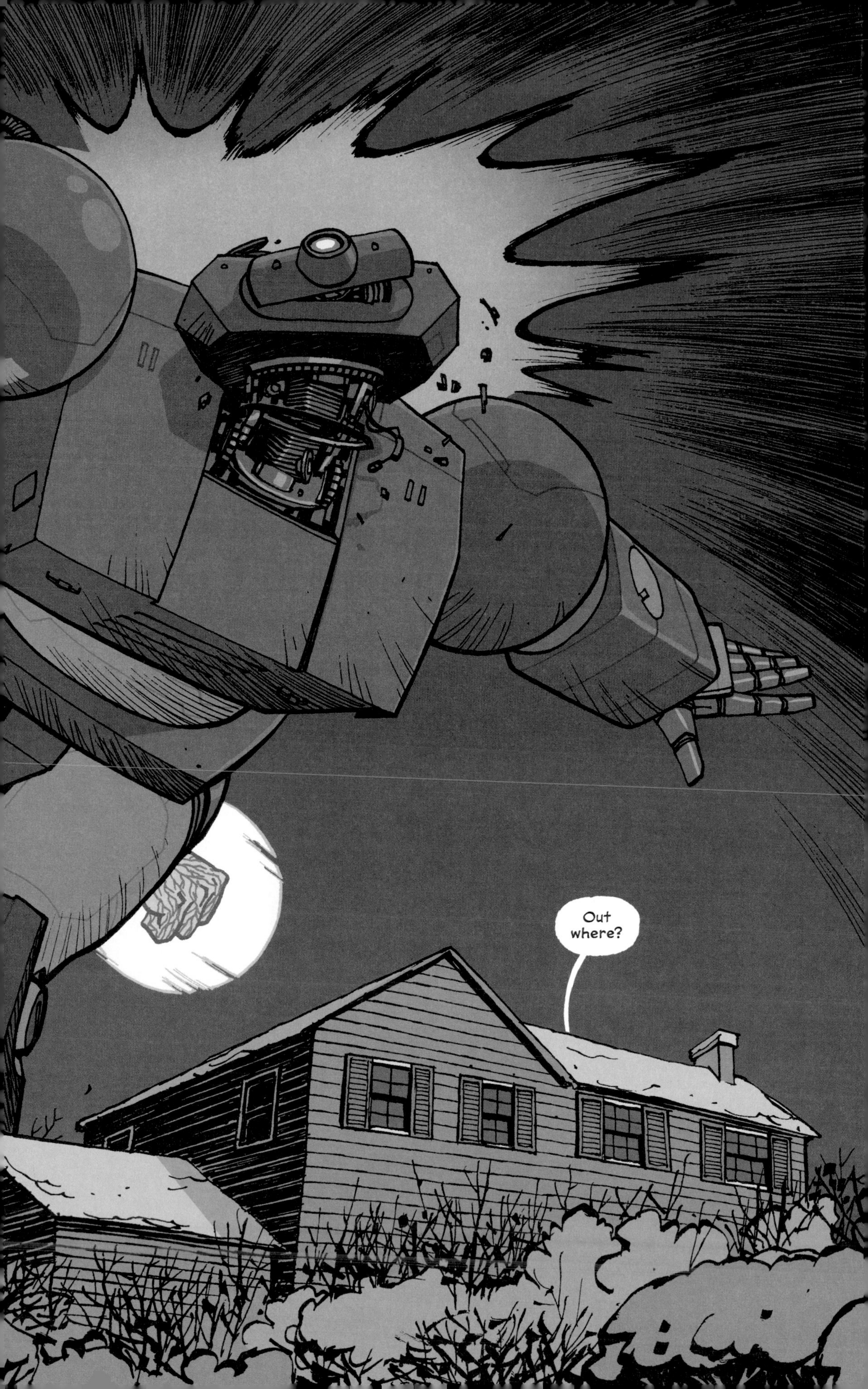
Out where?

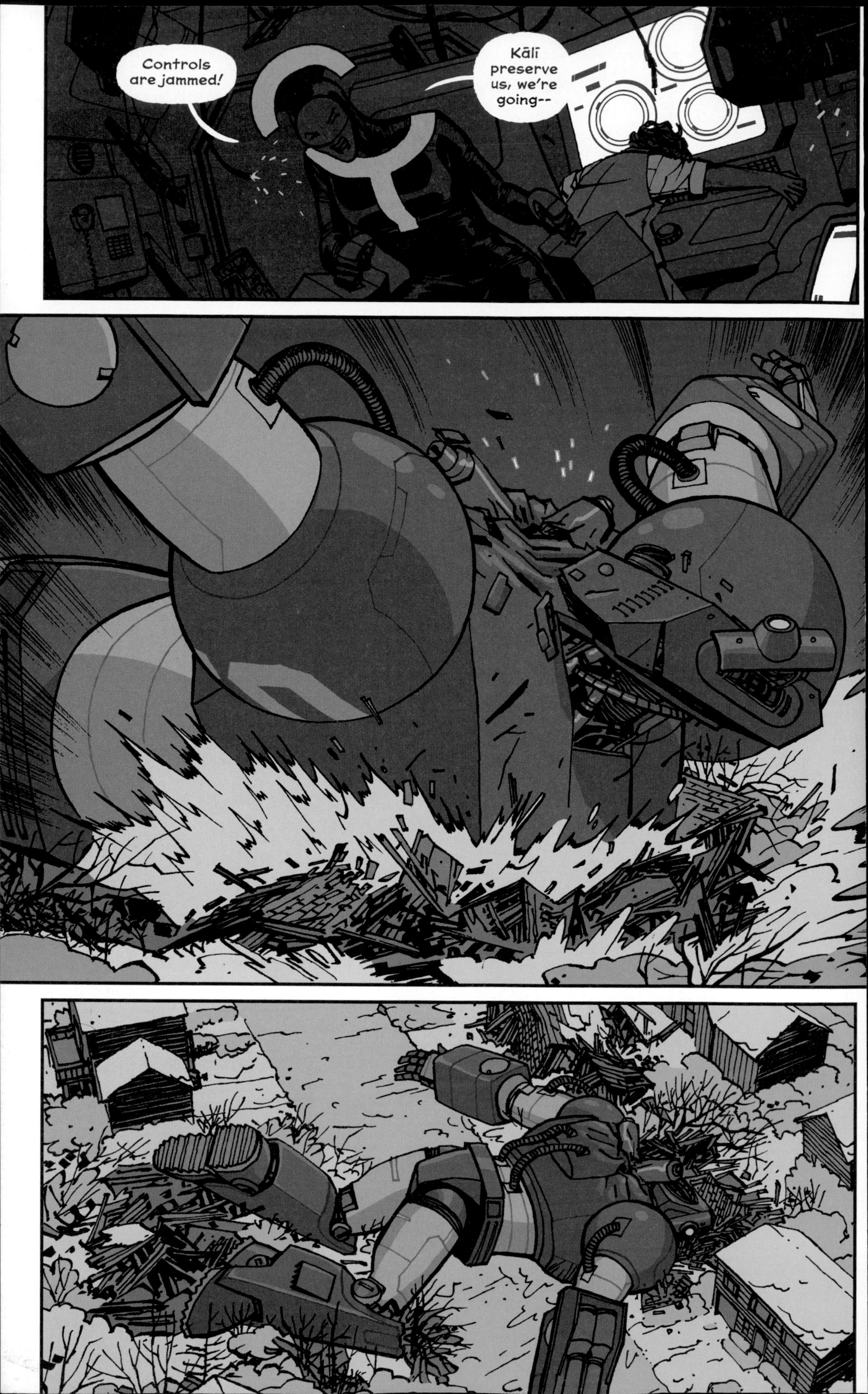
Controls are jammed!
Kālī preserve us, we're going--

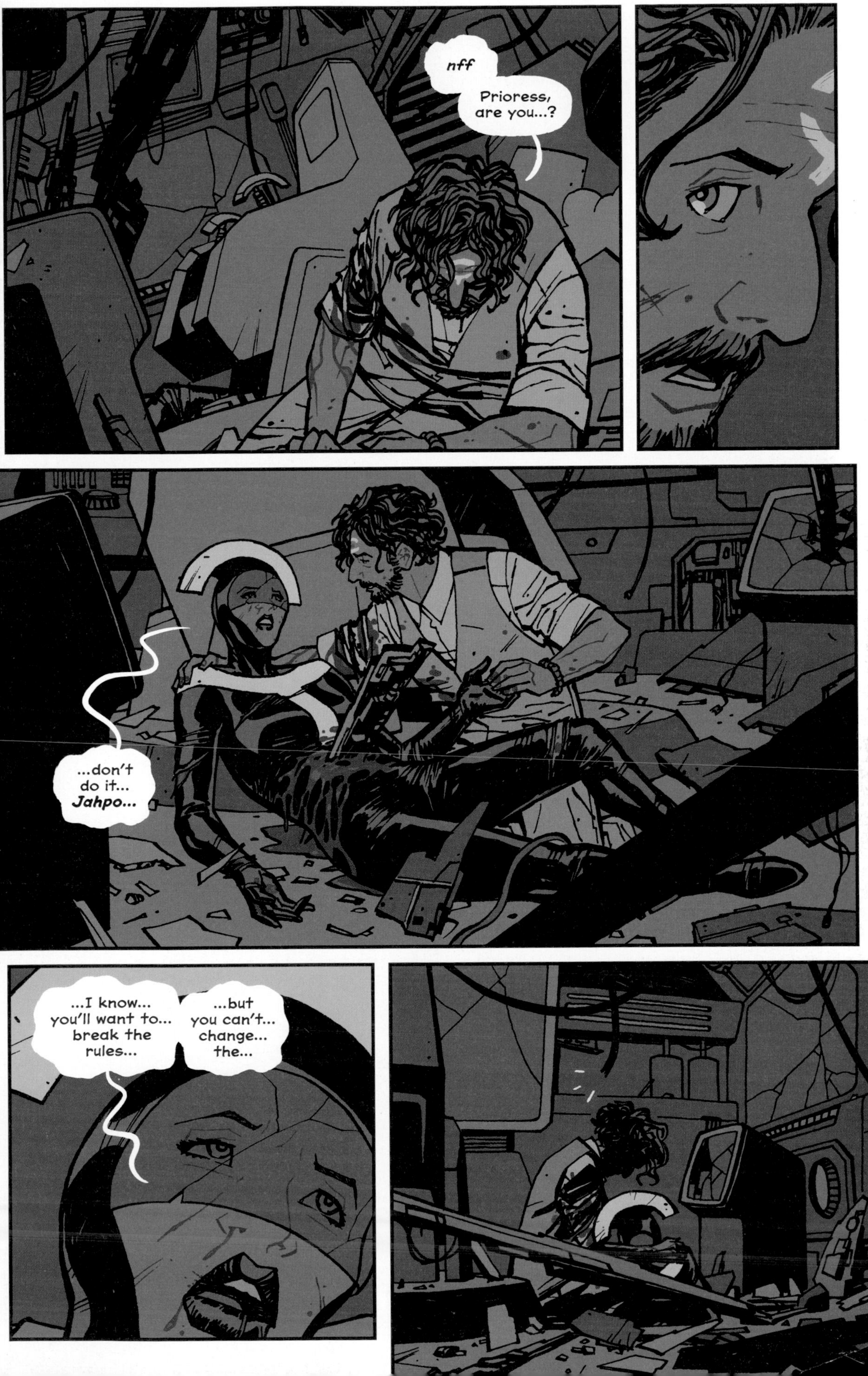

nff
Prioress, are you...?
...don't do it... ***Jahpo...***
...I know... you'll want to... break the rules...
...but you can't... change... the...

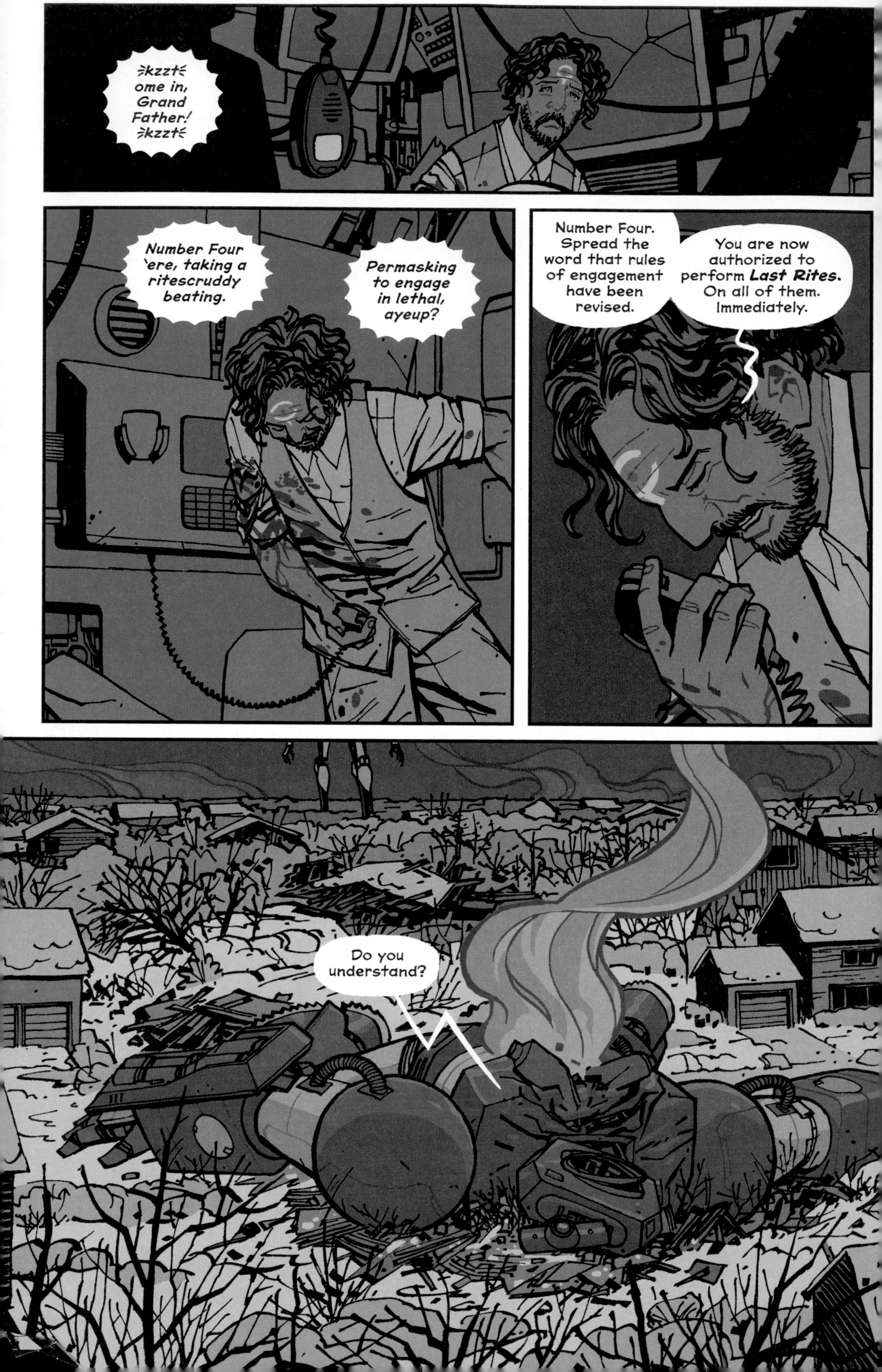

⊰kzzt⊱ ome in, Grand Father! ⊰kzzt⊱
Number Four 'ere, taking a ritescruddy beating.
Permasking to engage in lethal, ayeup?
Number Four. Spread the word that rules of engagement have been revised.
You are now authorized to perform **Last Rites.** On all of them. Immediately.
Do you understand?

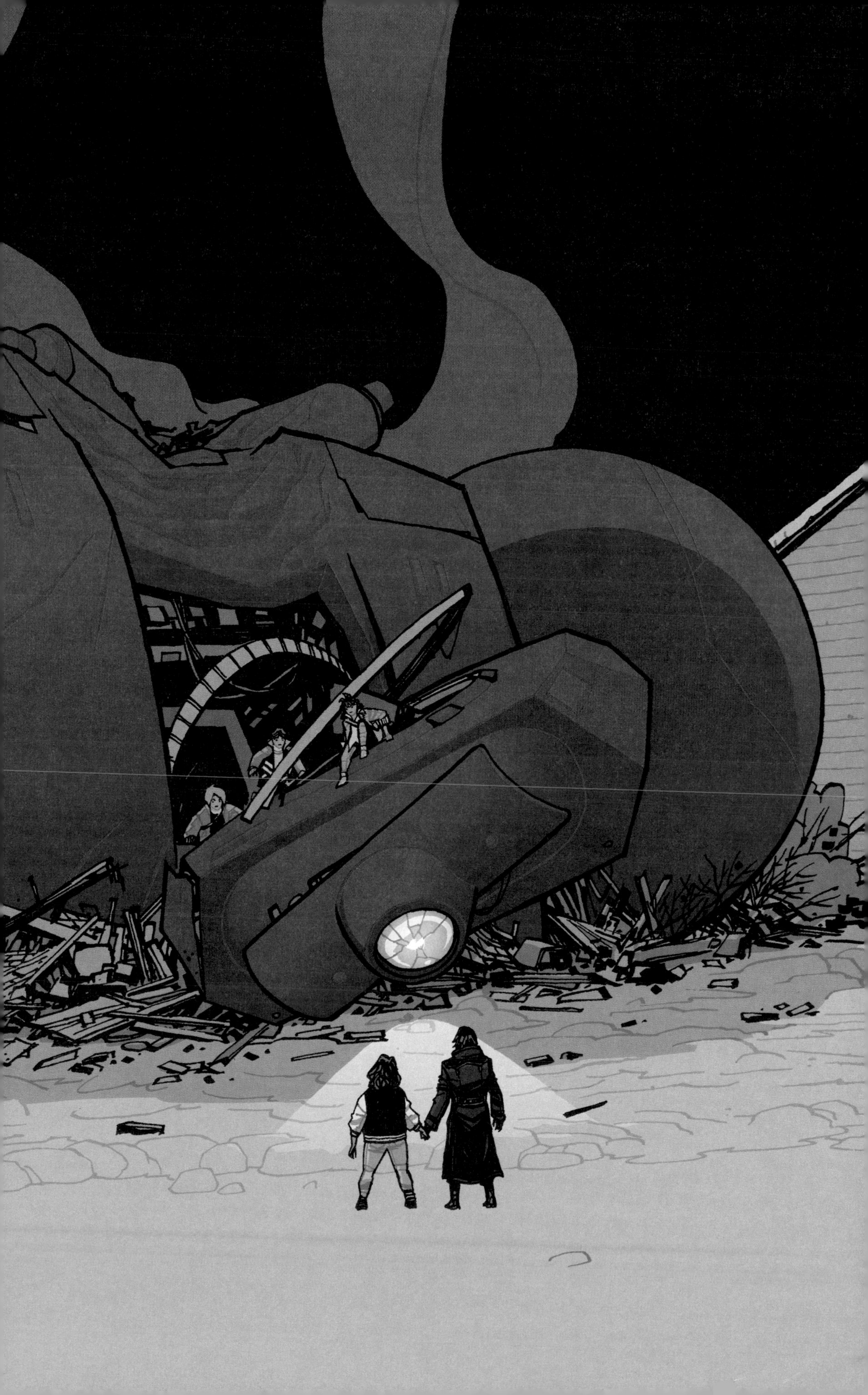

"Trump Orders Government to Stop
Work on Y2K Bug, 17 Years Later"

-**Bloomberg Politics** headline
 June 15, 2017

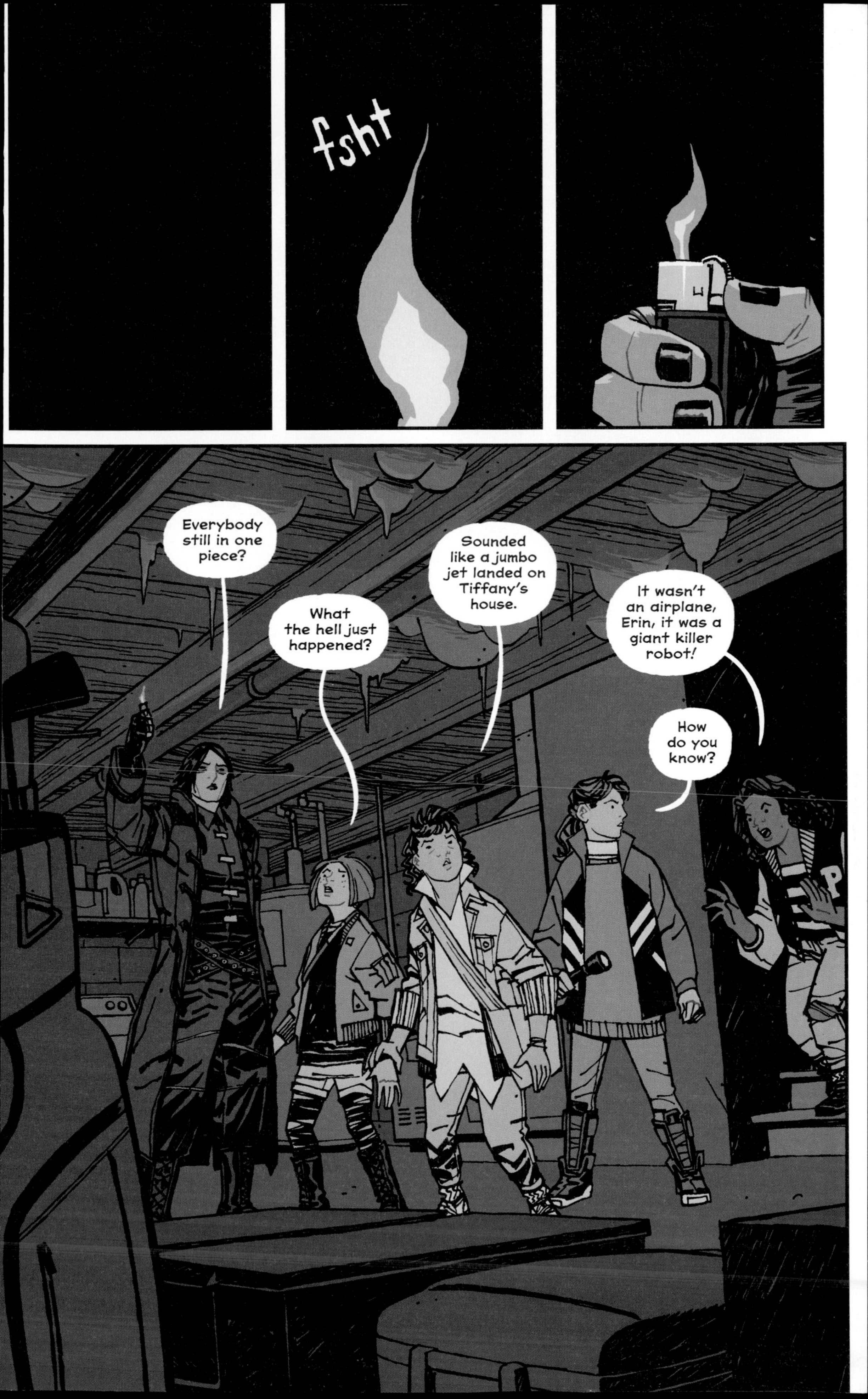
fsht
Everybody still in one piece?
What the hell just happened?
Sounded like a jumbo jet landed on Tiffany's house.
It wasn't an airplane, Erin, it was a giant killer robot!
How do you know?

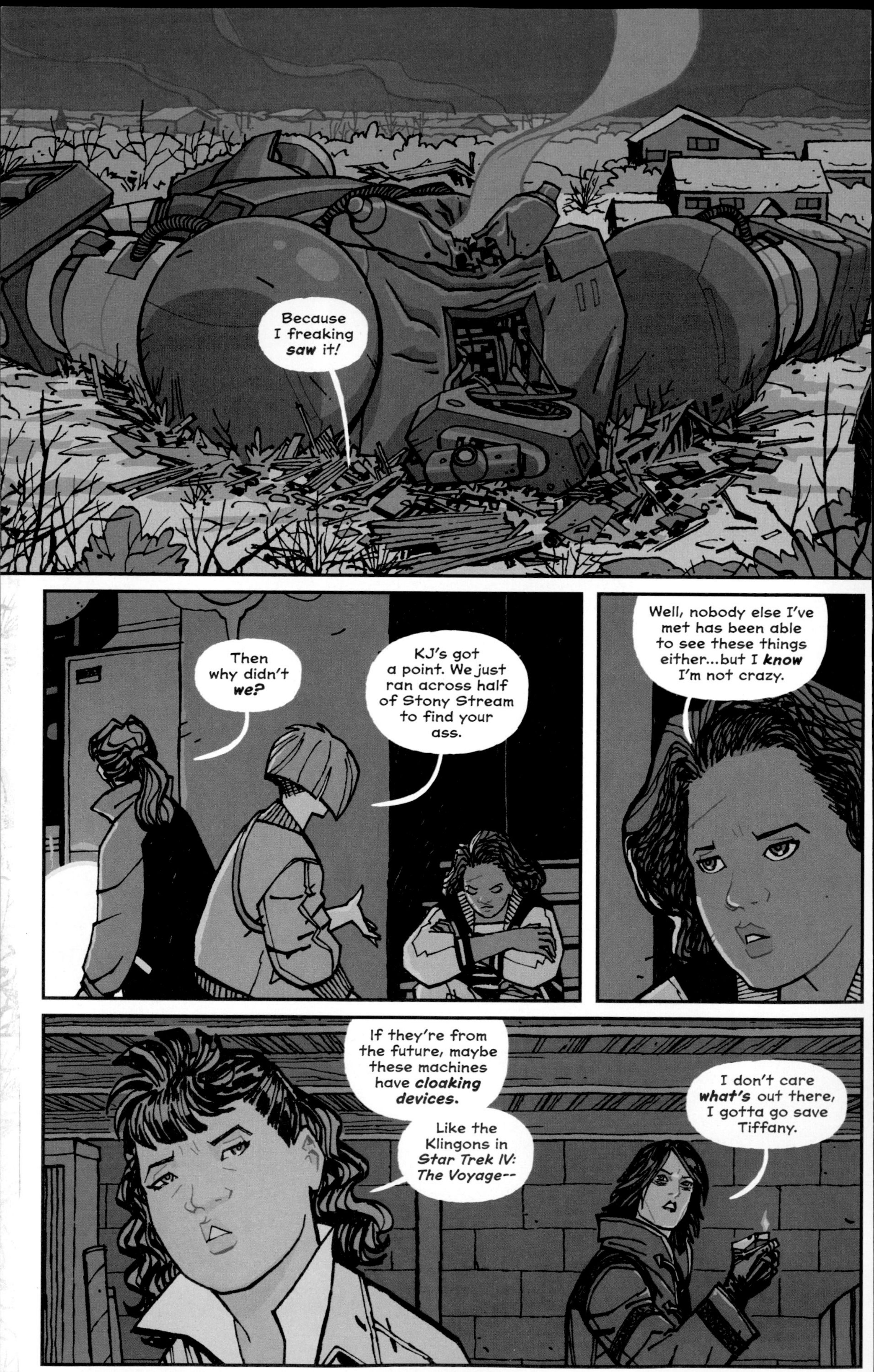
Because I freaking *saw* it!
Then why didn't *we?*
KJ's got a point. We just ran across half of Stony Stream to find your ass.
Well, nobody else I've met has been able to see these things either...but I *know* I'm not crazy.
If they're from the future, maybe these machines have *cloaking devices.*
Like the Klingons in *Star Trek IV: The Voyage--*
I don't care *what's* out there, I gotta go save Tiffany.

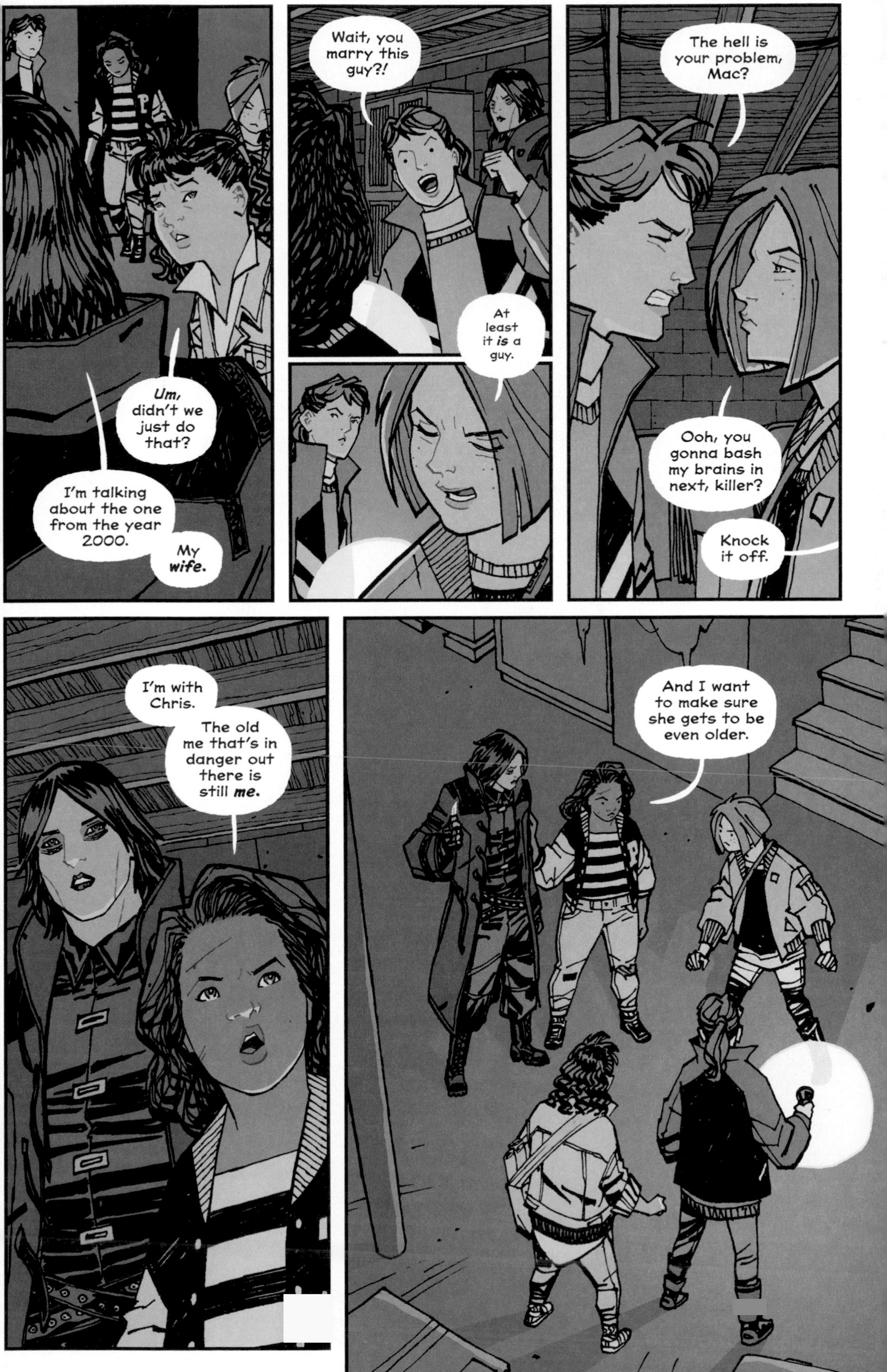
Um, didn't we just do that?
I'm talking about the one from the year 2000.
My *wife.*
Wait, you marry this guy?!
At least it *is* a guy.
The hell is your problem, Mac?
Ooh, you gonna bash my brains in next, killer?
Knock it off.
I'm with Chris.
The old me that's in danger out there is still *me.*
And I want to make sure she gets to be even older.

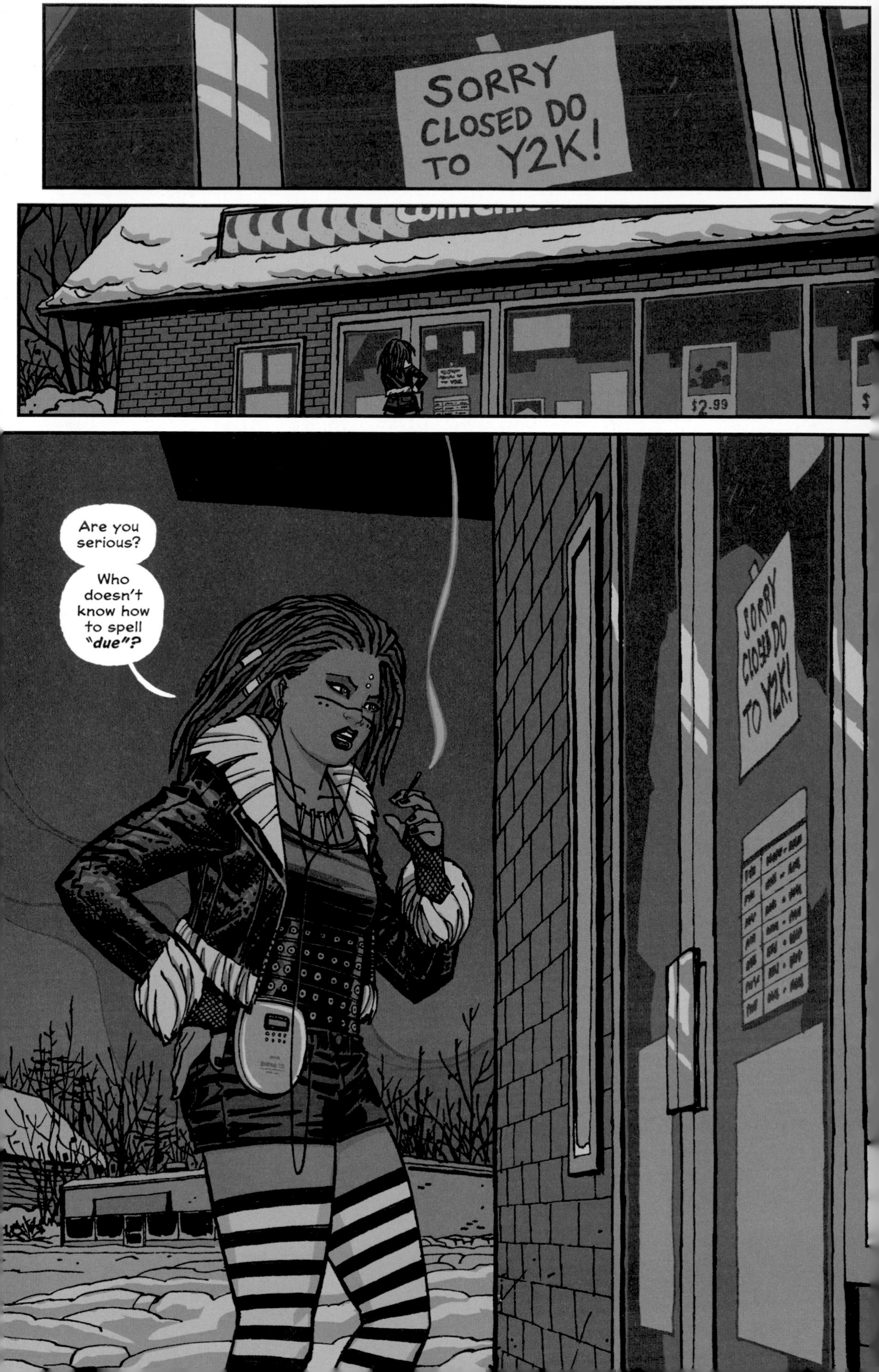
SORRY CLOSED DO TO Y2K!
$2.99
Are you serious?
Who doesn't know how to spell "due"?
SORRY CLOSED DO TO Y2K!

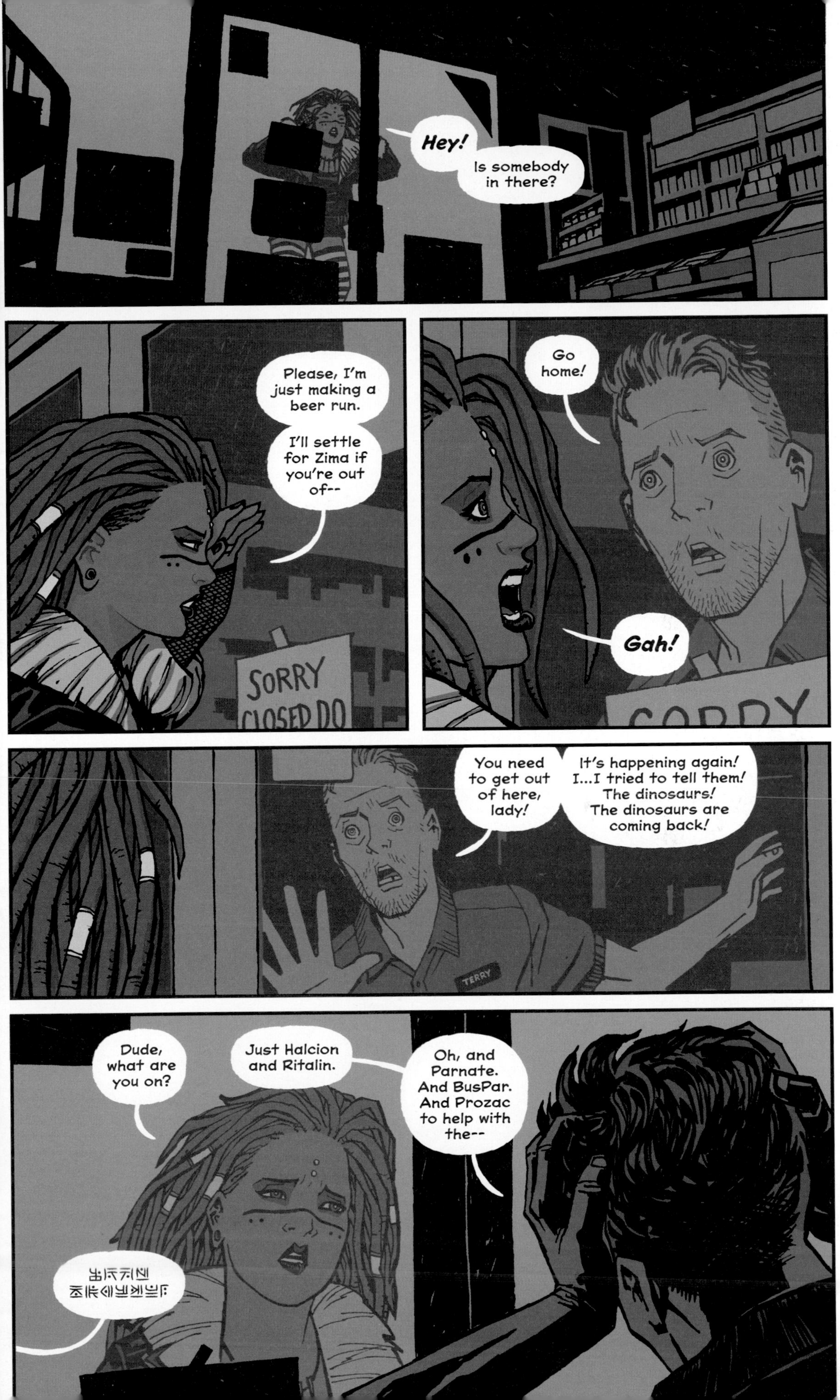
Hey!
Is somebody in there?
Please, I'm just making a beer run.
I'll settle for Zima if you're out of--
SORRY
Go home!
Gah!
You need to get out of here, lady!
It's happening again! I...I tried to tell them! The dinosaurs! The dinosaurs are coming back!
TERRY
Dude, what are you on?
Just Halcion and Ritalin.
Oh, and Parnate. And BusPar. And Prozac to help with the--

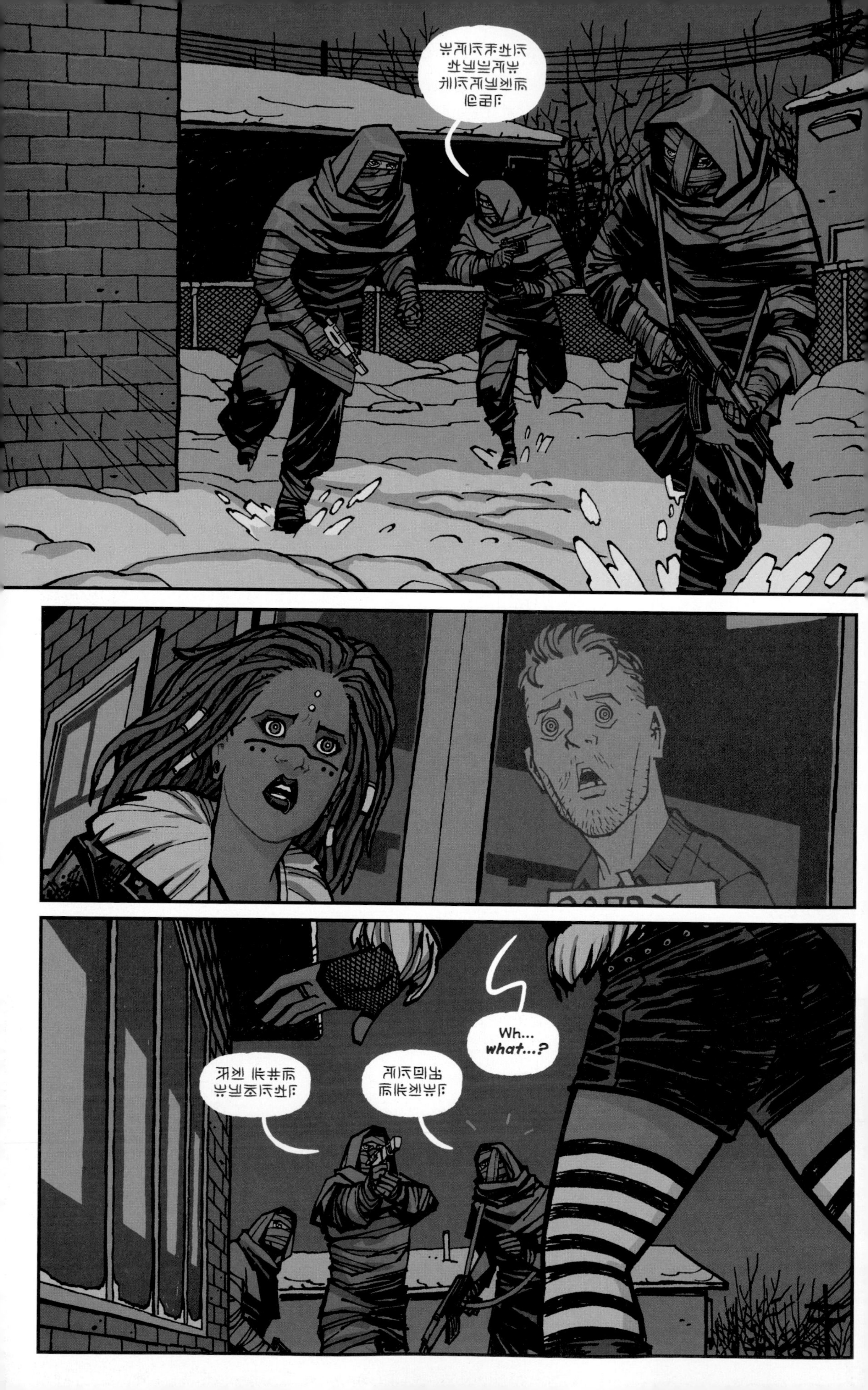
Wh... *what...?*

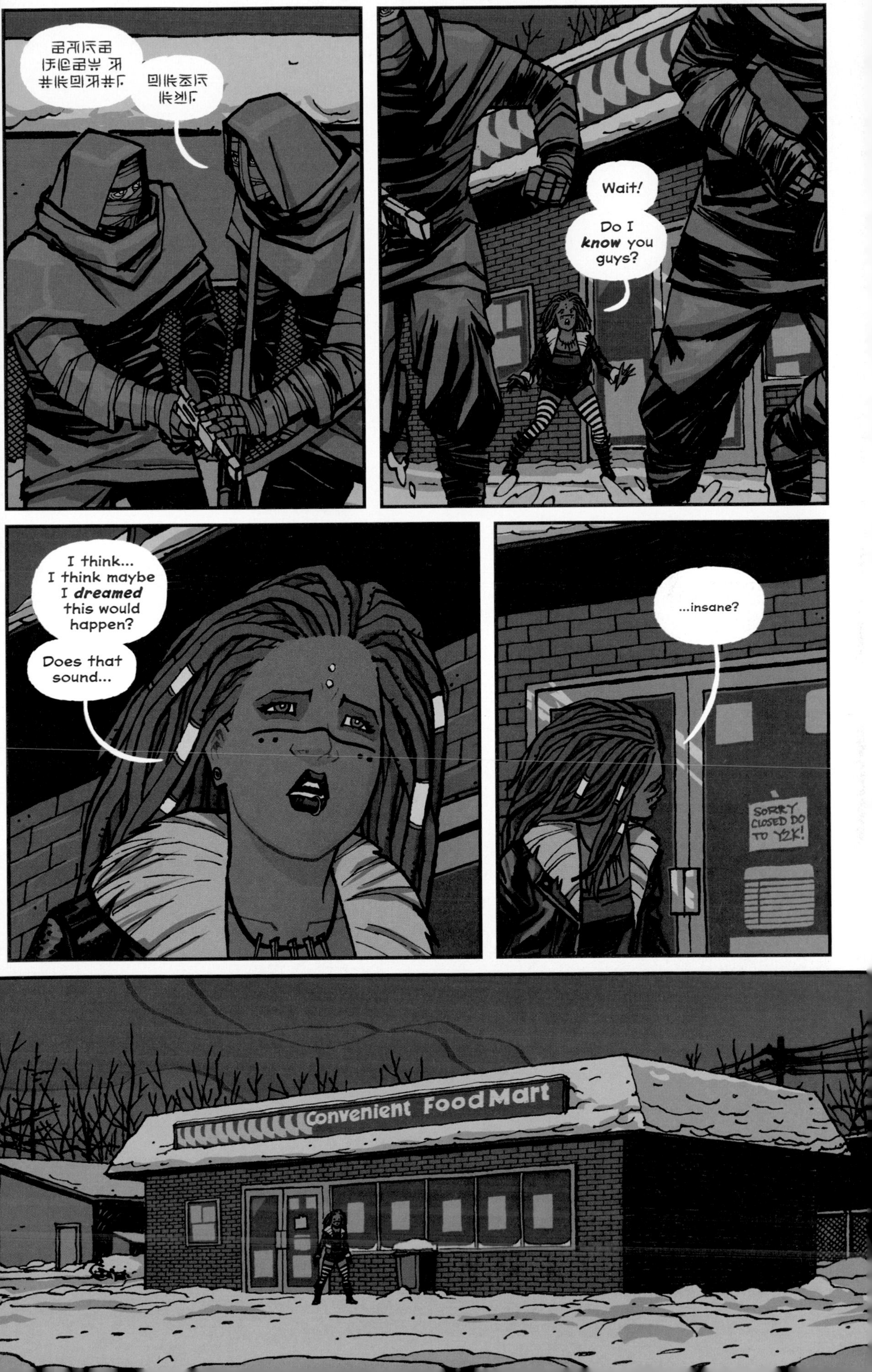
Wait!
Do I *know* you guys?
I think... I think maybe I *dreamed* this would happen?
Does that sound...
...insane?
SORRY CLOSED DO TO Y2K!
Convenient Food Mart

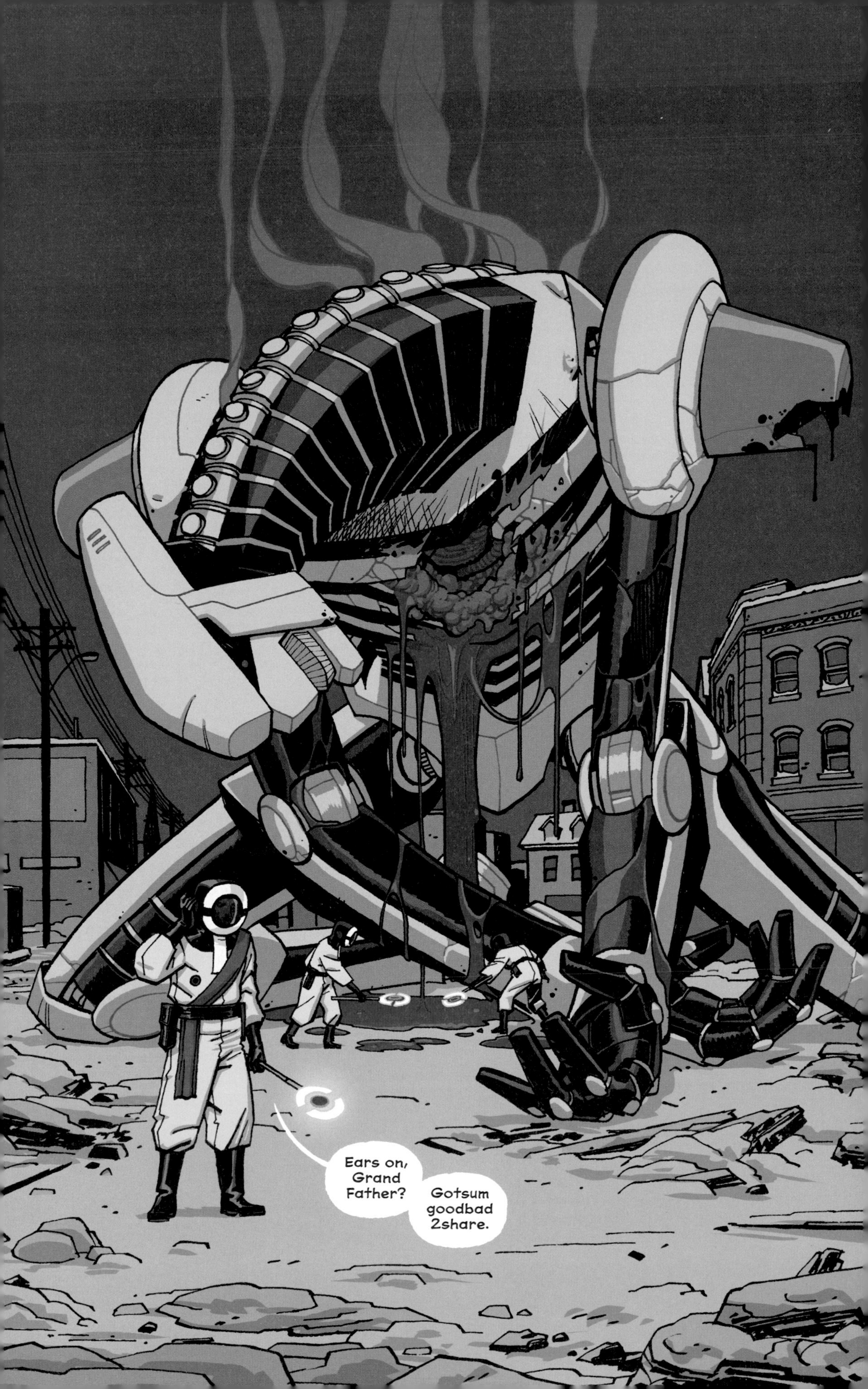
Ears on, Grand Father?
Gotsum goodbad 2share.

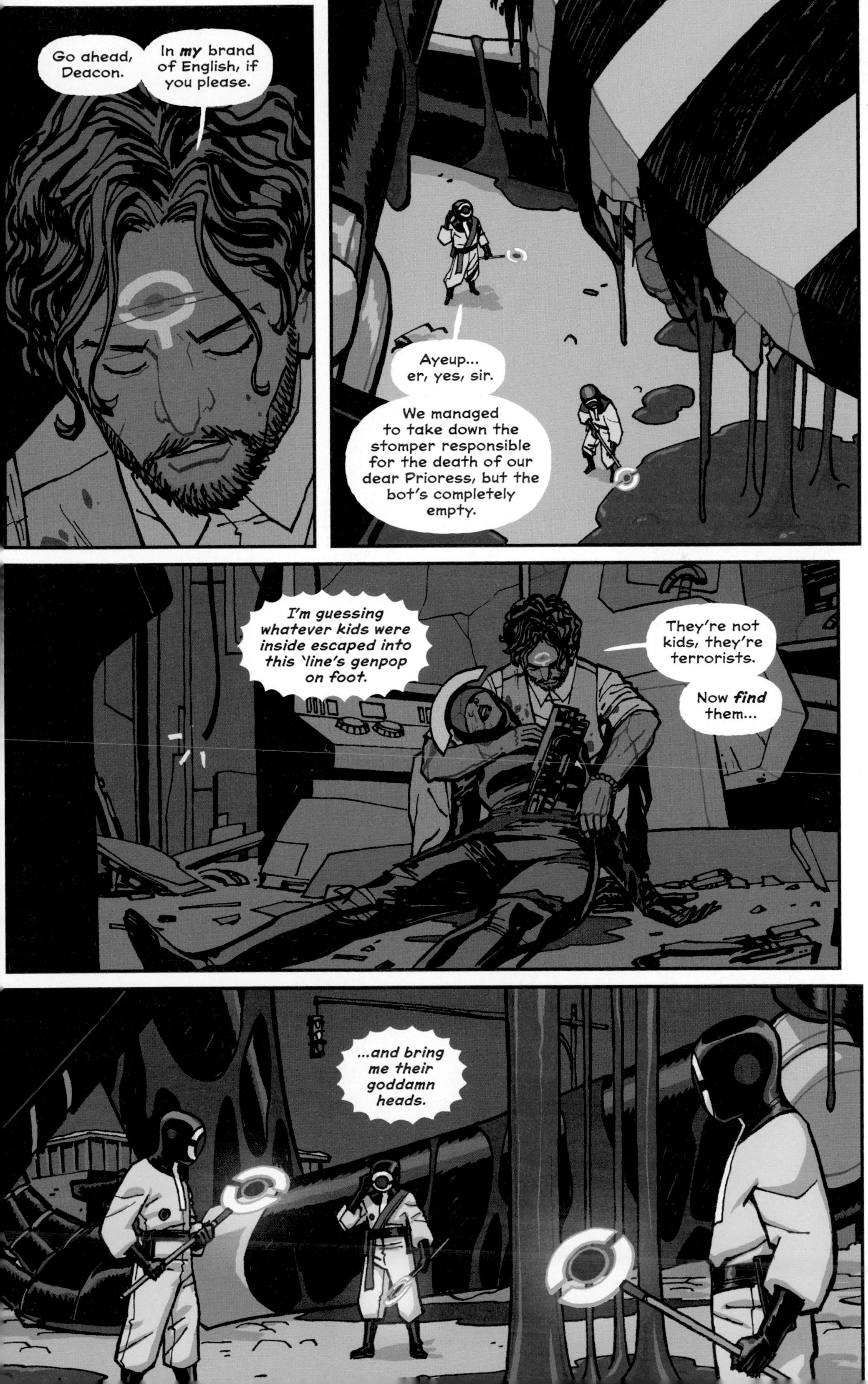
Go ahead, Deacon.
In *my* brand of English, if you please.
Ayeup... er, yes, sir.
We managed to take down the stomper responsible for the death of our dear Prioress, but the bot's completely empty.
I'm guessing whatever kids were inside escaped into this 'line's genpop on foot.
They're not kids, they're terrorists.
Now *find* them...
...and bring me their goddamn heads.

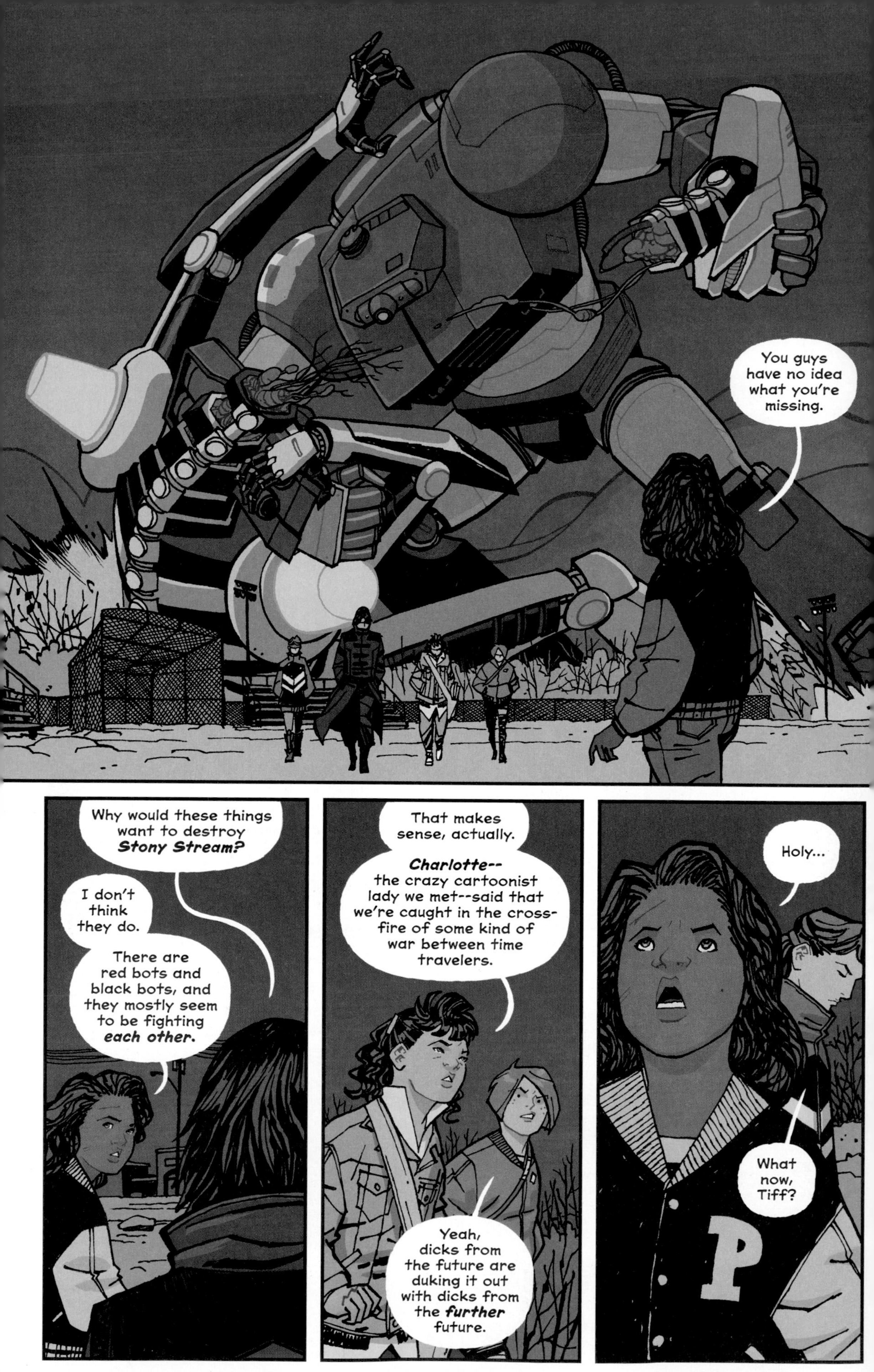
You guys have no idea what you're missing.
Why would these things want to destroy **Stony Stream?**
I don't think they do.
There are red bots and black bots, and they mostly seem to be fighting **each other.**
That makes sense, actually.
Charlotte-- the crazy cartoonist lady we met--said that we're caught in the cross-fire of some kind of war between time travelers.
Yeah, dicks from the future are duking it out with dicks from the **further** future.
Holy...
What now, Tiff?

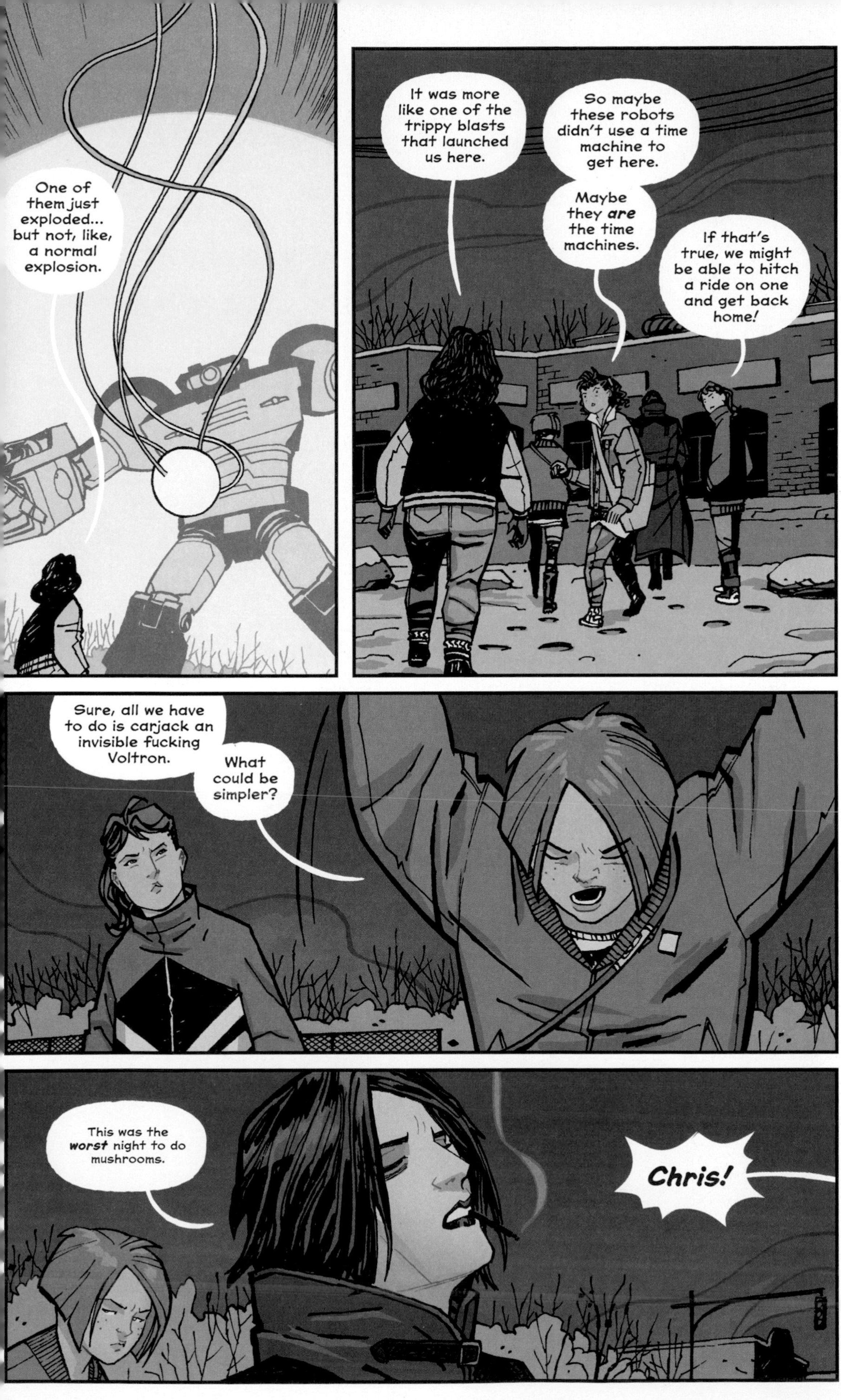
One of them just exploded... but not, like, a normal explosion.
It was more like one of the trippy blasts that launched us here.
So maybe these robots didn't use a time machine to get here.
Maybe they *are* the time machines.
If that's true, we might be able to hitch a ride on one and get back home!
Sure, all we have to do is carjack an invisible fucking Voltron.
What could be simpler?
This was the *worst* night to do mushrooms.
Chris!

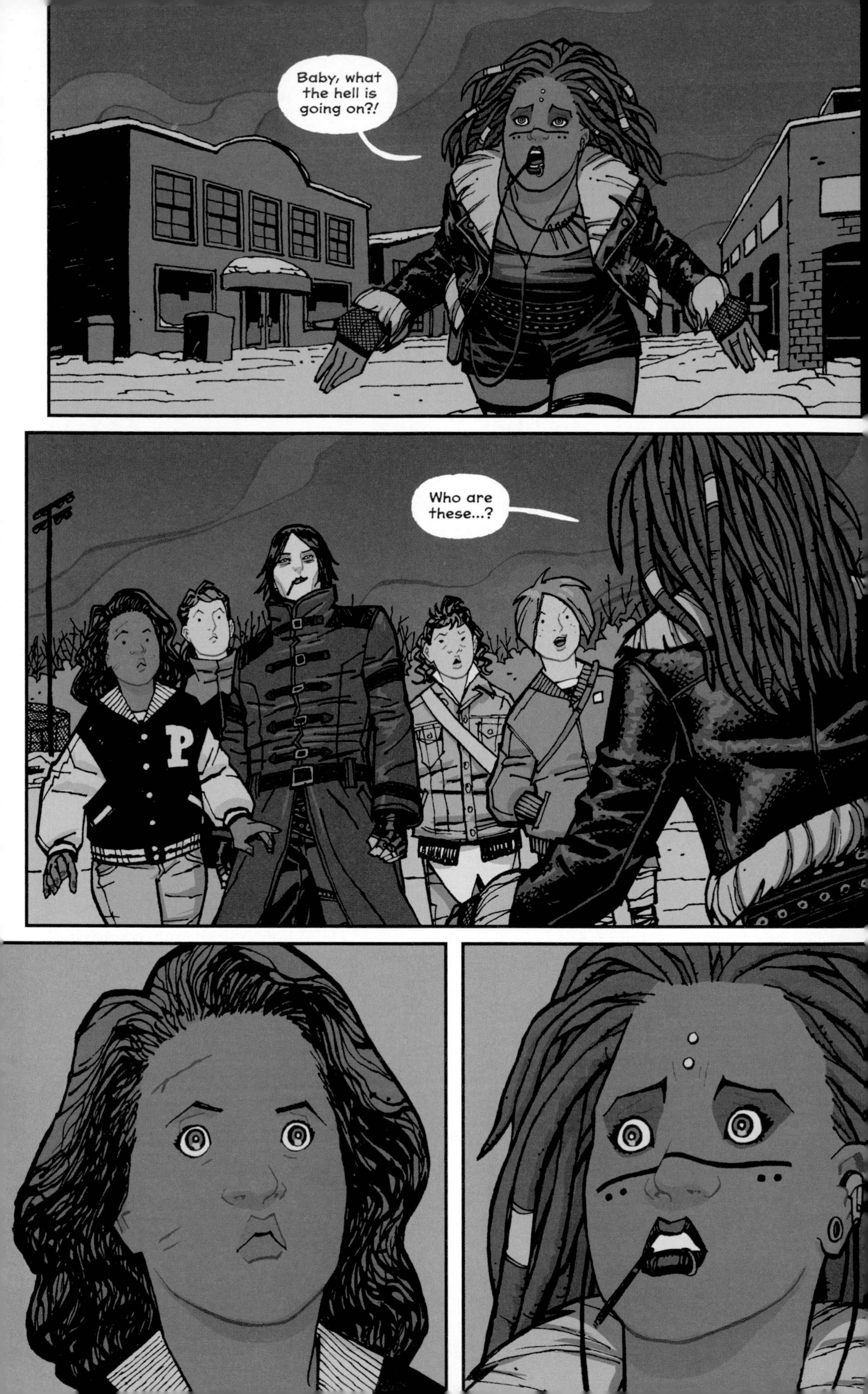
Baby, what the hell is going on?!
Who are these...?

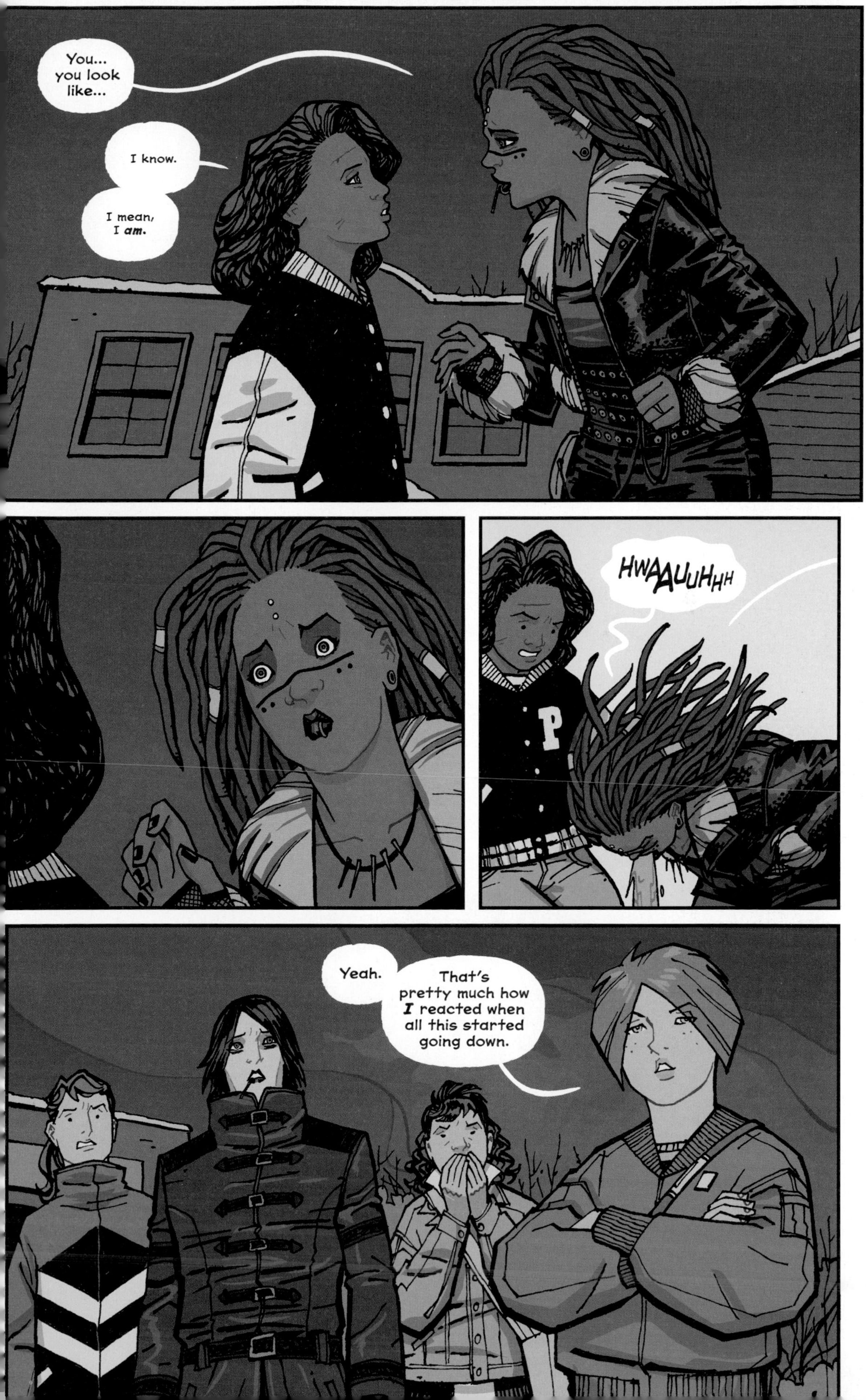
You... you look like...
I know.
I mean, I *am.*
HWAAUUHHH
Yeah.
That's pretty much how *I* reacted when all this started going down.

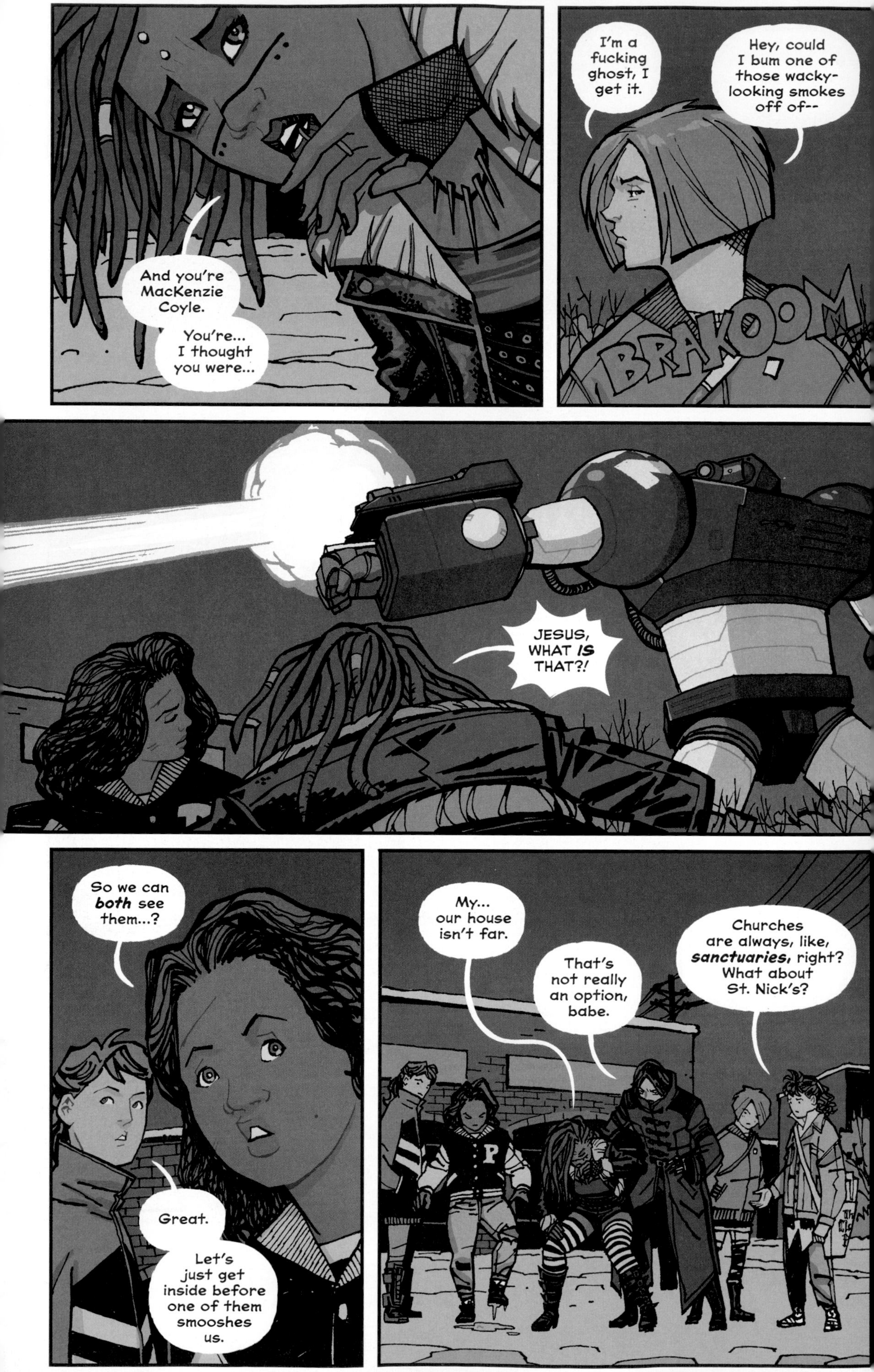

And you're MacKenzie Coyle.
You're... I thought you were...
I'm a fucking ghost, I get it.
Hey, could I bum one of those wacky-looking smokes off of--
BRAKOOM
JESUS, WHAT *IS* THAT?!
So we can ***both*** see them...?
Great.
Let's just get inside before one of them smooshes us.
My... our house isn't far.
That's not really an option, babe.
Churches are always, like, ***sanctuaries,*** right? What about St. Nick's?

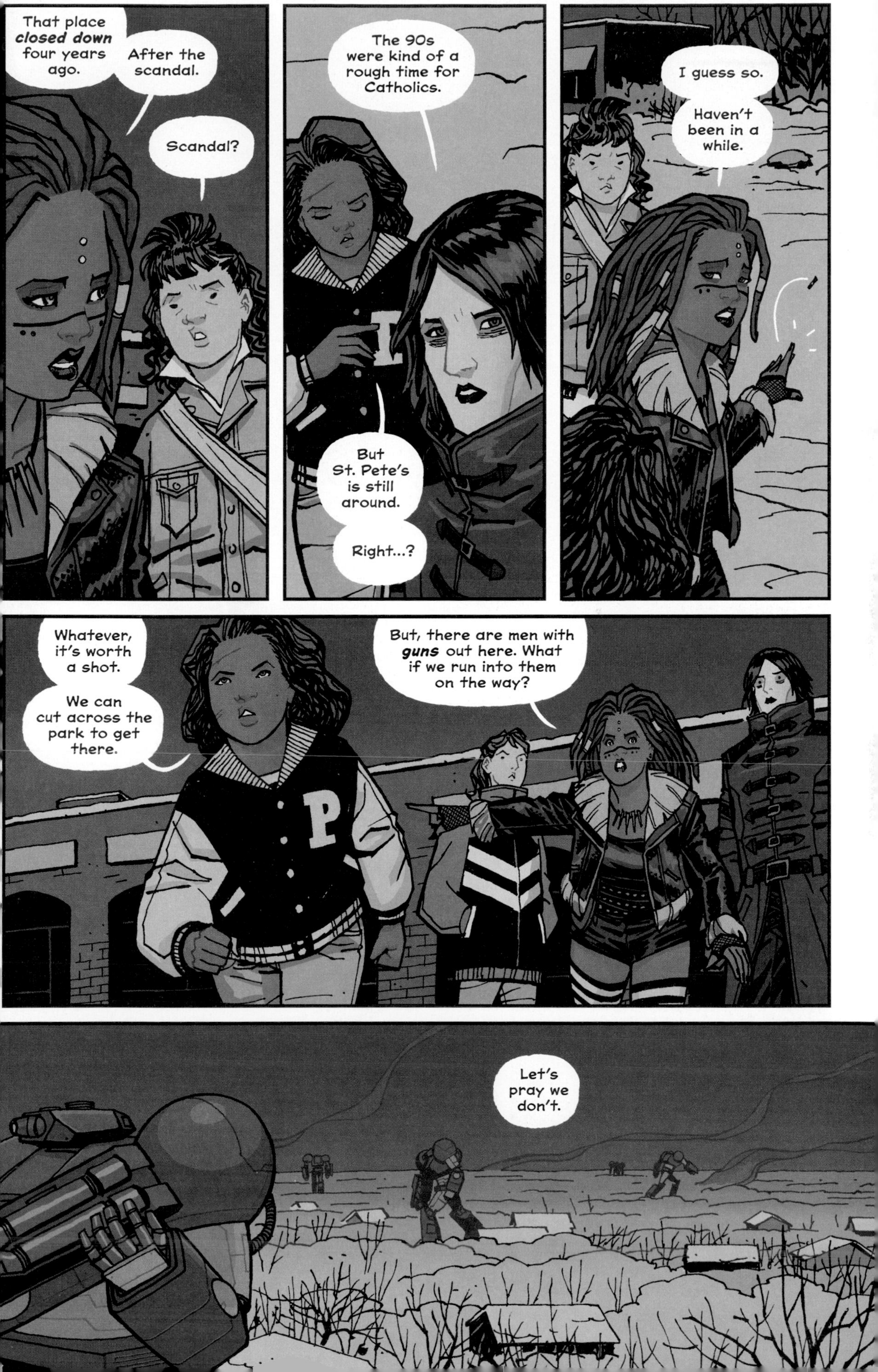
That place **closed down** four years ago.
After the scandal.
Scandal?
The 90s were kind of a rough time for Catholics.
But St. Pete's is still around.
Right...?
I guess so.
Haven't been in a while.
Whatever, it's worth a shot.
We can cut across the park to get there.
But, there are men with **guns** out here. What if we run into them on the way?
Let's pray we don't.

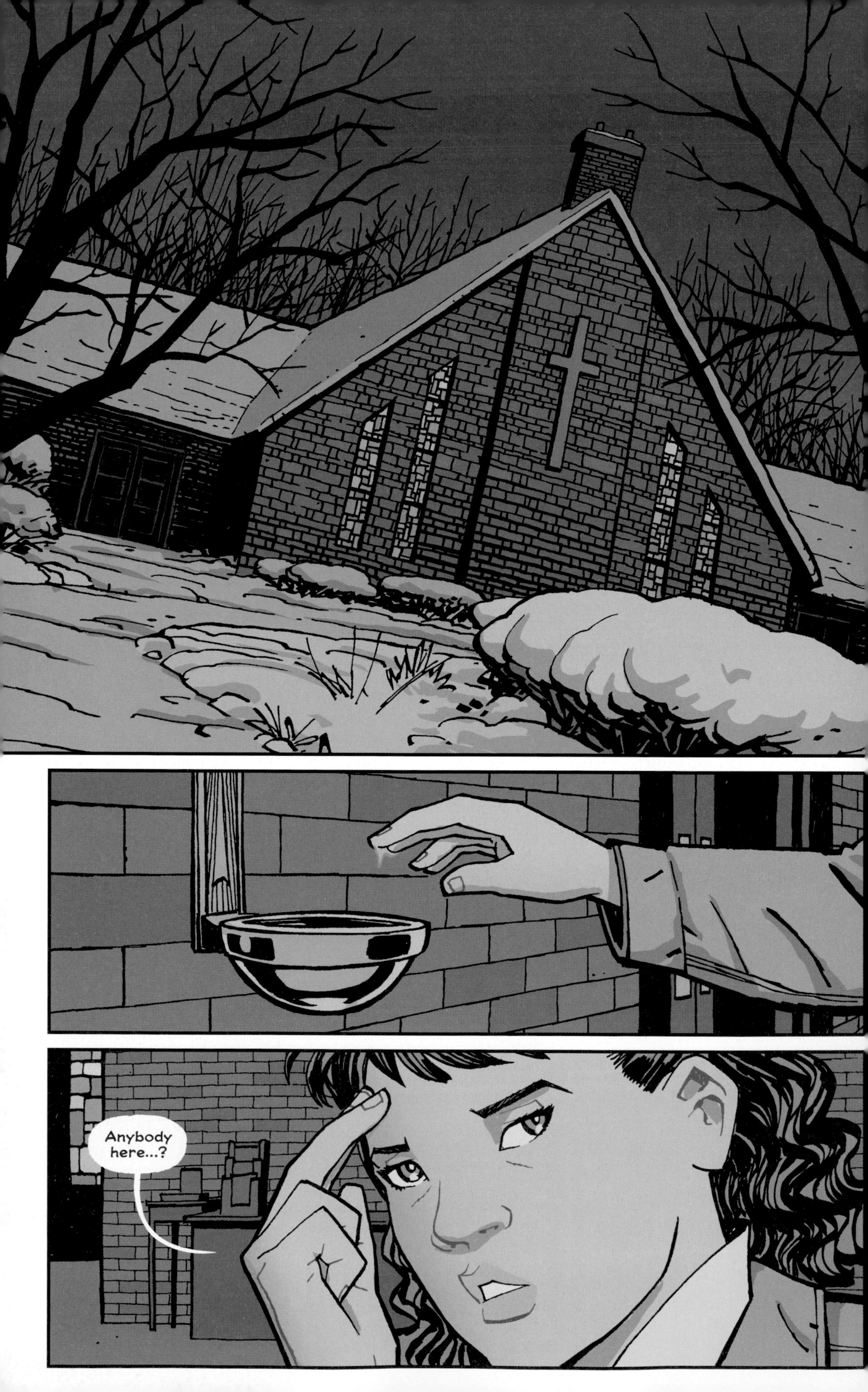
Anybody here...?

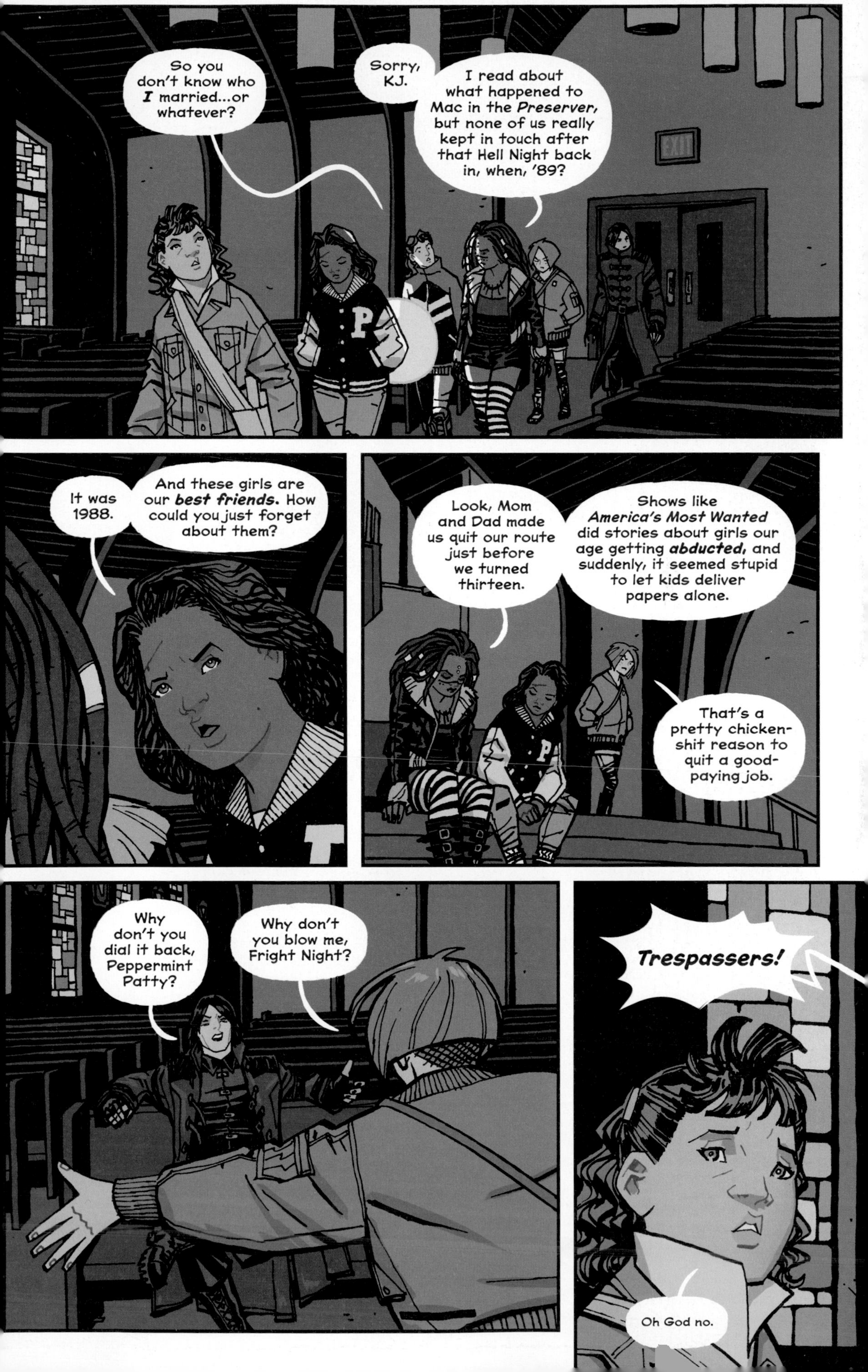
So you don't know who *I* married...or whatever?
Sorry, KJ.
I read about what happened to Mac in the *Preserver,* but none of us really kept in touch after that Hell Night back in, when, '89?
It was 1988.
And these girls are our ***best friends.*** How could you just forget about them?
Look, Mom and Dad made us quit our route just before we turned thirteen.
Shows like *America's Most Wanted* did stories about girls our age getting ***abducted,*** and suddenly, it seemed stupid to let kids deliver papers alone.
That's a pretty chicken-shit reason to quit a good-paying job.
Why don't you dial it back, Peppermint Patty?
Why don't you blow me, Fright Night?
Trespassers!
Oh God no.

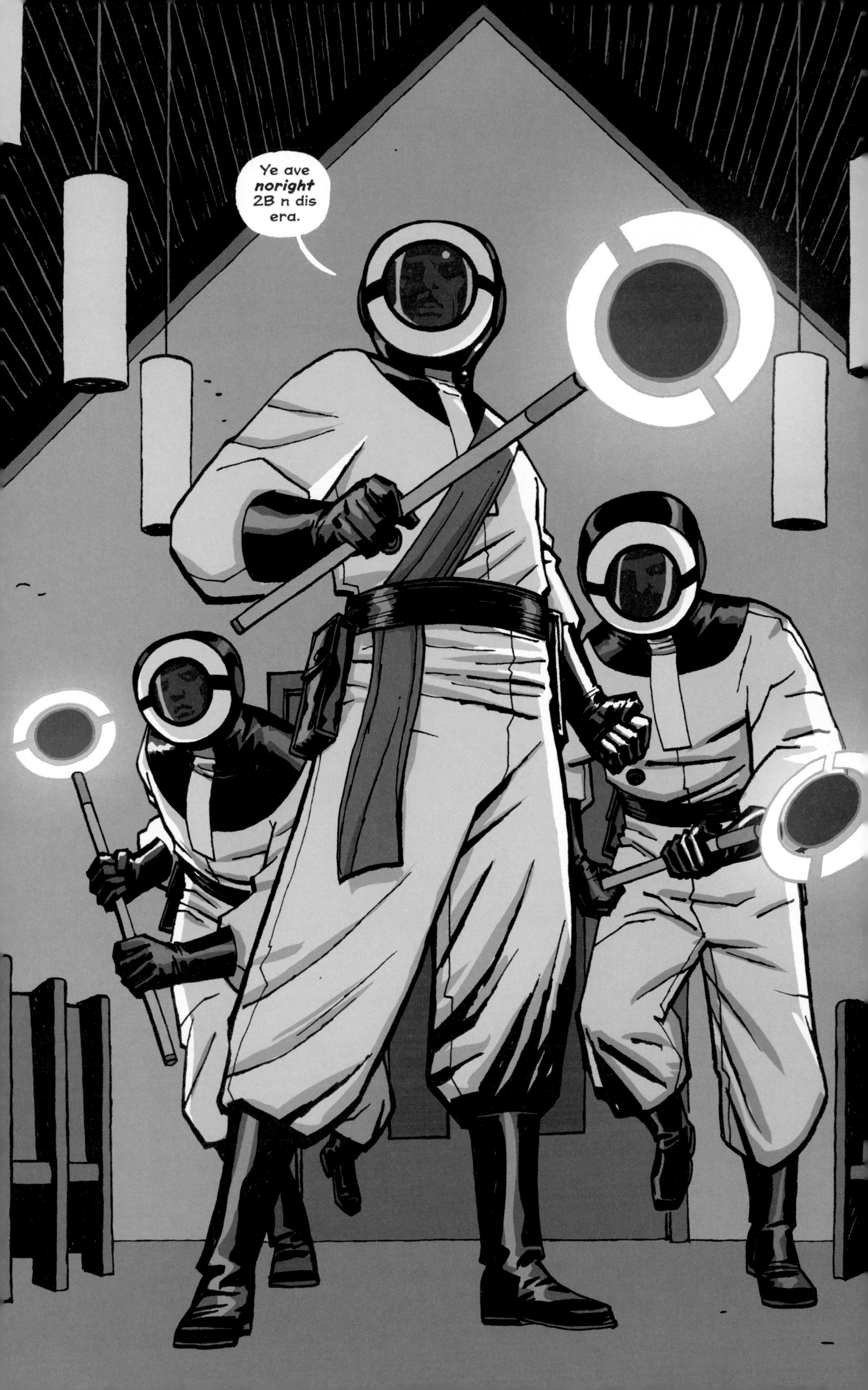
Ye ave *noright* 2B n dis era.

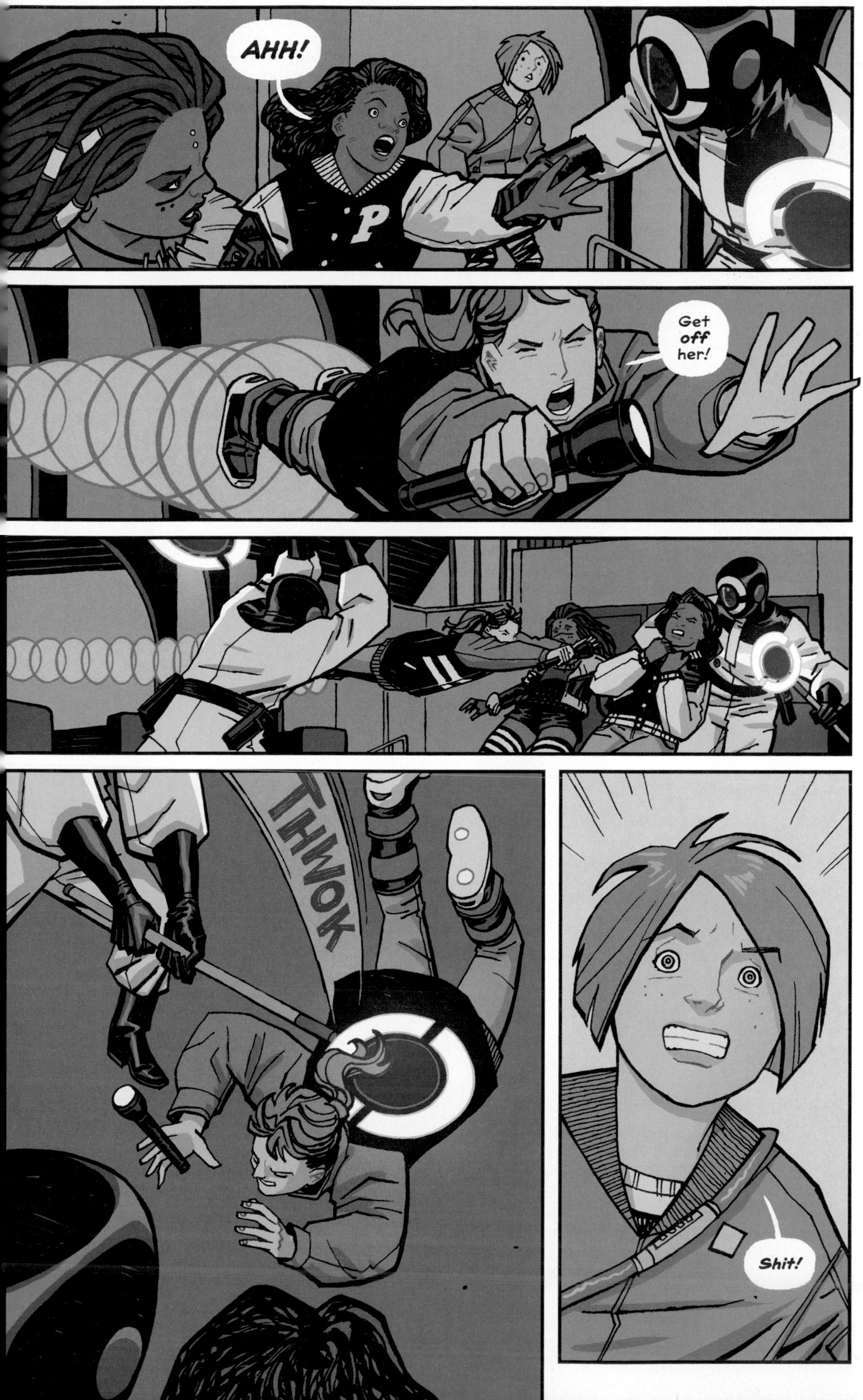
AHH!
Get off her!
THWOK
Shit!

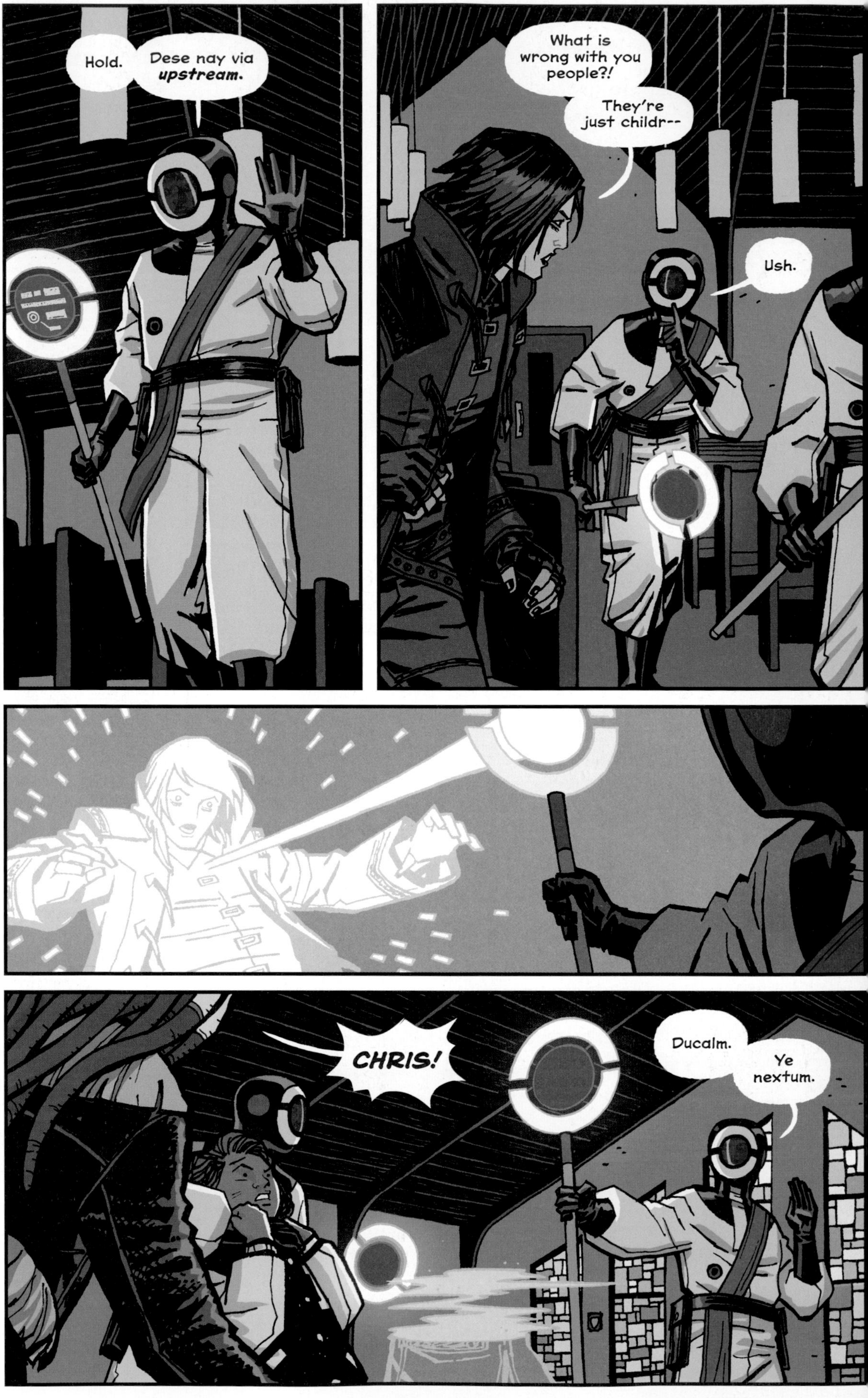

Hold.
Dese nay via *upstream.*
What is wrong with you people?!
They're just childr--
Ush.
CHRIS!
Ducalm.
Ye nextum.

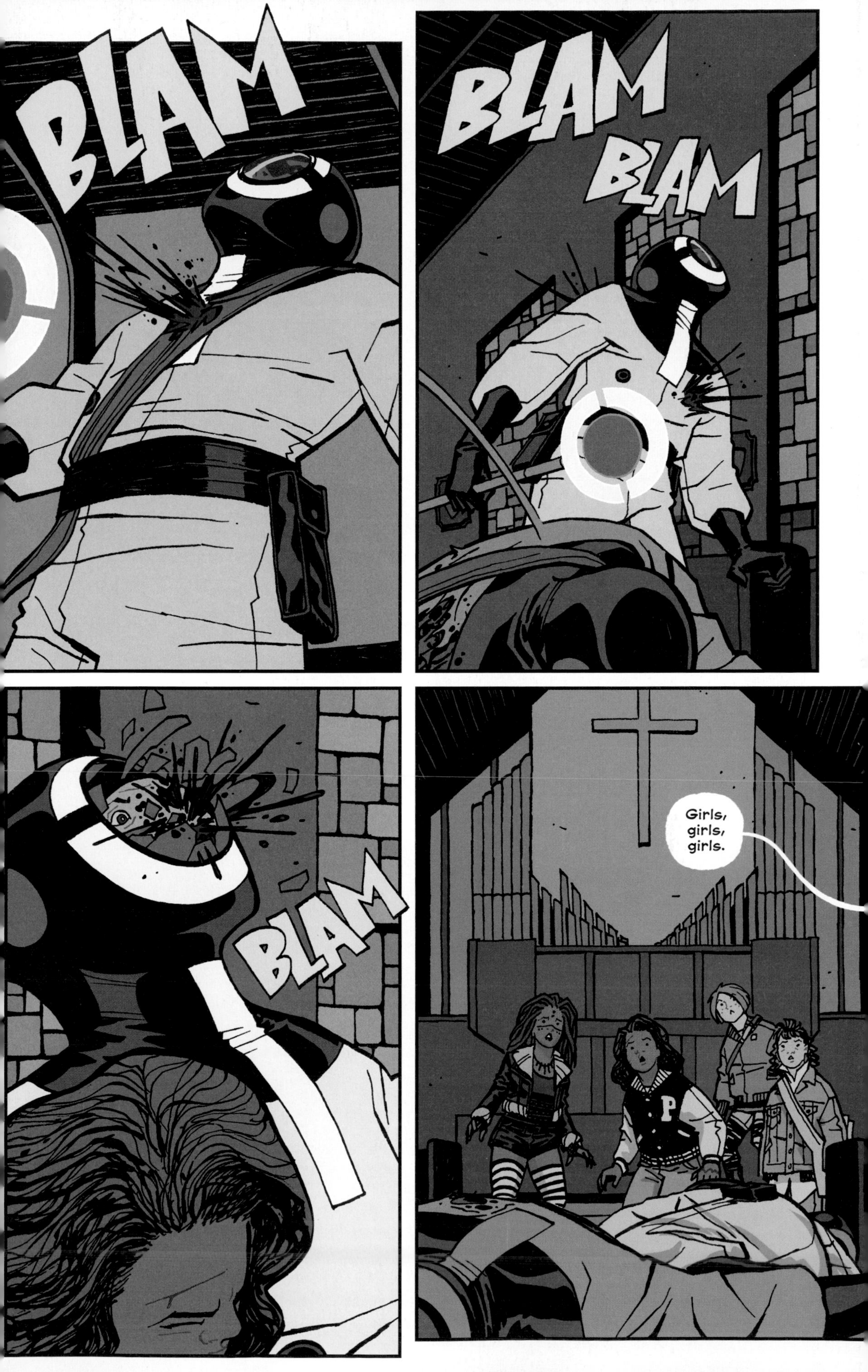
BLAM
BLAM
BLAM
BLAM
Girls, girls, girls.

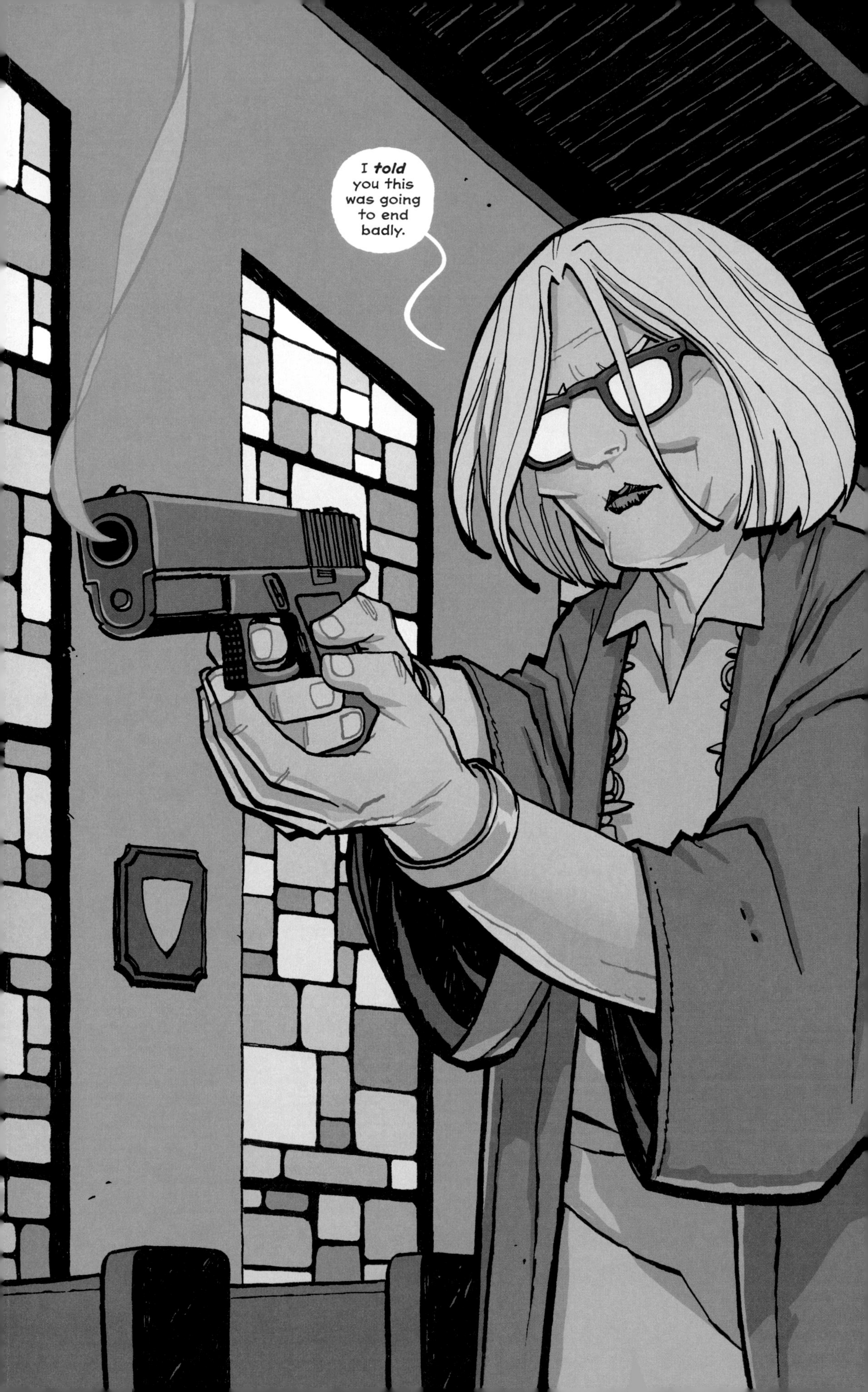
I *told* you this was going to end badly.

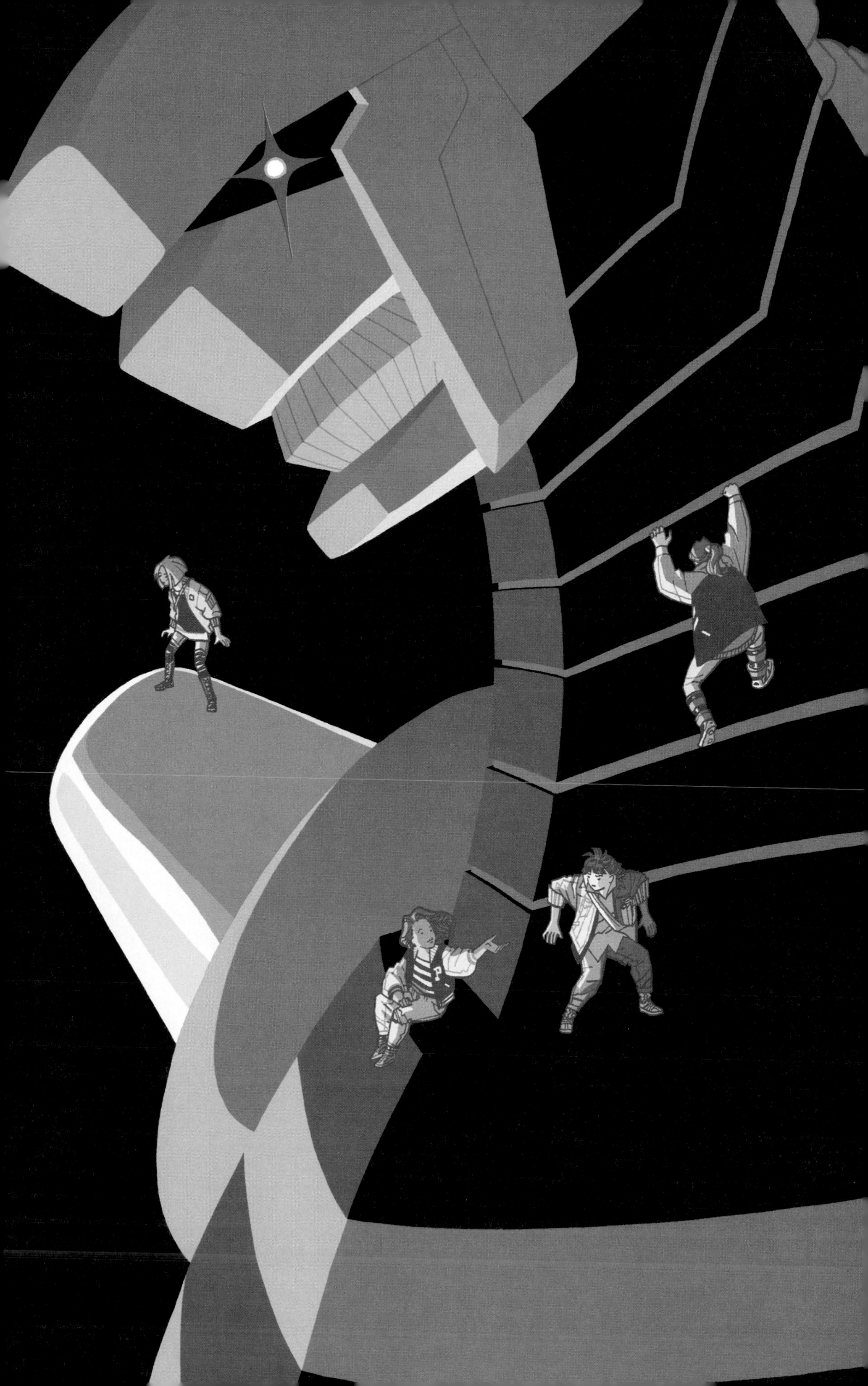

"ARMAGEDDON
Year 2000 Computer Bug
Will Turn Machine Against Man!"

-**Weekly World News** headline, 1999

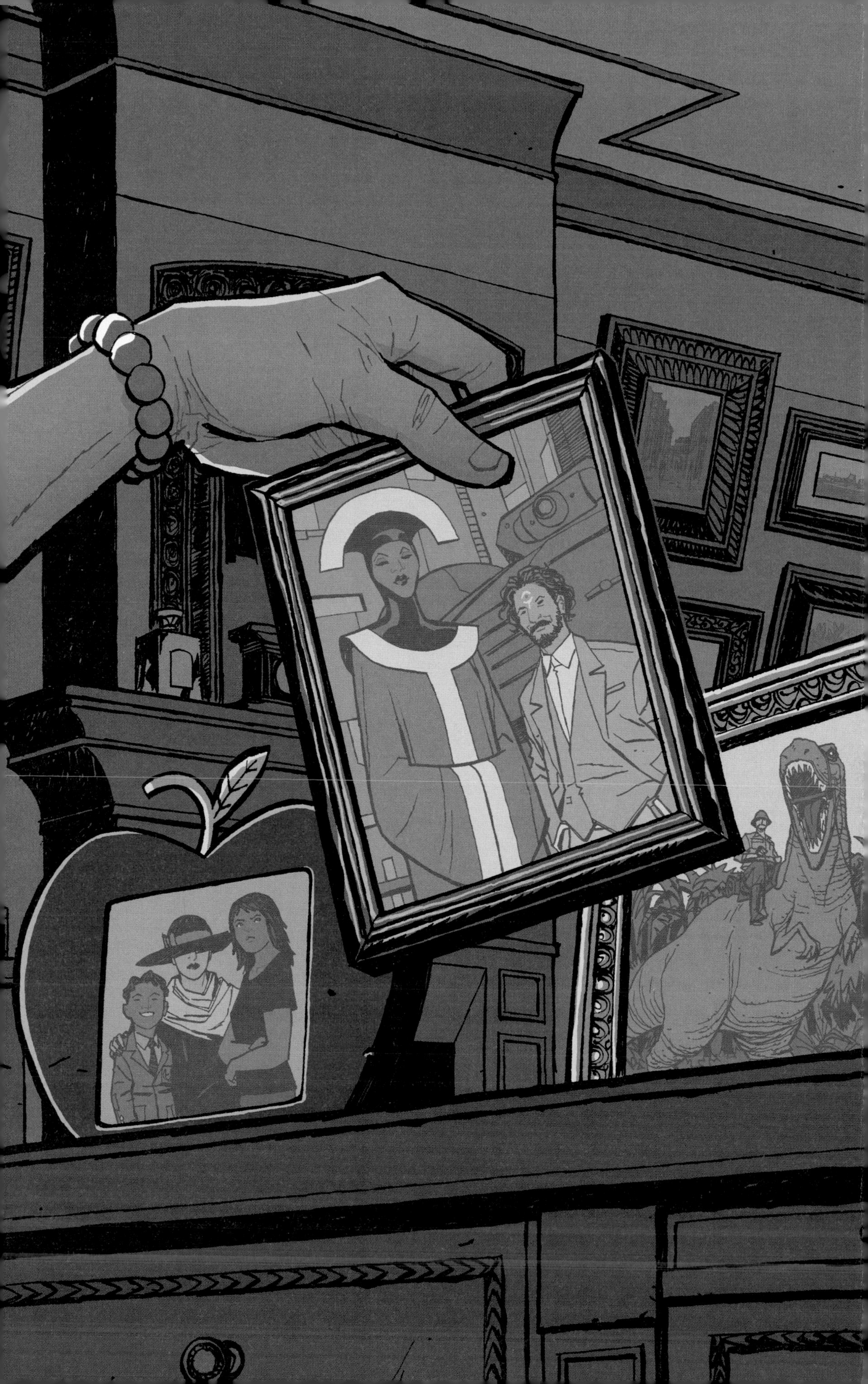

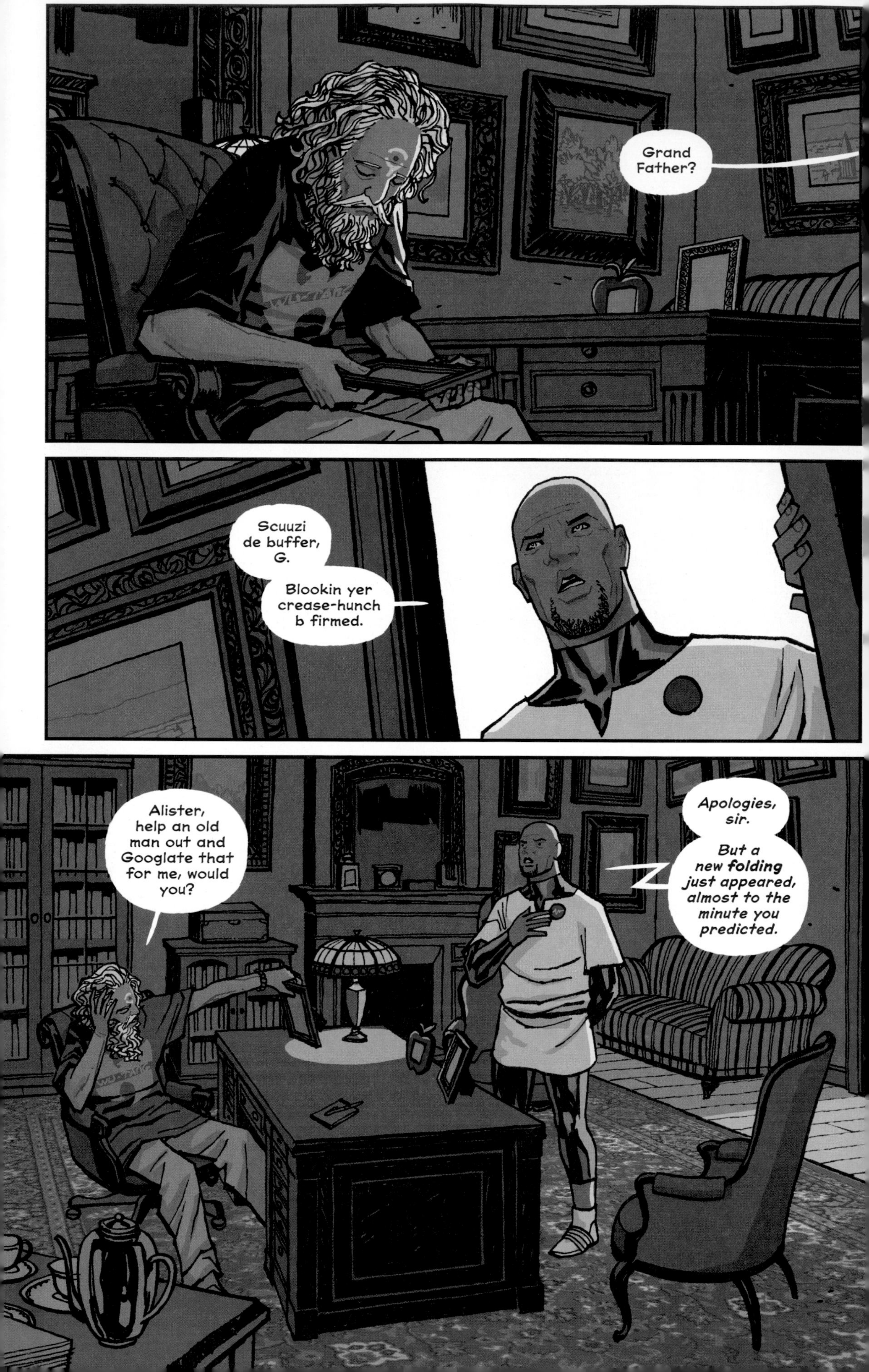
Grand Father?
Scuuzi de buffer, G.
Blookin yer crease-hunch b firmed.
Alister, help an old man out and Googlate that for me, would you?
Apologies, sir.
But a new **folding** just appeared, almost to the minute you predicted.

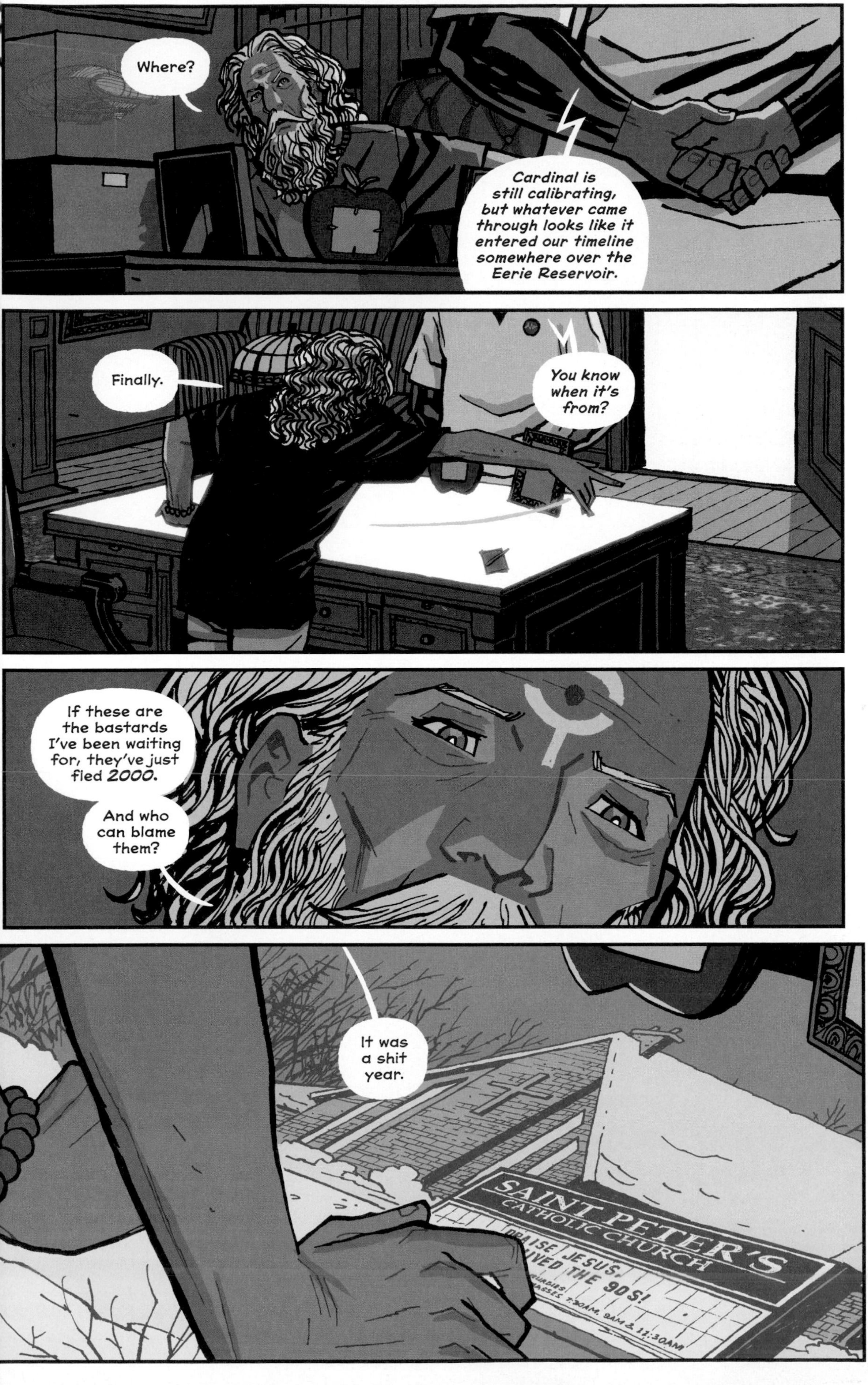

Where?
Cardinal is still calibrating, but whatever came through looks like it entered our timeline somewhere over the Eerie Reservoir.
Finally.
You know when it's from?
If these are the bastards I've been waiting for, they've just fled 2000.
And who can blame them?
It was a shit year.
SAINT PETER'S
CATHOLIC CHURCH
PRAISE JESUS.
THE 90S!
7:30AM, 9AM & 11:30AM

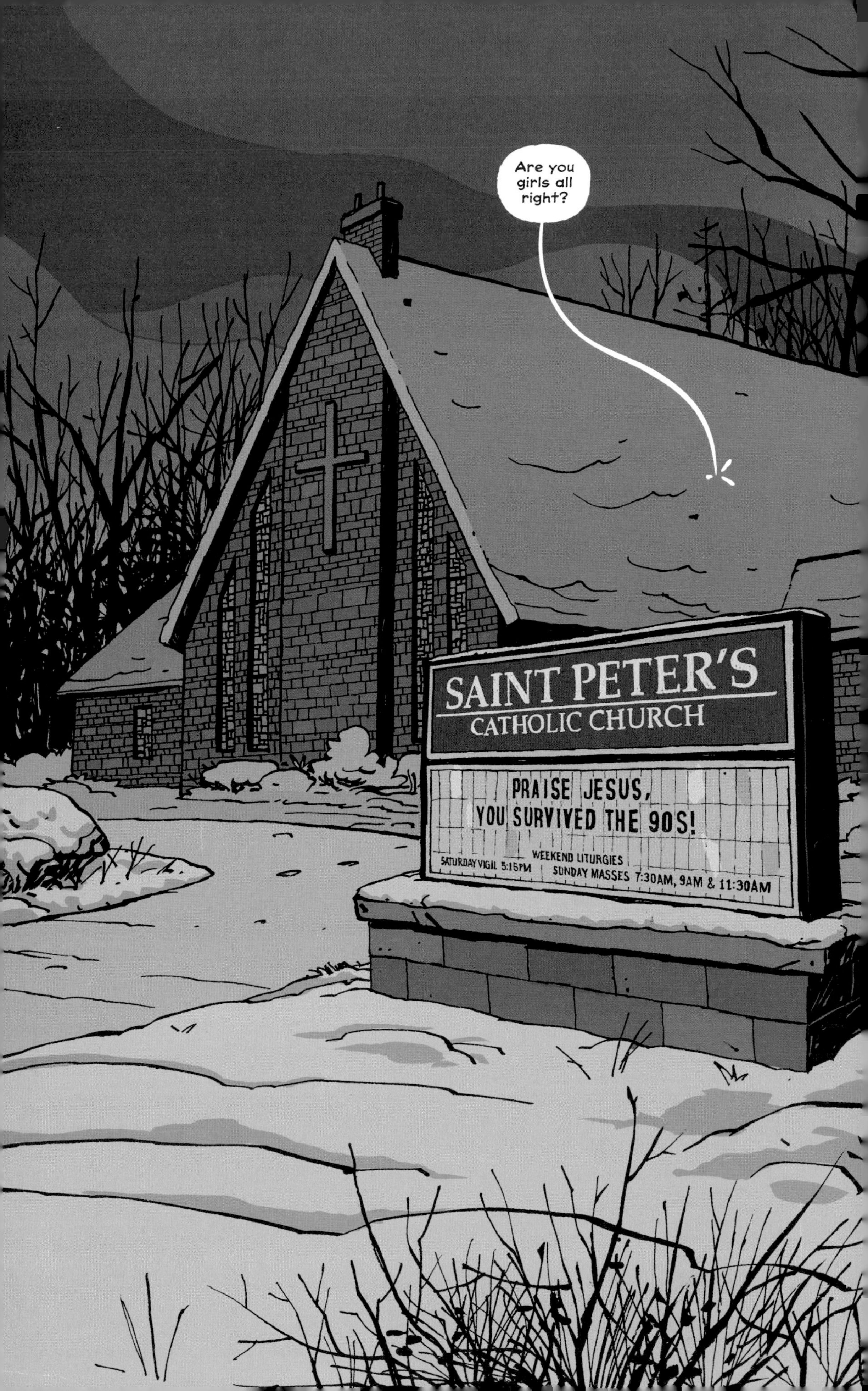
Are you girls all right?
SAINT PETER'S
CATHOLIC CHURCH
PRAISE JESUS,
YOU SURVIVED THE 90S!
WEEKEND LITURGIES
SATURDAY VIGIL 5:15PM
SUNDAY MASSES 7:30AM, 9AM & 11:30AM

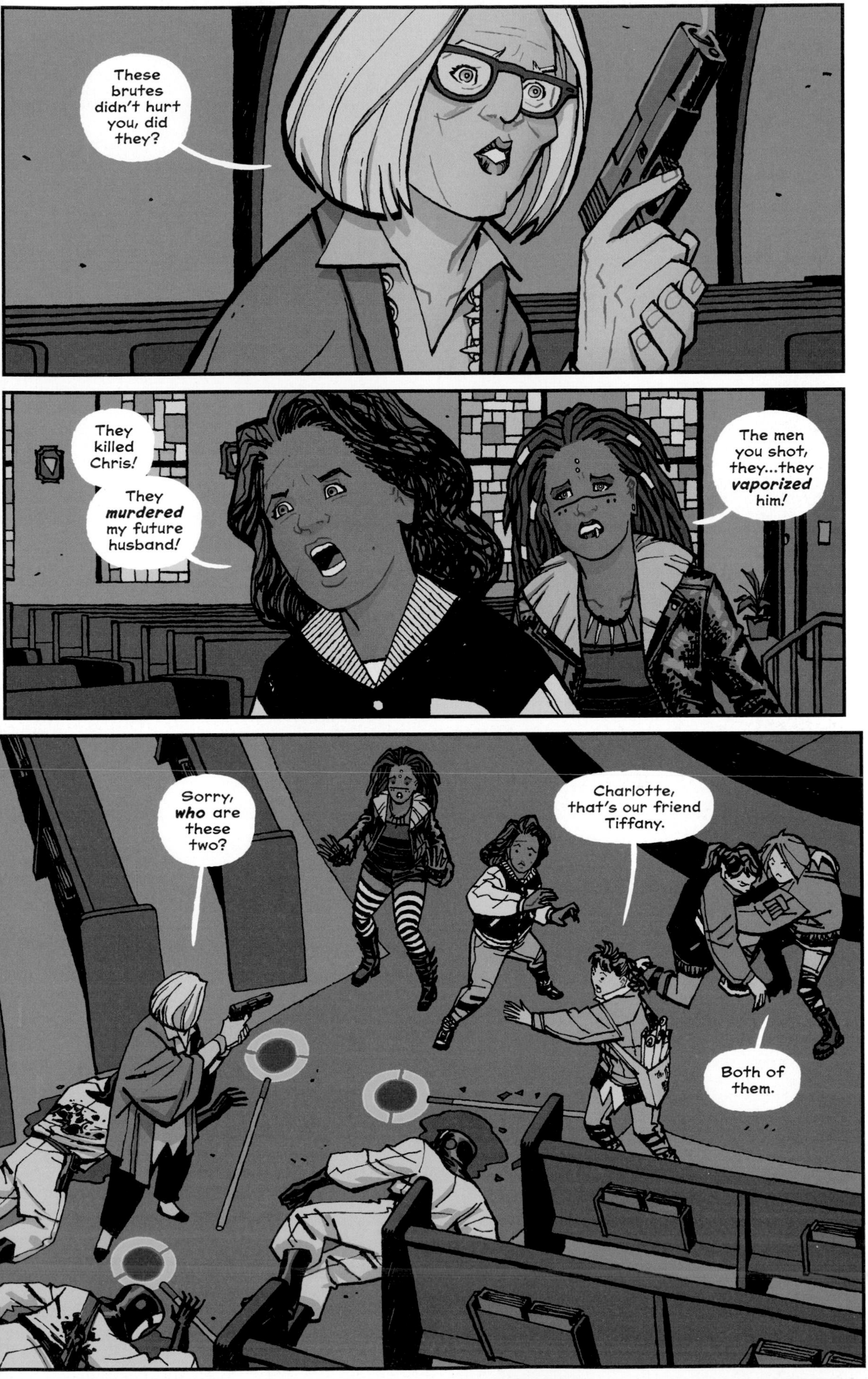
These brutes didn't hurt you, did they?
They killed Chris!
They **murdered** my future husband!
The men you shot, they...they **vaporized** him!
Sorry, **who** are these two?
Charlotte, that's our friend Tiffany.
Both of them.

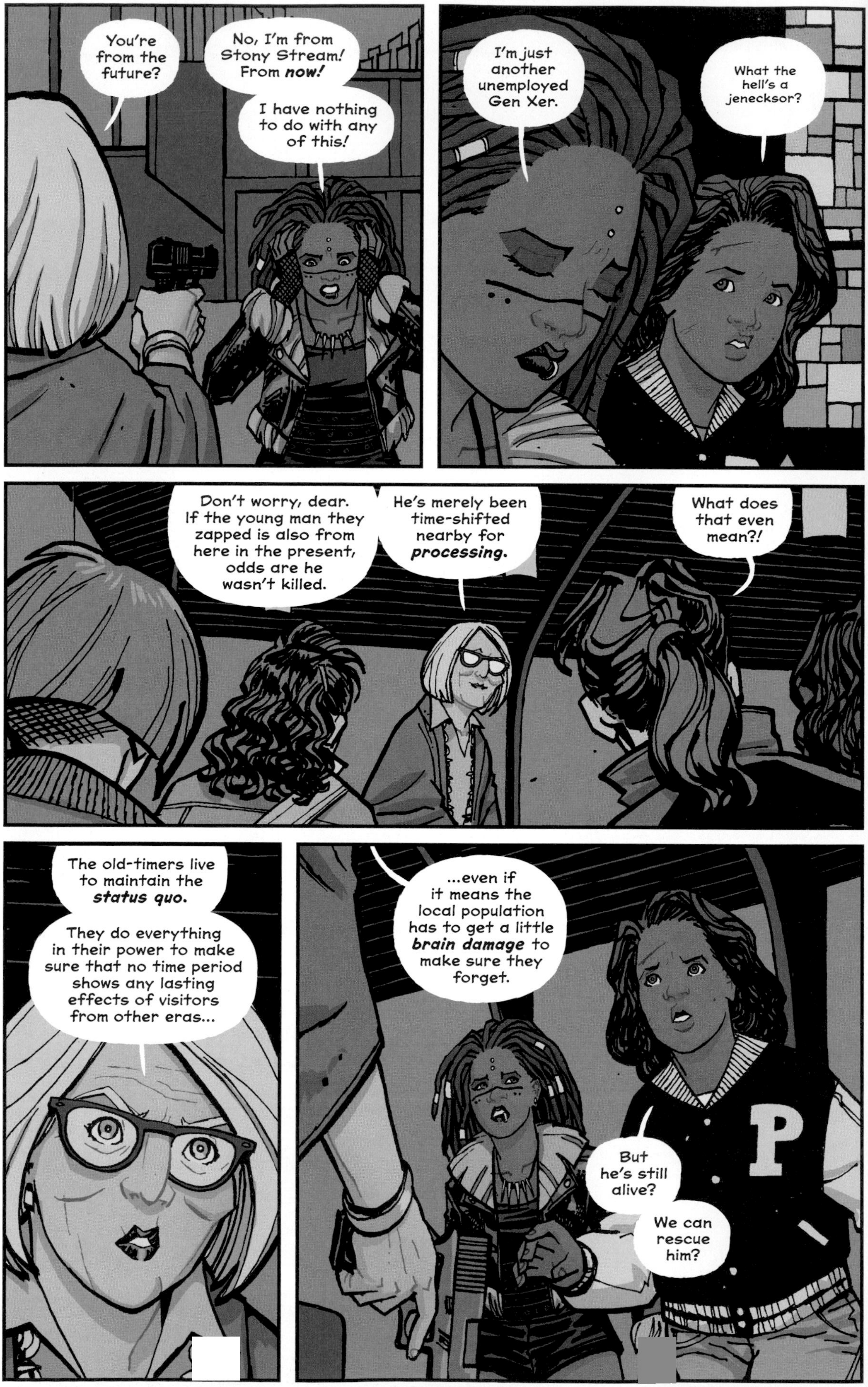
You're from the future?
No, I'm from Stony Stream! From *now!*
I have nothing to do with any of this!
I'm just another unemployed Gen Xer.
What the hell's a jenecksor?
Don't worry, dear. If the young man they zapped is also from here in the present, odds are he wasn't killed.
He's merely been time-shifted nearby for *processing.*
What does that even mean?!
The old-timers live to maintain the *status quo.*
They do everything in their power to make sure that no time period shows any lasting effects of visitors from other eras...
...even if it means the local population has to get a little *brain damage* to make sure they forget.
But he's still alive?
We can rescue him?
P

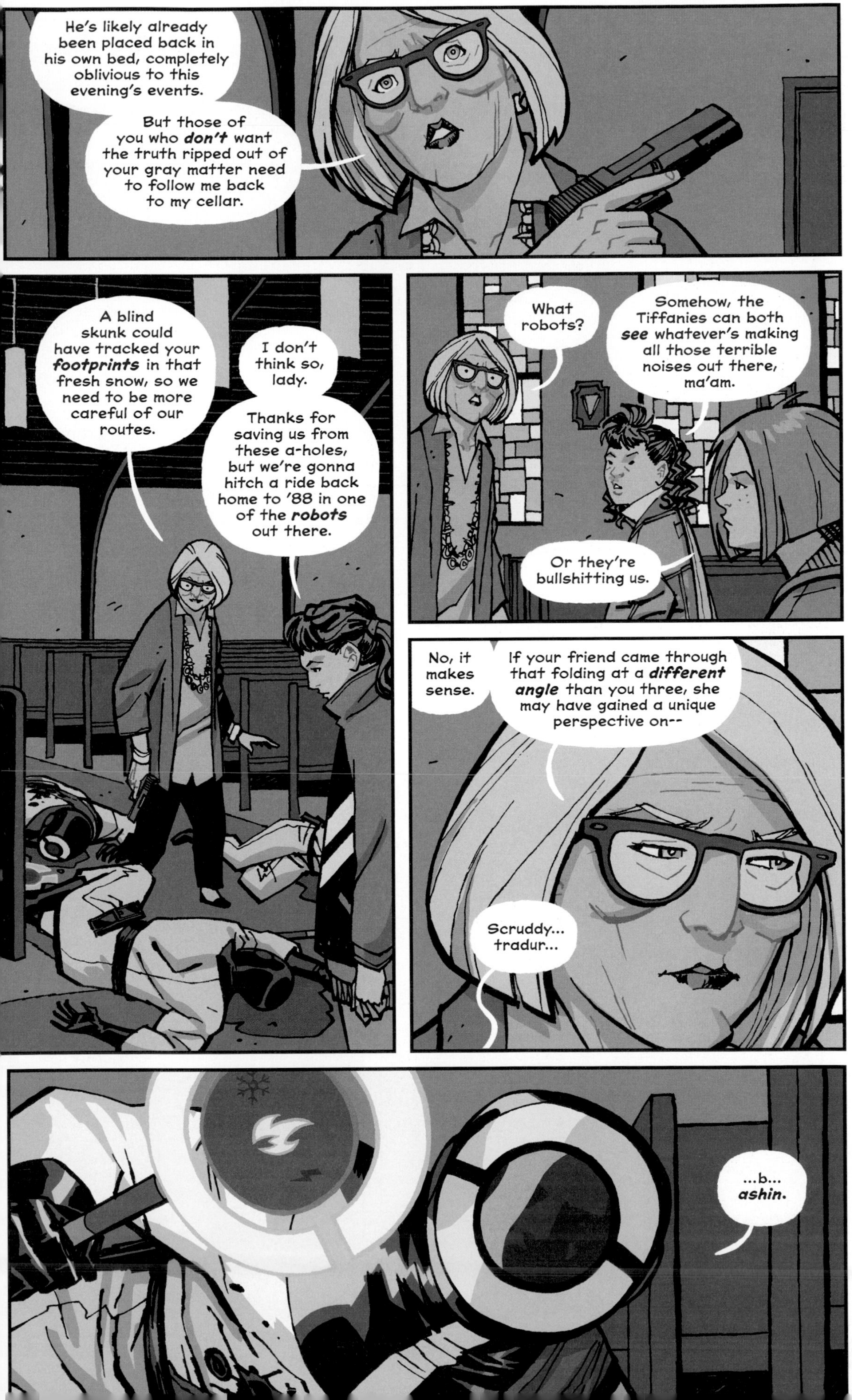
He's likely already been placed back in his own bed, completely oblivious to this evening's events.
But those of you who ***don't*** want the truth ripped out of your gray matter need to follow me back to my cellar.
A blind skunk could have tracked your ***footprints*** in that fresh snow, so we need to be more careful of our routes.
I don't think so, lady.
Thanks for saving us from these a-holes, but we're gonna hitch a ride back home to '88 in one of the ***robots*** out there.
What robots?
Somehow, the Tiffanies can both ***see*** whatever's making all those terrible noises out there, ma'am.
Or they're bullshitting us.
No, it makes sense.
If your friend came through that folding at a ***different angle*** than you three, she may have gained a unique perspective on--
Scruddy... tradur...
...b... ***ashin.***

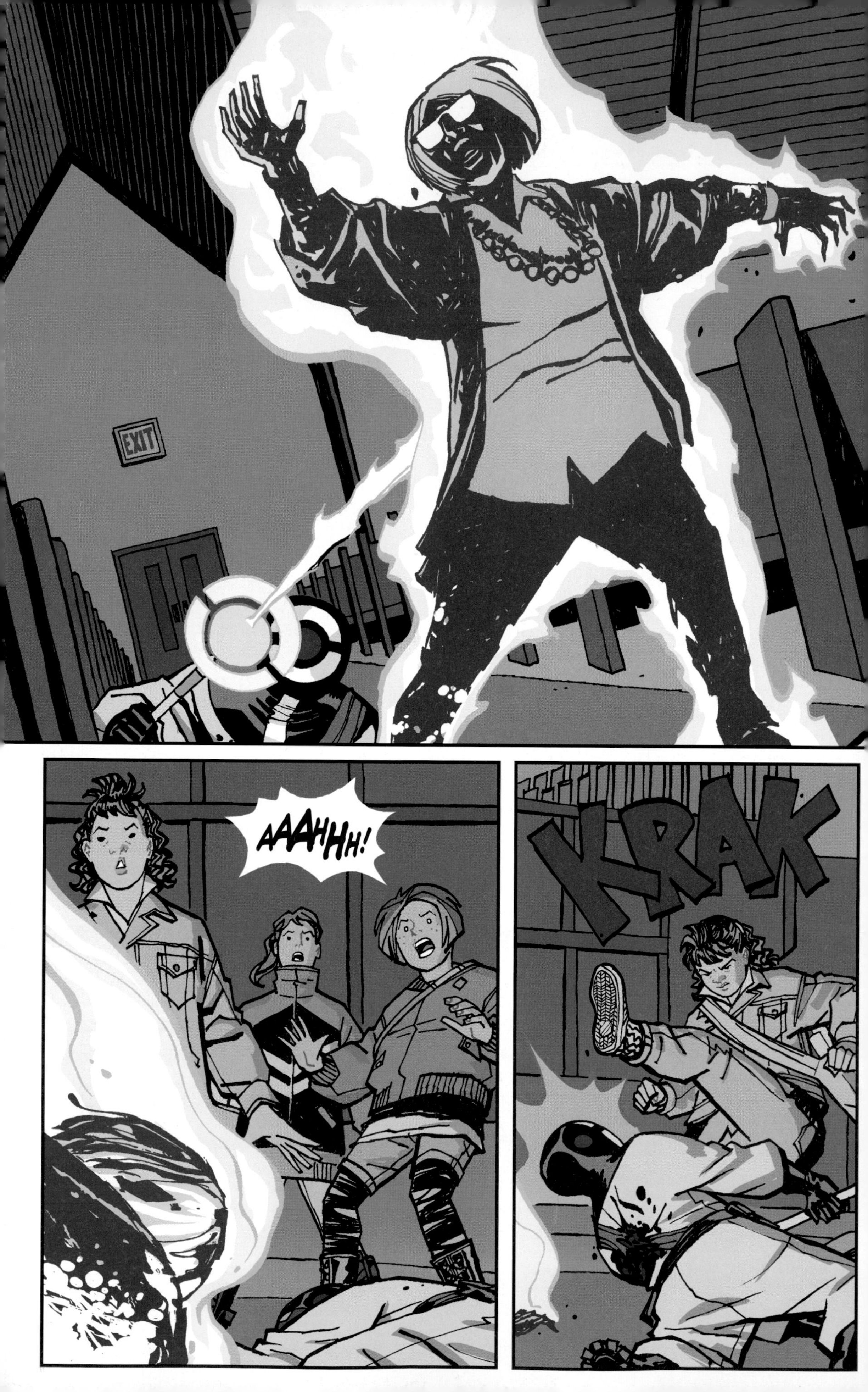
AAAHHH!
KRAK

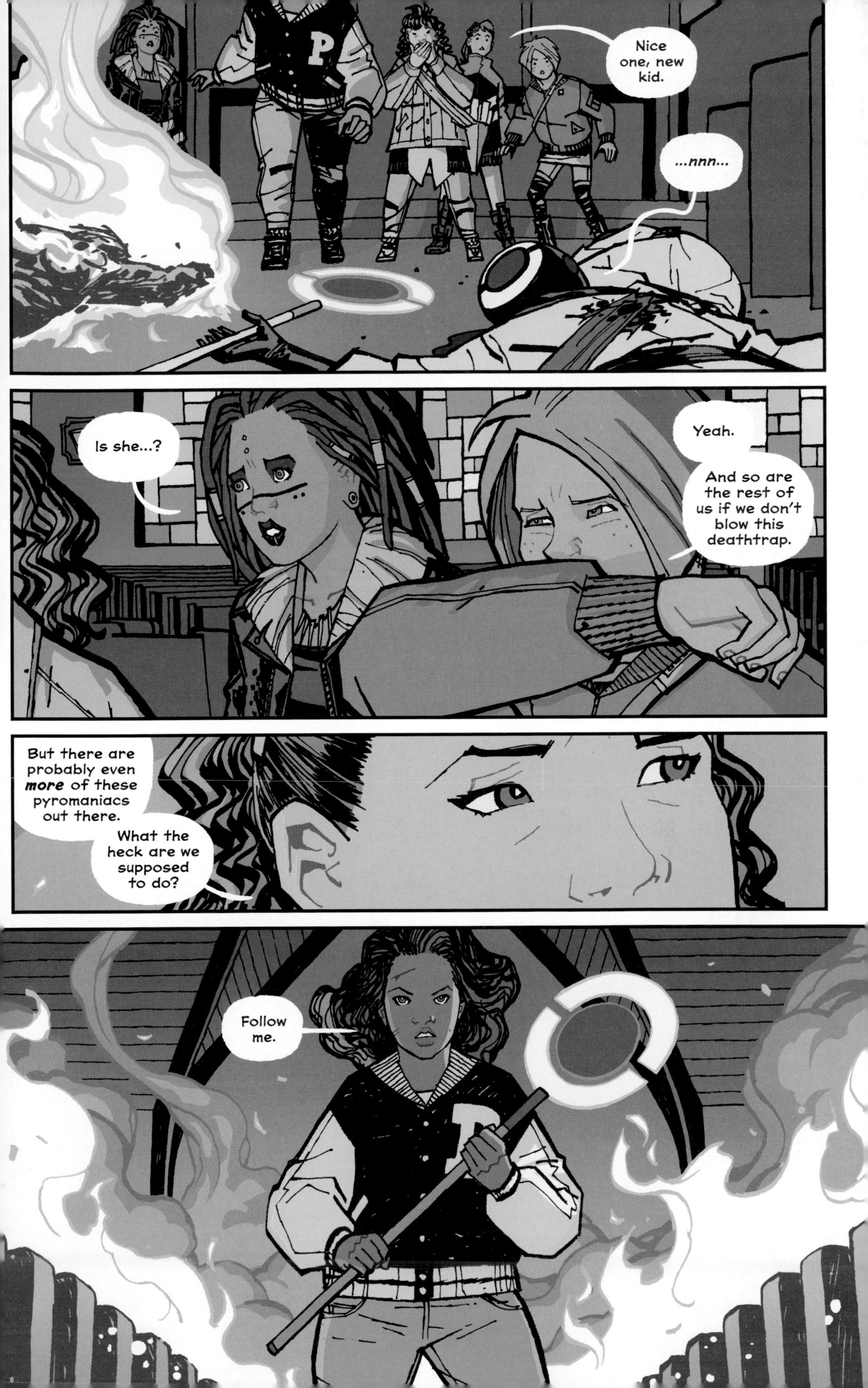
Nice one, new kid.
...nnn...
Is she...?
Yeah.
And so are the rest of us if we don't blow this deathtrap.
But there are probably even *more* of these pyromaniacs out there.
What the heck are we supposed to do?
Follow me.

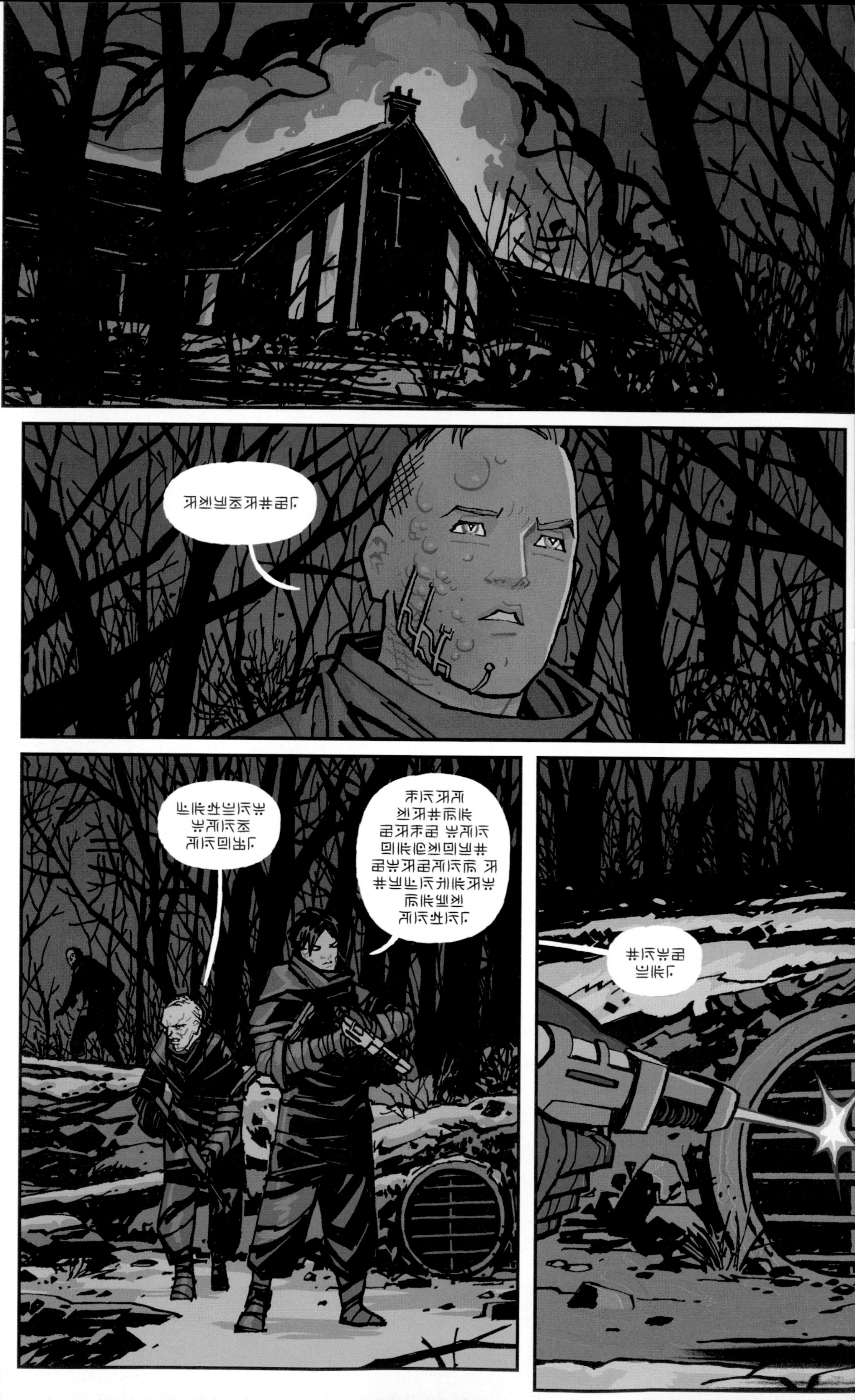

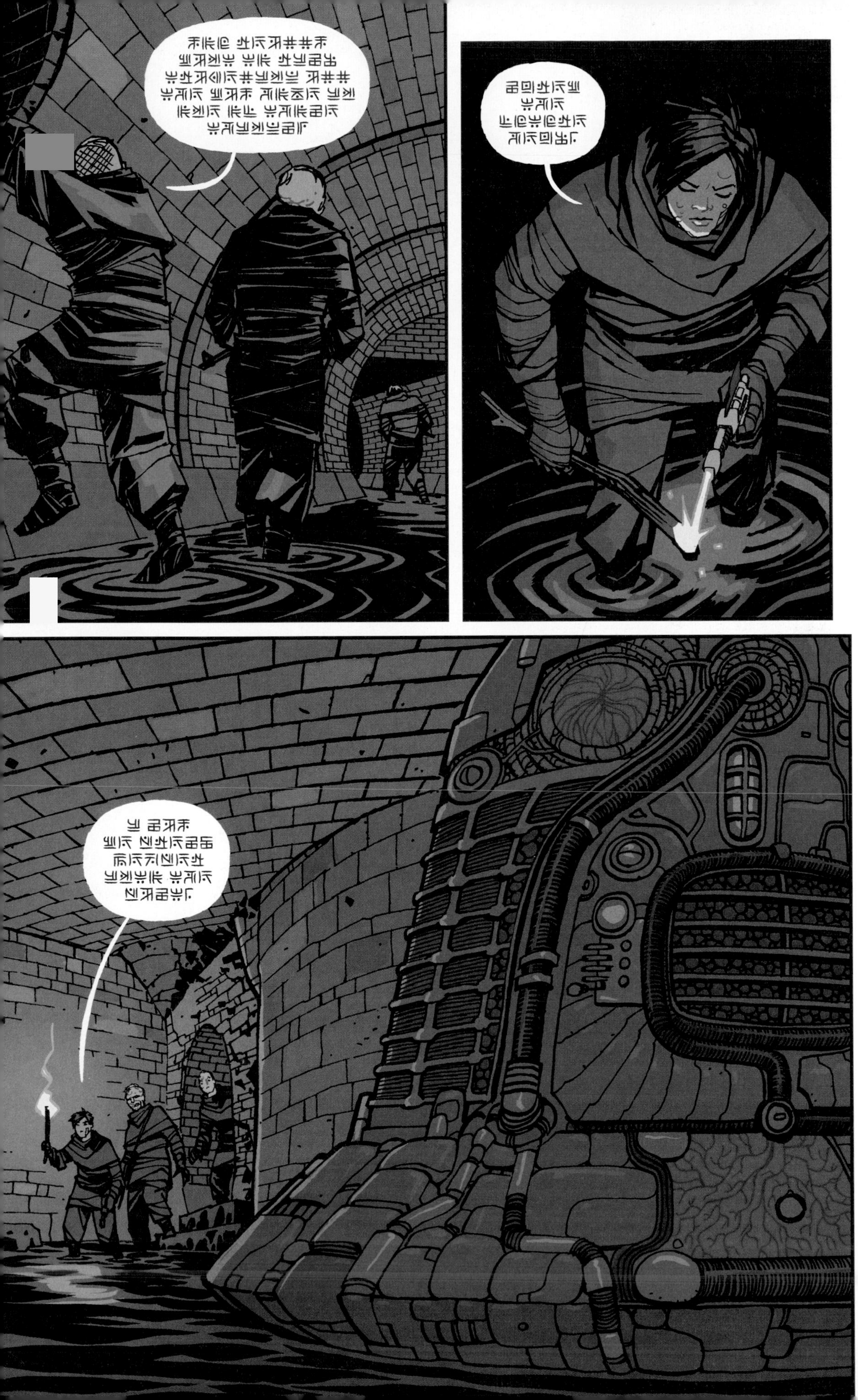

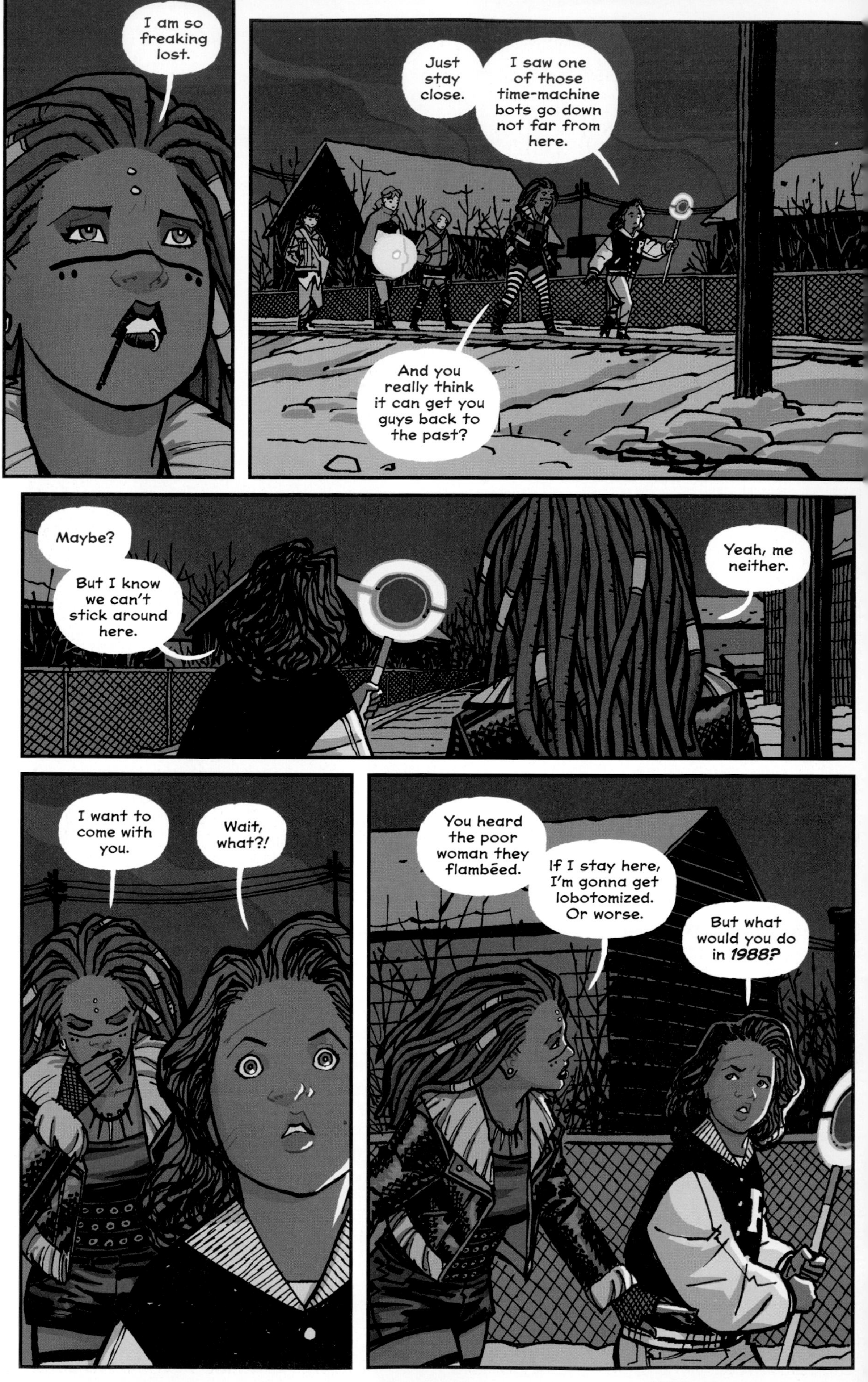
I am so freaking lost.
Just stay close.
I saw one of those time-machine bots go down not far from here.
And you really think it can get you guys back to the past?
Maybe?
But I know we can't stick around here.
Yeah, me neither.
I want to come with you.
Wait, what?!
You heard the poor woman they flambéed.
If I stay here, I'm gonna get lobotomized. Or worse.
But what would you do in *1988?*

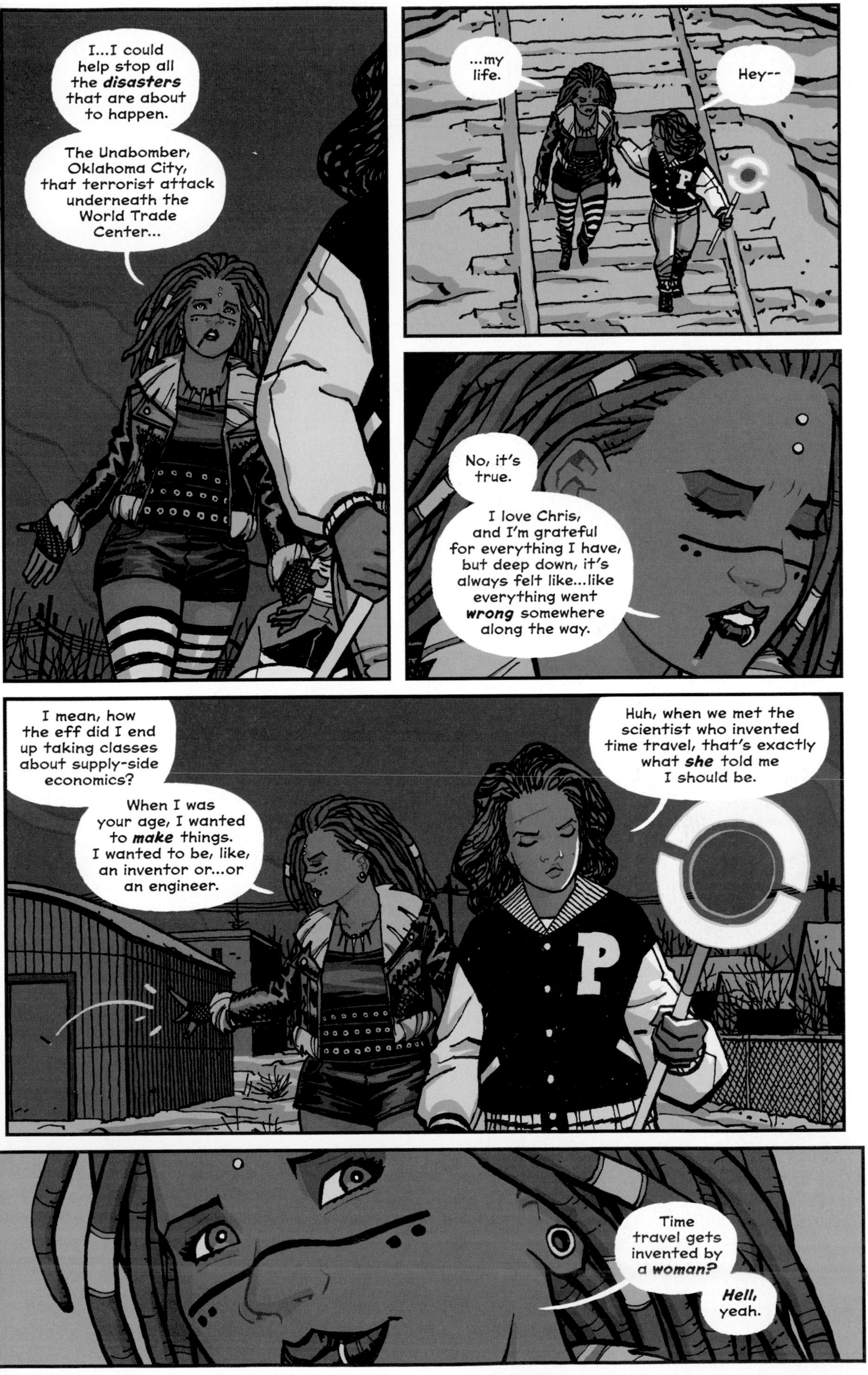
I...I could help stop all the *disasters* that are about to happen.
The Unabomber, Oklahoma City, that terrorist attack underneath the World Trade Center...
...my life.
Hey--
No, it's true.
I love Chris, and I'm grateful for everything I have, but deep down, it's always felt like...like everything went *wrong* somewhere along the way.
I mean, how the eff did I end up taking classes about supply-side economics?
When I was your age, I wanted to *make* things. I wanted to be, like, an inventor or...or an engineer.
Huh, when we met the scientist who invented time travel, that's exactly what *she* told me I should be.
Time travel gets invented by a *woman?*
Hell, yeah.

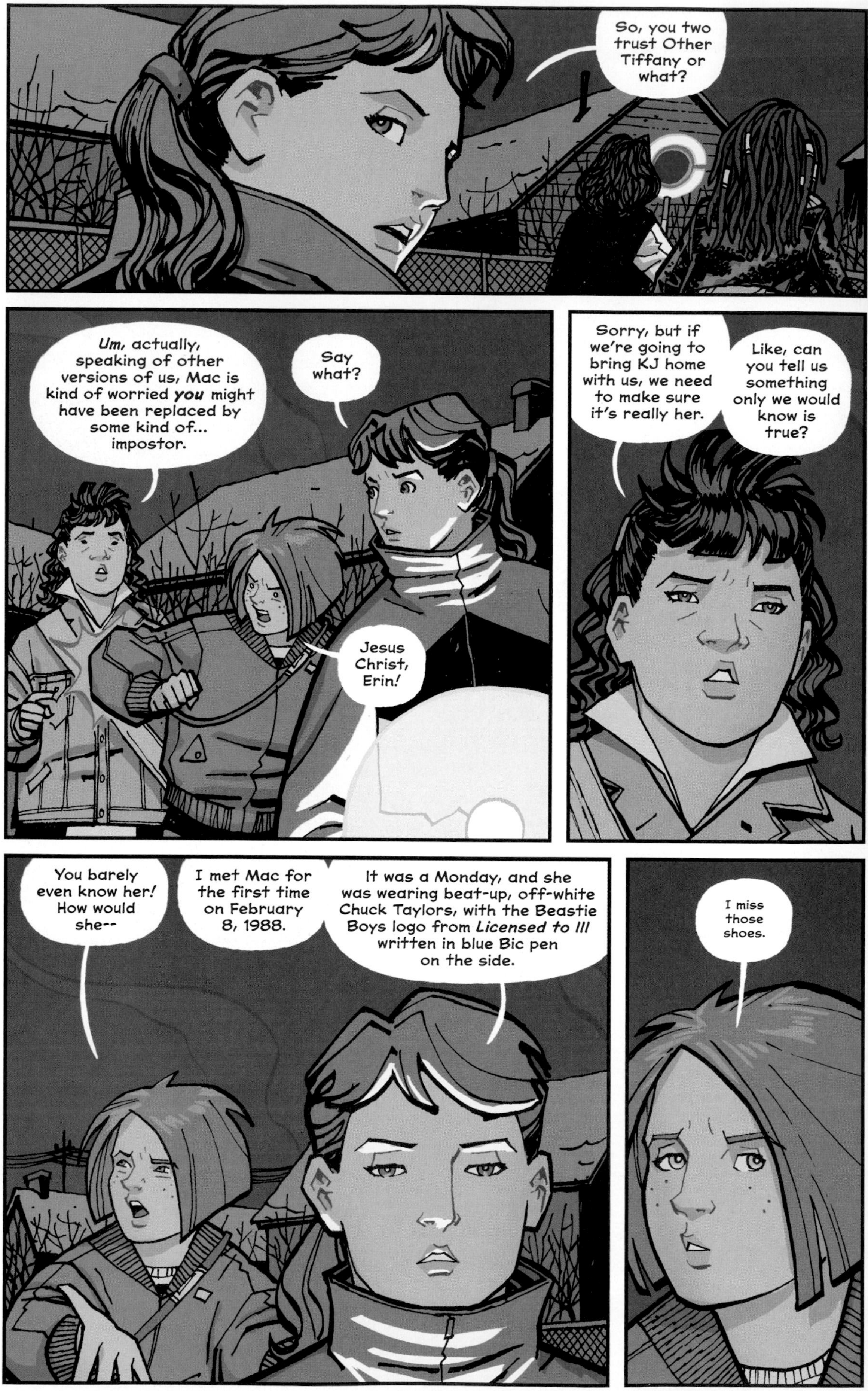
So, you two trust Other Tiffany or what?
Um, actually, speaking of other versions of us, Mac is kind of worried ***you*** might have been replaced by some kind of... impostor.
Say what?
Jesus Christ, Erin!
Sorry, but if we're going to bring KJ home with us, we need to make sure it's really her.
Like, can you tell us something only we would know is true?
You barely even know her! How would she--
I met Mac for the first time on February 8, 1988.
It was a Monday, and she was wearing beat-up, off-white Chuck Taylors, with the Beastie Boys logo from *Licensed to Ill* written in blue Bic pen on the side.
I miss those shoes.

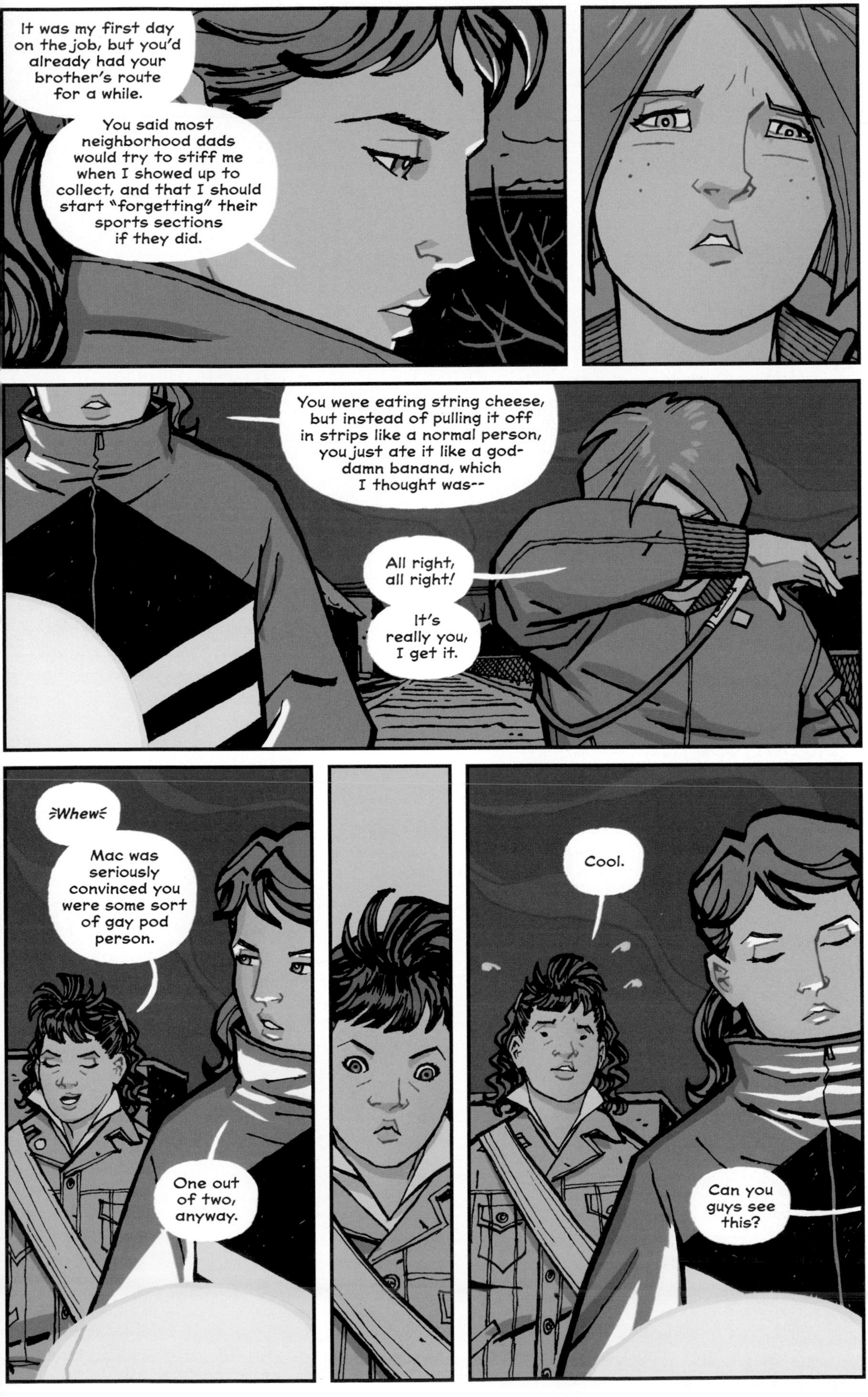
It was my first day on the job, but you'd already had your brother's route for a while.
You said most neighborhood dads would try to stiff me when I showed up to collect, and that I should start "forgetting" their sports sections if they did.
You were eating string cheese, but instead of pulling it off in strips like a normal person, you just ate it like a god-damn banana, which I thought was--
All right, all right!
It's really you, I get it.
Whew
Mac was seriously convinced you were some sort of gay pod person.
One out of two, anyway.
Cool.
Can you guys see this?

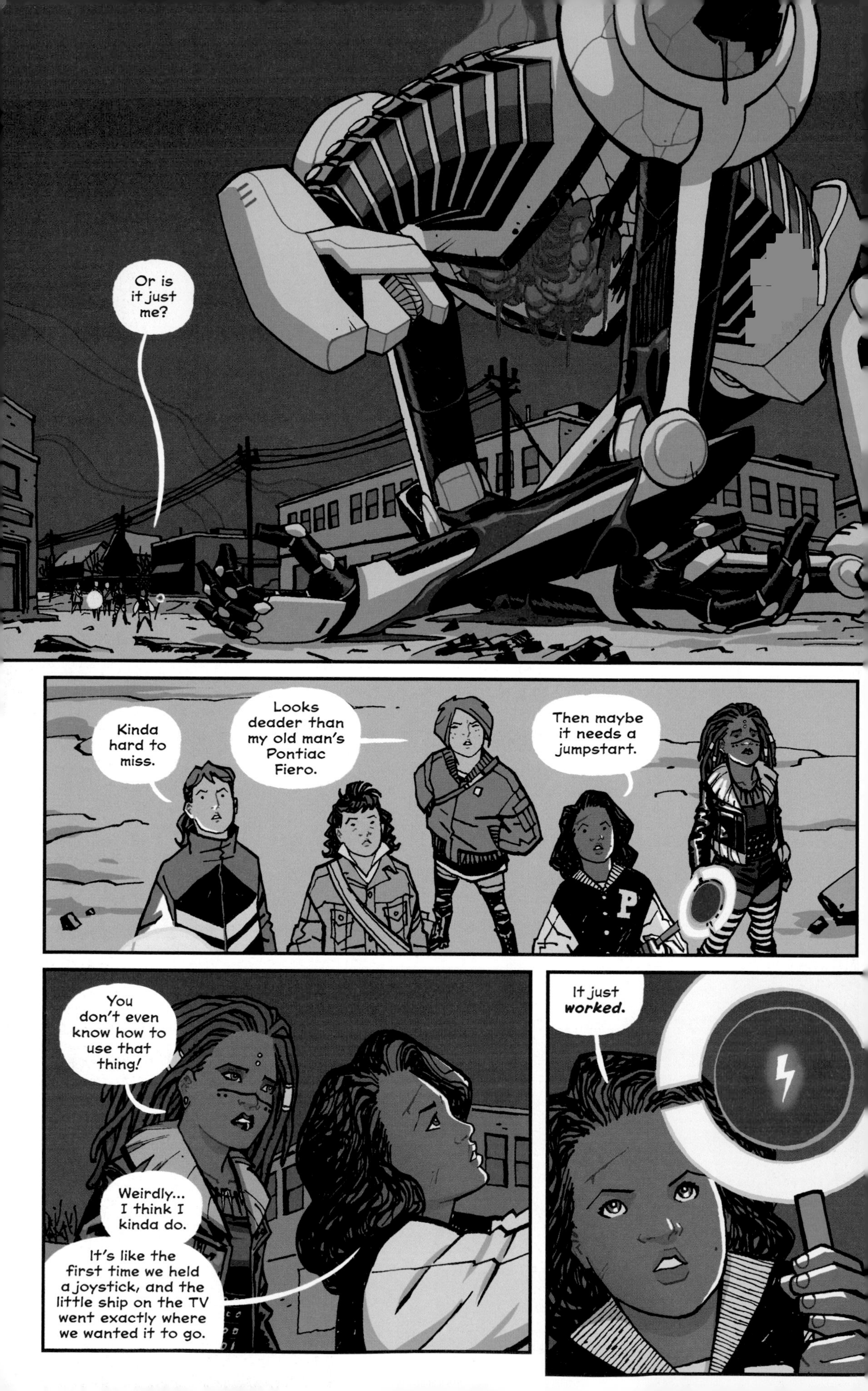
Or is it just me?
Kinda hard to miss.
Looks deader than my old man's Pontiac Fiero.
Then maybe it needs a jumpstart.
You don't even know how to use that thing!
Weirdly... I think I kinda do.
It's like the first time we held a joystick, and the little ship on the TV went exactly where we wanted it to go.
It just **worked.**

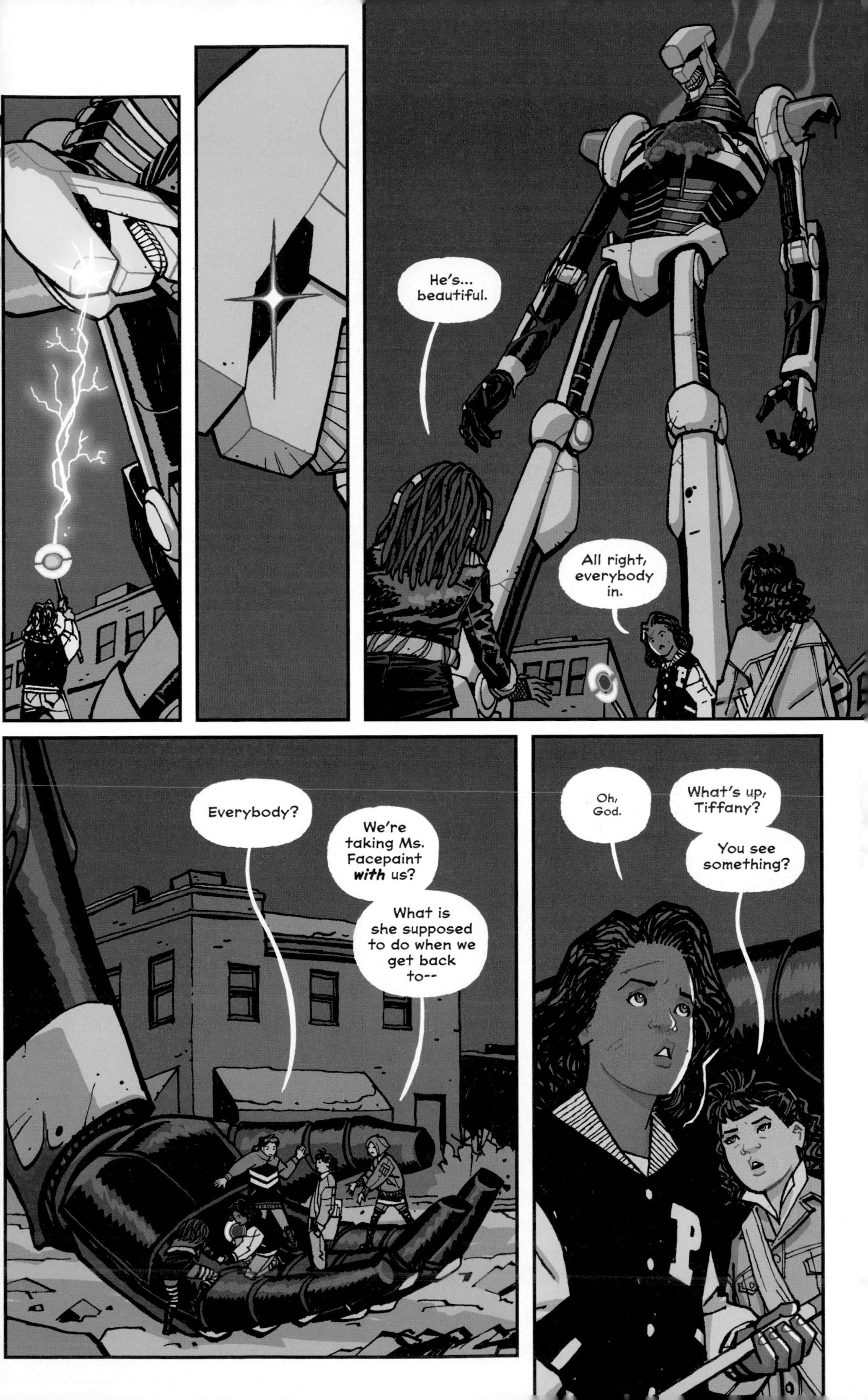
He's... beautiful.
All right, everybody in.
Everybody?
We're taking Ms. Facepaint *with* us?
What is she supposed to do when we get back to--
Oh, God.
What's up, Tiffany?
You see something?

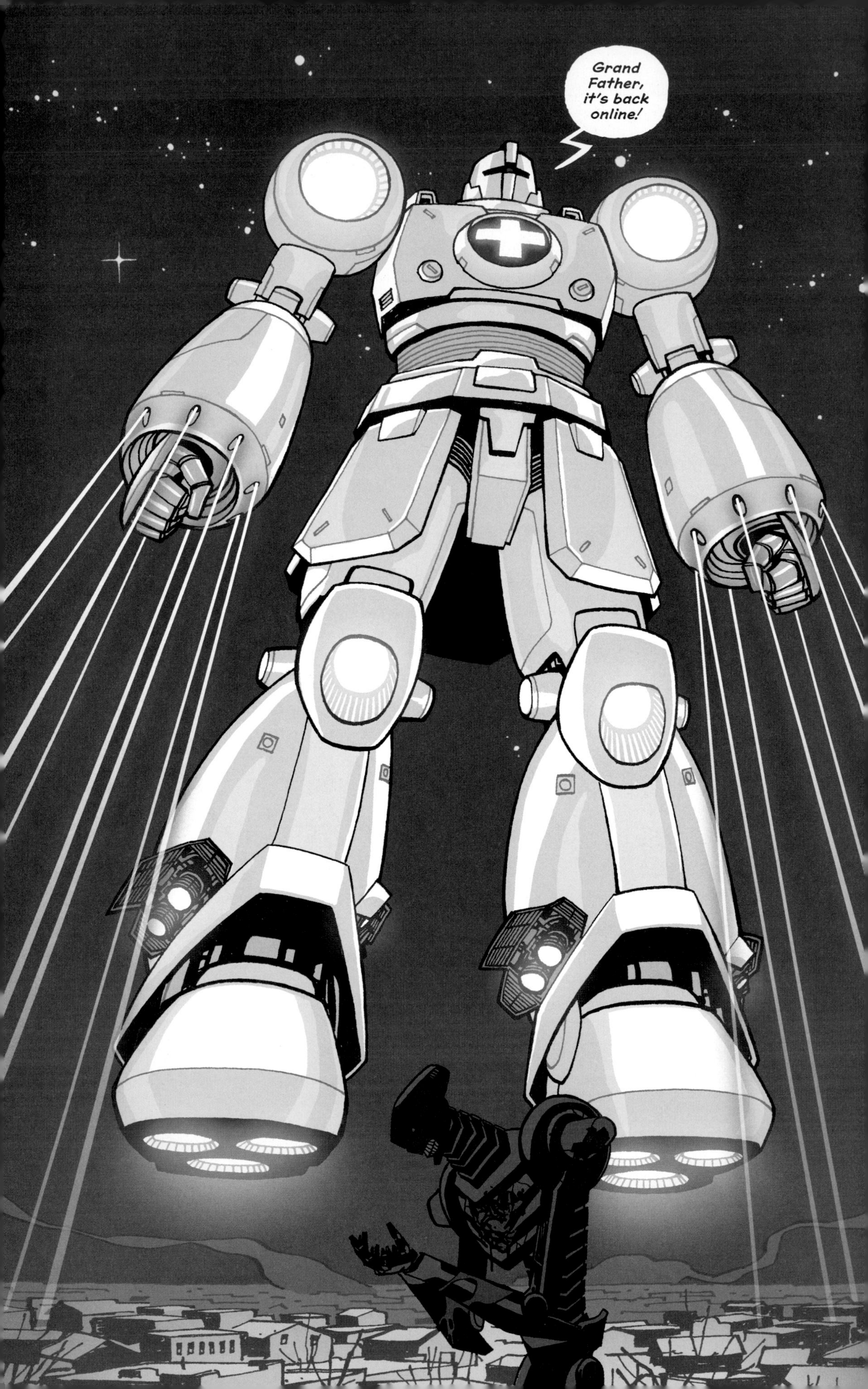
Grand Father, it's back online!

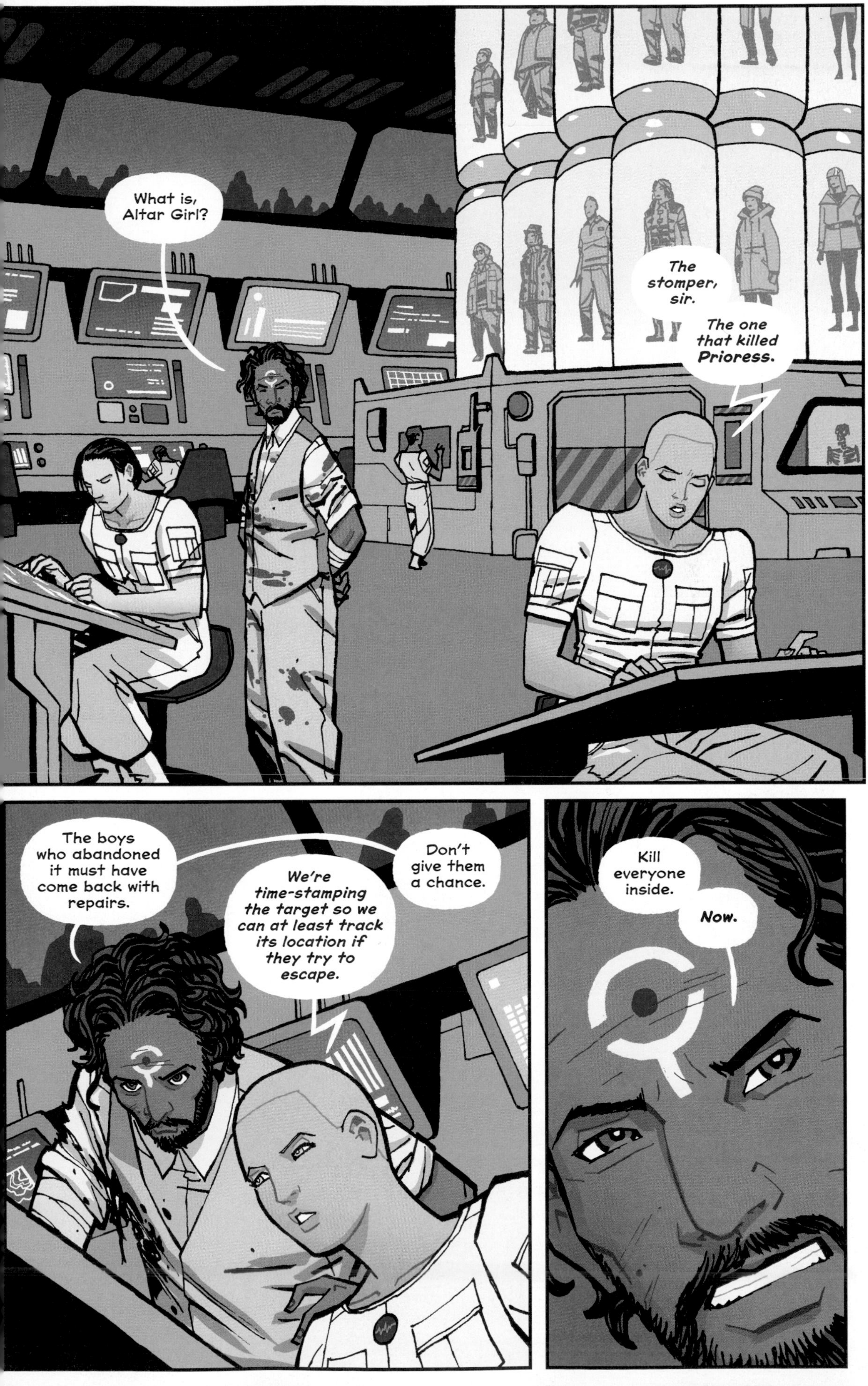
What is, Altar Girl?
The stomper, sir.
The one that killed Prioress.
The boys who abandoned it must have come back with repairs.
We're time-stamping the target so we can at least track its location if they try to escape.
Don't give them a chance.
Kill everyone inside.
Now.

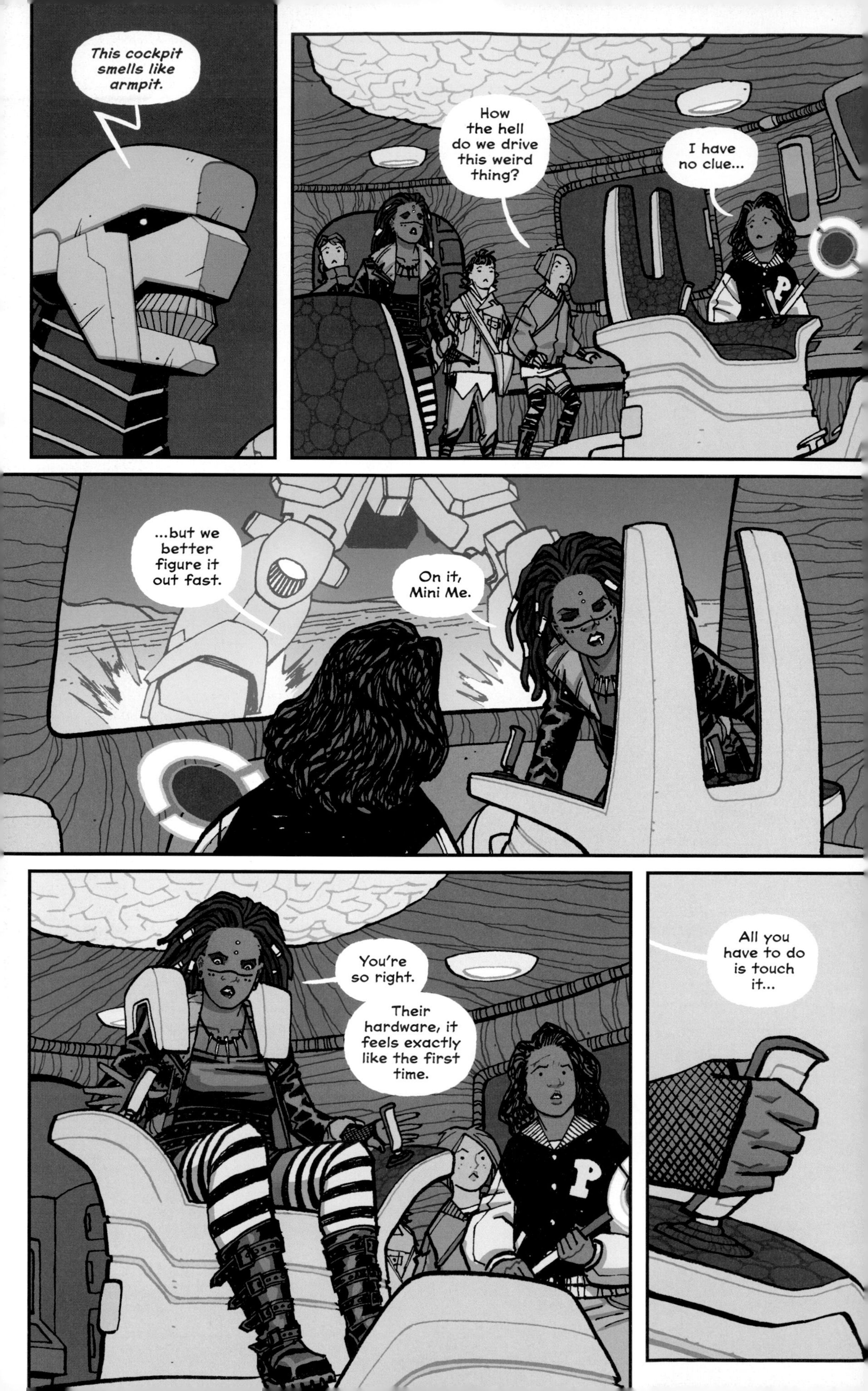
This cockpit smells like armpit.
How the hell do we drive this weird thing?
I have no clue...
...but we better figure it out fast.
On it, Mini Me.
You're so right.
Their hardware, it feels exactly like the first time.
All you have to do is touch it...

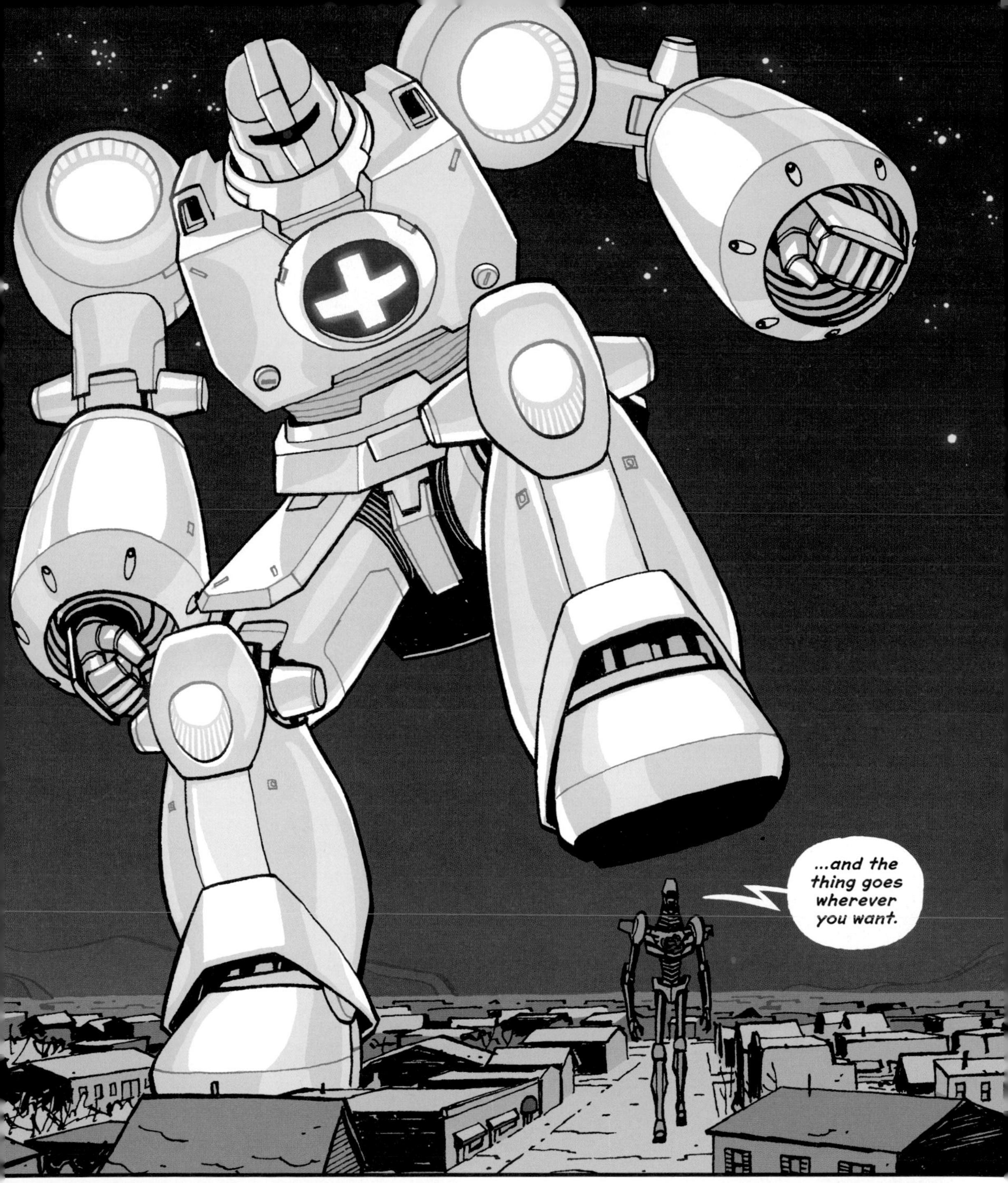
...and the thing goes wherever you want.
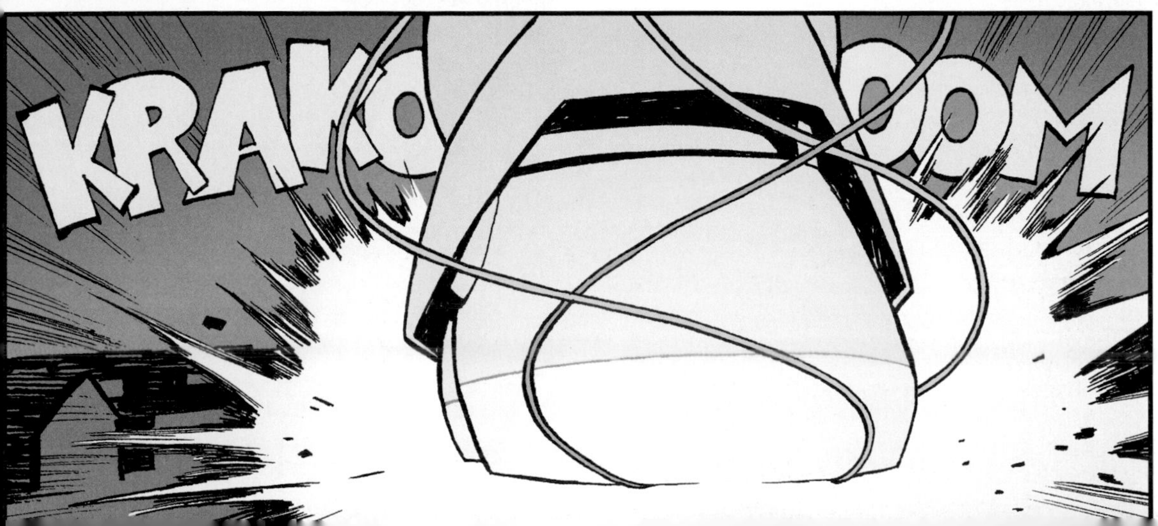
KRAKOOOM

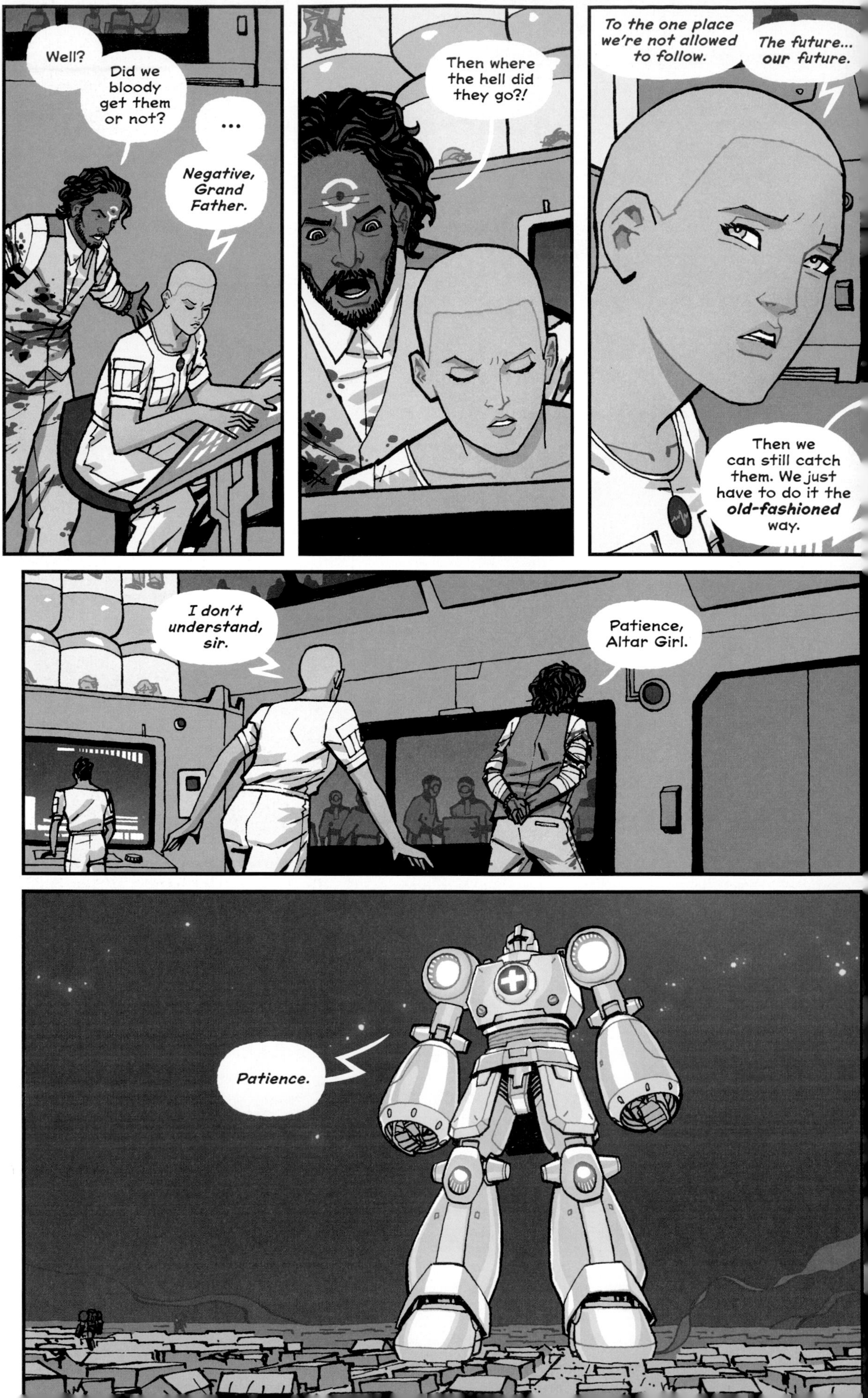
Well?
Did we bloody get them or not?
...
Negative, Grand Father.
Then where the hell did they go?!
To the one place we're not allowed to follow.
The future... our future.
Then we can still catch them. We just have to do it the old-fashioned way.
I don't understand, sir.
Patience, Altar Girl.
Patience.

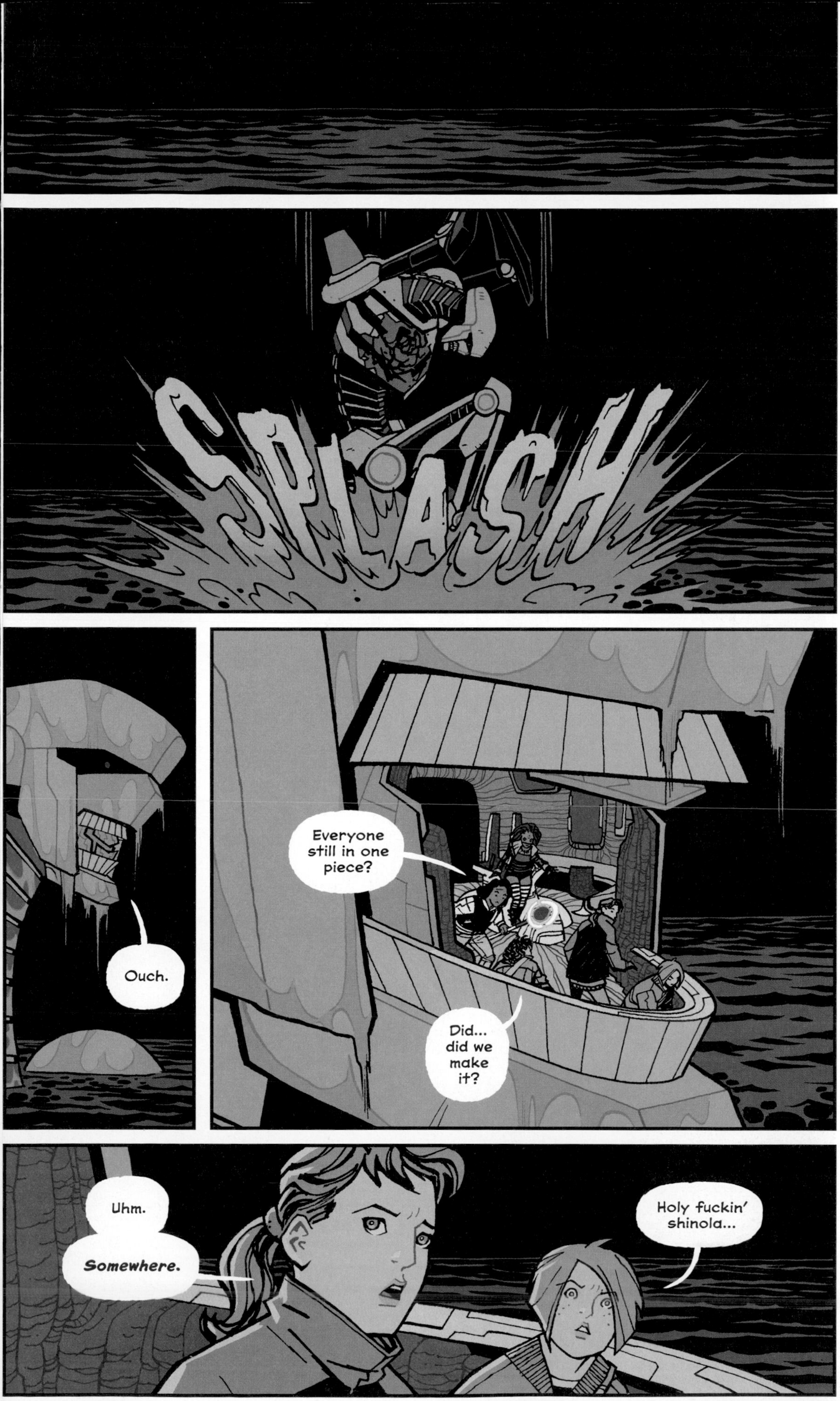
SPLASH
Ouch.
Everyone still in one piece?
Did... did we make it?
Uhm.
Somewhere.
Holy fuckin' shinola...

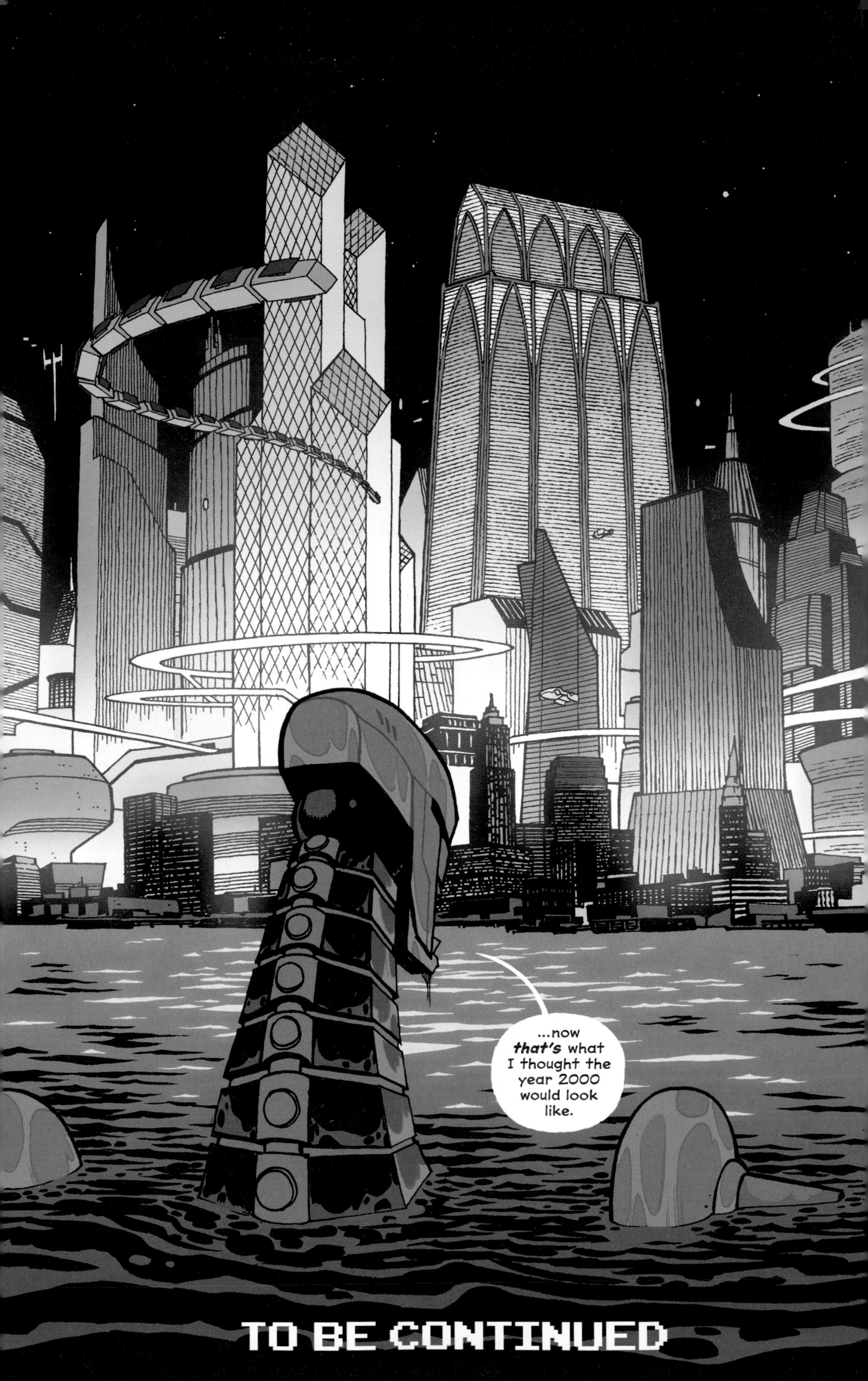
...now *that's* what I thought the year 2000 would look like.
TO BE CONTINUED

CREATORS

BRIAN K. VAUGHAN
Activities: Theater, Sci-Fi Book Club,
Power of the Pen
Worst Subject: Math, P.E. (tie)
Halloween Costume: Homemade
Spider-Man Symbiote Suit

CLIFF CHIANG
Homeroom: Miss Benson
Activities: Chorus, Ski Club, French
Cultural Society, Art Club
Favorite NES games: *Contra,
Double Dribble, Metal Gear*

MATT WILSON
Homeroom: Miss Pearce
Activities: Basketball, Art Club,
Taekwondo, skateboarding
Favorite toys: Battle Beasts, M.A.S.K.,
The Centurions, G.I. Joe, TMNT

JARED K. FLETCHER
Homeroom: Mr. Chandler
Activities: Sailing, Art Club,
Wrestling, talking too much
Favorite Lego set: Space Monorail
Transport System 6990

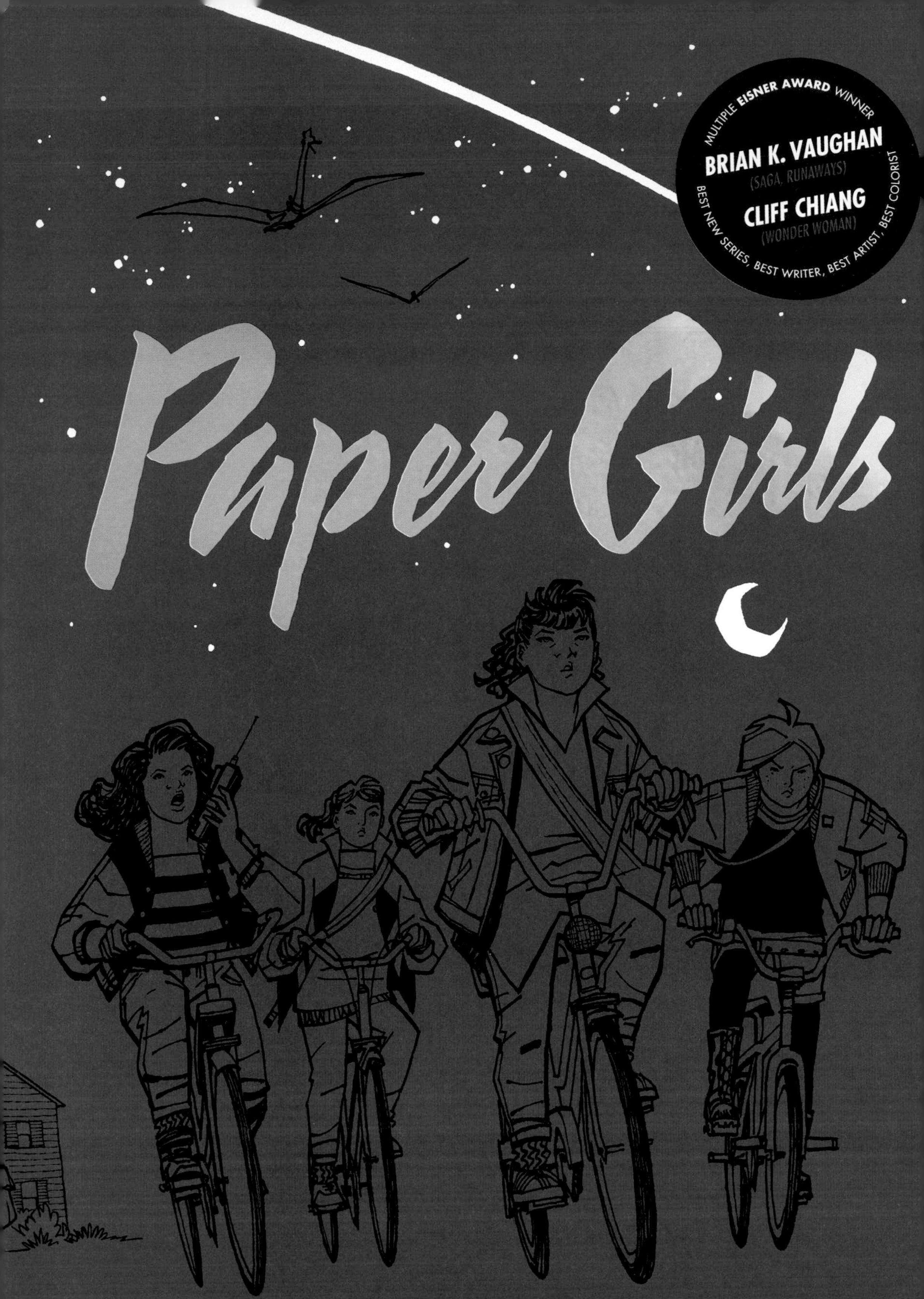
MULTIPLE EISNER AWARD WINNER
BRIAN K. VAUGHAN
(SAGA, RUNAWAYS)
CLIFF CHIANG
(WONDER WOMAN)
BEST NEW SERIES, BEST WRITER, BEST ARTIST, BEST COLORIST
Paper Girls